Rebecca Maizel holds an undergraduate degree from Boston University and an MA in English from Rhode Island College. She is currently pursuing an MFA in Writing for Young Adults at Vermont College. *Infinite Days* is her first novel – written when she was working nights as a bartender in New York, living like a vampire.

Praise for Infinite Days:

'*Infinite Days* is a grab-you-by-the-throat, ignore-the-world-around-you, fall-completely-in-love-with kind of book, the kind I haven't really read since *Twilight*. Yep. I just used the T-word' AllThingsUrbanFantasy.blogspot.com

'*Infinite Days* builds to an exciting conclusion, and leaves the door wide open for a kick-ass sequel' www.wondrousreads.com

'There is no other vampire book like it and if you have a love for immortals but are fed up with reading more or less the same story over and over again, then *Infinite Days* is the ideal book to pick up . . . Maizel's writing is beautiful . . . Her voice is very unique and has an eloquence to it that I wish we could see more of in young adult fiction' www.yabookreads.com

'I found myself thinking about this novel long after I'd put it down . . . It plays around but still retains the haunting and tortured tone of all the best vampire stories' www.amazon.co.uk

Look out for

Stolen Night

The second Vampire Queen novel

www.MyKindaBook.com

Infinite Days

Rebecca Maizel

MACMILLAN

To Mom and Dad:
Every word. Every single one belongs to you.
You always light the way.
And my sister, Jennie, who always has the right words.

First published 2010 by Macmillan Children's Books

This edition published 2011 by Macmillan Children's Books
a division of Macmillan Publishers Limited
20 New Wharf Road, London N1 9RR
Basingstoke and Oxford
Associated companies throughout the world
www.panmacmillan.com

ISBN 978-0-330-52042-3

1 3 5 7 9 8 6 4 2

A CIP catalogue record for this book is available from
the British Library.

Printed and bound in the UK by CPI Mackays, Chatham ME5 8TD

Part 1

'There's rosemary, that's for remembrance; pray you,
love, remember.'

— Ophelia, *Hamlet*, Act IV, Scene V

Chapter 1

I release you . . .
I release you, Lenah Beaudonte.
Believe . . . and be free.

Those were the last words I could remember. But they were formless, said by someone whose voice I did not recognize. It could have been ages ago.

When I awoke, I immediately felt a cold surface on my left cheek. An icy shiver rushed down my spine. Even with my eyes closed, I knew I was naked, stomach down on a hardwood floor.

I gasped, though my throat was so dry I made an unearthly animal sound. Three heaving breaths then a *thump-thump, thump-thump* – a heartbeat. My heartbeat? It could have been ten thousand fluttering wings. I tried to open my eyes, but with each blink there was a flash of blinding light. Then another. And another.

'Rhode!' I screamed. He had to be here. There would be no world without Rhode.

I writhed on the floor, covering my body with my hands. Understand that I am not the type of person to find herself naked and alone especially in a situation where sunlight shines down on my body. Yet there I was, bathed in yellow light, sure that I was moments away from a painful, fiery death – I had to be. Soon flames would erupt from within my soul and turn me into dust.

Only, nothing happened. No flames or imminent death. There was only the smell of the oak in the floor. I swallowed and the muscles in my throat contracted. My mouth was wet with . . . saliva! My chest rested on the ground. I pressed down on my palms and craned my neck to look at the source of my torment. Luminous daylight streamed into a bedroom from a large bay window. The sky was a sapphire blue, no clouds.

'Rhode!' My voice seemed to swirl in the air, vibrating out of my mouth. I was so thirsty. 'Where are you?' I screamed.

A door somewhere near me opened and closed. I heard a wobbling step, an uneven shuffle, then Rhode's black buckle boots stepped into my eyeline. I rolled on to my back and looked up at the ceiling. Gasping. My God – was I breathing?

Rhode loomed over me, but he was a blur. He leaned forward so his hazy features were within inches of my face. Then there he was, as though coming out of a mist, looking as I had never seen him before. The skin over Rhode's cheekbones stretched so tight it looked as though his bones would break through. His usually full and proud chin was now a thin point. But the blue of his eyes – they were the same. Even in the haze of that moment they pierced me, down to my soul.

'Fancy meeting you here,' Rhode said. Despite black bruises that ringed his eyes, a twinkle, from somewhere deep within, looked back at me. 'Happy sixteenth birthday,' he said, and extended a hand.

Rhode gripped a glass of water. I sat up, took it from him and finished it in three large gulps. The cold water trickled down the back of my throat, flowed down my oesophagus and into my stomach. Blood, a substance I was used to, trickled, but its absorption into the vampire body was a lot like a sponge soaking up liquid. It had been so long since I'd had a drink of water . . .

In Rhode's other hand was a piece of black cloth. When I took it from him, the cloth cascaded out to reveal a black dress. It was lightweight cotton. I pressed up from the floor and stood up. My knees buckled but I steadied myself by throwing my arms out to balance. I stood there for a moment, until I was firmly planted to the ground. When I tried to walk, a small vibration shook me so hard that my knees touched.

'Put that on and then come into the other room,' Rhode said, and lumbered unevenly out of the bedroom. I should have noticed that he had to hold on to the door frame when he walked but my knees and thighs trembled and I had to try to find my balance again. I let my hands fall back to my sides. My brown hair unfurled and, like seaweed, strands stuck to my naked body. Longer strands reached my breasts. I would have given anything for a mirror. I took a few breaths and my knees wobbled again. I looked around for a corset but there was nothing. How curious! Was I meant to walk around this place with nothing to hold me in? I slid the dress over my head and it stopped right above my knees.

I didn't look a day over sixteen, yet if someone had calculated my age on that particular day – I'd officially turned 592.

Everything was so crisp and bright – too bright. Beams of light trickled minute rainbows across my feet. I looked around the room. Despite waking up on the floor, there was a mattress in an iron bed frame covered by a black quilt. Across the room a bay window looked out at full leaves and swaying branches. Beneath the window was a seat covered in plush blue pillows.

I ran my fingertips against the textured wood of the walls and couldn't believe that I could actually *feel* it. The wood was layered and I felt the raised and jagged parts under my smooth fingertips. My existence as a vampire meant that all my nerve endings were dead. Only by remembering what things felt like as a human could my vampire mind understand whether I was touching something soft or hard. The only senses a vampire retained were those that heightened her ability to kill: the sense of smell was linked to flesh and blood; sight was super sight, detailed down to the minutiae, its sole purpose to find prey within an instant.

My fingers fluttered over the wall again – another rush of shivers rolled up my arms.

'There will be time for that,' Rhode said from the other room.

My heartbeat echoed in my ears. I could taste the air. As I walked, the muscles in my thighs and calves seemed to burn, twitch and then relax. In order to stop shaking, I rested my body weight on the doorway and crossed my hands over my chest.

'What century is this?' I asked, closing my eyes and taking a breath.

'The twenty-first,' Rhode said. His black hair, which had reached halfway down his back the last time I'd seen him, had been cut short and now stood up in spikes. Round his right wrist was a white medical bandage. Rhode gripped a side table and lowered himself into a crimson-coloured lounge seat.

'Sit,' he whispered. I sat down on a pale blue couch that faced the lounger.

'You look terrible,' I whispered.

'Thank you,' he said with the barest glimmer of a smile.

Rhode's cheeks were so sunken that his once masculine carved features now clung to his bones. His usual golden skin had yellowed. His arms quivered as he lowered himself into the chair, holding on to it until he was almost fully sitting down.

'Tell me everything,' I commanded.

'Give me a moment,' he said.

'Where are we?'

'Your new home.' He closed his eyes and leaned his head back on to the chair. He gripped the armrests and I noticed that the rings that had once adorned his fingers were now gone. The curling black snake with emerald eyes, the poison ring for emergencies (which meant it was always filled with blood) were missing. Only one ring remained on his pinky finger. My ring. The ring that I had worn for five hundred years. Only then did I notice that my own hands were bare. It was a tiny silver band with a black stone – onyx. 'Never wear onyx unless you want or know death,' he once told me. I believed him. Besides, up until that moment, I was confident no vampire enjoyed creating death more than I did.

I tried to avoid his gaze. I'd never seen Rhode so weak.

'You're human, Lenah,' he said.

I nodded once in acknowledgement, though I looked at the lines in the hardwood floor. I couldn't respond. Not yet. I wanted it too much. The last interaction I had with Rhode, before waking up in that bedroom, was about my desire to be human. We had an argument, one that I thought would last for centuries. It had, in a way, the argument had happened a century before that moment.

'You finally got what you wanted,' he whispered.

I had to look away again. I couldn't stand the cool blue of his eyes appraising me. Rhode's appearance was so altered – changed – as though he was withering away. When he was at his fullest health, his square jaw and blue eyes made him one of the most beautiful men I'd ever seen. I say man but I am not sure of Rhode's age. He could have been just a boy when he was made into a vampire, but through the years he'd clearly seen and done so much – it had aged him. Vampires, as they move into the maturity of their existence, become so ethereal in appearance that it is nearly impossible to guess their age.

Making sure to keep my eyes away from his, I examined the living room. It looked as though he had just moved in, though the atmosphere of the room felt like Rhode. Despite a few boxes piled next to the door everything seemed to be in its proper place. Many of my possessions from my vampire life decorated the apartment. Specifically, items from my bedchamber. On the wall, an ancient sword was held to a metal plate by golden clasps. It was one of Rhode's favourite pieces, the longsword from his days with the Order of the Garter, a ring of knights under Edward III. It was a special sword, one that was forged by magic, outside of the brotherhood. It had a black leather grip and a thick base that tapered down to a deadly and distinct point. The pommel, the wheel-shaped counterweight on the top of the sword, had an engraving circling its perimeter: *Ita fert corde voluntas.* The heart wills it.

On the wall, on either side of the sword, iron sconces made to look like roses linked by vines and thorns held white unlit candles. White candles should be burned in a house wishing to dispel evil spirits or energy. Every vampire had them for protection against other darker magics. Yes, there are worse things in the universe than vampires.

'I forgot your human beauty.'

I looked back at Rhode. He wasn't smiling, but his eyes sparkled and I knew he meant it. Seeing me now in my human form was a personal fulfilment. He had done what he had set out to do hundreds of years before.

Chapter 2

Evening of 31 October 1910, Hathersage, England – the Peaks

My house was a stone castle. There were halls with marble floors and painted ceilings. I lived in Hathersage, a rural town known for its rolling hills and gorges. My castle was set back from the road and watched over endless fields. That night was Nuit Rouge or, in English, Red Night. Once a year, vampires would come from around the globe and occupy my home for one month. For the thirty-one days in October, Nuit Rouge brought vampires of all races to my home. Thirty-one days of opulence. Thirty-one days of pure terror. This was the last night before everyone returned to their respective hauntings.

It was just after dusk. Above me the stars sparkled in the twilight – they glinted gold light off glass goblets. I pushed past guests sipping on blood and dancing to a string quartet. Rhode followed me out from the back of the castle and on to the stone terrace. Men and women, dressed in top hats, corsets and the finest silks from China, laughed and crowded Rhode's way. At the back of the house, a set of stone steps led down into the gardens. Two white candles stood tall on either end of the steps, their wax dripping tiny archipelagos on to the stone. The garden spread out wide and then down, out into the sweeping countryside. I was wearing an evergreen silk gown adorned with gold piping, and a matching corset beneath.

'Lenah!' Rhode called, but I was darting through the crowd. I was walking so fast that for a moment I thought I would spill out over my corset.

'Lenah! Stop!' Rhode called again.

It was just after dusk. I ran the length of the gardens down the sloping hill into the start of fields.

I led Rhode down the hill, out of sight of the vampires in the castle. I stood at the foot of fields that spread out for countless miles into the distance. Back then, I looked different. My skin was pale white, no shadows under my eyes or wrinkles on my skin. Just white, clear skin as if my pores had been buffed away.

At the crest of the hill, Rhode looked down at me. He was dressed in an evening suit, with a top hat and black silk lapels. He held a cane in his right hand. When he stepped down the side of the steep hill, the wispy grass bowed under his feet. I turned to look out at the fields.

'You have not said a word to me all evening. You've been completely silent. And now you run out here? Care to share with me what the hell is going on?'

'You don't understand? If I uttered a word I would not be able to conceal my intentions. Vicken is unnaturally gifted. He could read my lips from five miles away.'

Vicken was my last creation, that is, the last man I made into a vampire. At sixty, he was also the youngest vampire of my coven, though he didn't look a day older than nineteen.

'Dare I think that this might be a moment of clarity?' Rhode asked. 'That perhaps you realize Vicken and your band of ingrates are more dangerous than you anticipated?'

I said nothing. Instead, I watched the wind trace patterns over the grass.

'Do you know why I left you? My fear,' Rhode spat, 'was that you had truly lost your mind. That the prospect of infinite time had started to eat away at you. You were reckless.'

I spun round. Our eyes met immediately.

'I will not let you fault me for creating a coven of the strongest, most gifted vampires in existence. You told me to protect myself, and I did what I had to do.'

'You cannot see what you have done,' Rhode said. His strong jaw clenched.

'What *I* have done?' I stepped closer to him. 'I feel the weight of this existence in my bones. As though a thousand parasites are eating away at my sanity. You told me once that I was what kept you sane. That the curse of emotional pain released you when you were with me. What do you think happened to me in the hundred and seventy years you were gone?'

13

Rhode's shoulders fell. His eyes were the most blue I had ever seen – even in five hundred years. The beauty of his slim nose and dark hair always shocked me. The vampire essence heightened a person's beauty but for Rhode it radiated from within and lit up his soul – it made my heart burn.

'The magic that binds your coven is more dangerous than I would have ever thought possible. How did you expect me to feel?'

'You don't feel. Remember? We're vampires,' I replied.

He gripped my arm so hard I was sure he would break a bone. I would have been frightened had I not loved him more than I could articulate. Rhode and I were soulmates. Linked in a love bound by passion, the lust for blood, death and the unfaltering under-standing of eternity. Were we lovers? Sometimes. Certain centuries more than others. Were we best friends? Always. We were bound.

'You left me for a hundred and seventy years,' I said, through gritted teeth. Rhode had only returned from his 'break' from me the week before. We had been inseparable since his return. 'Do you not know why I brought you down here?' I asked. 'I can tell no one else the real truth.'

Rhode dropped his arm and I turned to face him directly.

'I have nothing left. No more sympathies,' I whispered, though there was an edge of hysteria in my voice. I could see my reflection in Rhode's eyes. His dilated pupils overwhelmed the blue but I stared into the blackness. My voice quivered. 'Now that I know you have the ritual . . . Rhode, I cannot think of anything else. That my humanity – that it might be a possibility.'

'You have no idea how dangerous this ritual is.'

'I don't care! I want to feel the sand beneath my toes. I want to wake up to the sunlight pouring through my window. I want to smell the air. Anything. Anything I can feel. God, Rhode. I need to smile – and mean it.'

'We all want those things,' he replied in a calm manner.

'Do you? Because I don't think you do,' I said.

'Of course. I want to wake up to blue waters and feel sunlight on my face.'

'The pain is too much,' I said.

'You could try again. Concentrate on me – loving me,' Rhode said gently.

'You, who leave.'

'That's not fair,' Rhode said now, reaching for my hands.

'Even loving you is a curse. I can't really feel or touch you. I look at the humans we take and even they can feel. Even in their last minutes of life they have breath in their lungs and taste in their mouth.'

Rhode held my palm in his and the warmth, the feeling of his passion for me, swept up through my hand and into my body. I closed my eyes, relishing the momentary

15

relief from the countless tragedies resting within me. I opened my eyes and took a step away from him.

'I am losing my mind and I don't know how much longer I can bear it.' I took a moment, careful in my wording. 'Ever since you discovered the ritual,' I continued, 'it's all I can think about. My way out.' My eyes were wild, I was sure of it. 'I need this. I need this. God help me, Rhode, because if you don't I will walk out into sunlight until it scorches me to flames.'

Rhode nearly lost his top hat in a gust of the wind. He ripped his hand out of mine. He still had long hair then and it fell past his shoulders and on to his topcoat.

'You dare to threaten me with your suicide? Don't be petty, Lenah. No one has survived the ritual. Thousands of vampires have tried. All – every single one – has died in the process. Do you think I can bear to lose you? That I could part with you?'

'You already did,' I whispered savagely.

Rhode pulled me close, so fast that I wasn't prepared for the force of his mouth against mine. One deep growl from him and my bottom lip split open as he bit into me. I could feel a rhythmic pull as he sucked the blood from my mouth. After a moment, he stepped away and wiped his bloody lip on his jacket sleeve.

'Yes, I left you. But I had to find the magic and science I needed. If we ever try this ritual – I needed to make sure . . . I didn't expect you to fall in love when I left.'

There was a silence. Rhode knew as well as I that I'd

never believed he was coming back.

'I do not love Vicken as I love you.' I said every word so it was clear and calculated. After a moment, I added, 'I want out.'

'You do not know what will come to you if you choose human life.'

'The air? Real breath? Happiness?'

'Death, sickness, human nature?'

'I don't understand,' I said, stepping back again. 'You have said yourself that humanity is what all vampires crave. The freedom to feel more than constant pain and suffering. Do you not feel this way?'

'It consumes me,' Rhode said, and took off his top hat. He looked out at the fields. 'There are deer, there.' He pointed. He was right. About ten miles away a herd of deer grazed silently. We could have fed off them, though I did love my dress, and blood would not match the green silk. Besides, I hated the taste of animal blood and would only feed on them if I were in a dire situation. With the creation of the coven, I had ensured that would never happen.

Rhode slipped his hands round my lower back and brought me even closer.

'Your beauty will be a powerful force in the human world. Your human face may betray even your best intentions.'

'I don't care,' I said, not quite understanding and not really caring either way.

17

Rhode reached out and ran his index finger down the thin slope of my nose. He then gently rubbed his thumb over my lips. I couldn't have looked away from his furrowed brow and piercing stare even if I had tried.

'When I took you from your father's orchards in the fifteenth century I saw your future laid out before me,' Rhode confessed. 'Swashbuckling vampire linked to my side for all eternity.' There was a pause. Somewhere behind us music from the party echoed down into the fields. 'I saw my own dreams.'

'Then give me what I want.'

Rhode's mouth was a thin line. He furrowed his eyebrows and looked out at the deer. They galloped deeper into the grassy hills. I could tell from his still mouth and dark expression that he was formulating a plan.

'One hundred years,' he whispered, but still looked out at the deer.

My eyes widened.

'Starting tonight you will hibernate for one hundred years.' Rhode turned back to look at me and pointed up the hill. I knew he was gesturing towards a cemetery. It was to the right of the terrace and protected by a wrought-iron gate topped by spiked points.

Hibernation only occurred when a vampire rested in the ground. The vampire sleeps and deprives herself of blood – there are a series of spells so the vampire remains in a meditative state, almost to the point of death. On a prearranged day a fellow vampire revives her. But only with magic is this possible. Only very brave (and some would argue very stupid) vampires have done this.

'The night before you are supposed to wake,' Rhode continued, 'I will unearth you and take you somewhere safe, somewhere you cannot be found. Somewhere you can be a human and live out your days.'

'And the coven?' I asked.

'You leave them behind.'

My heart throbbed, a familiar pain that I couldn't help but recognize. The magical binding between the coven and myself would force them to search for me. Just as I knew I would love Rhode until the end of the earth, I knew that the coven would search for me. I nodded once but said nothing. I watched the deer nibbling at the grass and licking their fur.

'You are not afraid to die?' he asked.

I shook my head. Rhode turned to face the house. I stopped him from walking up the hill by gently grasping his fingers. He turned to me.

'Will you be there?' I asked. 'If I die and we fail, will you be there?'

Rhode's fingers lightly grazed the top of my hand. He turned it over, touched my palm and whispered, 'Always.'

'How did you do it?' I was spellbound. Back in the dark apartment, my back pressed into the pillows. My fingers wandered over the fine velvet. My fingertips skimmed along the softness of the couch, which produced a wave of goosebumps over my legs. Before, I would have known the couch was soft but it would only have meant the fabric. It wouldn't have meant comfort or safety. Just soft.

'That night. The last night of Nuit Rouge. You went to bed . . .' Rhode started.

'After killing one of the maids,' I admitted, remembering the young blonde girl I'd caught off guard in the attic.

Rhode continued with a slight smile. 'I told Vicken that you had decided on your hibernation. That you would sleep for a hundred years and that I was to wake you on the last night of the following Nuit Rouge.

'Why did we decide one hundred years? I never asked you,' I said.

'Simply? Time. Vicken would be distracted enough that I could take you from your hibernating plot in the cemetery. All I had to do was wait for a night when he wasn't watching your tombstone. When that night came not long ago, I took you away.'

'So it's been one hundred years?' I asked, eager to place myself within space and time. 'Since I was last above ground?'

'Just shy. It's September. I spared you a month or so.'

'And you performed the ritual two days ago?' I asked.

'Two days,' Rhode confirmed.

'What about the coven? Do they have any idea I'm gone?'

20

'I don't think so. Vicken still thinks you are buried. Remember, I told him that you *wanted* to be buried – to make it official. He thought it was a wonderful idea. He wanted a chance to rule your coven.'

'I wouldn't have protested against that,' I said.

'Precisely why he believed me so willingly. It was a lie, Lenah. The moment you looked into my eyes on the fields and begged me for human life, I knew that my quest, my vampire life, your vampire life, what I had done to you, was coming to an end.'

'I shouldn't have begged you. Manipulated you like I did.'

Rhode laughed but the breath was short. 'That is your way.'

I looked at the bandage round his wrist and the dark rings circling his eyes. At that moment, I felt a surge of guilt. In my human state, I couldn't imagine bribing Rhode or threatening him with suicide. It had been so easy for me before. Easy because the emotional pain that clouded the vampire life prevented rational thought.

'Please tell me about the ritual,' I asked again.

Rhode unwrapped the white bandage, roll by roll, until his wrist was bare. There, on the inside of his wrist, were teeth marks, my teeth marks – two small indents. The one on the left was just higher than the one on the right. I'd always hated the fact that my bite was uneven. I could have recognized my teeth marks anywhere.

'The most important thing is the intent. The success

of the sacrifice, and *it is* a sacrifice, depends solely on the vampire performing the ritual. It takes two days.'

Rhode stood up. He paced whenever he was telling me something difficult. Sometime in the sixteenth century I'd asked him why. He said it was so he wouldn't have to look me in the eye.

'The intent is where most vampires fail,' Rhode continued. 'You have to want the other vampire to live. You, in turn, have to want to die. It is the most unselfish act you've ever committed. As you know, such selflessness is nearly impossible for the natural state of a vampire.'

'Who told you this?' I asked.

'When I left you for those years, I went to France. I searched for— '

'Suleen,' I said, though I was suddenly finding it very hard to breathe. *Rhode had met Suleen . . . in person.*

'Yes. He was coming out of a fifty-year hibernation. When I described you and then told him of my plan, he comforted me with a compliment. He said that I might be the only vampire with soul enough to succeed.'

I raised my eyebrows in surprise. It must have been quite a special moment in Rhode's life. I wished I had been there to see Rhode's reaction when Suleen said something so significant.

I imagined Suleen. He was an East Indian man, or at least he had been some time ago – when, I have no idea. He is the oldest vampire alive. Nothing in the grand scheme of life would or could ever rattle his soul.

Suleen is not hindered by death nor does he want to return to human life. All he wants is to live long enough so he may see the end of the world.

'There are a few more rules,' Rhode explained. 'The vampire performing the ritual must be more than five hundred years old. Suleen mentioned something about the chemistry of a vampire of that age. It is a crucial ingredient. But most of all he kept saying, "The intent, Rhode. It's the intent." The will and the desire to give up your life in order that another may live. Vampires are selfish, Lenah. Inherently so. I had to find that will within myself.'

'You sacrificed yourself?' I whispered. I was unable to look up from the floor. Rhode remained silent. He was waiting for me to look at him. I hated him for it. Finally, our eyes met.

'The ritual required that I give you all of my blood. After two days, you woke up, more or less, and bit into me. I had to allow you to finish it – well, almost all of it. But the important thing was the intent, the chemistry of my blood and my love for you.'

'I never would have agreed to those conditions.'

Much to my surprise, Rhode's stoical facial expression turned into a smile. A toothy, happy smile. 'Precisely why I did it when you were weakened and hibernating.'

I stood up. Now it was my turn to pace.

'So where is Vicken?' I asked, trying to think like a

23

vampire. Trying to place all the pieces together. I had been asleep for one hundred years.

'He remains at your house in Hathersage with the rest of the coven. I believe he is awaiting your return.'

'Have you seen him since my hibernation?'

'He is too young for me to converse with as often as he would like. His energy tires me. Yet, when I stayed with them, he was respectful. He's a fighter. Excellent swordsman. I can see why you loved him.'

My cheeks warmed, which surprised me. Then I realized I was feeling shame. I snuck a peek at Rhode's fingers holding the arm of the lounger. They were pruned and wrinkled as though all the liquid inside him had been sucked away.

'I do not blame you for loving another,' Rhode said.

'You believe Vicken loves me? As I love you?'

Rhode shook his head. 'Vicken loves your outward appearance and desire for thick, congealed blood. I love your soul. As a mate to my long search on this earth. You are – were – the most vicious vampire I have ever known. I love you for that.'

I couldn't respond. I thought of Hathersage, of the fields, of Rhode in his top hat and the deer grazing in the distance.

'Vicken will search for me,' I said. 'As you know, he is bound to me. And when he finds me the coven will destroy me. I created the coven to do just that. To seek, capture and obliterate.'

'That is the exact reason why I chose this place.'

'Yes. Where are we?' I looked about the apartment.

'This is *your* new school.'

'You intend for me to go to school?' My head reared in his direction.

'It is crucial you understand.' Even in his weakened state Rhode stood up and towered over me. He glared at me with such a passionate fierceness that I should have been frightened. 'Vicken will dig you up from the cemetery. I promised you would return on the final night of Nuit Rouge. The party ends on October the thirty-first.'

'So on the thirty-first he will find an empty casket. End of story.'

'It's not that simple. You were a vampire, Lenah. One of the oldest of your kind.'

'I know what I was.'

'Then do not pretend that you need a tutorial in the seriousness of this situation!' Rhode snapped, and continued pacing very slowly. I was silent. Rhode regained some of his composure and again spoke at a low decibel. 'When Vicken digs up the grave and discovers an empty casket, he will search the earth for you. As you've said yourself, the magic that binds the coven has made it so. You made it so. He will exhaust himself, so will all of the coven, until they find you and bring you home.'

'I did not foresee myself in this situation.'

'Yes, well, luckily, for now, the magic that protects you allows a few luxuries. Your vampire sight and your extrasensory perception.'

'So I did keep it, then,' I said, and stood up. I looked around the room again. Yes, as Rhode said, I could see all of the adornments in the room, down to the knots in the wood floor and the perfection in the paint on the walls.

'As you assimilate into this human existence, these accompaniments will fade.'

How was I to process not being a vampire any more but still retaining some vampire qualities? Could I be in the sun? Could I eat food again? These thoughts rattled within my head and I stamped my foot in frustration. Rhode put his hands on my cheeks and I was startled by how cold they were. It stopped my tantrum.

'You must disappear into human life, Lenah. You must go to school and become a sixteen-year-old girl again.'

In that moment, I couldn't cry no matter how badly I wanted to – I was too shocked. Vampires cannot cry. There is nothing natural in a vampire. No tears, no water – just blood and black magic. Instead, the tears that would spill over the cheeks of a normal person in the vampire are acidic pain which scorches the tear ducts.

I wanted to run or turn inside out, anything to curb the feeling that made my stomach burn. I balled my hands into fists and tried to fill the anxiety with a breath, but it caught in my throat. My gaze fell on a photo resting on top of a bureau. It looked tattered and old, though the last time I had seen the photo I was posing for it. 1910, the last night of Nuit Rouge. In the photo, Rhode and I stood hip to hip, arms round each other's waists, on the back terrace of my home. Rhode was dressed in his black suit and top hat, me in a gown, my long brown hair tied and styled in a long braid that fell over my left breast. We were more than human. We were frighteningly beautiful.

'How can I do that?' I turned away from the photo to look at Rhode. 'Hide?'

'Oh, I think you will find it easier than you expect. You have never been sixteen before. I snatched that away before you could.'

He stepped close to me again and kissed my forehead.

'Why did you do this for me?' I asked. He pulled away and the air shifted as the space opened up between us.

'Of course, you must know,' Rhode said, and cocked his head to the side.

I shook my head to say that I did not nor could I ever understand what he had done for me.

'Because,' he continued, 'throughout all of my histories I found no one I loved more than you. No one.'

'But I'm losing you,' I said, my voice breaking.

Rhode grasped me so my cheek pressed against his chest. I stayed there a moment and let my heartbeat echo between our bodies.

'And you think Vicken won't be able to find me?' I asked.

'I do not think in his wildest dreams he will understand what I have done. It will take the entire coven's effort just to follow us this far and I believe I have done my best to conceal our whereabouts. Also, why would he ever suspect you could be human?'

I stepped away and looked back at the portrait photograph of Rhode and me.

'When will you die?' I asked, turning away from the photo and sitting back down on the couch. I brought my knees to my chest and linked my arms round my shins.

'The morning.'

We sat together and I stared into Rhode's eyes for as long as possible. He told me of the changes in society. Cars, television, sciences, wars that neither of us, even in our vampire minds, could understand. He said that practical things were of the utmost importance to humans. I would now be capable of getting sick. He had placed me in the finest boarding school in New England. A doctor, he informed me, was only a few buildings away. He begged that I complete school and grow up, as he had prevented me from doing.

We talked and talked and, without knowing it, I fell asleep. The last thing I remember were his eyes looking into mine. I think he may have kissed my lips but that also felt like a dream.

When I awoke, the shades were drawn and the whole living area was shrouded in darkness. Across from me, red-lit numbers illuminated the blackness. A digital clock said that the time was eight in the morning. I was on the couch and Rhode wasn't in the lounger across from me. I shot up. My muscles were stiff so I stumbled and held on to one arm of the chair.

'Rhode?' I called out.

But I already knew.

'No . . .' I whispered. I spun in a circle. There were only four rooms: a bedroom, a bathroom, a living room and a kitchen. Off the living area was a balcony. The curtains were closed yet the way the wind drifted inward made the curtains billow. The door was open behind them. I pushed them aside and stepped out on to the wooden boards. I put my hand over my eyes as a visor. My eyes adjusted immediately as I scanned the balcony, hopeful for only a moment.

Rhode was gone. From my life. From my existence.

I saw the onyx ring lying in the centre. When I approached it, I realized it was in the middle of a tiny pile of glittering dust. It looked as though sand was mixed with mica or tiny diamonds. My Rhode, my companion for close to six hundred years, weakened from the transformation and self-sacrifice, had evaporated in the sun. I dipped my thumb and index finger into Rhode's remains. They were cool and gritty. I pulled out the ring and slid the smooth metal over my new sensitive skin.

I was alone.

Chapter 3

Grief is an emotion not completely foreign to vampires, but it feels more like a shift or a change in the direction of the wind. It is a silent flutter, a parasitic reminder of the many layers of pain that define the vampire world.

This was something entirely different.

The morning of Rhode's death, I scooped the glittering dust into an urn and placed it on top of the bureau. Rhode had brought my jewellery box from Hathersage so it was easy to find an old blood vial and fill it with a handful of his remains. I hung it from a braided chain round my neck.

I turned from the bureau and found a letter on the coffee table. I used a silver letter opener to slice the envelope and I started to read. It was nearly noon when I looked up from the pieces of paper. The letter held instructions for my new life, social expectations of the twenty-first century and what I was to do with my days before school started. The beginning of the letter warned that I should start with simple food as my body wasn't accustomed to eating and then digesting. I placed the

letter down on my lap then picked it back up again.
The last paragraph of Rhode's letter kept drawing me
to read it again and again:

Was it all worth it? Did we not have moments
of grace? No more are you bound to involuntary
suffering. Find peace in my death. Shed tears. There
is only freedom now. If Vicken and your coven
return, you will know what to do. Never forget, Lenah.
Evil be he who thinketh evil.
Be brave,
Rhode

There was an aching in my gut. Deep down where I
couldn't fill it. I tried to distract myself by looking out at
the Wickham campus. From my balcony railing I could
see a stone building with the words STUDENT CENTER on
the front. To the right and just behind it, was a building
with a high stone tower. The distraction wasn't working.
I looked back to the papers Rhode had left me.

One thing was certain: Rhode's savings were more
than anyone needed to survive in present-day society.
The problem? I couldn't touch them. My own money
remained in the control of Vicken and the coven. I
couldn't access it either because they would be able to
track my exact location. I wasn't sure of the workings
of banks and 'routing' as Rhode explained in his letter, but I was to deal exclusively in cash unless I had an

emergency. He left me a trunk's worth.

Rhode's instructions were clear. I was to work and to avoid spending his savings. '*You might need them one day,*' were the exact words he used. His letter also said '*immersion was key to survival*'. The thought of what Vicken could or would do seeing me, his former lover, his former queen, in this vulnerable state sent shivers down my spine. Vicken, like all vampires, has a lust for tragedy, a desire for tears, blood and murder. Most vampires want to reach out, inflict the pain that constantly haunts them and siphon it out on to others. Despite my hesitation, I could imagine the scenario. What Vicken could potentially do to me, as a human . . . I shook my head quickly to divert the thought.

I was about to pick up a manual for a laptop computer when a knock on the door startled me from my thoughts. Hanging on the arm of the lounger was a simple black sweater that had once belonged to Rhode. I pulled it on over a tank top I was wearing and walked back into the apartment.

'Reveal yourself,' I commanded to the closed door.

'Um . . .' a timid, male voice said in response.

'Oh, I mean, who is it?' I said a bit more gently. After all, I didn't command a ring of vampires any more.

'Car delivery for Lenah Beaudonte.'

I ripped open the door.

'*A car?*'

The boy behind the door was tall, lanky and clad in a

shirt that had writing scrawled across the front: GRAND CAR SERVICE. The hallway behind him was poorly lit and the wallpaper had some sort of nautical theme with sailboats and anchors.

'I'm just here to deliver it,' the lanky boy said with about as much enthusiasm as a person delivering news of a relative's untimely death.

After grabbing a set of very dark sunglasses from the coffee table (I can only assume Rhode left them for me) and a black floppy hat, I followed the boy out of the apartment, down the stairs and into the lobby. Once I was in the lobby, I hesitated in the doorway. Outside, birds chirped and the voices of students flew from all directions. The blazing sun blasted the cement walkway leading from the front of the building, out on to a grassy lawn. Perhaps the sensitivity to sunlight was much like my vampire sight? Would I still be affected by it?

Sunlight breaks down the magic that seals the vampire, though the danger of sunlight lessens as the vampire ages in years. As they move forward in their vampire life, the magic to withstand sunlight strengthens. Though I have heard that death by sunlight is supposed to be the worst pain, like being ripped apart and scorched to ash while conscious for every moment of it. Regardless of my age, I have never directly stepped out into the light without protection.

I nudged a toe out of the doorway and let my foot and leg hit the sunlight. I whipped it back inside and paused. I twisted my leg so I could see the back of my calf muscle. I also checked my shin. No red mark. No burns.

'You gonna go outside?' said a voice to my right. The security guard, a squat woman with thick-framed eyeglasses, watched me. The way she spoke was so strange. 'You gonna . . .' – the phrasing of her words was *interesting*. 'Gonna' . . . What could this possibly mean? I waited for her to say something else, but she just looked at me. Through my sunglasses, I moved my gaze to the car deliveryman. He raised an eyebrow at me from the sunny entryway. I was in a pair of thin sandals, wearing Rhode's oversized black sweater and a pair of shorts. I was ready. I took a deep breath and walked outside.

The summer heat was the first thing I felt. How glorious! Sunlight felt like a bath by a roaring fire, like sweat and happiness washing over me from head to toe. I exhaled happily.

Wickham's campus was enormous. Although it seemed pastoral at first glance, the buildings were brick with sleek metal and glass facades. There were meadows of green grass and serpentine pathways that linked throughout the campus. In the distance, through swaying, leafy branches, a colonial-style chapel shone white under the morning sun.

Seeker was the dormitory closest to the private school's entrance gates. It also had the largest lawn. Directly outside the front door, a collection of girls was lying out on a blanket in the sun. They seemed to be wearing only their undergarments but then after a moment I realized their ensembles were meant for this kind of activity. This was curious to me, as I had never seen anyone sunbathe before.

I watched the girls rub a white lotion into their skins, adjust their blankets and lie back down.

'So there it is,' the lanky boy said. He pointed past the sunbathers at the parking lot which abutted the lawn. In the row closest to the lawn was a baby-blue car. My car. I couldn't tell you the name or the make at the time, but just the idea that I had one was brilliant.

'You've got nice parents,' the kid said.

I started to walk towards the car when a group of students about my age (relatively speaking) ran by and pointed into the distance, past Seeker. To the left of my dormitory was a tree-lined pathway that led to the Wickham grounds. Later I discovered that there were many pathways just like this that snaked throughout the grounds. One of the girls yelled to another pack of students trailing behind her.

'It's one fifty-four! Come on! They're gonna start in six minutes.'

'What's the commotion?' I asked the car-delivery kid.

'Enos brothers. Kind of a daredevil group. They race their boats out in the harbour right in front of Wickham's private beach every Labor Day weekend. Been doin' it for two years. The youngest Enos had to turn fourteen before they could do it together.'

I signed my name, took the car keys and decided I would worry about driving later. I wanted to see the boat-racing Enos brothers.

I let the students run ahead of me; I wasn't exactly ready to mix with the group. Wickham's paths were lined on either side by tall oak trees. Even with the wide-brimmed hat and sunglasses, I tried to walk in the shade. On each side of the pathway were buildings that were designed in the same fashion as my dormitory, Seeker. Most were made from grey stone with great glass windows and doors. Some of the buildings were marked with red signs on their lawns that declared their names and specific functions. It was all quite regal, actually. Most of the students on the walkway were heading towards the far end of the path, past a greenhouse (this piqued my interest) and down a series of stone steps that ended on a beach.

There it was. The ocean during daylight. So many nights I spent watching the moon run a milky line across the top of the water. So many times I had wished it were the sun. Eventually I was old enough to withstand the daylight, though the beach was never a place I ventured. It's not that vampires stand in direct opposition to the natural elements of the world. But the ocean, sunlight and all of the happiness that comes with the beach during the day was just another place I couldn't be. Another source of torment.

It smelt like salt, earth and crisp air. The way the sun dazzled on the water made me wish I could touch the light, wield it with my hands. It looked how I felt – happy. The beach at Wickham had different-shaped boulders that were scattered about the beige sand. The waves were no more than two feet and rolled lazily on to the shore. There must have been fifty people dotting the coastline. Like Rhode said, my vampire sight was as clear as ever so I did a quick scan of the beach to find there were exactly seventy-three people standing about.

Not only that but the sand was made from thousands of colours, coral, yellows, browns and hundreds of shades of grey. Dark blue umbrellas were stacked and laid against the storm wall that separated the beach from the campus. I could see the fibreglass in the poles of the umbrellas and each thread of fabric in the tops. A wooden boat dock jutted out about twenty yards from the beach.

An island sat in the middle of the bay. The landscape was pretty sparse; just some tall oak trees and a sandy shoreline.

I turned from the water and approached the stone wall. It wasn't too high, about six feet. I stuck a foot in one of the holes between the stones and I climbed up with ease. I sat down on top of the wall with my legs crossed. I still had my sunglasses on and I felt a bit more protected as a branch from a large oak tree shaded my spot. I leaned back on my hands and stared out at the ocean.

While I looked out at the island and watched the branches of the trees sway in the wind, I had a sudden feeling . . . I inherently *knew* that someone was watching me. My thoughts immediately went to Vicken, though this would have been nearly impossible. In this century, Vicken would have turned 160. At that age, most vampires cannot be in a shaded room during the day but Vicken was different. He could be in the sunlight from a very early age. Also, he assumed I was hibernating. There would be no reason for him to search me out at Wickham. Although Vicken was my own creation, he was and always has been the most advanced vampire I have ever met.

I admit, it was a relief when I looked to the right only to find a group of girls staring at me a few feet away from the water. They looked me up and down, which was curious. I had friends who were female vampires but they'd never examined me as though there was something wrong with my appearance. One of the girls was quite pretty. She was shorter than me, and had long light-blonde hair. She was the one who was staring the most intently.

'Can I sit with you?'

An Asian boy stood on the sand. His blue jeans were ripped in a vertical line, showing his right thigh. He wore two different-coloured sandals, one red, one yellow, and a blue button-down shirt. His facial features showed him to be Japanese. I started to speak to him in his native tongue.

'*Why would you want to sit with me?*'

He pressed his lips together and his eyebrows screwed up. He ran a hand through his spiky, black hair.

'I don't speak Japanese,' he said in English. 'But my parents do.'

'Strange,' I said. 'A Japanese boy who only speaks English?' I took off my sunglasses so our eyes could meet.

'How do you know Japanese?' He leaned his right hand on the stone wall and kept eye contact with me.

'I know a lot of languages,' I said. I stared through the brown of his irises, forging a bond. Vampires use the gaze as a way to see your intentions. If the person stares back at you, you can trust them. Sometimes this failed me and I was lied to regardless. Once I discovered this betrayal, I had no problem ripping out their throats with my front teeth. But this boy, he had a white aura and an innocence to his soul.

'How many languages can you speak?' he asked.

'Twenty-five,' I said honestly.

He laughed, seeming not to believe me. When I didn't react but looked into his brown eyes quite earnestly, his jaw dropped.

'You should work for the CIA,' he said. He stuck out

39

his hand. 'I'm Tony,' he said, and I shook his hand. I snuck a peek at his inner wrist. The veins stuck out just fine – he would have been an easy kill.

'Lenah Beaudonte,' I said.

'Beaudonte,' he said drawing out the *e* so it sounded like *ay*. 'Fancy. So can I?' He gestured to an open spot on the wall next to me.

'Why?' I asked. I didn't enquire in a mean or accusatory way. I was genuinely interested in why this seemingly normal boy would want to sit next to a person like me.

'Because everyone out here pretty much sucks?' he proposed. He nodded in the direction of the pretty girls still looking my way. Now they were standing even closer together, occasionally peeking up at me. I smirked in response. I liked his honesty. I also liked the use of the word 'suck' in a non-vampire situation.

Communication in this century was fascinating. It was so casual and without the formality that I was accustomed to hearing in the beginning of the twentieth century. Now, as many times before, I would have to adapt. For hundreds of years I had listened to the parting of lips and undulations of tongues. I stood on the fringe and studied, translated, sometimes in many dialects, in order to find the best way to adapt and fit in. Understanding the way people spoke to one another ensured that I could interact and mingle in society without being noticed – it made it easier to kill.

I broke from these thoughts when Tony hoisted himself up and let his legs dangle over the edge of the stone wall. He kicked his heels back so they bounced off the stone. We sat there for a moment, and I liked the silence; in fact, it gave me an opportunity to look him over. He was a bit taller than me and burly, like a wrestler. Sitting this close, I was able to see the wispy lines of veins running along his neck. But that's not what kept my attention. He wore at least ten earrings in each ear! Some were so wide that they had stretched his ear lobe out and I could see right through it.

'So, why are *you* sitting over here by yourself?' he asked.

I pulled back quickly and put on my sunglasses. I thought it over a moment; the way I would speak, that is. I remembered the way the car-delivery boy had spoken, and the casual intonation behind Tony's words – both were quite easy to understand. Words so far were lazy and the formulation behind them held very little social expectation. Everyone seemed to speak this way, with very little concern for formality. *I could do this*, I thought. I would have to internalize contemporary cultural references but *this won't take long at all.* I exhaled as a smile crossed my face.

'Because most of the people here look like they pretty much suck,' I said.

Tony smiled in return. 'How old are you?' he asked.

'Sixteen, as of yesterday.' (Was I lying?)

'Cool! Happy birthday.' Tony's smile widened and his eyes twinkled. 'I am too. So that makes you a junior, right?'

I recalled some paperwork that I had seen that morning. I remembered an official letter that said I was a junior. I nodded in response. We sat for a bit and listened to the happenings around us. Some people chatted about the beginning of school and I concentrated on the way people spoke in this age.

I am so not going to even speak to him this year.

Are you insane? Justin Enos is the hottest guy on campus!

Why the hell is that girl wearing sunglasses and a hat? Incognito much? Hello?!

Then the chatter changed dramatically. Some people pointed out towards the harbour. I snuck one more glance back at the tall blonde staring at me. She looked away from me and started to jump up and down. I refocused on the water. After all, that was why I was there: to watch boat racing. Not to get the inquisition from a blonde girl who would have been a reasonably small lunch in my usual circumstances.

'Look!' Tony pointed. 'Here they come!'

I could see two boats coming from opposite directions in the harbour. They were strange boats made from white metal and shaped so the bow was a sharp point. One of the boats was painted with red flames running along the sides, the other had blue flames. During my existence all boats were made from wood. This was something new. Though Rhode had briefly explained cars and engines, I wasn't prepared for the intense roaring that came from these machines. Even on the beach it echoed, vibrating within my ears.

'What are they doing?' I asked. The boats were still roaring from opposite ends of the harbour. They moved so quickly towards each other that huge sprays of water propelled from the back of the boats up into an arc in the air.

'They race round the island twice. Whoever gets back to the dock first, wins. They smashed into it two years ago,' Tony said.

'What do they get if they win?' I asked.

'Respect,' Tony replied.

The boats moved so fast I couldn't tell who was behind the wheel. *Surely this must be some kind of sick joke*, I thought. The boats were coming closer and closer, the pointed bows aimed right at each other. A girl on the beach screamed. Then, within moments, maybe within inches of each other, both boats changed angle. Sprays of water flew in the air. I could see the curved underbelly of the boat with blue flames. They raced away from the beach, each choosing a side and tearing away round the island.

Everyone on the beach screeched, yelled and whooped so loud that the sound swelled in my ears. They all stood, jumping and waving, except Tony and me. Some were chanting the name *Justin* over and over, others the name *Curtis*.

The boats came round again and passed in front of the island. I held my breath because they criss-crossed within inches of smashing into each other. The bows just barely grazed. There was a collective gasp from the beach as the boats disappeared behind the island again.

'This is fun?' I asked. My heart fluttered from all of the adrenaline bashing about my chest.

'This is the least of what they do,' Tony said. 'The whole family is crazy. Thrill seekers.'

'They're brothers, right?' I asked, a memory of my coven leaping into my mind. 'They must be close, I said. 'Trust each other.'

Tony replied to what I said but I was barely listening. In my mind Heath, Gavin, Song and Vicken sat by a fire. We were at my home in Hathersage sometime around the 1890s. Rhode was still gone, angry with me somewhere in Europe, and I sat in the middle of my brotherhood. They surrounded me in a circle and were seated in black wooden chairs. Each chair was carved to match their personality. Gavin's was marked with many types of sword because he was a brilliant swordsman. Vicken's was covered in globes and ancient symbols. He was the strategist. My favourite was Heath's, which was adorned with words in Latin. Song's was notable as its only adornments were Chinese lettering. My chair was smooth, wonderful wood with only one adornment. The words of our coven, the lyrical sentiment that I twisted into malice and pain: *Evil be he who thinketh evil.*

I was wearing an aubergine-coloured gown. We were laughing hysterically about something that I cannot remember now. I do remember that behind us, passed out and chained to the wall, was a peasant man I intended to have for dinner.

'Here they come,' Tony said. I blinked, coming back to the moment. 'Wow, it's pretty close,' he said, and craned his neck to get a better look.

The motors were at full throttle. The powerful engines propelled the boats towards the dock so fast that I had the instinctive reaction to get up and back away. But Tony wasn't backing up, so I sat still. The blue and red boats were neck and neck. The sharp bows headed right towards the wooden dock.

'They're going to hit it!' I said.

'Maybe,' Tony said casually.

'They'll die!' I said, half horrified and half exhilarated.

They were now so close that even without my vampire sight I could see that driving the blue-flamed boat was a tall blond boy and behind the wheel of the red-flamed boat was a pudgy blond boy. I focused in, and the red-flamed boat came closer. The pudgy boy wore a necklace with a silver charm. He had silver hoops in his ears. A scar above his left lip. Then, at the last second, the boat with the tall boy behind the wheel skidded by the dock first. He turned his boat in the direction of the harbour so quickly that a huge arc of water rose and then splashed down, just touching the people by the waterline.

There was a collective scream of joy and almost everyone ran towards the dock. The pudgy boy and a significantly smaller version of him secured the losing boat to the dock. Out in the harbour, idling, was the victor, the tall boy. The engines of his boat went silent and then a splash. He was swimming towards the beach.

Tony leaned closer to me and pointed at the smallest of the brothers.

'That's Roy Enos. He's a freshman.' He pointed to the pudgy one. 'That one is Curtis Enos. He's a senior. Class joker,' Tony said. He was much rounder than the others. His fleshy middle pushed out his swimming trunks.

Finally, the tall, six-foot-three, blonde, gorgeous boy emerged from the ocean. He kicked his legs through the shallow water. He was taller than Rhode. I didn't know anyone, up until that moment, who was taller than him.

'And that's Justin Enos,' Tony grumbled. 'He's in our class.'

Justin had a long face with chiselled cheekbones and evergreen eyes. He had a broad chest and sculpted torso. It was the shoulders that kept my stare – square and broad, it seemed like they could do anything: raise a building, swim the English Channel, lift me up with

46

his bare hands. Every boy on that beach was envious of him. Every girl on the beach salivated at the sight of him.

'So you hate him?' I said, breaking my stare to enjoy the sentiment of jealousy – just a little bit.

Tony smiled in return. 'Every guy at Wickham does.'

Without another word, I hopped off the stone wall and started towards the steps that led back towards campus. The race was over and I wanted to reread Rhode's letter.

'You're just gonna leave like that?' Tony called after me. I turned. He was still sitting on the stone wall.

'I'm going home.'

'Generally, you say bye when you're gonna leave.'

I walked back towards Tony and he jumped down from the stone wall to meet me.

'I'm really bad at this whole *social* thing,' I explained.

'Where are you from?' Tony asked, but a voice towards the shore interrupted: 'I wanted to push it to eighty but I didn't need to! Just maxed out at sixty miles an hour.'

Tony and I stood side by side near the stairs. Neither of us could take our eyes off Justin. He took a duffel bag from another boy about his age, walked in our direction and then stopped at the group of girls that had given me the eye. He slung the duffel over his shoulder (his biceps were huge) and then slipped a hand round the

waist of the conspicuous blonde girl. She beamed, clinging to Justin's arm and swaying her hips as she walked.

Justin walked towards the stairs. When he saw Tony
and me, he stopped. He stared straight at me, not in a
dumbstruck way but as though he'd found something
on the ground and wanted to investigate it, hold it under a microscope and give it a thorough inspection. I
looked at Tony and then back at Justin. Justin was still
staring but now he was smiling. His lips were full and
he looked as if he was pouting. I wasn't sure what to say.
Thankfully, Tony spoke.

'What's up, Enos?'

Maybe Justin was waiting for me to join the group of
girls but I just stood there. The tall, blonde girl stared at
me, her slim nostrils flaring and her high cheekbones
reddened. Was this what jealousy looked like on a
mortal teenager? How wonderful! I couldn't help
feeling triumphant in her anger and pain. This was a
gut reaction. As a vampire, I loved others' pain because
it lessened my own. But now, as a human, as soon as
I recognized the pain within her, it flitted away – that
instant desire to reach out, inflict hurt – it was gone.
Instead I concentrated on Justin's green eyes looking at
the hat, the sunglasses and me. I knew the vampire aura
was capable of putting spells on humans, enrapturing
them so they believed they were in love or that they had
found peace. Did Justin Enos love me despite his better
judgement? Was this one of the 'accompaniments' that

had stayed with me through the transformation? I looked at Justin, eagerly awaiting what he would say to me.

Finally, he spoke. 'Next time you leave your room, think about putting on some trousers,' Justin said. He winked and started towards the stairs to the school campus.

I looked down. Rhode's oversized sweater made it look as though I wasn't wearing anything on the bottom. The girls cackled as they walked away, especially the blonde one. She turned her brown eyes on me. A burning spread in my chest. I knew anger. That emotion had haunted me my entire life, but this was, dare I think it, embarrassment? No one had dared to embarrass me before.

I walked quickly up the path in the direction of Seeker. I just wanted to be in my room, shut the door and go to sleep. I wanted Vicken, I wanted Heath, I wanted the familiarity of a dark room.

'Hey, wait!'

I kept walking.

'Lenah!'

I stopped. It was the first time in hundreds of years someone who wasn't a vampire had said my name. Tony jogged up the path from the beach.

'Remember the whole *saying bye* thing?' he said once he was in front of me.

'I hate those girls.' I crossed my arms over my chest. My cheeks burned with heat.

'Everyone does. Come on. Let's go do something.'

49

Chapter 4

'Do something'? *What did this mean exactly?*

'It's, like, three, right? Union is open. You get your books yet?' Tony asked. 'I'm headed over if you want to come.'

So many questions! Did I get my books yet? 'No,' I said. 'I don't have my books.'

Tony walked me back to Seeker Hall so I could grab what Rhode left me as my money holder. I also needed some official papers so that I knew what books to buy for class. Wickham students had two days before classes started. Rhode had left me some modern-day clothes, which were mostly all hideous (and revealing) but I slipped on a pair of jeans with the promise to go shopping as soon as I could figure out how to drive.

I spotted the blue car when I came back out of Seeker. Tony was sitting on one of the wooden benches that were on either side of the dorm entrance. He held his hands behind his head and stretched his legs out.

'That's mine,' I said. I stepped next to the bench and pointed at the car.

'Whoa,' Tony said. I could see that he was admiring

the sheen of the bonnet. 'Lucky. You can leave campus. Restaurants, the mall, Boston.'

'Maybe you could show me how to drive?' I proposed.

'You don't know how?' Tony stopped walking. I shook my head. Tony smiled. 'Your parents bought you a fancy car but haven't taught you how to drive it? I thought my parents were weird. Soon, Lenah. As soon as possible.'

'Excellent!'

As we passed Seeker, I looked back and saw my balcony, the door still open, and I wondered for one fleeting moment if any of Rhode's remains were swirling around the floorboards.

'You hungry?' he asked.

I thought wistfully of my tea bags at home and the oatmeal I was supposed to ease into. I also thought of my promise to Rhode. I did not want to meet any doctors so soon into this human experience.

'A little,' I said, noticing my stomach was doing that lurching, tingly thing, which meant that I needed to eat.

The Wickham union was constructed like the rest of the buildings on campus: made of stone and fronted by glass double doors with silver handles. The shape of the union was different from the rest of the buildings; it was a large circle. Shooting off from the main room were five or six hallways, all leading towards rectangular rooms. Tony opened the door of the union and I was met with the most amazing smells I had experienced since my mother's cooking during the fifteenth century.

The circular part of the building was a cafeteria. There were five food windows where students could pick out what they wanted to eat. Each one was different. In the middle of the room, underneath a circular skylight, were linoleum cafeteria tables.

'We can eat anything we want?' I asked. There were windows for Italian food, burgers, vegetarian options, salads and sandwiches. Behind each counter was a student or union employee in a white apron. My eyes were wide with amazement.

'Let's chow and then we'll get our books,' Tony said. Just as the door was about to close behind us he added, 'You act like you've never had food before.'

Hamburgers. French fries. Green beans. Lemonade. Chocolate. Pizza with pineapples. Rare steak. How would a person decide? I settled on some bland chicken soup.

'You think we're in some of the same classes?' Tony asked. I couldn't help but watch him chew the meat in his mouth into tiny pieces. The blood from the rare steak he was eating washed in a mix of saliva over his teeth. 'You're staring at me,' Tony said, swallowing.

'That steak has blood coming out of it. It's in your mouth.'

Tony nodded 'The bloodier the better. I love rare steak.'

As a vampire, I never yearned for animal blood, so I wasn't drawn to the blood in Tony's mouth, though it was strange that I couldn't smell it. I sniffed a few times, trying to hone in on the rust flavour that I used to love so dearly. I sniffed again, but too many different odours wafted up my nose: perfumes, chicken broth and fizzy drinks. The vampire sense of smell was limited to blood, flesh and body heat. Occasionally, I could smell herbs or flowers but that was rare the more time that passed. I could smell animal blood from miles away, though I hated the taste of it. The truth was that I hated its impurity. It took away from my status as the most pure, most powerful vampire in recent history.

After our early dinner, Tony talked me into ice cream. Food was so different, so packaged, and appeared without the work I had to put into it on my family's orchard back when I was first mortal. Even in the fifteenth century, obtaining food was easier than obtaining blood. During my vampire years, it took coercion to lure someone into my house or alleyway in order to suck their blood and leave them for dead.

'I'll have a rocky road, triple scoop in a cup with rainbow sprinkles,' Tony ordered.

Watching Tony eat his ice cream made me want to tell him that I was a vampire. He scooped and dug into the creamy mass with gusto and delicately savoured each bite. He closed his eyes and smiled each time – even if it was only for a split second. It filled me with an immediate affection for him. I, on the other hand, finished my one scoop of strawberry ice cream with four obnoxious digs of my spoon.

My vampire past was a secret lodged in my heart. I wanted to tell Tony so that someone would really understand me, see into my soul. Vampires are haunted by pain, longing and anger. Every imaginable sadness is pressed upon their shoulders. They are victims of torment and they cannot escape.

Love, oddly enough, is the one respite from this anarchy of misery. Yet, there is a catch: once a vampire falls in love, they are bound to that love. They will always love that person no matter what happens. They can fall in love again and again but each time a piece of their soul is given away. I fell in love twice. Once with Rhode and a second time with Vicken. The two loves were different. With Vicken it was less whole than it had been with Rhode. Either way, I was bound. Vampire love is an ache, a hunger, and no matter how much either of them loved me – it was never enough. No matter what is said or done it is in the vampire nature to be left completely unsatisfied. This was the kind of torment I experienced every day.

I placed my ice-cream bowl down when I heard the clacking of trays hitting the linoleum table next to me. One of the Enos brothers and a few of his friends sat down. The youngest one, Roy, sat with students who looked a bit younger than Tony. He kept looking over at me, then whispering to his friends.

'You're a hit,' Tony said, licking his spoon.

'A hit?' I asked. We got up from the table, dumped our bowls and spoons, and then we walked towards the bookshop where Tony clarified.

'All the guys are staring at you.'

'Is that a good thing?'

'I guess, if you're into guys wanting to date you or whatever.'

I couldn't reply because I had never been on a date before. Not in the human sense, at least.

'Want to see the art tower before you go home?' Tony asked. 'I spend all my time there. It's in the Hopper Building. You know, after the painter? On the bottom floor is the gym, some lounges, study halls and TV rooms. Everyone goes there. Chances are you'll need to do something and someone will tell you to go to Hopper.'

I kept peeking into my bag of purchases from the bookshop until we walked out of the union. Tony and I stepped outside and back on the path. He pointed at a building to the left and behind the union. It was an enormous stone building. Hugging the front entrance was a medieval-style stone tower. It stood directly to the right of the building and stretched up towards the sky.

It faced north, in the direction of the main entrance, but I knew if I were in the tower I could see a full view of the campus.

We crossed over a long meadow. As we got closer, I looked left at another dormitory. Most of the buildings I had seen so far were no more than four or five storeys high. It was dinner time so most students were picnicking outside.

Once we got to the glass door of Hopper, Tony held it open for me. In the foyer, I could either go straight into the building or up to the tower. There was a winding staircase just to the right of the main door. We started up the four flights towards the topmost floors of the tower.

'Wickham is so different to what I'm used to,' I said, holding on to the banister with my right hand, keeping my bookshop bag in my left. 'There are people everywhere.'

Tony looked back and smiled. He was ahead of me, leading the way up the circular staircase. 'I like your British accent,' he said. I didn't respond but a tingle crept through my chest and I knew that I liked the compliment.

At the top floor, we reached the art studio.

'Like I said, this is where you can find me almost any time,' Tony said, and placed his own bookshop bag on the floor.

Small, rectangular, castle-like windows lined the

circular stone walls. Easels were peppered about, though they were without art work as the school year hadn't started yet. Papier mâché masks dangled from the ceiling by thin wires. Some were made to look like bulls with horns, others like human faces. Paintbrushes and black charcoal stubs lay in metal and plastic bins and ten wooden desks circled the room, each with their own particularly unique splatter of paint. The room held a vibration, one of promise and creativity. I could tell, no, I could *feel* that wonderful moments had been experienced in that room. As a vampire, this would have enraged me.

How odd, I thought.

'I'm not a spectator to happiness any more,' I said, while running a hand across the top of an easel.

'What'd you say?' Tony asked.

'Oh, nothing.' I spun round to face Tony.

'You like Wickham?' Tony paused. 'I'm here on an art scholarship.'

'What does that mean?' I examined a painting of a vase of flowers to the right of a window.

'It means I'm too poor to pay for this place so they let me go to school for free. As long as I produce quality artwork. What about you?'

'I'm not on scholarship,' I said, watching Tony carefully to see if this would matter to him.

He shrugged. 'It's cool. Just promise me you're not one of those rich girls who only dates guys who play lacrosse or football and drive really nice cars.'

I had no idea what half of that even meant.

'I think I promise,' I said.

'I live in Quartz. We passed it on the way here – it's one of the guys' dorms,' Tony said. 'I have to live with all the jocks.'

'Justin Enos?' I offered with a sly smile.

'Yeah,' Tony said, rolling his eyes. But in *my* mind, Justin was bronzed and beautiful, pushing his way out of the ocean.

I turned to Tony. 'Well, don't worry, I won't be one of those girls circling around Justin, if that's what you're worried about.'

'His girlfriend? Tracy Sutton? They call each other the Three Piece.'

'Three Piece?'

'Yep, it's as stupid as it sounds. It's her and her two best friends. They each date an Enos brother and they hang out in the dorms in this annoying group. They're always together, and *always* making everyone around them want to poke their eyeballs out.'

'The Three Piece's eyeballs?'

'No, their own.'

I laughed at first but after a moment the sheer familiarity of what Tony was talking about echoed in my mind. My fingers grazed the crisp, dried hairs of a paintbrush as my eyes fell out of focus. That sounded familiar – too familiar.

'I was like that. At my old school.' I looked up at Tony who was listening politely. 'I wasn't part of the group. I *was* the group.' I shook my head quickly, to clear out the crazy thoughts. 'Anyway,' I said, 'I won't be like that here.'

'Can I paint you sometime?' Tony asked.

This was a new twist. 'Paint . . . me?'

I'd had my portrait painted in the early 1700s but nothing since, only photographs.

'Yeah,' he said, and leaned back against the wooden shelf that lined the circumference of the room. Above his head was one of the small, narrow windows. Outside, I could see the clouds darkening. 'Portraits are kind of my thing. I'm good too. I'm going to apply to Rhode Island School of Design next year.'

Tony was a good-looking Japanese boy, though the only face that I could see was Song's, a vampire in my coven. Altogether there were five in the coven, including myself. Song was the second-youngest man I'd made into a vampire. He was eighteen when I found him, a Chinese warrior I'd discovered in the eighteenth century. I saw him across a crowded room and decided to seduce him. When I chose someone for my coven I based my choice on stealth, endurance and capacity for giving death. Song was the most lethal martial artist in China. I chose him so I would never have to worry about protecting myself ever again.

My eyes refocused on Tony's high cheekbones and

smooth skin. Behind him, I could see the rain starting to fall in a steady rhythm. Even from here I could smell the wet earth, not because of any vampire senses but because it had been so long since my sense of smell included anything other than blood and body heat.

'Besides,' Tony said, still talking about the portrait, 'you have a different look. And I like different. I don't run with the crowd here.'

'I doubt I will,' I said. 'I'm reformed,' I finished with a smile.

Tony smiled. 'Cool,' he said, and crossed his arms over his chest.

'I should go.' I started back towards the door then turned to face Tony in the last minute. 'And yes on the painting. It'll be an exchange. You'll teach me how to drive and I'll be your model.'

Tony smiled and in that moment I noticed that his teeth were very white. This was a clear indication of good health and food intake. His blood probably tasted sweet and earthy.

'Deal,' he said.

I walked down the twisting and turning of the winding staircase.

'Crap. Crap. Crap,' Tony said, and ran past me down the stairs.

'Where are you going?' I asked.

'Just noticed the rain!' he said. 'Left my window open!'

Tony hopped two steps at a time so his bag of school-books swung dangerously in the air. His sandals slapped against the stairs all the way until he reached the ground floor. Then I heard a smack on the tile and the opening of a door.

When I reached the second floor, there was a window, much like those in the art tower. It was small and rectangular but it had a clear view of the meadow and student union. I placed my bag down on a step and rested my palm on the cool stone wall. I stuck my face close to the window and watched the raindrops hit the cement of the pathways below. Then it occurred to me – I hadn't stood in the rain and let it drop down my skin since 1418. The last time I'd felt the raindrops was the night I'd left my mother's earring in our apple orchard. The night I met Rhode and fell in love at first sight.

The night I died.

1418, Apple Orchard, Hampstead, England.
The rain fell on the roof of my father's house. We lived in a small, two-storey manor behind the grounds of a monastery. The monks were far off from the orchards, separated from our home by two great meadows of apple trees. My father was an orphan, entrusted to the care of the monks in his childhood. There they taught him about growing apples.

It was the middle of the night and the rain fell against the roof in an easy rhythm. I sat in a rocking chair, looking out at my family orchard. The house was silent despite the pattern of the rain and my father's snores echoing downstairs. The embers of the nightly fire still lingered and my feet were warm. It was the beginning of autumn and it was warmer than anyone had anticipated. Although it was early September, my family rested easier. We had already sent the first batch of our prized apples to the royal Medici family in Italy.

I was dressed in a white nightgown. In those days the nightdresses were flowing and sheer. If someone wanted to, they could see all of my fifteen-year-old self. My hair was still long and brown but it hung in a loose braid over my left breast and stopped somewhere near my belly button.

Through the wet window, rows and rows of orchards stretched into darkness and somewhere to the right, in the distance, I could see a tiny, orange glow of candle-light from the rectangular windows of the monastery. I rocked back and forth in the chair, lazily watching the rain. I reached up to remove my mother's earrings that she had let me borrow that morning. When I touched my earlobe, I realized the right one was gone. I stood up from the chair. The last place I'd had them . . . where was the last place I'd had them? My father had complimented the glint of gold in the sun in the . . . *last row of the orchard*!

Before thinking twice, I was out of the back door. I ran through the rows and fell to my knees. I crawled up and down the last row. I didn't care about the time of night or that my chemise would be sullied and dirty from the rich earth. I couldn't bring myself to look at my mother's face when I told her I'd lost one of her favourite earrings. She would caress my face, tell me it was only an earring and mask her disappointment. I had let the rain coat my face and was crawling from one end of the row to the other when a pair of black silver-buckled boots stepped into my view. These were not the high heels that we are accustomed to in the modern world. These boots were low-heeled, made from a thick hide and covered the man's leg all the way up to his shin. I followed the length of his leg, up his body until I looked into the most piercing set of blue eyes I had seen or ever would see. They were framed by dark eyebrows that highlighted the man's masculine jawbone and thin nose.

'Having an adventure?' he asked as casually as if he were wondering about the weather.

Rhode Lewin squatted down on his heels. He had shaggy hair then. As always, he had a proud mouth and a constantly furrowed brow. I was almost sixteen, had never left my parents' orchard, and the most beautiful man in the world stood in front of me. Well, he looked like a man, though he could have been young, perhaps my own age. There was something in the way he looked at me that told me this boy, despite his smooth cheeks and the youthful expression, was much older than me.

As though he had seen the whole world and knew of its many secrets. Rhode wore an all-black ensemble, which made the colour of his eyes pop out at me from the impenetrable night.

I fell back on to the ground. It was wet and I was soaked through. The mud squished under my heels as I pressed into the ground to move away from the man in front of me.

'This is private property,' I said.

Rhode stood back up, placed his hands on his hips and looked in both directions.

'You don't say,' he said, as though he didn't know where he was.

'What do you want?' I asked. I leaned back on to my hands and looked up at Rhode.

He walked closer so that there was only a foot of space between us. He extended a hand. I noticed an onyx ring on his middle finger. It was different from any gem I had ever seen before. It was black and solid, flat, without any glint or sparkle. He opened his fingers and in the middle of his palm was my mother's hoop earring. I looked at the hoop and then into Rhode's eyes. He smiled at me in such a way that I instantly felt something within me that I had never felt before. Something tingled near my heart.

I stood up quickly, all the while keeping my eyes on the man in front of me. The rain splattered on to the wet ground. I reached out for the earring, my fingers shaking. I was about to touch the gold when I thought for sure he would close his fingers around mine. The rain fell on to his hand, on to me, and his palm was slicked with drops. I looked up at Rhode and snatched the earring with a flick of the wrist, and placed my hand back by my side.

'Thank you,' I barely whispered, and turned back towards my family's home. In the distance, I could discern the flat shape of the roof even in the dark, rainy night. 'I have to go. And so should you,' I said, walking away from him.

Rhode turned me back to face him with one hand on my left shoulder.

'I have been watching you,' he said. 'For some time now.'

'I've never seen you,' I said, and raised my chin in defiance. I didn't realize I was showing him my neck.

'The problem, for you . . . is that I'm in love with you,' Rhode said, though it sounded more like a confession.

'You can't be in love with me,' I said stupidly. 'You do not know me.'

'Don't I? I watch you carefully tend to your father's orchard. I watch the way you braid your hair in your bedroom window. That when you walk, you glow, as bright as a candle flame. I have known for some time that I must have you near me. I know you, Lenah. I know how you breathe.'

'I don't love you,' I said, without a clue why I said it. My chest shuddered with every breath I took.

'Oh, come now,' Rhode said, and cocked his head to the side. 'Don't you?'

I did. I loved the way he looked rugged though his skin was flawless and completely polished. He could have told me he'd slain a dragon with both hands tied behind his back and I would have believed it possible. Perhaps it was the allure of being in the presence of a vampire. I didn't know at that moment that Rhode was a vampire, but the more time that passes, the more I am sure I fell for him in that very instant.

Rhode looked me up and down and I realized he could see through my nightgown. He ran a fingertip from my throat down through the middle of my breasts and ended at my belly button. I shuddered. Out of nowhere, he hooked a hand round my waist and brought me against him. It all happened so languidly as though it were choreographed. The slap of our wet bodies when Rhode brought me close, and the feel of his palm on my forehead as he wiped a string of hair out of my eyes. He groaned when he met my eyes. And, in that instant, Rhode sank his teeth into my neck so fast that I didn't notice the sound of my skin breaking.

The rain fell in gorgeous patterns outside the art-tower window. The campus was drenched and once my eyes refocused I watched students run for shelter or jump over puddles. There were dozens of students outside. But the ones closest to me, two girls and a boy about my age, were smiling, holding their hands over their heads. The boy linked his arm round the waist of one of the girls and they ran into the shelter of Quartz dorm. I stepped back from the window into the darkness of the art-tower stairs and looked at my inner wrist.

In moments of passion Rhode dug his teeth into my skin. 'Just a taste,' he would say. It was as if his lips were touching my ear. How his voice moaned at me in the darkness. I sighed and rubbed at my wrist unconsciously. My chest hurt, my muscles ached from the transformation and I wanted to punch my hand through the stone wall of the tower until my knuckles bled.

'Oh . . .' I said aloud, and my knees gave way. I sat down on the tower steps.

This was grief.

It was odd how much more acutely this emotion affected me in my human state. Human grief wasn't muted by other pain as in my vampire existence. As a vampire, grief was muddled by the presence of every imaginable sadness. I took deep breaths until the adrenaline running through my lungs and stomach subsided. Would I cry? I reached to touch my cheeks but they were dry.

I continued down the stairs, pushed out of the main foyer of Hopper and stepped back into the meadow. I walked away from the building and soon the raindrops were patting my head. After a few moments, my arms were drenched and Rhode's sweater was too. I could barely see in front of me, though I knew I was headed for the pathway at the other side of the meadow. I wiped the rain from my eyes.

Having an adventure?

See, the problem is I'm in love with you . . .

I stopped in the centre of the green. I kicked off my sandals and placed the bookshop bag on the ground. I put my arms out and let the rain fall. I thought of my mother's face, my father's laugh, Rhode's blue eyes and the coven's comfort.

The will and the desire to give up your life in order that another may live.

It's the intent, Lenah.

Tiny splashes hit my face and I could feel the drops run down my cheeks. A chill ran through my body. In my vampire state, I would have felt nothing but the drops hitting my body, like a body gone numb. I would have known I was drenched but feel nothing. This time, I raised my hands higher in the air and closed my eyes, letting the rain drip between my fingers and down my arms. The water drenched my jeans and eventually I was soaked through. I curled my toes into the mud and took in a deep breath.

'You do this often?' I heard a boy's voice call from afar. I wiped my eyes with the back of my hand. From the top floor of a dormitory across from me, Justin Enos smiled from an open window. I hadn't realized I was standing next to the boys' dorm, Quartz. I took a second to think of a retort.

'Maybe,' I called back.

'Glad to see you found your trousers,' he said, and folded his arms on the windowsill. 'What are you doing?'

'What does it look like?' A thrill of goosebumps shimmied over my arms. I noticed in a couple of other windows some boys were watching me as well.

'Like you've lost your mind.'

'It's not racing boats at a murderous speed but it's invigorating nonetheless.' I smiled, and a crack of thunder crashed in the dark sky. I didn't flinch at the sudden boom.

Justin smirked. 'All right. I get you,' he said, and closed the window. Maybe he was offended. I snuck a peek behind me. A hundred feet or so away was the union. I looked back at Quartz dorm. A stone arch framed a darkened alleyway leading to the lobby. After a moment, Justin came through the archway in no shirt and a pair of mesh shorts with the words WICKHAM in white lettering. He was barefoot and joined me in the middle of the green.

My arms at my side, I lifted my chin towards the sky. Justin smiled at me and then did the same. The rain slapped on the cement path and lightly tapped against the grass beneath our feet.

'Definitely not racing boats,' he said after a moment. I opened my eyes. His chest was covered in rain and we were both drenched. We smiled at the sky, then at each other and for the moment I forgot I was over five hundred years older than he was. 'What's your name?' he asked, his green eyes protected by long, wet lashes.

'Lenah Beaudonte.'

He stuck out a wet hand. 'Justin Enos.'

We shook and I held on a bit longer than I expected. His skin was rough on the palms but smooth on the top. He let go first.

'Thank you, Lenah Beaudonte,' he said, and put his hand by his side before I could sneak a peek at his inner wrist. We kept our eyes on one another and I didn't look away. I tried to decipher the new emotion coming up through my body. It was – strange. This boy wasn't Rhode but he was – *something* to me. I examined the curve of his upper lip, the way it sloped down and met a proud and full bottom lip. His nose was slim and his eyes were set further apart than Rhode's. They were well-framed beneath dirty-blond eyebrows. The green was so different from Rhode's blue. My Rhode. Who was gone forever.

'You look really sad,' he said, interrupting my thoughts.

Not what I was expecting.

'Do I?'

Justin lifted his face up into the air so the rain smacked his skin even more directly.

'Are you?' he asked, still looking up.

I nodded once when he looked back at me. 'A little.'

'You miss your parents?'

I shook my head. 'Brother,' I said. It was the closest I would get to the truth. Boyfriend was wrong. Lover was wrong. Soulmate was a bit dramatic.

'What would cheer you up?' He was almost smiling at me now, a crooked smile. 'Besides standing in the rain.'

This is helping, was the thought that came to mind. Thank goodness it was getting dark. He couldn't see me blush.

'I'm not sure.'

'I'm gonna have to do something about that,' he said. I could feel his energy. It was mischievous, yet he was harmless. I liked the combination.

He started to walk backwards towards his dorm. He admired me with a look of relaxed contentment and said, 'See you at assembly.'

I picked up my bag of books and headed towards the path to Seeker. Once on the pathway, I looked back at his dorm. He was in the archway of the building, leaning his shoulder against the stone and had one ankle crossed over the other. The rain was still falling and when our eyes met through the drops he cracked a smile and turned into the darkness of the building alleyway.

Chapter 5

Bleeeeeep. Bleeeep. I smacked the alarm clock with the palm of my hand. Saturday morning, *placement test* morning. As I hadn't been, well . . . *above* ground, I was required to take the tests when I arrived on campus. The night before, I read directions for various electronics and fumbled with timers and dials. It all worked and I was awake at 7 a.m. in time to get ready and walk to Hopper. Turns out Tony was right. According to my itinerary for the first few days before school started, anything and everything I needed to do was in that building.

With a backpack slung over my shoulder, I walked into Hopper and down the ground-floor hallway towards the administrative offices. As I walked, I noticed school advertisements and posters. A notable one said, BIOLOGY CLUB. WE LOVE BLOOD! I smiled but I wanted to tell Rhode. I wondered if he had seen what I was seeing.

I approached the headmistress's door at the end of the hallway. MS WILLIAMS was printed in gold lettering on the glass. I knocked and was called in. Ms Williams stood beside her desk looking through a file. Eventually she lifted her head.

'Come with me, Ms Beaudonte,' she said, and gestured to the open doorway. I followed after.

They made me take five tests. Yes, five. The headmistress herself stood over my right shoulder and watched me take the Japanese test. She didn't believe I could speak and write in every language that Wickham offered. In this world, the human, contemporary world, clocks are everywhere. Mortals live their lives by a ticking clock. Vampires spend days, even weeks awake. We're not truly alive. We look alive, though there is no circulation, there is no pumping heart, no reproductive organs that thrive. Our chests do not rise and fall because there is no oxygen in the blood to flow through our veins. In moments when I wanted to escape the pain and terror, I longed to inhale. If I felt the air hit the back of my throat, I could pretend I was alive. I never did feel it, though. There was just an eternal aching – a constant reminder that I was numb, turned off, no longer part of the living world. Being a vampire is an ancient magic. Nothing exists . . . nothing but our minds.

I have travelled the entire earth more than once, learned many languages, some that don't exist any more. Heath taught himself Latin in three months and, when he did, it was all he would speak. He was tall, blond and strong-boned, like a swimmer. He was so beautiful that no woman ever saw it coming when he whispered Latin into her ear and then ripped out her throat.

The smell of overly sweet perfume brought me back to the moment. Ms Williams returned to her office. I sat in a brown leather lounger facing the secretary's desk.

'What should we do?' I heard Ms Williams ask one of her colleagues, a stuffy older woman holding a clipboard. 'She's placed out of all the AP classes,' she whispered.

'I need a job?' I offered. Might as well offer my opinion. Also, I had a promise to keep to Rhode.

'What are your strengths, besides speaking languages?' Ms Williams asked.

'How about the library?' the stuffy colleague suggested.

They were speaking about me as though I wasn't there. Anger shot through me, which surprised me at first. I wanted to kill them both, though something within me told me it wasn't a good idea. In my vampire life, I would have drained their blood and murdered them just to release the constant anger that afflicted me. For an instant, I imagined pressing my hands into the arms of the chair, standing up and grabbing Ms Williams's head between my palms. It would take no more than a flick of my wrists and I could have snapped her head back, drained her blood and murdered her. Instead, I looked up and smiled lamely.

'The library sounds excellent,' Ms Williams confirmed, and she pulled some paperwork out of a drawer in her desk.

Library? That sounded reasonable. As my thoughts revolved around my days surrounded by books, something miraculous happened. My anger subsided. It ebbed away as the thoughts of books, pages and comfort entered my head. As the two women continued to talk, I realized that what I was feeling was simultaneous emotions. Feeling joy, hope and anger at the same time? That was enough to dissolve my anger instantaneously. I looked up at the stuffy administrator handing me a pen. On second thoughts, I wouldn't have sucked them dry – even if I were a vampire. I hated the taste of anyone over thirty, anyway.

31 October 1602, Hathersage
The living room was empty. A leather couch faced a crackling, lively fire. On the walls were paintings, and some portraits of Christ – for fun. Chatter, voices and incoherent sentences echoed from the hallway. I ran a long index fingernail along the top of the couch. My nail was pointed so sharp that it made the tiny fibres inside the soft upholstery stick out at jagged angles. The flames roared. The fireplace was more than five feet high and four feet wide with a mantel made of black onyx. I sauntered past it. The year was 1602, the dwindling years of the reign of Queen Elizabeth I. I wore dresses made from the finest Persian silk and corsets that pushed my breasts so close together I was astonished a breathing human could survive the pressure.

I swung my hips as I turned and sauntered down a long hallway lit only by wall sconces in the shape of two palms facing up. In the hands were candles that had burned almost into nothing. The waxy drops fell in succulent globs on to the floor. The train of my dress spread them across the wood in luscious zigzags as I headed towards a doorway at the end of the hall. When I glanced behind me, the grand fireplace threw orange embers of light into the dark hallway and outlined me in a tangerine line. I stopped in front of the doorway and listened. I could hear orchestral music and laughter. I didn't know it yet but that night, 31 October 1602, was the last night of the very first Nuit Rouge celebration.

I grasped the handle, which was shaped like a dagger facing downwards. I pushed the door open. Ancient greetings such as 'merry meet' and 'grand tidings' met my ears. There on the floor, in the centre of the room, was a portly woman sitting on her heels. She wore a white wool dress that covered her up to her breasts, and a white bonnet on her head. Her blonde hair fell across her face as she muttered something in Dutch. It struck me that she was most likely someone's servant, though I did not recognize her. She probably had no idea her master was a vampire, and now here she was, in my house.

The ballroom was lovely, I should mention. This servant's plump behind was seated on the finest wood floor in England. Tall torches rested high on the four circular stone pillars that supported the room. Their flames busily illuminated the dance floor, musicians played in the corner and two hundred vampires stood in a circle around the fat woman.

Rhode leaned against a pillar watching me, smiling. His arms were crossed over his chest. His ensemble was simple. He wore black leggings, solid black shoes with a thin leather sole that were flat with no heel. The clothing at the time was very rich in texture and wealthy vampires loved to show off. Rhode wore a black linen jacket fastened with a thick black ribbon. The muscles of his arms were well defined under the tight sleeves of the black jacket. He must have just fed because his teeth looked whiter than I had seen them in ages.

I walked languidly around the inner part of the circle of vampires. I held my eyes on Rhode until I reached the ballroom doorway, which was now open and showed the long hallway and the dance of light from the fireplace.

The woman in the middle of the room kept glancing at the hallway. I felt, as always with my vampire extrasensory perception, what this woman wanted. She wanted to make a run for it.

'Do you know why you are here?' I asked the woman, speaking to her in Dutch. I circled her very slowly, keeping my hands behind my back.

She sat on her heels, watching me. She shook her head, no.

'Do you know what I am?' I asked.

Again she shook her head. 'I want to – to leave,' she said, her voice quivering. 'My mother and father.'

I raised my index finger and placed it over my lips. Images from my human life drifted to the front of my mind. My parents' stone manor. The wet earth. An earring in a palm. I refocused on the servant's features. Her keen blue eyes, their round shape and short blonde eyelashes. I stopped circling and stood above her, looking down.

'You know,' I said, and smiled. The moment before the vampire will kill, the fangs lower. At first they appear as regular teeth but when the kill is happening, like an animal, the fangs are bared. I felt mine lower, as though slowly unfolding a blade. I bent over and looked deeply into her eyes. I whispered into her right ear, 'You're going to taste horrible. Look at your disposition.'

I pulled back and looked into her eyes again. 'I wouldn't dare sully my insides with what you are.' I stood back up. For a moment, relief swept over her face.

I walked past her, the low heels of my black leather shoes clicking against the wooden floor. The train of my gown swivelled behind me like a snake. I threw one long glance back at Rhode and smiled. It was silent in the ballroom. The musicians had stopped playing. I was midway back down the hallway when I lifted my right hand in the air, bent my wrist down and snapped my fingers.

Two hundred vampires descended upon her at once. I smiled all the way back up to my bedroom.

The library at Wickham was a gothic masterpiece with panoramic glass windows. I entered through the two double doors, taking in the plush chairs, rows and rows of books, and students investigating the stacks. Decorating the ceiling were three-dimensional octagonal tiles made out of black wood.

'Your job, Ms Beaudonte, is to sit here behind this desk. When people ask you questions, you answer them to the best of your ability. You can always direct them to a librarian if you can't answer something they want to know.' The librarian, who was leading me on a tour, was a tall woman with eyes shaped like a cat's and a thin nose.

These contemporary humans were so horribly misinformed. I was a former vampire who had been asleep the last hundred years. They expected me to act as reference guide?

'You get paid every Friday. I'll have your semester schedule at the end of your shift at seven p.m. Ms Williams also suggested you tutor some of the students in their language skills as you are so proficient. I'll make a sign for you to put up on the miscellaneous bulletin board at the union.'

Once she walked away, I collapsed into a chair behind the semicircular reference desk. Wickham private school certainly was going to keep me busy. In front of me was a computer, which basically blinded me with its blue light. There were all sorts of contraptions I had never seen before: staplers, ballpoint pens, paper clips, printers and electrical outlets. Keyboards, virtual desktops, search engines, these were just some of the hundreds of words that I had to learn in order to fit in – and quickly. To assimilate within Wickham, or as Rhode would say, 'to become a teenage girl again', would require all of my best efforts. This society was particularly complicated.

I glanced at the clock around 4.30 and realized I had two more hours on my shift. I decided to explore the library. I walked aisle after aisle, deep into the depths of the stacks, taking in the beauty of Wickham library. As I turned into the last aisle of books, a girl's laughter echoed from somewhere nearby. It was a kind of vibrating chortle that came from deep within her, bouncing under her ribs. Pure laughter. I wanted to see who she was. I raised on my tiptoes and peered over the tops of the books. Running parallel to the row were study atriums with glass walls and panoramic windows. Inside the room were deeply padded blue couches and study desks.

The row of books was a good hiding place because I could duck down behind the shelves, if I needed to. I peered over the top of the books again and kept walking, following the laughter.

I stopped short, just when I realized who the laughing girl was – Tracy Sutton, Justin's girlfriend. They were in the very last study atrium. Justin was relaxing in a lounger and Tracy sat on his lap. In chairs on either side of him were his brothers Curtis and Roy. Tracy laughed that same happy sound again. It struck me how easily people laughed in this age. How easily they could express their happiness. I had forgotten what that was like. Justin was tall, very tall, so Tracy looked tiny in his lap. If I had been in Tracy's place, my legs would have dangled over Justin's knees like a spider.

Tracy stood up and shrieked something unintelligible. The other members of the Three Piece, Kate and Claudia, stood on either side of her and pulled down the side of their matching jeans to expose their hip bones. I raised higher on my toes and stared. They were wearing matching undergarments made to look like leopard skin. Claudia hung an arm over Kate's shoulders and Tracy slipped back into Justin's lap. I couldn't help it – the staring, I mean. I was transfixed by their happiness.

I was especially drawn to Justin. He had this . . . aura. There is no other way to explain his life force. The image of his chest dripping with rain flashed through my head. And how his lips looked when he formed words. Especially when he'd asked me if I was sad. I wanted him to talk to me more.

'I am so not into morning assembly,' Tracy said, and then kissed Justin's cheek. She was now facing in my direction. I gasped and ducked down out of eyesight.

I didn't want anyone to see me. Not from that group anyway. I peered through the space between the shelf and the tops of the books.

I'd had a *human* reaction to Justin Enos. The flip-flopping of my heart and the way my breath skipped around in my chest. Would it have been this way for Rhode? Would Vicken, if he were human again, possibly have jitters when he looked at me?

Justin reached around Tracy and his palms rested on her thighs. As I examined him, by some horrible chaotic coincidence, Justin, who was looking at one of his brothers, furrowed his eyebrows and stopped speaking. His smile fell and he turned his head, so I could see not just his profile but his whole mouth. Then the sharp point of his nose, then his eyes, staring directly into mine.

'Ms Beaudonte.'

I spun round. The librarian with the cat-like eyes stood before me. She held a black crate filled with slim plastic cases. 'Please alphabetize these CDs in the listening room.'

'Listening room?' I asked, wondering what on earth a listening room could be. Had the modern world evolved so much that people sat in a room and simply – *listened*?

The librarian handed me the crate and pointed down the aisle of atriums to a room at the end. When I didn't move, she sighed.

'This way . . .'

I followed her. She shuffled when she walked – as though her hips and behind were too heavy for her to pick up her feet properly. As a vampire, I would have been able to murder her in less than ten seconds. She looked back at me and motioned for me to hurry up. I decided to stop thinking about her slow gait and my deft ability to lure my prey.

I peeked into the crate. The slim cases held names – some of which I recognized. I slid one of them out. On it read the name: George Frideric Handel. What was this? Handel was a musician, a composer – what on earth could those cases have to do with him? I flipped the case over. The artwork depicted a man wearing a white wig, a wig I had seen on countless men during the eighteenth and nineteenth centuries. The wig curled on both sides of the man's face and was held back into a ponytail. He held a small composing baton above a full orchestra.

Only when the librarian's clip-clopping heels came to a stop did I realize that we had come to the listening room. Justin and his friends were still in their atrium at the far end of the library. The librarian opened a black door with a paned window in the middle. She pointed inside the room; running over the walls was a thick, grey fabric that was very dense but soft to the touch. I let my fingers graze the plush material that crawled on the walls. Facing me was a towering black machine that took over the entire wall. The librarian pointed at a wall of shelves.

'Just place them on the racks and organize them by the last name.'

The wall was filled with cases just like the ones in the crate.

'Would you mind showing me how the machine works?' I asked, referring to the black tower to the right of the cases. On a desk in front of it were three computers.

'Which CD do you want to listen to?' she asked.

I picked up the CD that said HANDEL OPERA in swirling white cursive across the front of the case. The last opera I had seen was in 1740 in Paris. I shook my head – I remembered that night too well. And that was not a night I wanted to recall while I stood in a room with a stranger.

She pressed a button and a small tray slid forward all on its own. I felt my eyes widen. Everything that involved machinery in this age was so easy – one simple push and magic happened.

She opened the case and took out a silver disc.

'You place the CD in the slot, press the button on the stereo and there you go. You can turn it up to volume ten – no one can hear. This room is soundproof. The musicians listen to their CDs at an unreasonable volume.'

She turned the knob up to the ten setting and closed

the door behind her, leaving me in the silence . . . for a moment.

I stuck my hand into the box of CDs, waiting to line them up accordingly, when music came out of the speakers. I stood up and backed away from the stereo.

The aria was Handel's '*Se Pietà*' and it moved throughout the room, wafting over the fabric walls and carpeted floor. Finally, it settled into me. The feeling of the drawn-out strings, the vibrations of the cellos, flowed through my body like blood. *Violins* – many of them – how many I could not decipher. I could almost feel the bow moving across the strings. My lips parted and my breath escaped in a slow exhale. The cellos came next – the low melancholy strings made goosebumps roll over my arms. I reached forward and touched the tiny holes of the place where the music came out. I could feel the machine vibrating from the sound.

How on earth was this possible? Had so much time passed that humans were able to contain any music they wanted? Keep it somewhere so they could listen to it over and over again?

I brought my hand to my chest when a woman began to sing an aria. Her voice cascaded through the notes, soared with the violins and matched the cellos' harmonies. I couldn't help it – I slowly knelt down to the floor and closed my eyes. It was a kind of beauty I could not have fathomed before that moment – music that I could finally feel with my body and my soul.

In 1740, opera was popular but you had to travel to attend performances. Now it was in the listening room at Wickham Boarding School. I closed my eyes even tighter and let the sound pass through me. Like a whisper on bare skin, the tiny hairs on the back of my neck stood on end. I felt a pair of hands rest on my shoulders. I kept my eyes closed.

'Have you learned Italian yet?' a voice whispered in my ear. Except the voice was in my head and I was remembering the last time I'd heard that song – in 1740, in Paris, with Rhode.

'You're not really here,' I whispered.

'Didn't I tell you? Anywhere you go, I will go,' the voice whispered.

But I knew I was alone in that listening room in a century I knew nothing about . . . the ghost of Rhode my only company.

'What are you doing?' said a voice that was clearly not Rhode's.

My eyes flew open. I looked right. Justin Enos held the door open and the Three Piece passed behind him, looking in at me through the glass. I had the sudden realization that I was on my knees and I stood up from the floor immediately.

'Listening,' I said, though it was more like a yell.

Justin gestured to the stereo. 'Can I?'

I nodded, unsure what he was doing there. I fiddled aimlessly with the CDs. He turned down the volume so the song was no louder than a whisper.

'Why are you here?' I asked.

'I wanted to know what you were listening to because the look on your face was like you were in pain or something. But it was just classical music.'

'It's not just classical.'

His eyebrows furrowed and I looked away towards the CDs again.

But I had to look back.

Justin's shirt was unbuttoned just one button too far – just enough so I could see the cleft in between his chest muscles. A deep ravine of bronzed skin. I wanted to run my finger over it. It was just a simple, small button but it looked as though it was a forgotten button, as if getting dressed in a hurry was something he did often.

He followed my eyes, looked down to his shirt and immediately reached his long fingers up to button it. I grabbed a CD from the crate – disappointed.

'You looked like you'd never heard music before,' he said.

'I haven't,' I said. 'Not like that.' I focused on the last name on a CD in the crate. Madonna, a composer I'd never heard of – I placed the CD with the other last names beginning with M.

'You've never heard music on a stereo?'

'Not exactly.'

'And you chose opera?'

I looked up – Justin's expression was a mix of amazement and sheer confusion. Perhaps he thought I was strange but in that moment I could feel it – he was enthralled. My eyes travelled over his shoulder to one of his brothers peeking into the listening room, the older one, the one with earrings in his ear. Behind him, members of the Three Piece giggled to one another, hiding their mouths by turning their heads when I caught their eyes.

'I have to go,' I said, shoving the last CDs carelessly at the end of the row. I pushed past so my shoulder grazed Justin's arm – it was warm, as though he'd been sitting in the sun. As I walked away, past them, I didn't look back. Even as they laughed at my expense, I could feel the vibrations of the woman's soprano in the middle of my chest – somewhere very close to my heart.

Chapter 6

First day of classes. What to wear?

Wickham didn't have uniforms so it was a bit of a gamble. The weather was still so warm despite it being early September. Jeans and a simple black tank top – that seemed like a safe bet. No odd colours that were out of fashion. Just simple. Tony said he would meet me outside Seeker so we could walk to assembly together. *Strength in numbers*, I thought, after my debacle in the listening room with Justin.

The morning of the first day of school, I had a few minutes before I had to meet Tony. I went into my kitchen. It was a small alcove with modest wooden cabinets and a small counter space. Rhode had stocked it with pans, silverware and other kitchen tools. Yet the most important items were on the counter to the right of the sink.

Spices and dried flowers were stacked neatly in black, circular tins against the wall. The smallest black canister read DANDELION. *Of course*, I thought. Dried dandelion. The dried flower head is no larger than a dime and is meant to be carried for luck. If I was to assimilate into human life, as Rhode had requested, I needed all the luck I could get. That, and a clock, seemed to reside in my mind. During moments of silence when the distractions of this new age subsided, I could hear the seconds click past. Each tick-tock brought me closer and closer to the final night of Nuit Rouge. I shook my head as though to rid myself of these thoughts, stuck a dandelion head in my pocket and grabbed a bundle of rosemary that was tied together.

I stuck a tack in the door and hung the rosemary from it. I did this so that every time I came back to my apartment, the safe place that I would call home, I would never forget where I came from. And how much further I still had to go.

With my backpack on, I locked the door behind me. I stepped out of Seeker and found Tony on the lawn, lying on his back with his hands behind his head, basking in the morning sun. I pulled the wide-brimmed, floppy hat over my head. Tony was wearing the ripped jeans again and a belt decorated by metal spikes.

'Aren't you afraid of getting burned?' I asked, and placed my sunglasses over my eyes.

Tony hopped up. He pointed at me so that his back-pack dangled off his right elbow.

'OK, the security guard told me that you live in Professor Bennett's old place?'

'If that's the top-floor apartment, then yes,' I said.

'The top-floor apartment,' Tony mocked, exaggerating my British accent. He blinked twice and his jaw dropped. 'Professor Bennett died in July,' Tony clarified. His eyes were wide and his thin lips parted. He was waiting for me to react. When I didn't, he continued, 'They still don't know how he died except he had two holes in his throat. Made all the psychics and nut jobs in town claim vampires.'

I rolled my eyes . . . Rhode.

'So?' I asked. 'What does that have to do with me moving in?'

'It's September. The guy died two months ago. That doesn't freak you out at all?'

I shrugged. 'Not really. Death has never really bothered me.'

'Why doesn't that surprise me, Lenah?' Tony asked, and threw his arm over my shoulder. 'I guess you don't care about vampires either.'

'Do you believe they exist?' I asked him.

'Anything's possible.'

No, Tony, I thought. *Not anything. Some things, dangerous things.* Other vampires could have lived in Lovers Bay though I had never heard of any in that part of the world. Vampires generally know about one another, geographically that is, and either way what could I have done if they were there?

'Do you?' he asked. 'Believe?'

'Why not?' I replied.

Tony hugged me close to him so my left shoulder

pressed against his ribcage and I could feel his body heat. The sudden closeness made my mouth water. In the vampire state a kind of salivation takes place. The fangs come down and then the vampire feels the instinct to bite. I pulled away and pretended to reach into my backpack.

The pumping in my heart echoed within me and I pressed my hand over my chest – as if it would quiet it down. I pulled out an official document from the bottom of the bag and pretended to look at it. Was I salivating because of Tony's body heat? Did I want his blood? I concentrated on some sharp blades of grass. I swallowed to make sure the saliva had died away.

I looked up at Tony. He had walked up the path just ahead of me. I couldn't help but notice the way he walked: a long step with a small hop. His feet were a little big for his body too. He was wearing a pair of black boots that day, though one was different to the other. I'm not sure if anyone with regular sight would have noticed, but the stitching round the right boot was different to the one on the left.

'You coming?, Tony called. Assembly will start without us.'

No, I decided. I most definitely did not want his blood.

I stood and jogged to catch up. When I reached Tony's side, he smiled at me and we continued up the path. His breezy attitude made it easy for me to hide my vampire instincts. He didn't seem to mind when I acted strangely. I ran my tongue over my front teeth before speaking. I had to make sure . . .

'Are you from Lovers Bay originally?' I asked, trying to distract myself from what had just happened.

'Yep,' Tony sighed. 'My parents live right on the border of Lovers Bay in the really, um, interesting part of town.'

'Interesting?' I asked.

'Let me put it to you this way: you'd be scared just looking down the street.'

I smirked. Right . . .

'So how'd you score a full-floor apartment like that?' Tony asked. 'Everyone else has to live in regular dorm rooms.'

'My dad rented it for the two years I'll be going to school here,' I explained.

'Wow,' Tony said, raising his eyebrows. He navigated through the pathways towards Hopper. As we walked the twists and turns of the walkways, I glanced at Tony's face. He held his jaw loosely but smiled in a happy, re-laxed way. Tony's disposition was gentle and I could feel his energy. Vampires can feel human energy and pick up on the emotional intentions of those around them. Tony had never in his life hurt someone as I had nor had he felt unrelenting fear. I wanted to protect him in any way that I could and before I knew what was hap-pening, my hand was reaching for his. I dropped it back at my side and pretended that nothing had happened. Luckily, he didn't notice.

Outside dorms, in walkways and on the lawns, *more* students flung themselves at one another, crying in happiness and taking pictures of each other on cell phones.

Tony held out his arm towards me. He used his index finger to pretend he was snapping a photo.

'Oh my God!' he cried, and grasped his hand to his heart. 'I have to take your picture because, like, I haven't seen you in five minutes. Pose!'

I placed my right hand on my hip and smiled genuinely. Tony dropped his arms by his side and his face fell.

'You can pose better than that!'

'How should I pose?' I asked, not sure which kind of pose was acceptable in this century.

'Forget it, Lenah,' he said, laughing.

Tony grabbed my hand and led me back towards the path. I let him pull me and I smiled at his fingers grasped around mine. They had no age. Black smudges of paint dotted his hands. They were soft, without wear, and I realized that Rhode was the last person to hold me that way. I let go of Tony's hand.

'I was in Switzerland for two months!' a younger girl shrieked next to us while grasping her friend in a tight hug. 'And your hair is so blonde!'

Tony looked at me from the corner of his eye and then stifled a laugh.

My extrasensory perception was a bit like a radio signal; it kept picking up the emotional reads from the people around me. There were so many: excitement, longing, shame, anxiety – I could list a whole host of emotions.

The walkway we were on snaked in front of Quartz dorm. I couldn't help but peek at Justin's window. It was dark, though the window was open and a coffee mug sat on the windowsill.

As I kept stride with Tony, I obsessed over the students interacting with one another. If I was supposed to be one of them, I had to act as one of them. They wore bejewelled rings, expensive silver, gold watches and accessories of every kind. A lot of the girls held their hair back with elaborate tortoiseshell clips. Perhaps I could find some for me in the clothing shops. I almost forgot Tony's promise to teach me how to drive. With the introduction of my new job and my fascination with how-to manuals, I hadn't taken Tony up on his promise.

'I got a job!' I said while we waited in the line of the students congregating to get into Hopper.

'That explains Saturday. I came by Seeker to see you,' Tony said. 'You must have been working. Where at?'

'Library.'

'Rough deal. I work for the yearbook. Kind of a work-study thing,' Tony explained.

'Yearbook? What's that?' I asked. We stepped underneath the shaded awning of Hopper and I pulled my hair off my shoulders and fastened it with a black clip.

'You don't know what a yearbook is?' Tony gave me a look that said how could you NOT know what that is? But it faded fast. 'It's this book that comes out at the end of every school year. We take pictures all year, record what happens and put it together. To, like, remember. What happened.'

'So you take the photographs?'

Tony nodded.

'I should take some pictures of first assembly. Everyone always wears their best clothes. It's really annoying.'

'Is that your best spiked belt?' I asked, smirking.

He slid a camera out of his pocket so fast I didn't even know what was happening. Then a light flashed in my eyes. I yelped so that the back of my throat burned. The scream was quick and short but enough to have all of the students standing in line turn to look at me. Tony laughed and laughed.

'Wow,' he said. 'I should scare you more often.'

'Are you crazy? You can't just flash a bright light at someone. It could hurt them.'

Tony placed a hand on my shoulder.

'Lenah, it's just a camera. Maybe you like my fake one better but this one won't hurt, promise.'

Right, I thought. *Must learn to control that.*

The line of students started to move.

'Thanks for walking with me today,' I said.

'You don't have to thank me. I like it. All the guys on

campus think you're hot, so this makes me look awesome. I'll follow you to class, your dorm, Main Street,' he said with a smile, as we moved into the doorway of Hopper.

There was a tug on my heart. I looked to the ground as the image below my feet went from the grass to the tile of the Hopper foyer.

Anywhere you go, I will go . . . echoed in my head.

I walked with Tony in a sea of students, though I wasn't part of it – I didn't feel like I was, anyway. I couldn't jump, hug, or tell anyone anything that wouldn't scare them out of my life forever. And there, in the slow-moving line into the auditorium, the memory of the opera came back to me.

Opera intermission, 1740, Paris, France
I extinguished the candle flames with the tips of my fingers and then I waited in the darkness. There, in the shadow of the velvet seats and gilded gold railing, a couple stepped into the balcony. I killed them both before an utter of a scream left their mouths. I'd never murdered anyone in a public crowd before. They were a refined royal couple and their blood tasted sweet and surprisingly satisfying. I used their bodies as foot rests for the first and second act of the opera: *Julius Caesar,* my favourite.

A line of blood dripped down the front of my silk gown, spotting my tangerine-coloured shoes, but I waited for something else – the relief from the sheer agony that lived in my mind; that is what happened after murdering a victim. There was an instantaneous but brief relief from the emotional pain. I sat down on the plush seat and rested my feet on the chest of the young man I had killed. Surely it would come now, any moment . . .

Another crimson droplet fell, clinging to the white pearl beading that circled the hem of my gown. The dress itself was a deep red colour, the finest silk in Paris. I waited, uninterested in the chatter of the crowd awaiting the final act of the opera. I only realized that a long drop of blood fell off my chin when it splattered on to my cleavage.

It seemed as though an invisible hand pressed on every inch of my being. My shoulders and my arms were tensed like hard stone. I waited . . . and waited for the relief. I sighed out of habit and looked down at the unmoving palm of the young woman under my feet. *It will always be this way*, I thought, and kicked her hand out of spite. Even if she were still alive, the maniacal pain rushing through my veins would never calm – there would always be this tempest, never a breeze.

The curtain rose and I closed my eyes, waiting to be engulfed by blackness and sound. It would be safe there in the darkness of my mind. The only place I knew I could go to forget even just for a moment what I had become. The orchestra began to play and I let the violins make colours of peace – whites, blues and a whole symphony of colour. Violins swirled in my head. I could see the ivory fibres of the bows as they crossed the strings, over and back again.

The woman's operatic soprano filled the room from the stage. She began her aria, '*Se Pietà*'. She hit a surprisingly high note, but I had no physical reaction to its beauty. The collective reaction of the crowd told me that she was no common opera singer – she was able to move people through their bodies, through their souls. For me, the aria put out the light. It dimmed the spark so I could sink into the sound.

I gripped the chair when I sensed a shift in the air and a pair of hands gently caressed my shoulders. Then Rhode's lips were close to my ear. He sat down behind me.

'Have you learned Italian yet?' he whispered.

I shook my head, my lips parting.

'Too bad,' he said. His chin almost rested on my shoulder.

'What is she saying?' I whispered.

'That she is Cleopatra . . . and her grand plan is collapsing around her.'

The love Rhode felt for me coursed through my shoulders, down to my feet, and I wished I could shiver. The vampire emotion of love works in just this manner, as a reaction – a fulfilment – relief. Murdering my victims for their blood wasn't working any more. The love Rhode and I shared was all I had left.

'She thinks her love is dead,' he said.

I opened my eyes to Rhode's stare – that rugged face whose features softened only for me. He had sat down next to me. The singer, dressed in an Egyptian costume, raised her hands from her sides and knelt before the stage bed.

'The game has lost its sport,' I said.

Around Rhode and me, the singer's voice crescen-doed with the orchestra – it was a deafening beauty. I felt the crowd's swelling emotion, the union of their happiness. I ached.

'The music calms me. But I know I will forget myself again. The savagery prevails, the pain returns and the longing to hurt takes over . . . it always does. How do you bear it?' I asked. 'I'm on the brink.'

'You,' he said calmly, plainly. He took my hand into his and brought my fingers to his mouth. Under my nails was some leftover blood – he licked it away. 'I think about you and it's enough.'

'How?'

'We are allowed very little, Lenah. I focus my ener-gies not on the pain but on what I can do to avoid it.'

'So I am your distraction?'

'You,' he said, his face coming within inches of mine, 'are my only hope.'

I surveyed Rhode's beautiful features. His eyes probed mine for a reaction. I placed a hand on his cheek.

'I'm unravelling. I know now. No amount of blood

or violence will alleviate the loss I experience every day. I want to run my fingers along skin and *feel* it. I want to sleep, wake, laugh with a crowd. This,' I pointed to the dead couple, 'is no longer enough.'

Rhode brought my fingertips back to his lips. He closed his eyes as the aria swelled around us.

'Let's go,' he said, opening his eyes and then standing up.

'To where?' I asked.

'Anywhere,' he said. His eyes set into mine and bored deeply into what would have been my soul, if I'd had one. 'Anywhere you go, I will go,' he said. We turned from the balcony, the only indication of our presence . . . the carnage.

'This way, Lenah,' Tony said, and I shook my head, focusing on the doorway into the auditorium.

Once we entered, I could see why Rhode sent me to Wickham. It was easily the most elegant school I had ever seen. The auditorium rivalled some of the more beautiful homes I had experienced over the last five centuries. The walls and ceilings were modern. Nothing in my home in Hathersage was made from metal, just stone and wood. Wickham was different. It was the kind of place where lights were encased in stained glass and they brightened with the easy push of a finger. The seats rose up and away from a single podium in the centre of the room. The stairs leading up to the many rows of seats were lined with a red carpet and track lighting.

'Just the upper school has an assembly here,' Tony explained as we walked up the stairs. Many of the students congregated in tight groups. 'Sit over here,' Tony said, and showed me to a few rows of seats to the far left. All the kids already seated there were dressed like Tony. Some had interesting shades of hair and one older boy had his mouth and eyebrow pierced. Gavin, a vampire in my coven, loved stakes and knives. He would have enjoyed piercing himself. Perhaps he had by now.

I didn't see Justin. I have to admit that I hoped to. Though I did see his horrible girlfriend, Tracy Sutton, and her two friends sitting across the aisle. The self-proclaimed Three Piece were sitting together, heads close, whispering. Tracy looked up and caught my eye. I looked away. When I sat down, I removed my backpack and placed it at my feet.

I couldn't help it. I turned back to look at her and watched her mouth move. She leaned to the smallest of the blonde girls and said, 'That new girl is sitting with the art kids.'

The small blonde girl turned her head and I looked away just quick enough. 'She's pretty,' she said.

Tracy scoffed. 'Whatever. She's paler than me in mid-November and what's up with that tattoo on her left shoulder? Can you say weird?'

It was a palm-to-the-forehead, stupid-things-I-had-completely-forgotten-about moment. My tattoo. An expression is tattooed on the back of my left shoulder. Only those in my coven had these words tattooed on their skin:

Evil be he who thinketh evil.

I pressed my lips together and looked about the room. What was I going to do? How would I explain that phrase to everyone who saw it? Especially the girls in the Three Piece. I pressed my back into the seat so no one else would be able to see the tattoo. I let my hair down, though I knew when I walked or moved anyone would be able to see it. The straps of the tank top were extremely thin. It was a poor fashion choice but I had no time to run across campus and change.

I hated my ability to read lips. I hated my vampire sight. I wished I had worn a sweater.

Tony must have noticed I was staring at them because he leaned over to me. 'Bunch of bitches.'

'Why do they call themselves the Three Piece again?'

'Because they are always together. The three of them. Tracy Sutton, Claudia Hawthorne and Kate Pierson. Rich, popular and dangerous. Kate is a weekday student. She lives with her family in Chatham.'

'How can those three girls possibly be dangerous?'

Almost as I was saying the words, I understood what Rhode meant that day in the fields as well as what Tony meant. These girls were effortlessly beautiful. They flipped their hair with ease and a carefree swipe of their hand. They were dangerous because in their beauty they believed they held all their power.

Ms Williams spoke and ruined my examination of the Three Piece.

'Students and faculty, please take your seats,' she said over a microphone.

The chatter slowed, there was a bustling of bodies and after a few moments everyone sat down. I still didn't see Justin anywhere.

'Welcome back. It is my privilege this morning, as it is each year, to welcome you to another academic year at Wickham. What is my wish? For you to achieve the highest level of education available. For you to grow not only academically but as young adults. Here at Wickham you are the best example of this country's future. And, as the upper school, you are the example for the rest of Wickham Boarding School.'

'Blah blah blah,' Tony whispered in my right ear and my chest warmed. I was grateful to have him by my side.

'Before we dive into the highly anticipated schedule changes, there is some preliminary news. We have accepted only four new students to join the upper school this year. Can you all come down to the podium please? Lenah Beaudonte, Anne McKiernan, Monika Wilcox and Lois Raiken.'

My stomach dropped. This was not going to be good.

To my left, three students stood up and began the

walk down the long aisles towards Ms Williams. I looked to Tony, my eyes wide and my mouth dropped. He held his hand over his mouth. His big shoulders bounced up and down. Even though his mouth was covered, I could see the apples of his cheeks were red with glee. If only he knew what my tattoo meant . . . once I stood up everyone would see it. Everyone would ask.

I stood up. *Don't fall*, I prayed. *Don't you dare fall*. I stepped down, one sandalled foot at a time. I ripped off the floppy hat so the brim squished in my right hand. Slowly, but surely, I made my way to Ms Williams. I was careful not to look anywhere but at the stairs in front of me. I could already hear some whispering. The tattoo was small. No larger than average textbook print, but the scrawling cursive was specific. It was Rhode's handwriting etched into my skin with ink, blood, candle flame and a small needle.

Ms Williams stepped to the left of the podium to allow room for us. The other three students faced the audience. I did the same. Then I felt a hand on my left shoulder.

'Why don't you go first, Lenah? Just tell them a little about yourself,' she whispered. I stepped up to the microphone. I could only assume I was supposed to talk into it, as I had seen Ms Williams do. It exaggerated her voice and I already had an even, smooth cadence.

The student body stared. Hundreds of mortal eyes looked at me and waited for me to say something that

105

would define me within their world.

'I'm Lenah Beaudonte and this is thoroughly mortifying.'

Laughter erupted. I could feel that they were laughing with me and not at me. My hands gripped the side of the podium. I searched for Tony who gave me a thumbs-up. It was then that I noticed Justin Enos sitting in the seat directly behind mine. My heart thumped in my chest and I had to look away. He had also seen the tattoo. He must have. Either way, he looked unbelievable. Delicious, even. His skin was bronzed, a golden colour that one could only achieve from being in the direct line of the sun. I wondered for an instant if I touched him how warm he would be.

'I'm from a small town in England if you couldn't tell from the accent. I'm sixteen and . . . well, I guess that's it for now.'

I walked back to my seat, this time exposing my tattoo to the teachers who were seated behind me. The whole time I stepped up the stairs I locked eyes with Justin. His lips made it clear what he was thinking. I felt like a hybrid: half beast, half human, because it was easy for me to read him. He looked straight at me, with a smirk. One where his lips just rested on the edge of a smile. He didn't have to speak to me in the rain. He didn't have to say anything out loud because he said it all with his eyes.

I want you.

Chapter 7

As soon as assembly was over, everyone started to move towards the exits. I didn't want to seem eager to Justin, so, when Tony and I finally stood up to make our way to class, I turned round casually. But Justin had gone. I didn't like this position. Wasn't he supposed to be following me? I wasn't supposed to be wondering about him, hoping he was behind me. How frustrating.

Once we were in the hallway, I pulled my backpack close to my body so that my tattoo was covered.

'That tattoo is really cool,' Tony said, confirming my fears. We walked out of the auditorium down the main hallway of Hopper.

'Oh, it's nothing,' I replied.

'Nothing? That tattoo is *not* nothing. When did you get it done? Who did it? That's some serious ink.'

'An artist in London,' I said, though my mind flashed to a memory. I was in Hathersage, stomach down on the floor of the living room. Underneath me was a scarlet Persian rug Rhode had brought back from India sometime in the sixteenth century. A fire roared in the oversized fireplace. I was topless but only my back was exposed. Rhode was on his knees working the scripture into my back.

Around Tony and me, students wandered the halls, most with Wickham folders in their hands. There must have been a hundred middle schoolers wandering through the building. The moment reminded me of a castle in Venice during *carnevale*. Hundreds of costumed Venetians held masks over their faces. Lions, feathers, sparkling gems and flowing goblets spilt on to the floor. Just like this moment, it was disarming to be surrounded by so many strangers. There was no face I recognized, just eyes catching my gaze. Though, in 1605, in my confusion, I murdered the great Doge Marino when he refused to stop following me throughout the castle. I ripped his neck out and was quite full before dawn crept over the canals of Venice. I greatly regretted it all that next day, as I'd had no idea I had murdered my host. What was a girl to do? He kept following me around telling me how beautiful I was. Also, I was so bored.

'So, she's sitting there on her knees. Like, crying,' a voice said, tearing me out of my memory. Tracy stood in the hallway and flipped her hair over her shoulder. She was talking to the members of the Three Piece as well as Justin. They stood around her at the base of some stairs. There were a few other girls standing about that I didn't know. Tracy hit Justin casually on the shoulder. 'Justin

goes in there and says, like, what the hell is wrong with
you?'

'What did she say?' one of the girls I didn't know
asked while she sipped on a fizzy drink. Tracy looked to
Justin but he simply shrugged in response.

'She *lied*. She said she'd never heard music on a
stereo before.'

Justin looked up from the group and when he
locked eyes on me his eyes were polite – surprised even.
My cheeks warmed and I felt a stirring in my chest – I
wanted to scream at Tracy and throw her to the ground.
Instead, I sighed and turned to Tony who smiled apolo-
getically.

'The English floor is up there,' he said, and pointed
at a staircase. 'I can go up with you if you want.'

The position I was in with Tracy was not to be taken
lightly; I needed to go up alone. 'No,' I said, though my
tone was thankful. I looked back to the group but they
had started up the stairs. 'I'll be all right,' I said, grateful I wouldn't have to pass by them after they had just
talked about me in that manner.

'I'll see you tonight. Dinner?'

I nodded and started to climb.

'Don't forget!' Tony said, calling after me. I turned
round. 'B – O – B,' he said, sounding out the letters.
'Bunch – o' – bitches.'

I laughed and ascended the stairs.

*

Advanced English. Apparently, when I took the placement test that Saturday morning, I had scored 'higher than last year's valedictorian'.

The doors on the second floor were made out of mahogany with glass windows. I walked down the shiny tiled hallway, past two or three glass doors, and looked down at my schedule. I pressed on a wooden door with the numbers 205 painted in black and entered AP English. This classroom had a semicircular shape with a chalkboard in the centre of the room, and the teacher standing in the middle was a man named Professor Lynn. He was a short man, with a slight build and a receding hairline. His bald spot was the size of a half-dollar.

Most students were just taking their seats. I didn't see anyone I knew except Tracy. I sat as far away from her as possible. As I walked in, I noticed a familiar curve of a spine seated next to Tracy. The person had a wide, well-toned back that was hidden underneath a black shirt. It was Justin. I sat down without glancing in their direction.

Professor Lynn turned to the class from writing on the blackboard.

'Kate Chopin. *The Awakening.* 1899. Can someone tell me if this novel is a romance, a thriller? What genre is this?' Professor Lynn asked, catching my glance. *So I guess we're just going to jump right into this*, I thought.

I didn't respond. Instead, I pulled the book from my bag. It was a brand-new paperback copy that I had bought with Tony at the bookshop.

'Anyone?' Professor Lynn pressed. Again, no one responded. 'How about our new comedienne?' He referred to his class roster. I knew what was going to happen, luckily retaining my vampire ability to read people's emotional intentions. I knew, like an instinct, that Professor Lynn wanted to challenge me. He came towards my desk and crossed his arms over his chest. 'Did you read the first fifty pages? You should have received a letter and syllabus over the summer with instructions.'

I nodded. Although I'd received no letter while I was hibernating six feet under the ground, I thought it best I didn't mention that particular detail.

'Why don't you tell us what you think, Ms Lenah . . .' He referred to his roster. 'Ms Lenah Beaudonte. What are your initial reactions to *The Awakening*?'

'What would you like to know?' I asked without removing my eyes from Professor Lynn's. He was using me as an example, setting the stage – a power struggle. After the incident by the stairs with Tracy, I was going to win. Our stare was resentful, his eyes unforgiving. If Professor Lynn had ever been made into a vampire, he would have been frightening.

'I asked what you thought of *The Awakening*. The initial fifty pages. Any aspect of it,' Professor Lynn said. The smugness in his voice was sickening. *Just another example of human nature*, I thought.

Justin sniggered. I had never been in a classroom before this moment and already I didn't like it. Tracy rubbed her knee against Justin's and they both smiled at my stymied response. I shot a glance at them and then looked back to Professor Lynn.

'Well,' I said, 'I'm not a girl that likes to be controlled. The main character, Edna Pontellier, was controlled her whole life. That's the book. Edna acts out against the social restrictions against her. She feels trapped. Now, if you are truly asking my opinion and not anticipating my failure in completing the assignment, I think it's a dreadful book.'

Silence. Then chuckles.

'Dreadful?' Tracy whispered in Justin's ear, mocking me.

'You can tell all that from the first fifty pages?' Professor Lynn asked, his eyebrows raised.

'I've read the book before, sir.'

Now they weren't laughing. I scooched down further into the seat and crossed my left leg over my right knee. My legs looked long and spindly. Professor Lynn walked to his desk and then turned back to face me.

'You've already read *The Awakening*?'

I have a first copy, hard cover edition in my home in Hathersage, you fool.

'Yes, sir. Three times.'

An hour later, I dropped my English books into my bag.

After scanning the room for Justin, I walked towards the doorway.

'Miss Beaudonte?'

I turned. Professor Lynn held out a handwritten note on a piece of paper. I slung my backpack over my shoulder and walked towards his desk to retrieve it.

'Because you are so experienced in *The Awakening* and the rest of the class is not, I am going to assign you a few more written tasks than everyone else. It's not fair, Lenah. Your literary experience puts you at an advantage.'

I nodded, though I was silently kicking myself. I could have easily pretended I had never read the novel if I hadn't made a spectacle of myself, and if Professor Lynn hadn't singled me out. It didn't seem very fair. Though what could I say, really? Until a few days ago, I wasn't much educated in the business of justice.

I wouldn't dare sully my insides with what you are.

My voice echoed in my mind. I took a deep breath and closed my eyes as a wave of relief flowed through me. I couldn't access that kind of evil in my human state. Not yet, at least. It was with that thought I reached the door of the classroom.

'You think she's pretty,' Tracy said in an accusatory way. I stopped walking immediately.

'No,' Justin replied, though I knew he was lying. I knew what a lie sounded like. I was brilliant at telling them.

'Yes you do. I know you do. You were staring at her in class.'

'Professor Lynn was grilling her.'

'She's a slut,' Tracy said. 'And I heard she's dating Tony Sasaki.'

'Yeah, great, she's a whore. Can we go?' Justin asked.

'She's been on campus for, like, five minutes. She skulks around with her sunglasses on and doesn't talk to anyone except Tony. Freaky bitch,' Tracy added.

Heat circled and swelled under my heart. These human feelings, these *hormones* bubbling up under my skin . . . how annoying. I ran my tongue over my teeth, expecting my fangs to come down. I waited – no fangs. I sighed.

'Can we stop talking about it?' Justin asked. 'I have a scrimmage.'

I gritted my teeth, threw on my sunglasses and burst out of the classroom, purposely bolting directly between them. Justin's eyes flinched. He gasped, just barely, but I heard it as I stormed by.

I descended the stairs as quickly as possible and rushed down the long hallway. Just before I pushed out into the meadow, I looked left. I was directly across from the art-tower staircase. My anger rose in me so high that I wished for one horrible moment that I were a vampire again. That I had the strength of my coven to scare the life out of both Tracy and Justin.

Instead, I went up to find Tony.

'I don't understand. What the hell is wrong with these people?' I asked.

Twenty minutes later I was watching the clock and pacing back and forth. Tony and I were alone in the art studio, which was nice because I could say whatever I wanted without censoring myself. I didn't even care about my tattoo any more. I peeked at the clock again. I had fifteen minutes before my next class: history. Not that I had to worry about being late, the clock was everywhere – mocking me. I'd never had to even think about time before. I'd had as much as I'd wanted.

I'd had forever.

'I've heard music before,' I said, still pacing. 'Just not like that – in a *listening* room.'

Or on a stereo . . . I thought to myself, but decided not to mention it aloud.

Tony was sketching me, despite my reminder that he hadn't yet taught me how to drive.

'Saturday,' he said, and turned up the radio on a counter to his left. 'Saturday and then we can drive all over Lovers Bay.'

'Who do they think they are? Slut!' I scoffed. 'I've never even had sex.'

(OK, so I'd never had human sex.)

'Tracy Sutton and Justin Enos are, like, together,' Tony said from behind the cover of the sketchpad. 'Tracy Sutton is a bitch. Justin Enos is a rich kid who happens to be good at writing papers. They're going to hate you. You're smart and just trumped them at their own game.'

He squinted up at me and then furiously started sketching again. A different kind of music was playing on the stereo in the art tower, something with a lot of drumbeats and repeating rhythmic sounds.

'You're blushing, though, so maybe they should piss you off more often. Helps with the portrait,' he said, and reached for a peach-coloured pencil.

I rubbed at my cheeks as I walked towards the windows. Students walked to and from the many Wickham buildings. I could tell it was close to eleven by the position of the shadows on the grass. Vampires are not innately able to tell the time based on the shadows cast by the sun. It is a talent grown of necessity. Many vampires have been burned to a crisp by miscalculations.

In the meadow beyond Quartz, boys ran up and down a field slamming each other in the head with a stick that had a net attached to the end. On the back of their jerseys was a number and their last names. Two of the Enos brothers were doing this ridiculous activity. One was Justin and one was Curtis, Justin's older brother.

'What are they doing?' I asked, and pointed at the boys. Tony got up with a pencil in hand and bopped in time to the music over to the window.

'Lacrosse. It's religion at Wickham.'

'Seriously?' My eyes were wide. 'What is lacrosse?'

Tony laughed and I could see that I was a bit too literal for my own good.

'When you get to the library, Lenah, *please* look it up. If you don't know what lacrosse is, you're going to be in trouble here. Not with me,' Tony clarified, 'but with the dumb asses who care about that crap.'

'Lacrosse. Got it,' I said, and went to the door to gather my things. 'You see,' I said, turning back to Tony, 'I'm already in trouble. So far, just today, I'm a slut, a know-it-all and ugly.'

Tony sat down and squinted at me. Then he shaded something on the page with the tip of his ring finger. He was seated again, sketching away.

'Definitely not ugly,' he said, and reached for a charcoal.

Chapter 8

At around 3.30, I finished my last class of the day. As I stepped out of Hopper, I put on my sunglasses and wide-brimmed hat and walked into the grassy meadow that spread out towards Quartz. I headed to the library for work.

Instead of obsessing over Justin Enos calling me a whore, I tried to think of my new job, the prospects of the life ahead and how many of my days would be occupied by my transition back into living, *breathing* life. Did I miss waltzing through my Hathersage home? Did I miss alleyways in London and other European cities, murdering and hurting innocent people as I went? No. I did not. Yet I yearned for the faces of the coven. The men I had known for centuries. The men I had trained to be killers. My brothers.

Now that I was human, I had to think about dates and time. It was 7 September. There were fifty-four days before the last night of Nuit Rouge. Fifty-four days before Vicken anticipated my awakening. Fifty-four days before the hunt for me would begin.

*

After taking my spot at the reference desk, I took out Professor Lynn's assignment. It seemed simple: 'Write a five-paragraph essay discussing one way in which Edna is "awakened" in Chopin's *The Awakening*. Use SPECIFIC examples.' I had time after all. My shift was from four until six. I dived into research on five-paragraph essays. I gathered some books from the reference section and had already outlined an idea for the paper when a voice said, 'Can I talk to you?'

I looked up. There stood Justin Enos.

'No,' I said, and looked back down at the outline. Really, I could not look at him. His eyes and mouth were unbelievably beautiful. He was still wearing his practice uniform and pair of muddy trainers. I wanted to touch the thick pieces of golden hair that stuck to his head in swirls and sticky mats. His cheeks still held a flush and beads of sweat trickled down into his sideburns.

'I have, like, nine hundred things I want to say,' Justin tried to explain. Why did his lips have to pout like that? So naturally?

I picked up some books and made my way into the maze of Wickham stacks.

'I want to apologize,' Justin said, following me. I shoved a book into a spot on a shelf and continued on through the stacks. I focused on placing the four books in my hand in their proper places.

'What Tracy said was stupid and I shouldn't have—'

'Save it, will you?' I said, and continued on. 'Do you

do that to everyone? Stand outside in the pouring rain and ask a girl about her sadness? Then make fun of her? Why even apologize?'

Justin stopped in the middle of the aisle. 'Tracy's just jealous. You didn't deserve that.'

You didn't deserve that . . .

The phrase rang in my ears, sending vibrations through my head and echoing in my mind. I shelved the last book randomly. Then I turned towards Justin and crossed my arms across my chest.

'You know what I don't understand about people?'

Justin shook his head and his brow creased – he was genuinely curious.

'That they revel in the sadness of others. That they genuinely want to hurt one another. I don't ever want to be that kind of person again and I don't associate with people like that any more.' My embarrassment revealed itself through a sigh.

'I'm not that kind of person,' Justin said, though the expression in his eyes said that he was confused.

At that moment I noticed bold gold lettering out of the corner of my left eye. I turned my head to look at the binding of a book. The title read: *The History of the Order of the Garter.* I picked it up and placed it under my left arm. Justin took a few steps down the aisle and stood directly across from me. His chest heaved under his tight T-shirt.

'You're really something,' Justin said. 'I mean, the way you talk. It's—'

'British?'

'No. I like listening to what you have to say. You're smart.'

I don't know if he took a step forward or if I did but we were suddenly standing so close, Justin's lips inches from mine. He smelt sweet, like sweat. I knew that his heart was still pumping quickly and his blood was running through his veins faster than usual. I wished I could stop these calculated vampire thoughts but, as they say, old habits die hard.

'I'm smart enough to stay away from you,' I whispered, though I was looking at Justin's lips.

Justin leaned forward and just when I thought he would kiss me he reached underneath my arm to take the book. I took a breath. The scent of grass was embedded in his skin. He was dangerously close to my mouth. The instinct to bite. I waited for my fangs to lower. I opened my mouth, baring my teeth only slightly. The moment Justin pulled away, I shuddered and exhaled, shaking my head quickly, and shut my mouth.

'What are you reading this for?' he asked, and then flipped the book over and back.

'For history class,' I lied.

'So, can I make it up to you?' he asked, handing me the book. He rested his right hand on the stack and kept his left hand behind his back.

'Make what up to me?'

'For Tracy. And me. For making fun of you today,' he

said, a hue of pink rising on his cheeks.

'How would you do that?' I asked.

'There you are!' said a high-pitched voice. Justin spun round. Tracy and the other two girls in the Three Piece stood at the end of the row. Tracy's hand was on her left hip. It was clear they had coordinated their outfits. They all had on different-colour leggings that clung to their small bodies and similarly matched tank tops.

I felt like an underdressed giant.

'Curtis said he saw you come into the library,' Tracy said, coming forward to slide her arms round Justin's midsection.

I turned away from Justin and headed back to my desk, pretending the conversation never happened. I would not interact with Tracy. I would not be, dare I say it, the inferior one? The other two girls, who remained at the end of the row, stared me down. One of them, the shorter one from the morning assembly, Claudia, smiled at me as I walked closer.

'Nice tattoo,' she said. She turned to the other girl, Kate, and shared a devious glance. 'Can we see it up close?'

Once Claudia was at my side, I leaned closer to her and whispered, 'You have something in your teeth.'

There wasn't anything in her teeth but Claudia whipped out a tiny mirror to check. I glanced back at Justin who now had both of his hands occupied by Tracy's hips.

Later that night, I ate dinner with Tony. I took a final bite of that night's American Flair entrée: chicken breast with a kind of cream sauce. I couldn't stop smiling while I was eating. There were so many tastes in my mouth. The woody flavour of thyme. The sharp pungency of oregano. And, of course, sugar.

As we finished up dinner, I recounted what had happened with Claudia in the library. Tony was laughing so hard I could see his back teeth. He wore a baseball hat backwards and the same white T-shirt from that morning except now it was covered in smears of charcoal and paint.

'That's great! Claudia Hawthorne is such a bitch!'

As Tony finished chewing on a bone, I noticed over his right shoulder that Justin was walking into the union with Tracy on his arm. They separated when they got inside and the Three Piece headed towards the salad bar. They sashayed their hips and although they were only dressed in jeans and T-shirts I wished I had changed out of the clothes I'd worn all day. Tony's eyes followed mine, so he turned his head to look.

'Justin! Save us a seat!' Tracy called, and blew Justin a kiss. Claudia and Kate linked on to each of Tracy's arms and they got in line behind the rest of the students waiting to pile their plates with salad.

'He's on this kick to go snorkelling,' I listened to Tracy say.

123

'It's still eighty degrees out,' Claudia replied, and flipped her hair over her shoulder.

'Yeah, but in September?' Tracy asked.

'August was, like, two weeks ago, Tracy,' Kate said, and grabbed a plate from the salad bar.

I looked at Justin to see his eyes sweep over the semi-circular union. He did a survey of the tables and when his eyes fell on to mine he broke into a small smile. His eyes were happy, expectant. He made a beeline for our table.

'What did you do to the poor kid?' Tony asked, turning to me with a mouth full of chicken. As he took another bite, I noticed that his fingertips were stained with charcoal.

'What do you mean what did I do?'

'He's coming over here.'

All I had time for was a shrug in response because Justin was next to us in a second.

'What's up, Sasaki?' he said with a casual nod to Tony.

Tony nodded back. Justin leaned both palms on the table.

'Can I talk to you?' Justin asked me.

'Didn't you already? In the library?'

'Yeah, but I want to ask you something.'

Justin's eyes did a quick stab at Tony and then back at me. Tony couldn't see it because he was looking at me.

'Anything you need to ask me you can ask in front of Tony,' I said.

Tony smiled at me but with both lips closed because he was still eating. His eyes were warm and I knew I had done something right.

'Whatever. I didn't get to ask you in the library. I really do feel bad about what I said. Would you want to come snorkelling with us on Saturday?'

Justin's expression was calm but there was an eagerness in his eyes. The phrase, *snorkelling kick*, echoed in my head and I thought of the way Claudia flipped her hair over her shoulder.

'A full day of you and your nice friends? No thanks,' I said.

Tony scoffed and looked down at his plate to hide his smile. I had no idea what snorkelling was but as usual I decided it was best if I didn't mention this. I also noticed that at the salad bar Tracy kept throwing glances my way. Justin wouldn't take his eyes off me.

'My brothers are coming so you won't be stuck with just me and Tracy,' he added.

I appraised his expression and remembered the complex emotions behind the human gaze. The way that someone's eyes can burn into you and mean something just for you – that's what Justin's look was doing – he was speaking to me without saying anything aloud. But he was holding back, I could sense it. He was looking at me casually but feeling something much more on the inside. My ability to read other people's emotions and intentions told me this and for that I was grateful.

'I'll come if Tony does,' I said, while raising my chin. Tony, who was munching happily on the remains of a salad, stopped chewing instantly. The corners of his mouth fell and he grabbed for a napkin.

'Nice! Meet us in Seeker parking lot at one p.m. on Saturday.'

Once Justin had turned towards the salad bar to join Tracy, Tony swallowed and then reeled on me.

'OK, so, Lenah, that was the first time since eighth grade or something that Justin Enos has said a word to me. I hate those guys. Every fibre of my being hates those guys. Whenever I know they're going to something, I don't go. On, like, purpose.'

'Just think of all the things you will see while snorkelling,' I said. 'All the things you could draw.'

'Wait.' Tony blinked, the realization hitting him. He put down his fork. 'You think, on the boat, Tracy will wear a really revealing string bikini?'

So snorkelling involved a boat. Interesting . . .

'Yeah,' I said, leaning in close. 'You'll have all kinds of body models,' I said with a smile. Tony turned to look at the salad bar.

'This could be really good,' he said. 'I can stare at their boobs all day and pretend it's for my art.'

I laughed out loud, a real laugh, from the middle of my gut.

Nighttime was the most comfortable time of the day. My

breathing was smooth and rhythmic. My eyes blinked more slowly – it was easier to relax. The minutes passed too quickly, though; my new human body needed more time to sleep than I would have liked. That night, I sat on the couch with my feet curled underneath me. White candlelight flickered on to the hard cover of the Order of the Garter book that sat closed on the coffee table.

I leaned forward and lifted the heavy leather cover with my index finger. Inside, the title page read, *A Complete History*.

I placed the book in my lap and ran my fingers across the thick leather. The title was raised in gold lettering. Before I knew what I was doing, I was flipping to the chapter titled: '1348: The Beginning'. There, beneath the original names of the order was a crude engraving of a portrait of a man. And underneath that engraving was the name *Rhode Lewin*. The British knight who pledged allegiance to King Edward III. There were his fine features and his angular jaw. The engraving did no justice to the vampire I was privileged to know. I ran my fingers over the engraving, yet all my fingers could feel was the smoothness of the page.

I looked at the bureau. There were the two photographs; one was called a daguerreotype because it was a photo on a mirrored surface: a piece of glass no larger than a portrait photo. The daguerreotype was of the coven and me but I wasn't interested in that. I looked at the photograph of Rhode and me. I narrowed in on

Rhode's ethereal glow, the regal glance in his eye and, of course, the smirk. My stomach lurched and I took a breath. I got up from the couch and walked with my head down into my bedroom. There was an aching in my gut.

'Where are you now?' I whispered to the empty room.

I left the book open on the coffee table so Rhode's engraving would continue to look up at the ceiling of the living room. The candles flickered, throwing moving shadows about the apartment. The wicks snuffed out sometime in the middle of the night but I fell asleep while they burned. I watched the flames shiver by an invisible wind. The dance of their dark shadows reminded me of home.

Chapter 9

'Claudia!' Roy Enos yelled. Claudia clutched a pair of boy's tight white underwear in her hand and held it high above her head. She sprinted back and forth in front of Quartz dorm with Roy trailing in her wake. Eventually he tackled her, bringing her to the ground, and rubbed her nose in the underwear. The rest of the group sat in a group laughing so hard Kate had to hold her hands over her stomach.

I sat behind a tree – watching. Although the girls continually called me a freak and a bitch, I was fascinated. Why did women in this age judge one another so bitterly? Perhaps they always had and I'd never known – I was forced to watch it through the ages from the outside.

The days of September seemed to move with a lazy second hand. I hoped this would continue because every day that passed was one day closer to the start of Nuit Rouge. I admit I was easily distracted. Between my classes and my library job, my days at Wickham were fixed on one thing: following Justin Enos. I suppose you could say that people have auras, that the energy they harbour inside radiates from within and casts a colour around their bodies. With Justin, his aura was a bright, gold light. He raced speed boats and drove a fast car. He played difficult sports and a couple of times, in those first few days, he came off the lacrosse field with blood on his uniform.

It wasn't that hard to follow him. Most of the time he was at his usual spot in the library, in that little atrium. Over the tops of the books, I stared at his white teeth and his spiked hairstyle. I didn't even care that he was always with the Three Piece and his brothers, Curtis and Roy. Together, they moved like a pack of animals. The ritualistic behaviour, the touching, the social interaction . . . I couldn't explain how comfortable this made me. This is what I did as a vampire: watched you, stared at you until I knew how your chest looked when you breathed. Then I killed you.

At Wickham, Tony was my only companion. His friendship kept me company as well as all the memories of my vampire life, piling on and on in my mind like a stack of books, each memory a leather binding, reaching higher and higher towards an endless ceiling.

Wednesday morning, I had anatomy class at 9 a.m. The day before, at breakfast, Tony and I had happily discovered we had this class together. Anatomy would meet twice a week for two hours.

'Skull and crossbones?' I asked Tony when I walked out of Seeker. He was sitting on the bench facing the parking lot, wearing a black T-shirt covered in skulls and crossbones. He was also wearing black trousers and his two different black boots.

'In honour of blood and guts,' he said, referring to his T-shirt. Together, we walked away from Seeker and down the path towards the science buildings. He sipped on a cup of coffee. We followed the winding path for a quarter of a mile. I, of course, walked under the shade of the branches.

'What are you gonna do in the winter?'

'What?' I asked.

'When the leaves are off the trees and you don't have any branches to hide beneath.'

Well, there was a stumper. Tony turned off the path.

'I'll get a bigger hat,' I said, trying to smile and keep the conversation light.

Science classes were held in the buildings right before the stairs to the beach. The buildings were made of red brick and shaped in a semicircle. In the centre was a fountain, a bronze sculpture of Madame Curie, a scientist who'd discovered the element radium. She sprayed water in an arc from her hands. We walked past her and into the middle building.

Tony looked me up and down. 'We're inside. You can take those off.'

I shoved the glasses in my bag. Tony and I walked

past posters for safe sex and Biology Club, and various students passed us, younger and older (again, relatively speaking), and I watched them as much as they watched me. Tony pointed to a door at the end of the hallway. The science classes were on the first floor.

'If you could be anything when you grow up, what would it be?' Tony asked.

I looked down at the linoleum floor as I walked. It was newly waxed and my boots made a sharp click as Tony and I made our way down the hallway.

'I don't know,' I said. 'My life's been really . . . complicated.'

It was true. I'd never had much to do besides read, study and, well – murder.

'Come on, there's gotta be something you like,' Tony said as we finally approached the science lab door.

What *did* I like? I twisted the onyx ring round my finger as I thought it over. I had almost forgotten I was wearing it. Though I was reminded of it in moments like this, when I wanted to think. I liked biology and anatomy. I loved to investigate the workings of the human construction. Mostly for my own appetite. I looked down at my fingers working the onyx ring in circles and I stuck my hands in my pockets.

The anatomy classroom was simple enough. There were lab tables, each with two at a seat. A line of windows faced the Madame Curie sculpture and underneath were cabinets. Each table had its own sink and Bunsen burner, which was a small flame used for science experiments. I followed behind Tony into the back of the room where there was a free table. I never got a chance to answer his question because the rest of the class filed in behind us.

I slid into the seat next to Tony. He sipped his coffee and then took out a book from his bag. I did the same. A young teacher came into the room followed by a few latecomers, including Justin Enos. My heart thumped at his unexpected appearance. This was the only other class we had together besides English. I looked down, away from him, and at my blank notebook. I smoothed back my hair and threw the longer strands over my shoulder. Tony was chatting up someone in front of us but I tried to stay focused. I wanted to stare at Justin, talk to him some more. I wanted to snorkel. I wanted it to be Saturday.

'AP anatomy is the toughest class at Wickham. I tried to call out sick for the placement test last semester but when my sister found out she hit me on the head with a violin bow until I left to take the test,' I heard Tony say to the person in front of us.

'Your sister?' I asked. 'I didn't know you had any siblings.'

'She's really into education. Rides my ass.'

Odd. No one had made me responsible for myself in so long that it didn't seem to matter what I did or didn't do. After all, the only reason I was there at Wickham was because Rhode loved me and had died proving it.

The teacher placed a briefcase on the table. Everyone reached for their notebooks, but the teacher smiled.

'You can take out a piece of paper and pen but you don't have to. Not yet.'

She reached down to the floor and lifted a cooler up to the top of her desk.

'I'm your AP anatomy teacher, Ms Tate. I'm brand new to Wickham Boarding School. I hope you'll give me not only your attention but respect.' No one said anything, which I suppose was appropriate. 'Today, I am giving you an example of what you will be doing in my classroom this semester.'

She reached into the cooler, took out a white thing in a plastic bag and placed it on the main desk so we could all see it. The bag was so cold that it was foggy inside. We couldn't see what it was, not even me. I couldn't see through fog.

'Now,' Ms Tate said, and dimmed the lights. She pulled down the screen to begin her lecture. The white thing in the plastic bag was still on the desk. I didn't want to look – I already had a hunch that it was something dead. In the moment, I couldn't have scripted it any better. Justin, who was in the front row, glanced back at me and smiled. I felt a tingle in the pit of my stomach. I smiled too but just barely.

Ms Tate asked if anyone had done the pre-summer reading. No one had.

'Well, if you did, you would know we're starting this semester with blood.'

Despite everything in my body, I rolled my eyes.

The lights clicked off. I instinctively looked around me – at the classroom now shrouded in a grey light. Ms Tate flipped on a switch at the back of a small machine at the front of the room. There was a low, fluttering sound, kind of like a hum. Then an image of a human heart, a real heart, shone on to a screen. It was like a magnifying glass only very large – another piece of technology, another marvel of the modern world.

'Now,' Ms Tate said, 'if any of you had done the summer reading then you would be able to identify the key elements of the heart. They are the . . .' Ms Tate was leading.

No one answered. But I knew.

I could hear Rhode in my mind. We were in London in a tavern late at night. I had only been a vampire for four days and I had so many questions. Even though I was watching Ms Tate point at the three unmarked sections of the heart, I could only hear Rhode.

'You will have instincts now that you didn't before.'

'Like?' I asked.

The rain pelted the windows of a British tavern in the fifteenth century. The flicker of the candles made Rhode's porcelain features glow and I wondered if I looked the same in his eyes. Around us, men and women clinked glasses and ate stew from ceramic bowls. I looked at the hearty stew but turned away, un-interested.

'You will know exactly which part of the neck to bite. You will become an expert on creatures that you never knew existed. You will feed and you will sink your teeth with such precision that your prey will die instantly.'

Over the years, this technique was perfected but Rhode was right. If you bit into the jugular vein on the neck then it would be connected to the right ventricle, which was responsible for pumping blood in and out of the heart. It was the most direct way. The most pleasurable way. Because the vampire bite was not painful – it was the most complete feeling of satisfaction that a human could ever experience.

The lights clicked back on in the anatomy classroom but the mood had changed dramatically. Ms Tate was monstrously disappointed that no one had done their summer reading. After snapping on plastic gloves, she took the white mass out of the bag. A couple of the girls gasped and one of them shrieked. Ms Tate dropped the dead body of a cat on to a metal plate.

'Yes, I know, shocking. But this is anatomy so you'd better get used to the idea of dealing with dead specimens in this class.'

I couldn't help it. I was rising up in my seat to get a better look.

'Furthermore, you should all recognize this as a cadaver of a cat.'

A girl in the front row burst into tears, gathered her things and ran out of the room. As the door closed behind her, Ms Tate looked back to the room and spoke in a much softer tone.

'This is an AP-level class. Achieving an A will not only ensure that you will be in advanced classes in your college years but put you ahead when compiling your applications. If anyone else has a problem cutting open or dealing with dead specimens, they should leave now.'

Ms Tate moved the cat to the top of a rolling cart. The cart was similar to those in the library except underneath it were scalpels, tiny knives and assorted tubes.

'Anyone want to brave the cat? Cut her open so we can take a look inside and see for the first time perhaps what it means to see how a body works?'

No one did.

I looked left at Tony who was staring at Ms Tate with wide eyes. I glanced forward at Justin's rigid back.

Cut it open? It was dead already so there was no sport in it. Besides, I felt no fear of something dead. I looked around. A guy in the front row doodled on a piece of paper. A girl next to him flipped through pages in her textbook and kept her eyes to the desk. Death was the ultimate fear for mortals. I breathed a weighted sigh. I could take breaths and feel the warmth of my fingers, but I was not truly human. I was a killer, a vampire stuck in the body of a sixteen-year-old girl.

I raised my hand. What would be so hard about dealing with a dead carcass?

Ms Tate smiled wide.

'I didn't anticipate anyone actually being brave enough. Ms Beaudonte, please come up.'

Every single person turned round to stare directly at me. Justin raised his eyebrows. I walked up the centre aisle and reached my hand out to take the knife.

'No, no, Lenah. You need gloves.'

'Oh, right. Of course,' I said, and took a pair of latex gloves in Ms Tate's outstretched hand.

The cat was shorn of fur, and had been preserved in formaldehyde for so long that it didn't even really look like a cat any more. The skin was pruned as though all the water had been sucked out of it. The mouth was open and the tongue was yellow and a pasty white. In my past life I would have ripped the thing open with my teeth but this was a mortal life now. Bacteria and germs mattered.

I put on the plastic gloves, which smelt like rotten eggs. I used the tiny knife and cut the rubbery carcass so it exposed the preserved insides. As the tiny knife cut through the skin, I felt a slack in my shoulders and I exhaled for one brief moment. I was doing something I knew: cutting open a body.

The carcass had already been pre-cut but I wanted to make sure I could expose the heart. So I used my fingers and pulled the skin open a little more. The pressure of the rubbery, dead skin against my fingers reminded me of the many nights the coven spent digging holes in the earth. I helped them pick up the bodies and heave them into the ground. This cat had been dead six weeks. A few people gasped behind me. A lens suspended above the tray projected the image of the cat on to a screen.

'Yes,' she explained. 'The cat's innards are so small I have to project them. So, Tony Sasaki,' Ms Tate said, checking a class roster. 'Where should Lenah point if she wants to show us the right ventricle?'

Tony immediately started flipping through his textbook.

'Um . . .' he said, stalling.

'I see Mr Sasaki has also not done the reading.'

A couple of students laughed.

'What about the left ventricle, Tony?' I thought Ms Tate was kind of relaxed initially but now she was picking on Tony, my friend. His cheeks were red and students were starting to stare, even Justin.

'The way you phrased the question is confusing, ma'am,' I said without giving her time to stop me. 'The right ventricle is on the left but only to the animal. To us it's on the right side, facing me.' I just kept going. 'This is the ventral part of the cat.' I pointed at the body of the animal. 'Because the cat is on its back and the stomach is exposed.'

Ms Tate crossed her arms in front of her body and

let me finish explaining the particular portions of the heart that I could remember.

'What is the system called?' Ms Tate asked. Her blue eyes were fixed on me. I could tell she wanted me to be right. She wanted me to explain it correctly, not like Professor Lynn, the English teacher who'd wanted to make a fool out of me.

I thought of the books in my Hathersage library and the nights looking at diagrams by candlelight.

'The circulatory system,' I said honestly, and handed the tiny knife over.

'Thank you, Ms Beaudonte,' she said.

I knew I'd ripped that cat open as a test – for myself. To see if being human would make death and decomposition more difficult to bear. It didn't. My heart fluttered and I blinked my eyes. I ate, drank and slept. I did what a human did, sure. But so far humanity was mocking me. In the moment I'd prised the folds of the cat's skin open, I'd felt nothing but a relief from frustration. When I sat back down next to Tony, Ms Tate continued with her lecture.

'What Ms Beaudonte discussed today is in chapter five of the reading. Clearly she has had some experience with cat dissection.' Ms Tate paused and I felt Tony lean closer to me. He smelt like musk. A human musk – earthy.

'We are so going to get As,' Tony whispered. My eyes darted to the front of the room where Justin Enos was looking back over his shoulder and smiling at me.

Chapter 10

'You realize we're partners, right? That you have to help me because you're required,' Tony said. It was right after class and Tony jumped and skipped up the pathway back towards Seeker.

'And you're still supposed to teach me how to drive,' I reminded him.

'Speaking of that,' he said. 'I need you to sit for me. For your portrait.'

'This was supposed to be a trade.'

'Come on. An hour. You don't have to work till four,' he pleaded.

'I have to go get my wallet. Come see famous Professor Bennett's room. Lunch, then portrait.'

'Nice!' Tony said. I took out my hat and sunglasses and we started to walk. 'I wonder if his ghost is in there.'

The early morning sun was just starting to beat down on Wickham campus when Tony and I stepped into Seeker hall. He showed his ID to the security guard, we headed for the stairs and started climbing.

'You know they have elevators. They go up and down just by the push of a button. Kind of amazing,' Tony said between laboured breaths as we climbed towards the fifth floor.

'Never been in an elevator.'

'What? You are one weird chick, Lenah.'

Was I acting as I should? Perhaps I had stepped over the line with the cat during anatomy class. Tony continued to follow me up the stairs.

'I still cannot believe you not only ripped a cat open no problem but you're not freaked out to live in Bennett's old place. Guy was a real nice teacher, don't get me wrong. But, seriously, Len, that's creepy.'

I stopped in front of my door and slid the key in the lock.

'Doesn't bother me,' I replied.

'A guy *died* in there,' he said as we stood outside. Before I pushed it open, Tony leaned forward and sniffed the rosemary I had nailed to the door. 'I don't know about you but I believe in ghosts, spirits, all that. And *everyone* says Bennett was murdered.'

'The school administration probably wouldn't let me live here if that were true. Besides, people die in lots of places,' I said.

'What are the flowers for?'

'It's rosemary,' I said, opening the door and stepping inside. I placed my sunglasses and hat on the black lacquered foyer table, which sat to the right of the front door. 'It's a flower you put on your door to protect you. To remind you to stay safe.'

'Safe from what?' Tony asked as I shut the door behind us. 'Whoa! This is so cool! My roommate smells like crap and you live *here*.' Tony ran a hand over the soft couch and jumped in his step from painting to painting on the wall. Rhode's longsword was of particular interest. Tony walked right up and stood in front of it.

'What does *ita fert corde voluntas* mean?' Tony asked, sounding out the Latin words inscribed on it.

He ran his fingers down the middle of the blade with his index finger.

'Be careful,' I said. 'Don't touch the edge or it will cut you.' Tony placed his hands back by his sides. 'It means, "the heart wills it".'

'So this is real? What era is it from? Who gave it to you?'

I didn't say anything. Instead I walked away and looked for my wallet in my bedroom.

'This looks so real,' I heard Tony say again. His eyes were inches from the blade. I walked into my bedroom and found the wallet resting on my night table. When I came back into the living room, Tony had left the sword and was standing over the Order of the Garter book, looking down at the engraving of Rhode. He was so close to the bureau. My photographs. My eyes snapped back and forth from the photos on the bureau and Tony's back. My mouth was suddenly dry – parched. My tongue stuck to the roof of my mouth. Tony was silent, his back remained to me.

'R-ready?' I croaked.

'Is there any subject you don't like?' Tony asked, and turned to me. 'You're a history geek too?'

I sighed with a smile. He hadn't noticed the photographs.

'Let's go,' I said. 'I'm starving.'

'OK, Lenah. Turn the engine on,' Tony coaxed. That Saturday, Tony and I sat in the Seeker parking lot. My hands gripped the steering wheel so hard that my knuckles turned white and sweat formed under my palms.

The key dangled from the ignition. I turned it and the engine purred to life.

Tony explained the workings of the gas and brake pedal, turn signals and the importance of reverse. It was very interesting and not unlike the commands my father had taught me in the fifteenth century when I watched him manoeuvre the cows and horses in the orchard. The 1400s in England were marred by the end of the Plague. There was less male labour because of all the deaths and my father refused to let me out of his sight. My disappearance must have killed him. I never found out what happened to my family.

After an hour or so, I eased the car into a parking spot that faced Seeker and turned the engine off. We rolled down the windows and I stuck my feet out so they rested on the frame.

'Do all people sunbathe?' I asked, happy to be under the shade of a nearby tree. I looked at Tony through the shadow of my sunglasses.

'You don't like the sun, do you?' Tony asked. He had reclined his seat all the way back.

'I don't like things that make me uncomfortable,' I replied.

'Well, Justin Enos pretty much makes everyone uncomfortable. Kinda why I stay away from him and all the soccer freaks, lacrosse junkies and football nuts. Kinda why I hate you for making me go.'

'I've met worse,' I said with a laugh. There was silence between us for a moment. I looked down at my clothes, hoping what I wore wasn't another giveaway that I was anything less than 'normal'. I wore black shorts over a black one-piece that Tony insisted I buy. He came with me to the store and it took ten minutes to shut him up about buying a thong bikini. Even though Tony was wearing his swimming trunks he was still . . . well, Tony. He wore silver rings with crossbones and dragons. His swimming trunks were black with flames rising all over them.

'What is that?' Tony asked, sitting up and looking down at my chest. I followed his gaze. Before I had time to wonder if he was looking at my breasts I realized he was looking at the vial necklace. In it, Rhode's remains. They were ash and gold and sparkled in the light glinting through the windshield. I held the small pendant, which was crystal, shaped with a small silver stop. It looked like a clear dagger. I took a breath, rolling the vial between my thumb and index finger.

'If I tell you, promise not to tell anyone?'

'Yeah . . .' Tony said, though the tone was a bit more excited than I would have liked.

'A friend of mine died. And these are some of his remains.'

Tony's smiled faded as though I'd slapped it off him. He sat up and leaned towards me, like he was going to inspect the vial. He stopped.

'Can I?' he asked. He had leaned his body closer, his eyes looking straight at my chest.

'Sure,' I said, almost in a whisper, and held the vial in my palm, though I left it round my neck.

Tony came so close I could see the minute embers of light dance in the black pupils of his brown eyes.

'Should it be sparkling like this?' he asked, taking a quick glance at me.

'Yes,' I whispered, and sat back in the seat so the vial fell on to my chest. I also wished I wasn't wearing the onyx ring. I hoped he wasn't so observant.

Through the window, I could hear happy voices and the sound of passing cars out on Main Street. When I looked up, I could see the lines in the leaves and the fibres of the bark of the trees. I could distract myself with driving lessons and friends, but Rhode was still dead and his beautiful ashes were all I had to prove it.

146

'I had a brother who died,' Tony said unexpectedly. His sympathetic gaze surprised me. He sat back in his seat.

'When?' I asked, suddenly hearing a thump of bass from a car stereo. It was far away but I could hear it nonetheless.

'When I was ten. One day he was alive and the next – dead. Car accident.'

I nodded, not exactly sure how I could respond to that.

'Kind of why I can't always go along with everyone's happy attitude all the time. Life sucks sometimes and most people don't get it. They think – well, all of the people at this school anyway – they think everything is just handed to them. Real easy, ya know? Like, the day is never something you have to fight through.'

I placed my hand on top of Tony's and let it rest there for a moment. What could I say? I was a death giver. Happy to do it. I had been so good at being dead.

'I used to think I could talk to my brother after he died. When I was a kid, I lay in bed and whispered to him. Told him all my problems. Sometimes I dreamed about him right after, when I fell asleep. Do you think it's possible he was talking back to me?'

The dewiness of Tony's skin and the innocence behind his eyes made me want to lie. But I had seen death. Really seen it. And when someone died they were gone – for the rest of time.

147

'Like you said the other day. Anything's possible.'

Boom-boom-boom. The bass thumped from somewhere on Main Street now. I turned and looked behind us just as Justin's SUV came through the Wickham gates and pulled into the spot next to mine. Justin rolled down the window.

'You guys ready?' he asked.

I glanced at Tony, whose eyes said that we had reached a new understanding of each other. Were we ready?

I think we were.

Chapter 11

I wish I could tell you that I sat in bright sunlight on the bow of the boat with my feet dangling over the edge. I wish I could say that I watched the spray shoot up from beneath Justin's luxury motorboat and that the cold drops tickled the bottoms of my feet. No. From the moment we backed out of the boat slip, I was hidden away in the cushy cabin.

This boat was not the same as Justin's racing boat. This was Justin's father's boat, used only for lounge riding and, in our case, for snorkelling. A set of stairs led down from the boat deck into a hallway. I remembered small cabins and cottages from my human life but this boat interior was amazing – it was *meant* to float. On either side of the hallway were two booths, a kitchen, and a bathroom. I walked towards an open door leading to a bedroom.

I sat on the bed and folded my clothes so they were neatly piled in my bag, along with my necklace of Rhode's remains. I tucked that at the bottom, safe from prying eyes. I slid a white tube of sun block out of my backpack. Bold black letters read: SPF 50. I looked down the long hallway again. The sun's rays cast gleams of light on to the steps that led up to the main deck of the boat. I sighed, flipped open the cap and squeezed the tube just a little too hard. The creamy substance spilled all over my hands so it oozed between my fingers and dripped on to the carpeted floor.

The white liquid contrasted sharply with the royal blue of the soft carpeting and I tried to rub the sun tan lotion into the carpet with my big toe. To make matters worse, the motors slowed above and I knew we were coming close to the snorkelling spot. Soon people would come downstairs and see that I had rubbed a palm's worth of lotion all over my pale thighs.

I stood up and furiously rubbed my calves, my ears, my arms. I was starting to sweat. If I missed a spot, would it be like before? Would I burn easily? Maybe the trans-formation needed a few more days. The lotion smeared everywhere. It wouldn't rub in!

'Are you ever coming up from down there? You have to actually go into the water if you want to snorkel,' Tony called down to me.

Tony came down a few steps so he was standing in the boat stairwell. I rubbed the suntan lotion on to my feet. He laughed, his smile sweet.

'You have that stuff all over your face,' he said. He walked forward and rubbed the tip of my nose and the creases on each side of my nostrils with his index fin-ger. He smelled like coconut, just like the lotion I was rubbing all over, and he smoothed it in so it melted into my skin. 'This was your great idea,' he said, and sat down on the bed, crossing one ankle over the other. He wasn't wearing a shirt so I couldn't help but look over his physique. He wasn't sculpted like Justin but he was stocky and in shape.

I sat down on the bed but kept my back upright. My fingers clasped the SPF 50 sun block.

'Are you all right?' Tony asked, sitting up and looking at me.

I nodded but remained silent.

Tony pushed his sunglasses to the top of his head and tried to meet my eyes but they were hidden behind my sunglasses.

'Have you ever been on a boat before?'

'Long – time – ago,' I barely whispered.

'Are you freaking out on me right now?'

I nodded again, once, and swallowed. My mouth was very, very dry. Hadn't I brought some water with me? Where was it?

Tony turned me by my shoulder so I faced him.

'Lenah. We're going, like, three miles away from the beach. It's totally fine. Nothing bad's going to happen on the boat.'

I lifted the sun block. 'Will you put this on my back?' I asked. I didn't mention to Tony that it wasn't the boat or the ocean beneath us. It was the sun, the blaring sun and what it could do to my rejuvenated body, only a few days old. I heard the motor slowing once more and the roaring zoom was now a quiet purr.

As I mentioned, the bathing suit I'd bought was black, very low cut in the front and had very high cut outs in the hip. The vampire life is not tainted by body issues and fat. We are what we eat, if you will. I was a purist and was relentless in my pursuit for perfect blood. The outside of my body was a true reflection of the purest blood I could possibly find.

Tony's index finger was callused. I knew this was because of all his painting and sketching. His footsteps were different on the boat too. Without the lumbering specificity of the different boots, he was just a clumsy teenager to me. He rubbed the lotion over my back with his rough palms but I didn't say anything. He was the first *person* to touch my skin. He continued to rub the lotion over my back in wide circles. My tattoo was exposed and I noticed he spent a few more circular motions than usual on my left shoulder. I knew he was reading and rereading it, wondering when I would explain what it meant.

The motors stopped completely at the same time as Tony said, 'So, what does evil be he—'

'Thanks,' I said, interrupting him and spinning round. I took the sun block out of his hand and tossed it on to the top of my bag.

'Come on!' I heard Roy Enos call, and then a moment later a hefty a splash of water.

I stepped up and out of the cabin. There were two double engines and a few seats on either side of the boat.

Tracy stood on top of the rim of the boat and jumped into the water. She was wearing a red two-piece, which was tied together over her hip bones by two tiny strings. I suddenly hated my bathing suit and wished I had bought a bikini instead. The other members of the Three Piece, Claudia and Kate, were already in the ocean. Tony had climbed over a ladder and was doing breaststroke out to the others.

After Justin had dropped an anchor into the water, he readied the snorkelling equipment. He turned round with a red plastic mask hanging from his right hand.

'Wow,' he said, and his eyebrows raised. His eyes travelled up and down my body and I tried my hardest not to pose.

Justin turned away rather quickly. He fiddled with clear masks, blow tubes, flippers that looked like they belonged to creatures I had seen on display in museums at the beginning of the last century. Justin laid them out on top of a small cooler.

His feet were strong; they held his frame well and they were tanned from the sun. Roy Enos, who had a smaller head and a slimmer face than Justin, was treading water. He called to his brother back on the boat.

'Throw me those flippers, Justin,' he said, and rolled on to his back so he was floating. I looked down over the boat and realized that there wasn't much of an ocean below us at all. We were in a harbour and when the trees swayed in the wind I could see some of the familiar redbrick buildings of Wickham. The harbour was like an alcove just parallel to Wickham beach. I could specify beads of sand and blades of grass. But I tried to forget about my vampire sight so I focused back down on the water. Most of the girls were standing on their tiptoes; Tony was doing a handstand next to Tracy.

Claudia, the smallest of the Three Piece, swam around the boat wearing a snorkel mask. She peered down into the five or six feet that was directly below.

Ah yes! I thought. *Snorkelling in action.*

'You know you have to jump in that wet stuff, right?' Justin asked.

'I know,' I said casually and came out from underneath the protection of the awning over the driver's seat. The sun washed over my back and shoulders when I leaned forward to peer at the water. Tracy arched backwards, dipping her hair into the water. Wasn't I supposed to be the beautiful one here? I felt my stomach tighten. Instinctively, I placed my palms over my belly button. I was still surprised my body reacted this way. That the muscles would link to my emotions.

'Usually, this is fun. I didn't know you were afraid of boats,' Justin said, and lifted his right foot in order to prepare to step up and stand on the edge of the boat.

'I'm not afraid of boats,' I said, and dropped my hands.

'Sure you're not,' he said, smiling in a devilish, challenging way.

Before I could even begin to defend myself, Justin stepped up on to the rim of the boat. I watched his knees bend and the bottom of his feet press on to the wooden rim. He pushed up high. Before he hit the water he flipped so he did a somersault in the air and then splashed in so the spray came up high over my head.

What on earth could be the point in that? Those in the water laughed and clapped. Seemed a bit useless to jump for sheer amusement.

'My turn,' said Roy, and he swam back towards the boat.

'Don't crack your head,' Justin said to Roy. 'Be careful.'

Much to my surprise, one by one they all somersaulted off the boat. Why didn't I want to jump? Other people seemed to find such happiness in it. I turned away from the acrobatics and walked up to the bow. I sat down with my feet dangling over the edge. Behind me, there were more happy yelps and splashes but I focused on the small waves slapping against the boat's underbelly. Even though I was wearing my floppy hat I could still feel the sun shining down on me, heating me up. I glanced back to see Roy and then Justin somersault, in perfect circular movements off the boat. He was something, wasn't he? To be able to do that – and in the bright of day.

1850, Girvan, Scotland.

I lay in a field hidden behind a series of houses. I always dressed in the most luxurious fabrics. That night's dress was black and ankle length, made from China silk with a corset brocaded with flowers of red, green and purple. The iridescent satin gathered on each side and created a tier of ruffles. I wore my hair long, in a braid.

It was just after 9 p.m. and the houses on the street ahead of me oozed a dreamy light from their small windows. Girvan was a coastal town. A close-knit community with sweeping, endless hills. We, the coven, were in a meadow behind a stone wall that ran parallel to the main street. Song was pacing, keeping watch as always. Heath lay on his back, watching the stars move through the sky. Gavin threw tiny knives into the bark of a tree. He always held a collection of daggers in his boots or pockets. On that night, he picked a tree about one hundred yards away, threw the knife, and then retrieved it to do it all over again.

'We need someone knowledgeable,' I said. I stood up from the grassy ground next to Heath and started to pace. I was ruminating again. 'Five is a strong coven. After all, there are five points on the pentacle star. North,' I pointed at Heath. 'East,' I pointed at Song, 'and South,' I pointed at Gavin. We need a West; we are missing our West.'

Four protectors, with me the crux, the centre. With

five members, the pentacle would be complete. Once the coven was fulfilled the bonds between us would be unbreakable. The magic would require the coven to remain ruthlessly committed to one another until their deaths. All three of them – Gavin, Heath and Song – knew I wanted one more to join our unit. Though I think Gavin, the more careful of us, feared the power of the magic. Binding magic is lethal. It creates an invisible bond that ties to your soul. Breaking the bond is impossible. It means death – this was exactly my intention when making the coven. No one would betray me unless they wanted me to kill them. If I made the right choice and made the right man a vampire, we would be unbeatable. I wanted to ensure that we never had to worry about our survival. Survival? Could I even call it that?

'Above us is Andromeda,' Heath said, only in Latin. He was my second vampire, after Gavin. 'Next to her is Pegasus,' Heath continued, and pointed up at the many stars linked together to form the mythological winged horse.

'Take me, Pegasus,' I called, and started to spin in a circle, my arms out to my sides. 'Take me high in the sky at noon so the sun can shine down on my back. Let me reign on your wings.'

I laughed so my voice echoed through the meadow. I kept spinning and spinning until finally I collapsed on to the ground next to Heath. He rolled on to his left hip and faced me.

'They say that Andromeda appears as a woman holding a sword,' he said, and ran his hand along my body from shoulder to thigh. I smiled and then turned on my back. I could not see Andromeda. To me, stars were tiny bright lights that I could not wield.

'Also you can only see her by the five brightest stars in the galaxy.'

Interspersed in the silence, there was a *thunk* every time one of Gavin's knives hit his target. Song paced and paced, almost growling under his breath. We had no need to feed as we had decimated a boarding house the previous night. It would be a few days before the magic of the blood waned and we would have to feed again. As Heath continued to name the stars individually, I got up out of boredom and paced again. That's when I heard a man singing a lively Scottish song.

Straight ahead through the trees was a one-storey tavern made from stone. Small, rectangular windows threw candlelight towards the meadow. It had been fairly quiet but as I walked through the trees in the direction of the tavern, the singing grew louder. Soon the voice was clear. It was gravelly but carrying the whole tavern in song.

'Here's to the sodger who bled, and the sailor who bravely did fa'!'

I held the hem of my gown so I could walk with ease over roots and branches that stuck up from the mossy ground. I knew my coven was watching me but my extrasensory perception told me that they were at ease.

'Their fame is alive, though their spirits are fled. On the wings o'the year that's awa'!' sang the man again. The singing voice was quite good despite the slurring of his words.

I threw one leg over the stone wall and stepped down on the other side. I was a few feet away from the tavern and I approached the window as silently as possible. The candlelight from inside was a glowing orange. There were wooden tables with bar stools. Men and women held glasses filled with ale or whiskey. I peeked from the right-hand corner of the window and saw a tall man, in full British military uniform, dancing on top of a table. He couldn't have been older than eighteen or nineteen though there were wrinkles on the sides of his eyes when he smiled. His arm muscles pushed out and gripped the cloth of his uniform. I wanted to run my hand down the line of his spine.

The uniform had a red jacket and black trousers. He kicked out and jumped. He took a blue felt cap and threw it into the crowd. He kicked his right leg then his left and jumped up and down so his feet slammed on to the table top while he danced a traditional Scottish step. He brought his knees up and down and repeat-edly kicked his legs.

The cuffs and collar of the uniform were gold. The buttons glinted in the torches circling the tavern. I turned. The music came from a group of men hitting drums and playing bagpipes in the back of the room. The soldier kept dancing on top of the table while the guests in the tavern clapped in time to the music. His face was red, filled with life – filled with blood. He was tall, like Rhode, with slim features and a pouted mouth. His hands were strong and the right one grasped the handle of a mug of ale.

'Their fame is alive, though their spirits are fled! On the wings o' the year that's awa'!'

After the final resonating note he jumped from the top of the table to the ground so his beer sloshed out of the mug and on to the wooden floor. He had brown eyes that even in the darkness of the pub glimmered at the tavern guests.

I walked away from the window and round the perimeter of the building. I was going to go inside and talk to this man. Except, right before I pulled on the door, it banged open and hit the side of the building with a shudder. I raced across the street and leaned against a tree near the tavern door. The trees were green and leafy, but skinny. Their tops bent towards the sky in a thin point.

The man walked outside, took a deep breath and placed a cigarette between his lips. He inhaled and when he exhaled the smoke into the sky he held the cigarette in the corner of his mouth. He squinted one eye and wiped the sweat from his forehead. Taking the cigarette out of his mouth, he narrowed his eyes at me and took a step forward.

'Is someone there?' he asked. He had a husky voice with a deep Scottish accent.

I took a step away from the tree.

'Hello, soldier,' I said.

His eyebrows raised and he bowed in an exaggerated motion. When I did not curtsy in return, he smiled but with curious eyes. I stepped across the dirt street and stood in front of the tavern door.

'I shake hands,' I said in response to his bow, and stuck my right hand out as I had seen hundreds of men do in my time. Men in society during the 1850s did not think it proper for a woman to shake hands as an equal. This is a fact that remains preposterous to me.

He looked down at my outstretched palm and then up at my eyes. I was smiling with my lips closed. This was always effective whenever I wasn't getting what I wanted.

'Shake hands?' I asked. He stretched out his arm and when he did I looked at his inner right wrist. Thin blue veins protruded from the skin and ran away from his palm and up his arm.

We grasped hands and he looked me up and down. In that moment, I wished I could have felt the touch of his strong hands. I could sense his firm grip, but no skin-to-skin contact. Nothing definite, anyway. He let go first and backed away slowly into the tavern doorway. While I could certainly feel the heat of his stare I would have loved to know what his fingertips felt like running down my skin. Or what his breath smelled like or his hair. Even though I knew all of that was impossible, I wished it anyway. All I could smell was upturned earth and musk, the scent of his flesh still lingering on my clothes.

'Your hands are cold,' he said.

'There is something special about you,' I replied, walking closer so that the light from a torch on the door illuminated my face. He came closer again. He squinted a bit, turned his head to exhale smoke and then examined my face again, his eyes stopping on my mouth.

'No, my dear. There is something special about *you.*' This young man was looking at me with deep interest. The jovial tone was gone. 'What are you?' he whispered.

I admit this threw me. No one yet had mentioned my appearance, my smooth skin and wide, black pupils. No one dared admit that I was something other than normal. Most humans were transfixed by my beauty.

'No one of consequence,' I said casually, and started to circle him, swaying my hips in my usual way and looking him up and down.

'I'm a Scots Fusilier. A man of maps. I have travelled the world to verify the locations of the earth for the British army. I have looked upon many faces. Noses, eyes, all of intricate specificity. Your features, lassie, are not of these parts.'

'Nor any that you have ever known,' I said, stopping my circling so that I stood in front of him. 'What is your name?'

'Vicken, dear.' He stepped closer. The gruff edge to his voice was so strong, much harder than Rhode's, whose gentle cadence was burned into my brain. 'Vicken Clough of the Twenty-first Regiment.' Vicken held my gaze. He didn't flinch; he just blinked, calmly.

Either my ESP was extraordinarily off or this man was not afraid of me. I had to leave. This was something I couldn't fathom or understand. My eyes flickered to the meadow beyond the tavern.

'I must go,' I said, and walked past him, away from the tree and back in the direction of my coven. He grasped my forearm.

'I beg you not to trifle with me, miss, for you may get exactly what you want.'

This man was powerful – forthcoming. He knew exactly what he wanted. I ripped my arm away and headed back into the meadow. I stepped over the stone wall and towards the coven who I could see were still in their same spots, relaxing far off in the middle of the field. If I brought this man into the meadow, he would be instantly murdered. Not that I was against this but I was too intrigued to have him killed just yet.

'Wait!' I heard him call. His footsteps stopped at the edge of the meadow. 'Who are you?'

By the time Vicken had reached the field, I had

moved too far into the darkness for him to see me. I stood on the side of the meadow protected by the shade of tree branches. Vicken gripped the stone wall, lifted a foot and then placed it back on the ground. He craned his neck to see into the darkness. He swore under his breath and turned away. I walked back towards the coven.

'Who was that?' Song asked.

I couldn't help a smile of satisfaction. 'One of interest,' I said, and peeked over my shoulder. Vicken was walking back towards the tavern. 'Meet me at the inn at dawn.' I looked up at the sky and the position of the moon. 'We have four hours.'

With that, I turned from the coven and without him knowing it I followed Vicken home.

Vicken did not live far from the tavern. I climbed back over the wall, making sure to stay in the shadows and trail behind. When I got to the road, he was only a few yards ahead. He swerved a bit from the amount of ale he had consumed. He lived seven houses away from the tavern. He bumped his shoulder on a tree when he turned down a small dirt road. As I followed after, I looked ahead; the drive to his house ended with a sharp cliff and then miles of ocean.

Vicken's home was set on the edge of a dense forest that abutted the sea. There was a main manor made of white stone. It was two storeys and capped by a black roof. Behind it was a smaller one-room cottage made of a grey stone. It was considerably less grand than the main manor. As I silently followed, I passed a stable where I could hear horses neighing comfortably and the sound of the ocean hitting the rocks somewhere over the cliffs.

Vicken walked into the cottage and shut the door behind him. I turned the handle and followed after. It was true what he'd said. He loved maps and they were everywhere. At least a dozen were on the walls and on a small wooden desk in the right-hand corner of the room. In a closet were military uniforms. Even a bright blue globe sat on the desk.

The back door to the cottage was open and in the backyard I saw Vicken setting up a contraption made of brass. It was based on three legs, a kind of tripod.

I walked past a washtub. The curtain was pulled open and a pair of white socks hung over the basin. I stepped into the doorway and Vicken looked up. He didn't smile or frown; he simply stared for a moment and then went back to assembling the machine.

'You have no fear of beasts? Monsters?' I asked.

'You are no beast,' he said, matter-of-fact, and continued to fiddle with a long tube that was positioned towards the sky. He looked through the lens, checked the direction of the tube and then glanced at me again. 'I am more afraid, miss, of the things that I cannot see with my eyes.' Vicken gestured with a wave of his hand that I join him. I walked towards the telescope and looked through the lens. The moon was crisp and clear, though the moon's cracks and crevices were another land to me.

'Beautiful,' I barely whispered. I looked up into Vicken's eyes – he smiled a bit. I backed away in the direction of the main house.

'Why aren't you afraid of me?' I asked.

Although Vicken claimed that he was not riddled with fear, he kept his distance. He kept his fingers on the telescope, busying his nervous energy with the parts of the machine that needed to work to see the night sky. I followed the strong frame of his wide shoulders. Kept my focus on his dangerous glance. His masculinity was intoxicating.

'You intrigue me,' he said, meeting my eyes again.

I threw my head back and laughed deeply so my voice echoed in the silence.

'Intrigue you? Is that what this is? Curiosity?'

Vicken kept his gaze on the telescope.

'Tell me, Vicken Clough of the Twenty-first Regiment. What would you say if I told you that you could search this earth and record it all? Be the most powerful navigator the world has ever known? That as long as the earth existed, you would exist?'

Vicken's slim nose and square chin pointed at the ground. His brow was furrowed and he kept both his hands loosely behind his back.

'Eternity, miss, is not possible.'

'And if I told you it was?'

He looked deep in my eyes and I waited for him to break our stare but he stayed firm.

'I would believe you.'

I walked a few steps and stood across from him so our faces were inches apart.

'What do I have to do,' he asked, 'to stay with you?' He wanted to kiss me. I could see it in his gaze, that longing that brown eyes sometimes get. His lashes curled out from his lids so when he blinked he looked like a little boy. I smiled, this was my favourite part. He would surely feel terror after this. I let his lips brush over mine so gently that it barely registered even to me that we had touched. My fangs came down ever so slowly and I whispered, 'I'm going to have to kill you.'

Vicken's breath shuddered and he stepped away from me. There was a twinge of fear running through him but not the kind of horror I expected. No desire to run. The only fear he felt was for his own actions, what he could or would do – for me. This was mind-boggling. Preposterous. I checked the moon. Three hours until dawn.

'I'll give you a night to think about it,' I said, heading away from Vicken and back in the direction of the main street. 'This time tomorrow I will come for your answer.'

'The way you speak tells me, no matter what I say, this isn't a choice.'

Vicken had stepped out from behind the cottage to see me. Under the smooth light of the moon, I could see the sweat on his forehead.

I turned back.

'Why do you even consider this?' I asked, sure that there must be a reason for his compliance to my wishes. Vicken's smile was crooked, so only the left half of his mouth raised. He leaned a hand on the side of the little cottage.

'You,' he said.

There was a moment of silence. I looked at his strong arms and how his hair fell about his face in a lazy, haphazard way.

'Say your goodbyes, then,' I said, and turned away from him, disappearing into the darkness.

That next night, I approached the main manor. Through the window, I saw Vicken eating dinner with his family. Long white candles decorated both ends of the table. There was an open animal carcass and various bowls of greens. Vicken's father sat at the head of the table and Vicken was seated directly to his right. His father, a great round man with thickets of white hair, laughed heartily and took Vicken's cheek into the palm of his right hand. The familiar anguish rose in my throat. I hated families. So often this sadness made me enraged enough to murder, so I would kill whoever could possibly remind me that my family was the life I'd left behind.

Why didn't I want to kill this man? Why did I want to leave him in the confines of his house with his mother and father and collection of maps? Had I dared to find another that I loved besides Rhode? Yes, he would be free, I decided. As I turned from the window to rejoin my coven at the inn, I caught Vicken's eye.

He shot up from the table and ran after me, but I hurried down the dirt pathway, away from the ocean and back towards the main road.

'Wait!'

'I changed my mind. You're free,' I said, turning to him in the middle of the path. On either side of me were tall trees. 'Do you know, you were right? You're the first man I've ever allowed a choice. Go back inside with your family.'

Vicken walked up to me so fast I was surprised for the moment that he was only human. He placed his hands on my cheeks.

'I don't want that,' he said, so passionately that he was gritting his teeth. 'I've let them go. I don't want to be here, die here, and see nothing else of the world.'

'What is it, then? What do you want?' I asked.

Vicken grasped me by the shoulders – I didn't move. He took a deep breath.

'You,' he said, almost panting. 'Just you.'

I stared deep into his eyes and saw such a need in his gaze. He needed me. I looked down at the strong muscles of his neck and shoulders and then back up to his eyes. He leaned forward, lightly grazing his lips over mine. I took a deep breath just so I could smell his flesh – there was that smell again, musk and salt. Soon it would run through me.

'It will be done,' I said, opening my eyes. I grasped his wrist and led him away from the manor. 'You will be joining the ranks of vampires so ancient in history that no one knows of our origins. But you will be powerful. Beyond your imagination.'

I walked towards the woods beyond the small cottage.

'Will you be there?' he asked.

I took his hand into mine. 'Always.'

Perhaps Vicken fell in love with me because of my vampire presence. I don't know. I'll never know. Rhode once told me that the aura of a vampire is so powerful that most men were spellbound without knowing it. I can assure you that when I took him into the woods behind his cottage he was holding my hand. And when I bit into his neck – he was looking up at the stars.

Chapter 12

'Lenah!' I shook my head and my eyes refocused on the water lapping against the bottom of Justin's boat. 'Over here.' I looked to the left.

Justin Enos bobbed up and down as he trod water. The sunlight reflected off the smooth surface and into his eyes so he squinted a bit, but he was smiling.

'Don't make me come up there and get you,' he said.

As he said this, Tony floated by on an inflatable raft and snapped pictures of me.

'Who brought the paparazzi?' Claudia asked. She was doing laps round the boat.

I stood up carefully and stepped back towards the body of the boat. I tried to shake the images of Vicken from my mind, but that invisible clock, the one echoing in my head, reminded me that the days leading to Nuit Rouge were near. Soon, Vicken would try to dig me up from the ground. Justin swam towards the ladder and by the time I got there he was climbing up to join me.

'I've never seen the sun shine on the ocean like that before,' I admitted once Justin had climbed back aboard. He was dripping from head to toe.

'I've never seen someone as pale as you before,' Roy said from the water.

'Shut up, Roy,' Justin spat over the laughter of the others. Roy called him a swear word I'd never heard before and swam away. Tracy was staring and so were the other girls in Three Piece, though they were trying to hide it by splashing each other. There was a calm satisfaction in my mind. I remembered . . . gratitude. Justin had defended me.

'Come on,' he said, and extended a hand. Before I took it, I looked at his palm. His fingers were so smooth. Some vampires, though not all, believe in palmistry. Justin's lifeline, which is the line on the palm that runs between the thumb and index finger, was very long – it almost ran down to his wrist. It does not indicate how long you shall live. It is an indicator of your commitment to life, or, in other words, your life force. He would have been a perfect member of my coven. Justin grasped my hand before I could think any more and pulled me on to the top rim of the boat.

'You scared to jump?' he asked.

I nodded. He gripped my hand even tighter. His warm palms, hot skin. My life had been so cold before now. My toes curled over the side of the boat and I gripped Justin's hand.

'It's not like standing outside in the pouring rain or anything,' he said, referring to our conversation in the meadow. 'But it's really fun, I promise.'

'A promise from the boy who called me a whore.'

Justin sighed but kept his gaze on me.

'You gonna let me make this up to you or what?' My jaw dropped. I had no response to that.

'I'm sorry,' I said. 'You're right.'

'Do you want flippers?' he asked.

I shook my head.

'OK. Well, this water is pretty shallow. You can stand on your tiptoes, so don't dive. Just throw yourself in.' Justin met my eyes and waited for me to look back from the water to him. 'You ready?'

I nodded.

'Gotta start somewhere, right?'

I looked at Justin's assuring glance. 'Right,' I said. Justin's body propelled upward so I closed my eyes, felt my knees bend and jumped into the air. The sun was on my back and I threw my hands up and slid into the ocean so it enveloped me. The water felt like a thousand tons of prickly pressure sweeping over my body. All I could hear was the whoosh and hum of it. My ears and nose filled with water but I held my breath. When I felt the sand squish beneath my toes, I shot up towards the surface, gasping for air. Once I broke the surface, I opened my eyes and laughed and laughed. After I'd wiped my eyes I caught Justin's smile.

He pushed through the chest-high water in my direction. Tracy was swimming towards him on his right, though his back was to her. He was smiling brightly and I was too. He opened his mouth and for a moment, just a moment, it seemed that he had lifted his hand towards me. Then Tracy wrapped her arms round his chest and pressed herself to his back. She had bright pink nail polish on and like claws her fingers pressed on to his chest. Although Justin stopped reaching for me and instead held his hand over Tracy's, he never moved his gaze from me. Just when he turned to face Tracy, Tony popped up from the water and snapped a picture two inches away from my face.

'So, Lenah, where did you get that necklace?' Tracy asked from the passenger seat of Justin's SUV. She turned in her seat to look at me. We were on our way back to Wickham. It was late afternoon, sometime around four, based on the position of the sun. I placed the chain back round my neck.

'It was a gift,' I said.

'It's so cute. Pixie dust,' Claudia said, from the seat behind me.

Tony scoffed.

'That vial looks really beat up. You should take it back and ask for a new one,' Kate chimed in.

I didn't say anything. We had turned on to Lovers Bay's Main Street. The section closest to Wickham's campus was quite lively and filled with shops. That particular Saturday there was a farmers' market.

'I haven't seen anyone wear pixie-dust necklaces since, like, third grade. How retro of you, Lenah,' Claudia said.

We passed a section of vendors selling plants and flowers. One of the signs said: WILD HERBS.

'Can you let me out?' I asked.

'You don't have to go,' Kate said to me, but she threw a smirk to Tracy in the rearview mirror.

'Yes. *Please* don't go,' Tony said, but Justin was already slowing down. He pulled to the right side of the road. I could see the Wickham entrance gates just a few feet up from where we were. I stepped out of the car, catching a glimpse of Justin's eyes in the rearview mirror.

'Talk to you later, Tony,' I said, and slammed the door behind me. I was sure I would get a mouthful for leaving Tony with the vultures but I had to do something. Something I should have done when I'd first got to Wickham.

At the farmers' market, I walked past carts of apples and pumpkins and various blends of apple cider. Finally, I stopped at the cart filled with herbs and wild flowers. Orange marigolds, purple pansies, asters, and bright yellow chrysanthemums lay in small wicker baskets. A brown satin ribbon held the stems together in a delicate bow.

'Would you have any lavender?' I asked a woman sitting on a patio chair behind her cart. 'A small bundle?'

The woman handed one to me with a smile. 'Four dollars,' she said.

175

I paid and walked in the direction of campus. The lavender smelt heavenly and I pressed it to my nose all the way from Main Street until the great arches of the Wickham campus. I walked through the gate, smiled to myself and took a deep sigh. The campus was teeming with activity. Some people were lying out on blankets, others studied in groups, passing notebooks back and forth. I took a deep breath and listened to the voices echoing around me.

I can't read your handwriting! Just email me.

Bio is going to kill me.

I want that sweater Claudia Hawthorne was wearing.

Here's to the sodger who bled!

I nearly tripped over my own feet. I spun round to look behind me.

And the sailor who bravely did fa'!

I held my breath. Who was singing that song? A collection of girls on a blanket were reading from their textbooks. One of them had headphones over her ears. There were dozens of people on the pathway. Two younger boys passed by me but they were talking about the upcoming basketball season. I turned back round to look across the green but no one was singing. I took a step and then another. Just when my steps were even enough and I was in jumping distance of Seeker, I heard it again.

On the wings o' the year that's awa'!

I dropped the lavender on to the ground and held

my hands over my ears. I could feel my heart thumping in my chest. I looked at the students around me again, just to make sure. Most of them were walking towards their dorms and enjoying the warm weather out on the green. I took my palms off my ears and bent down to pick up the lavender.

Call me later!

Dinner in twenty!

The conversations were normal. The Scottish man singing was gone.

Ghosts have a way of misleading you; they can make your thoughts as heavy as branches after a storm. It was Vicken's voice that swirled in the trees, haunting me from my memories. Even all the way in Lovers Bay, Massachusetts, I knew it – he missed me.

Once I got to my door, I tacked the lavender right next to the rosemary. Lavender, if you are hunted, will protect you from evil forces. It will bless the house of the door it decorates.

Chapter 13

Have you ever in your life wanted to do something terrible? I mean, earth-shatteringly terrible? Because, that next morning, it took everything in my power not to call my coven. When I woke up, there was a silence. A hush to the room and to the world outside on Wickham campus. I focused on needless things. The ceiling in my bedroom was smooth and white. The birds chirped and tree branches swayed from a light breeze. More than anything, I was aware that I was alone. No trip to the water could cure me. I yearned for Song's quiet musings, the way Vicken would look at me from across a crowded room and I would know just what he was thinking. I missed the way the hills rolled away from my house and spread so far into the distance that during sunsets, just when it was safe enough to approach the windows, the grass looked like it was on fire.

I gripped the soft sheets of my bed in my hands and rolled on to my side. Rhode's words slithered through my mind. That final night we had talked about so many things. One was a warning:

'You must not contact them, Lenah. As much as you might

want to. As much as the magic that you created yearns for them. Calls to them. You must deny yourself.'

I looked at the telephone on the night table. Did they even have a telephone? If I called and one of them answered, would they know it was me? But I didn't call. Instead, I rolled to my other side, away from the telephone, and faced my bedroom windows. My thoughts drifted away from the coven. Maybe I would shower. As a vampire, I'd had no need to shower. There was nothing organic about me; I was magically sealed, inhuman, a dead body, enchanted by the blackest of magic. Now, in the human form, hot water rolling down my arms and back was the closest I came to finding some peace.

I stepped out of the bed, away from the doorway, making sure not to allow my eyes to fall on Rhode's sword just outside the bedroom door. I did that a lot – for comfort, mostly. I rubbed sleep from my eyes and stepped on to the cool tiles of the bathroom floor.

'Ahhhhhhh!' I gasped, and threw my back on to the wall behind me.

The reflection in the mirror. My skin. It was a honey colour. A deep bronze. The top of my nose had a sheen of glimmering gold across the bridge. I had *tanned*.

I stepped within two inches of the mirror. I pulled my skin tight with the tips of my fingers. My eyes narrowed, I checked my cheeks, my chin, even my neck for redness of the skin. Even with the SPF 50 I had tanned, though I wasn't scorched as I had expected. I hadn't evaporated either.

I bounced out of the bathroom and hopped into the living room – though I stopped in the doorway. Rhode's sword remained still on the wall, its plaque holding it frozen in place. Then I looked to the bureau and the photographs of my coven. They stared at me with a melancholy emptiness. But everything was empty, wasn't it? No one occupied the couch or the lounge seat. No one made the coffee or asked me what I wanted for breakfast. There was only me.

I sat down on the couch. It was too early for breakfast and Tony had said he wouldn't be up and ready to eat until almost noon. Weekends were different at Wickham. The weekday students went home and mostly everyone else took the time to study. The first week of classes had been uneventful except for anatomy class. I looked down at the coffee table. The book I'd taken from the library was still open at Rhode's engraving. I glanced at Rhode's eyes, those beautiful eyes that would haunt me forever – they stared out at nothing. There was no one who could understand.

Suddenly I was tired again and I wanted nothing more than to curl up for a while. *Yes, sleep would be nice,* I thought. As I walked to my bedroom I hoped that maybe I would dream of Rhode.

That night, I went to Tony's room to find that his family

had come by to pick him up for dinner. So I wandered the campus alone. Although it was warm for September, I could smell something in the air; it was cooling off.

Despite the twilight, Quartz dorm was full of activity. Boys passed footballs back and forth in the meadow, soccer balls too. Rock music echoed from the art tower. Boys and girls walked along pathways and chatted near windows in various buildings.

As I walked, two girls passed by me. I recognized one of them from English with Professor Lynn.

'Hi, Lenah,' she said.

'Um. Oh, hello,' I replied, and found myself smiling. She was a junior too. That was it. A hello – just for me.

I think I was heading for the beach to watch the stars when I noticed the greenhouse directly past the science buildings. With the scent of lavender still fresh in my mind from yesterday's purchase I headed over another grassy patch towards it.

The building was made from glass and stretched back and away from the pathways. I pressed my palms on the glass panels and peered in, but it was dark inside. I focused on the various plants that were in my direct eyeline. I gasped and adrenaline dashed in my chest.

'Nasturtium! Roses, lilacs, marigold and thyme,' I whispered. All of the herbs I missed and so desired to have back in my life. The double-door entrance was glass, just like the rest of the building, and I tugged on the black handles. The doors shuddered back at me. I wanted nothing more than to go inside. As a vampire, you would think I would be completely removed from the natural elements of the world. I could wield nothing natural myself – no need for breath or water – but I loved all herbs and flowers, plants. All flowers have a natural power. All stones have a natural power. Everything, the flowers, the plants, the soil, even the black magic that ran through me as a vampire, came from the earth.

'Greenhouse is closed.'

I spun round.

'Why don't you stop following me?'

Justin Enos was freshly showered and alone. He came from the grassy patch between Quartz meadow and the science buildings. He was wearing a blue button-down shirt and khaki shorts. He looked like he was glistening.

'I'm walking to the parking lot,' he said, and pointed up the pathway. 'Why do you want to go in the greenhouse?' He stepped next to me and looked into the darkened building. 'It smells like dirt in there.'

'I love it,' I said with an edge of a whisper.

'Do you?' He gave me a surprised glance. I looked back into the greenhouse and didn't answer. I didn't want to explain my love for flowers and herbs. 'Still mad at me?' he asked.

'One snorkelling trip and I'm supposed to swoon?' I replied. He rested a hand on the greenhouse and leaned forward, almost inches from my face.

'You smell amazing,' he said.

'Thank you,' I said with a flush of breath in my voice. Justin's eyes pulsated into mine and then he pulled back to an appropriate distance. If I didn't know any better I would have thought he was testing me, as vampires do, through a locked gaze.

'Still gotta do something about you, don't I?' he said, almost growling. It made me want to purr, if it was possible.

'Justin!' called a voice.

Both of us spun round. Tracy and the Three Piece headed towards the greenhouse, coming from the direction of the union. All three were dressed in short black cocktail dresses, though each one was just slightly different in style from the other.

'Hi, Lenah,' Tracy said when she got to the pathway.

'You tanned so fast,' Claudia said to me.

I looked down at my arms.

'I guess I didn't notice,' I replied with a shrug.

'Staying in tonight?' Tracy asked, looping her arm through Justin's. I looked into Tracy's eyes as a vampire would. A stare that pierced deep into the pupil. Though I saw no depth to her soul. She was flat, a child of the secular universe. In fact, every one of the Three Piece was a victim of her own self-absorption. Justin on the other hand had a light in his eyes. A window of sorts where I could see that he was much, much more than an average boy. He had stealth and courage – like Rhode. He had soul. I tore my eyes away from Tracy's. There was a tug in my chest as though a spell had been broken.

'Yes, I'm staying in,' I said, and refocused on Claudia and Kate. 'Sunday isn't a big night out for me.'

'Just hanging out outside the greenhouse?' Kate asked. She was in an extremely short dress.

'Too bad,' Tracy said to me, and then looked at Justin. 'Let's go. I want to get to the club and back before curfew.'

And, with that, they started walking up the path. I didn't want to follow behind so I pretended I was looking at something in the greenhouse.

'Night,' Justin said with a glance back at me.

'Night,' I said, and soon they were enveloped in the blackness of the path and I was walking home.

9 a.m., Monday morning and I found Tony at the library. Turns out he had been there for hours. He was surrounded by hundreds of pictures. I mean it, hundreds of pictures – of *me*. After I put my backpack behind the desk I looked down the long aisle of books towards the back study area. I took off my sunglasses and started down the row of books towards Tony.

I stood above the table but Tony didn't look up. The pictures were from the snorkelling trip. There must have been two hundred photos, each from a different perspective. Tony's head was down and his fingers tightly clenched a stumpy piece of charcoal. I looked at a white sketchpad on the table and saw the outline of a pair of eyes that looked very much like my own.

'You realize this could be categorized as an obsession?' I said with my arms crossed over each other.

Tony shot back into his chair and I have to admit I took a step back out of surprise. His usual happy-go-lucky attitude was nowhere to be seen. His smooth skin had a few lines of charcoal on it and a black smudge on his forehead where he must have been resting his palm while working.

'I've never done a portrait like this before,' he said, and then bent over, back at the sketchbook. 'I gotta get the perspective right,' he grumbled, though it seemed Tony was talking more to himself. He looked at me, back down at the sketchpad and ripped out the page. He crumpled it into a ball and dropped it to the floor. I slid one of the photos off the table.

In it, Justin Enos and I stood on the rim of the boat. Justin's hand was in mine and, the way our profiles looked, it was as though we were washed in sunlight. I was looking into Justin's eyes and I was smiling. The water directly below us cast a glittery, gold glow on our faces. Before I had a moment longer to look at the curve of my mouth and whiteness of my teeth, Tony snatched the photo out of my hand and threw it carelessly into the pile.

'Hey!' I protested.

'Wrong. The perspectives on these are all wrong.'

'Tony, how could that be? Look how many there are. I'm sure you can find—'

He shook his head quickly and with one sweep of his arm pushed the photos into a canvas bag and stalked away up the long aisle and towards the front door. His backpack fell off his arm and dangled over his wrist. He brought it back over his shoulder just as his baggy jeans slid off his backside, showing me his boxer shorts and the top of a very small butt crack. He took a small hop and hiked up his jeans. With a flourish, he pushed open the library door.

'Tony, wait!' I called, and pushed out of the library.

I tried to hold in the laughter as I jogged to catch up.

'You don't get it, Lenah,' he said to me, but kept walking. 'I have to get this right. I mean, it's not just your portrait. It's a big part of my scholarship. Every project I choose has to have some kind of learning curve. You know, where I'm applying something new to my work.'

'So painting a portrait of me has to push the envelope in terms of your artistic ability?' I asked. Our gaze met and Tony's frustration eased into a smile. He rested his arm over my shoulder.

'When you put it that way and talk so fancy, yeah. Also, you're easy on the eyes.'

We started walking towards anatomy class but there

was foot traffic. Students gathered together in a large group so we had to walk slowly.

'The prince and princess are having a fight,' said a junior in front of Tony and me. I did not know her but she had poor blood flow (dull blue vein – that colour was always a clear indication).

Tracy and Justin were in the meadow in front of Quartz. Tracy was pointing at Justin so that one French-manicured nail was inches from his nose. He crossed his arms over his chest and looked at the ground. As we turned left towards the Madame Curie statue, I caught only a snippet of the fight.

'You're always suggesting the library these days. Let me guess, Justin, to see the one girl on campus who doesn't throw herself at you!'

'Tracy! That's not it!'

'She's really rich. I assume that has something to do with it. Sorry, not everyone can buy their way into a private apartment, Justin. I know you and Lenah have singles but roommates are, like, part of the deal here.'

'What are you even talking about?'

'You never want to come to my room any more. And don't try to deny it! You think she's pretty; I've seen the way you look at her in English class!'

'Whoa,' Tony whispered as we walked into the science building for anatomy. I couldn't help feeling a burn of satisfaction.

*

During class, my thoughts jumped back and forth between Justin and Tracy's fight and Vicken's voice echoing through the campus. After obsessing over Tracy's accusations about Justin's feelings for me, I would revert back to thoughts about Vicken. How and why did I hear him so clearly? I knew I wasn't crazy and hearing voices. A vampire in love can communicate with his mate telepathically, though Vicken's connection should have been severed with my transformation.

Vicken's willpower and determination when he was alive were powerful forces; they were part of the reason I changed him into a vampire. These aspects of his personality would have exaggerated as the years went on – perhaps he *could*'ve reached me even though I was thousands of miles away.

'Sit,' Tony said after anatomy class. My thoughts were interrupted by the sharp sound of wood dragging across wood. Tony slid a stool from one side of the art tower to the other. After a few moments, I was sitting on the stool while Tony worked away. He abandoned the charcoals, deciding he couldn't grasp my features well with them. He came from behind the easel and bent forward close to my face. He took a pinky finger, decorated by a silver band, and moved a strand of hair out of my eyes. He checked the accuracy of a paint colour by dabbing it on his palm.

'You look great. This is gonna be perfect,' he said

with a smile. I liked the smell of paint in the room and the fresh grass outside wafting with the breeze through the open windows. Tony smelt a little like a boy, musky but covered in paint. I looked into his eyes – he stared into mine. A smile crept across his face. Soon, before I knew it, I was lifting my chin towards his and our lips were inches apart.

Then someone knocked on the door frame.

'Lenah?'

Tony jumped backwards. He spun round to the door-way. Justin Enos walked into the art studio. I smiled, completely unable to help it.

'I went to the library to look for you,' Justin said, striding across the floor towards me.

'First the greenhouse, now this?'

'The librarian said you're usually up here with Tony.'

'Just for work,' I said, and stood up. Tony was already putting his paints away. I was smiling so much I felt giddy.

'Are you painting Lenah?' Justin asked, and craned his neck to peek at the easel.

'Yeah,' Tony said curtly, and gathered his paint-brushes in his hands.

'Cool. Can I see?'

Tony picked up the canvas. 'No. Totally not even ready yet.' He moved the easel so it faced the wall.

'He's a little sensitive,' I said, still smiling.

'What's up, Enos?' Tony said. 'You don't usually come around here.'

'I'm here to see how brave you are,' Justin said, but he was talking to me.

'Brave?' I asked, turning to face Justin more directly.

'Saturday. We're going bungee jumping.'

I looked from Justin to Tony. Tony shook his head quickly.

'Don't do it, Lenah. It's suicide.'

'What's bungee jumping?' I asked.

'Seriously?' Justin asked, and now leaned against a studio desk. He crossed one ankle over the other. A pose I had seen him do before. This was a comfort position, a way he stood so that he would feel as though he was in a position of power. I sighed – this ability to read positions was a vampire trait. A habit that, thus far, I could not turn off. 'You jump from a bridge to a lake. It's fun.'

Tony stepped between us and put both hands up. One hand was still gripping all of his brushes. 'You wear a strap round your ankle. It's a really elastic cord and then you jump from a high bridge or a building—'

'It'll be worth it,' Justin interrupted.

Tony placed his paintbrushes in a water basin. He washed off his paint palette and turned. 'To who, Enos? Just because you have a death wish doesn't mean Lenah does.'

'All right,' I said. 'I'll go.' Justin's face lit up immediately. 'But only if Tony goes.'

'No. Nope. No way,' Tony said. 'No,' he repeated with a kind of maniacal laughter. He stood in front of some of the student cubbies and pushed a red curtain aside. The curtain sectioned off Tony's art cubby. All of the art students had them. He threw his palette into a metal bin. 'No,' he said, laughing again and shaking his head. He threw his black leather portfolio book under his arm and blasted past Justin and me. 'No,' he said, stepping into the stairwell. 'No. Ha. Ha. I mean, *no*,' he continued, saying it all the way down the stairwell.

That night, I came home and collapsed on to the lounge chair. My eyes rested on the bureau across the room and I stared at the daguerreotype of my coven. My body just couldn't run for endless hours any more. There were blood and muscles now and my everpresent thumping heart.

It was so quiet. My eyes grew heavy. Outside, it was silent but every once in a while I could hear chatter from people walking in the stairwell of my dorm. I listened to my breathing because it actually mattered if I had oxygen in my lungs. In and out. In and out . . . the rhythmic whoosh of the air was comforting. My eyelids slid down for the hundredth time and, finally, I let them fall. Then there, in my mind, coming out of the blackness, was the first-floor sitting parlour of my home in Hathersage, though it looked dramatically different.

A hundred years ago there were large Oriental rugs, deep-red curtains, furniture upholstered in plush velvet. In this dream, the room remained the same but accessories had been added, like flat-screen televisions and computers.

In the corner, Vicken, dressed in a pair of smart black trousers and a black shirt, paced back and forth. He walked to the window and pressed a button on the right side of the wall. The curtains opened mechanically. Outside, directly below the window, was the cemetery washed in a blood-orange glow. On a tombstone was my name, Lenah Beaudonte.

'Something is amiss,' Vicken said, though he spoke in Hebrew. 'Rhode's materials are gone. His bedroom stripped.'

'She will rise,' Gavin said, speaking in French from the doorway. 'Patience.'

Vicken did not turn to look at him.

Their speech was a mishmash of languages, cultures and accents.

'We've gone over this,' Heath said, joining Gavin in the doorway and of course only speaking in Latin.

'Yes, but every day as we come closer to Nuit Rouge, there is a rising doubt in my mind,' Vicken explained.

'Fear,' Song said, slipping past Gavin and Heath and sitting down in a brown leather lounger that faced the window. He spoke in English.

Vicken scoffed.

'Fear is what holds you to that window,' Song said.

Vicken's fingers dug into the window frame. His nails cut a line of ridges in the wood. He turned from the window rapidly and collapsed into an empty armchair. On an end table was a dish filled with dried lilac. He picked some up with the tips of his fingers and let the purple petals fall like grains of sand back into the bowl.

'I need her. If in five weeks she does not rise, I will dig her up with my bare hands,' he said, and that's when I opened my eyes in the living room, gasping for breath and smelling lilac in my hair.

Chapter 14

Nickerson Summit is a bridge suspended 150 feet over a river. That Saturday we left in Justin's SUV for Cape Cod Bungee, which was only half an hour from Wickham. Most people had to get parental consent to bungee jump – I just forged Rhode's signature. After an hour's tutorial and a lot of papers, which we signed to say that if we died our parents wouldn't sue, we took our lives into our own hands. We lined up to bungee off Nickerson Summit.

'I can't believe you talked me into this. *Such* a bad idea,' Tony said, pacing back and forth in front of the bridge. He stopped every few paces and shook his shoulders. 'You can *do* this,' he mumbled under his breath.

'Are you gonna jump with me?' Tracy asked Justin, while hanging all over him.

'We're all gonna jump alone, babe,' Justin said. Tracy leaned in for a kiss. I noticed that her mouth was open and that Justin kept his closed. It was an odd sort of kiss, not equal.

'I want to go first!' Tracy squealed, and hugged each member of the Three Piece.

'Thank God,' Tony said under his breath, and sat down on the kerb of the bridge.

'Promise you'll jump right after me?' Tracy asked Justin. Her eyes took a stab at me, then she kissed Justin on the cheek.

'Sure,' he said, and Tracy took her position on the bridge.

She stood on the ledge, held both arms out and then leaned forward. She shrieked and then she was gone. All of us ran to the edge of the bridge. The ends of Tracy's hair just barely touched the river. She held her arms above her head and her body flowed with the movements of the cord. She rose up, almost to the height of the bridge and then back down. The way her body was so limp, I could tell she completely trusted the technology. How on earth would I do that? As the cord started to slow, she soared through the air more languidly, side to side, so her hair swayed and flew in the wind.

As the bungee company people came in their dinghy to untie her from the bungee cord, Claudia and Kate grasped hands and jumped next. They shrieked the entire way down. After Curtis, then Roy, soon the only people left to bungee were Justin, Tony and me.

'Come on, Tony, you can do it!' Tracy yelled from the river's edge.

I peered over the edge, surprised that Tracy had actually said something nice to Tony. When I looked, I saw that the girls were sunbathing. Underneath their clothes they were wearing matching red bikinis. All I had was my bra and underwear.

Tony stepped up to the bridge. He clenched and unclenched his hands.

'My hands are sweating. My back is sweating. I'm nasty.' He turned and tossed me his baseball hat. 'I can't believe I'm doing this. I wanna puke.'

The bungee guy, standing next to Tony, handed a blue bucket to him out of nowhere. Tony took a deep breath. 'I am an artist. I can *do this*.'

'Are you ready yet?' the bungee guy snarled. He was squat with a beard, and wore a T-shirt that read, FAT GUYS LOVE MEAT.

'Nice shirt,' Tony said to the bungee guy, and then looked back at me. 'I can hear my mother, Len. "Tony, why you wanna kill yourself?"'

I laughed so hard my chest hurt.

Tony placed his arms out at his side, closed his eyes and screamed so that his voice cracked the entire way down. I heard a splash and then the Three Piece whooped and cheered.

Justin and I were the only ones left. The bungee man tied me into the harness. Behind me, on the ground, I could feel Justin watching me.

'You did this on purpose,' I said to Justin as the man continued to strap me in.

'Maybe,' he said.

'What is it you're playing at? Your girlfriend is

down there at the river.'

'Let's jump together.'

'Come on, Lenah!' Tony called from below.

'If you jump with me, Tracy will know.'

Justin stood up. 'Know what?'

'I mean, she'll think you did it on purpose.'

'I did do it on purpose,' he said.

'You two,' the bungee man said. 'Keep your eyes open if you're jumping together. Don't bash heads or anything. I hate cleaning up blood.'

'If you jump with me—' I started to say.

'I don't care any more.'

Justin grasped my hand and we stepped on to the bridge ledge. I didn't look at Tracy and the Three Piece because they were utterly silent below. Justin had waited to jump with me and now everyone knew it. I saw him lift his right foot.

'No – wait,' I said, feeling the enormity of the distance from the bridge to the river. Then Justin squeezed my hand and I refocused on the river below. The way the little waves swept together and moved. I watched the curl of the white caps from the dinghy's motors. It came into my mind at that moment – the dream of the coven. It wasn't real, though it had *felt* real. I suddenly imagined Rhode's enraged face. He'd sacrificed his life for me and I was going to throw myself off a bridge?

'I feel like you've never gone outside your house,' Justin said, and he broke the spell of my thoughts. With my hand grasped in his, I looked at him. 'That's how you're looking at the river.'

'I'm not sure I did before now,' I said.

'You can't hide under a boat cabin for the rest of your life. Right?' I looked down at Tony who pumped his fist in the air. 'You gotta let go . . .' Justin said.

I looked back at Justin and pushed the image of the coven out of my mind. I was ready. With my right hand in his left . . . we both broke into the smallest of smiles.

'Ready?' he asked.

We jumped.

My body was . . . free. My hands broke with Justin's when we jumped. I felt my torso rising and falling and the air rushed by my ears and between my fingers. Through all the cheers it was Tony's I could hear the clearest. My hips were pulled by the elastic bungee up and then down. The wind rushed over my cheeks and over my scalp. I looked to my right and saw that Justin's eyes were closed, his arms above his head. I mimicked him by closing my eyes and a chill rushed over me. I smiled, unable to help it. When the elasticity of the bungee slowed, I looked over at Justin, upside down. He was smiling at me.

'Sad any more?' he asked.

As they helped us into the boats and drove us to the riverbank, Justin wouldn't break my gaze. No, in that moment, sadness was not possible.

Chapter 15

'Lenah! Wait!' Tony called from the top of the art-tower stairs. It was the day after our bungee excursion and Tony had spent the morning sketching my eyes. When he came into the doorway, there was a green streak of paint across his nose. 'Thanks for today,' he said. 'I finally got it . . . I think.'

'Any time,' I said. Before I got to the bottom of the stairs I heard Tony say to the other students in the tower, 'Ladies! Don't let my ass cheeks and sexy stride distract you. I'll be here all day.'

'You have paint on your nose, Tony,' someone said, and a slew of giggles erupted from the art tower.

I stepped outside and looked up. The clouds were deep, layer upon layer of grey swollen puffs. As I walked across the meadow, I was surprised to see Curtis, Roy, Claudia and Kate sitting on a blanket. As I walked past, ready to smile at the girls, Kate leaned to Claudia and hid her mouth with her hand. Over the tops of Kate's manicured fingers, Claudia's eyes gazed into mine. She cocked her head to the side, listening to Kate, but instead of smiling and sharing some devious secret as they usually did Claudia's eyes softened. I looked back to Kate – her eyebrows drew together and though I could not see her mouth I was sure she was sneering. Claudia, though . . . there seemed to be a shift. Claudia and I shared this moment until Curtis leaned back on his elbows and looked me up and down. He smirked. He was tall like Justin but fuller, with a pouting mouth and double chin.

I walked slowly. Kate tossed her blonde hair over her shoulder. Roy, Claudia's boyfriend, stared at me too. He was smaller than both Justin and Curtis.

'Nice jump yesterday?' Curtis asked.

Kate scoffed. Then it hit me, a slap so hard that it burned my cheeks. I had no extrasensory perception. I couldn't access how they felt. I knew disdain was oozing from Kate, but that was obvious. I concentrated on the group, but no sensation came over me. No clear idea of their emotional intentions.

It was gone.

I looked away swiftly and quickened my step. I looked down at the blades of grass and the wings of a passing fly. OK, my vampire sight was still there. I sighed in relief. I headed over the meadow towards the science buildings. *Thump-thump. Thump-thump. Thumpthumpthump.* Stupid heart. The beating fluttered in my ears, making them throb. Adrenaline rushed up and down my chest so that my fingertips tingled. I walked faster, past students headed towards their classes. I hid my eyes from anyone coming my way. It was very hard to breathe. I brought my hand to my chest and felt the shudder of my lungs.

My body was rebelling against me. This physical reaction – what was this? Anxiety? Fear? I gritted my teeth. I was going to go to the greenhouse for some control. I'd almost walked by the archway to Quartz, intending to pass by without stopping, when I heard a very familiar voice.

'I knew it. I knew this would happen,' Tracy said.

'Knew what? This has been a long time coming, Trace.'

'Long time? Like a few weeks, right? Since you met her. Everything was fine before Lenah Beaudonte came to school.'

I gasped and rested my back against the stone of the building. My heart was still thumping like crazy. My ESP! Why, when I really needed it, was it gone so completely? And without warning?

'It's not Lenah,' Justin tried to explain. I refocused on the conversation.

Tracy scoffed. 'Come on. The minute that girl opened her mouth I knew you wanted her. Lenah this, Lenah that. The whole damsel-in-distress crap. Who's never been on a boat? Who hates sunlight?'

I snuck forward so I was just to the left of the archway. The looks from Claudia, Kate and Curtis made sense now. They must have known this was going to happen.

'I just don't get it.' Tracy's voice broke and I could tell she was going to cry. I peeked round the corner of the building and saw Justin and Tracy in the shadow of the alleyway. The glass doors of the dorm opened and closed when students walked past. Most kept their heads down while whispering quietly to each other. Justin drew her close, which made my stomach burn.

'What about me?' she cried. 'I saw you up on Nickerson Summit. You didn't want to bungee with me.'

'It's just different now. I feel different.'

Tracy's head snapped up and her eyes landed on me. I whipped round so my back rested against the building.

'Lenah!' Tracy squealed.

I groaned.

'What?' Justin said.

'Lenah. She's at the top of the alleyway. What the hell is wrong with the both of you?' Tracy said. The sound of her heels on the pavement clicked up and past me. She ran fast through the meadow and was on a pathway before I noticed that Justin was standing next to me. I wanted to follow Tracy and tell her how sorry I was. I had a tingle in my stomach, a squirming feeling, and then Justin's fingers touched my shoulder. I stepped away from him into the meadow.

'Lenah . . .' Justin's eyes burned with desire – to comfort me.

'I didn't want to hurt anyone,' I said.

'You didn't.' He reached out to me. I wanted him to wrap his hands round my back and hold me close, but everything felt heavy in my chest. I pointed to where Tracy had run off.

'Just now, I did.'

'No – that was me.'

I stepped deeper into the grass. Through the sporadic drops of rain falling in front of me, Justin and I held each other's gazes. How could one set of eyes show me so much? Justin's passion for me and his connection with my heart allowed me to see far into his soul. Through the green of his eyes, deep into the pupil, there was an entry way, a place where I could see and then feel all of Justin's intentions. I gasped and hoped, no matter what happened to my vampire sight as I became more human, that I would never lose that connection to him. *Please*, I thought. *Please never let me forget how he makes me feel.*

I had to look somewhere else so I focused on Justin's mouth; his lips were set in a straight line. I would have given anything to stop the guilt running through my veins. To stop all the world and time moving with it and kiss him right there in the middle of the campus. But that was my curse, wasn't it? To always know the feeling of guilt and know it was my fault. Feeling as though I was ripping myself away, I turned and took off for the greenhouse.

Pit pat. Pit pat.

The greenhouse was quiet except for the rain starting to pepper the curved glass ceiling. It had been hot before the rain shower so the windows were covered in fog. Above me, dozens of potted purple ferns were suspended from metal hooks. The leaves were green with a lavender fringe. I walked underneath them down the main aisle of the greenhouse. On either side of me, twelve-foot-high shelves lined each side of the walls. The misting mechanisms came on every few minutes, keeping the plants watered and warm. For the first time in a very long while, I felt safe.

I knew the magic of my ESP had faded while bungee jumping. When we were standing on that bridge and his hand was grasped round mine, I'd abandoned my fear of the coven in that moment and chosen to participate in the real world. Another sacrifice. Rhode was right. It is always the intent that matters.

These thoughts came sifting in and out of my mind as I was walking. Vicken's face came to my head and, because of the fear that came with it, I reached for some rosebuds. Rose in your tea will bring you love. I stuck the petals in my pocket. Next, I would look for apple blossoms for luck. Hanging and growing around me were cacti, orchids, ferns, leafy plants all growing in standard green pots. Some leaves were big and stretched over into the aisle while others were small and barely visible to the eye – the non-vampire eye, that is.

It smelt like wet earth. Yet it was no longer something I envied. Perhaps for once, in a very long history, I understood that I came from that dirt. I was natural too.

'You glad you jumped?'

I spun round. Justin stood in the greenhouse doorway. The double doors eased to a close behind him and we were alone. I turned to face forward. I didn't move. He walked towards me so that his trainers made a slight squish on the wet floor. Then he was so close his chest rested on my back. Justin's body was strong and sculpted, so different to a vampire's, which remains in the exact state it's in at the moment of death.

Justin took slow breaths that sent shivers down the back of my neck. Goosebumps swept over my back and shoulders. I looked right to see an orange flower, with puffy petals. Some had a blood-orange hue, others were bright yellow. The petals were full with a slightly jagged edge, so the lot of them made the flower seem like a plush seat.

'Calendula,' I said, feeling the heat of Justin's body against mine. 'More commonly known as marigold,' I barely whispered, short of breath.

Justin reached a hand round my stomach and pulled me towards him. I was so close I leaned my head back on to his chest.

'Unbelievable curative properties. Good for bites,' I continued.

He didn't say anything. He just held me close and wrapped both hands round my waist. My body tingled, my hands and fingertips alive. I stepped forward, took a breath in, and then in again, finally exhaling. I walked slowly, and Justin walked behind me.

Another flower caught my eye on the shelf to my right. I turned slowly all the way round and met Justin's eyes. I looked down at the flowers that were directly below his fingertips.

'Nasturtium,' I said, and reached down. I plucked a dainty yellow flower bud from a long green stem. There was no more room between us. This was as close as we could get. I held the tiny flower up to him in the palm of my hand. 'You can eat it.'

Justin looked down at the flower and then at me. He opened his mouth, waiting. I placed the flower on his tongue and he closed his lips.

I brought my face closer to his without even thinking of the consequences. He swallowed the petals and I watched his Adam's apple rise and fall. Soon his hands were on my hips and my face was tilted up towards his.

'What does that one mean?' he whispered. Our mouths were a hair's breadth apart.

'Happiness. Right where you are.'

A human kiss. A mouth hot with the peppery taste of nasturtium. He was leading my lips, open and closed, the pressure of his lips against mine – I had never been kissed before. Not like this. Not like I was alive.

There were petals, saliva, breath and pressure. Heartbeats and my eyes – closed.

Justin's hands pressed on my hips, slowly travelled up my back and threaded into my hair. I can't tell you how long we kissed like that. I know that when I finally stepped back Justin moaned, just a bit.

I heard footsteps, one slightly heavier than the other. A sound that only I would be keen enough to understand. A shoe that was just microscopically different in construction to the other. I peeked over Justin's right shoulder and met Tony's eyes. He blinked once, turned away and stalked back towards the lacrosse field in the direction of Hopper.

A raindrop rolled down my arm, over my wrist, down a knuckle and then dripped off my finger on to the floor. I stood in the doorway of my apartment for a good five minutes before I stopped replaying the kiss over and over in my mind. I was soaked so deeply that my clothes clung to my body. I giggled, bringing my hand to my mouth, surprised by the way it sounded, and the blood rushed to my cheeks. Justin Enos had kissed me . . .

I looked up, not meaning to, but my eyes fell on Rhode's sword. I walked slowly, step by step until I was so close to the sword that I could lick it. I watched my smile fade in the reflection of the metal. Even now, I could see tiny bloodstains ingrained in the metal.

I reached for the vial necklace, considering a moment if perhaps I needed Rhode's remains round my neck. I dropped my hands and turned to head into my bedroom. Of course I did. Justin Enos may have kissed me but I wasn't ready to let go of my past. I was still comforted by the memories of my life dealing out destruction and death. As I walked away, I considered what it would mean to take down that sword and put it away, place it in a trunk to remain in the dark with all the rest of my old intentions. No. I wasn't ready. Though it was time to do *something*. Even if it was something small.

Chapter 16

CRASH – smack!

Metal cracked against metal. I spun in a direct circle – keeping my eye on my opponent. 'Always keep your focus,' Rhode had told me. I threw my weight into my left arm, raising my sword in the air, making sure to keep a firm grasp round the handle. I was wielding Rhode's longsword. With a resounding thud my sword hit Vicken's and stopped. Our blades met and both of us froze.

'You have been practising,' he said. I stepped back and lowered my sword. The year was 1875. Vicken and I stood in the weapons room in Hathersage. On the wall were hundreds of swords, daggers and various kinds of weaponry. There was an apothecary table and a room in the back for magic, sectioned off by a black curtain.

My loose-fitting gown allowed me to manoeuvre with ease. It was a sea-green colour, bright when the rest of my world could not be. Vicken loved practising his swordsmanship, positive that one day he would need it. That day he wore a white shirt and a pair of leather trousers. 'Easier,' he said, 'to advance with the sword.' The weapons room was on the first floor and faced the main drive to the house. It was when I placed my sword back in its sheath that I heard laughter. Vicken was already at the window.

'Who is it?' I asked as I joined him.

'A couple,' Vicken said.

They walked hand in hand. She was a young creature in a bright peacock-blue gown. Her companion was dressed in a light brown suit.

I raised my eyebrows and took a step back from the windows when the young man looked about him, stopped walking and gathered the woman into an embrace. He kissed her so hard that when they pulled apart she gasped. Then he did it again.

'Lust,' I said. 'The downfall of any woman with a mind of her own.' I turned and rested my back against the wall. Vicken leaned against the window frame and looked at me. He had such deep-set dark eyes. Even as a vampire they were still warm.

'That is not lust, Lenah.'

'Kissing her in that manner? To take her breath away?'

Vicken stood in front of me and ran his hands down the length of my arms. I wished I could feel his touch, but it was just wind against a tombstone to me. As of late, Vicken's company was the only reason I maintained any semblance of sanity.

'Don't you wish sometimes,' he asked, his eyes eager, 'that you could feel me?'

I looked down at the smoothness of Vicken's hands and was reminded of a moment in an opera balcony when I'd had those same desires. When I looked up to Vicken's face, I noticed that his mouth was turned down. Perhaps he knew as well as I that I no longer had the capacity to wish. I turned away from him and looked out of the window.

'I do,' he said. 'I miss touch. I mean *really* touching, so that all my nerves stand on end.'

Out of the window, the couple had turned to walk off the property. The man stopped, picked a wild flower and presented it to the woman.

'That's human love,' he whispered.

I scoffed.

'Has it been so long that you cannot see it?' Vicken asked.

A dark shadow passed over my eyes. He was right. It was love and Rhode had been gone so long that I could no longer see it. I gritted my teeth so hard one of my back molars cracked.

'Come on,' I said, and started for the doorway.

'Where are you going?' Vicken asked, and a smile spread across his face. His fangs lowered.

'To meet our new friends,' I said, and spat out part of the broken tooth so it jumped along the floor. 'Let's have a bite to eat.'

I shook my head and refocused on the anatomy table.

It was Monday, and I was back in class. I felt the caverns of the broken tooth in the back of my mouth with the tip of my tongue and sighed. I had got to class early. I hadn't had much sleep since Justin Enos had decided to change everything and kiss me. When I'd first arrived, the classroom was empty but during my daydream almost everyone had shown up. A pair of sunglasses slid across the table and bumped my notebook. I looked up to see Tony half smile at me and then take his seat.

'I didn't see you at breakfast,' I said.

'You forgot those. In the art tower yesterday,' he said, pointing at the sunglasses.

'Oh,' I said. 'Thanks.' *So that's why he followed me into the greenhouse . . .*

'Are you ready?' he asked, taking out a pen and paper.

I did the same but wondered why we weren't getting out our books.

'For what?' I asked.

'Frog day. We have to dissect a frog,' he said.

'Is it alive?' I asked with interest. There was a jolt of excitement in my chest. Would I have to kill the frog? Would I care?

'It's like our first test or whatever. Do you even listen in class?'

Not really, I thought.

'It's really bad luck to look into its eyes. So don't,' Tony explained.

'What's so bad about it?'

'My dad says killing a frog is like killing a soul. It's just bad. But listen. More important business, Lenah. Way more important.' Tony turned to face me. I expected this to be it. The moment he would confront me about Justin Enos. Tony's features were all business. 'I need you to sit for me again today. My teacher wants me to get one more thing right in the portrait.'

'I have, um, an appointment,' I said, thinking of my small promise to myself the night before. 'After class.'

'What do you have to do?' Tony asked. 'Hang out in the greenhouse?'

'No. I'll tell you later.'

'Secrets, Lenah. So many secrets,' Tony sighed. 'Come by Hopper around dinner?'

'Sure,' I said. Just when I took out my lab book and pen, I felt a kiss on my cheek. I looked up. Justin towered over me. He looked good – too good. There were crinkles on the sides of his eyes.

'What up, Sasaki,' Justin said with a nod.

Tony nodded back once and flipped open his anatomy notebook.

I didn't need ESP to tell his mood was icy.

'I have practice after class but you're coming to dinner with us tonight, right? I have to ask you something and I don't want to forget,' Justin said as Ms Tate walked into the room.

'Yeah,' I said without a thought.

'I thought you said you would help with the portrait?' Tony said, and I could see a rising shade of red creep up his neck.

'That's right, I did,' I admitted, before Justin could say anything. 'You think we could do it tomorrow?' I asked Tony.

'Whatever,' Tony grumbled.

'Don't forget, Lenah, dinner. I have to ask you something. It's about Halloween weekend,' Justin said as he made his way up towards his seat. Why did he always have to look so good?

'He probably just wants you to watch him play lacrosse,' Tony scoffed. The idea of watching Justin run up and down the field, cradling a lacrosse stick, sweating and jumping while I sat by and watched? In my fantasy Justin was dripping with sweat, glistening from the sun. It seemed like a really great idea.

'You're becoming one of them,' Tony added, just as Ms Tate started to unpack a cooler.

'Who?' I asked.

'One of those girls who follows Justin Enos around. An official member of the Three Piece. Or is it something even more lame if you join, like, Foursome?'

'I'm not one of those girls.'

'I wasn't the one bungee jumping with Justin Enos. You were. Why did you even make me come?'

'I thought—' I started to speak but Tony interrupted.

'Soon you'll be sitting on the sidelines watching him play sports. You'll be coordinating your outfits, melting your brain. Just wait and see.'

My mouth dropped from the surprise of the return of two old friends – pain and shame. They pooled in my stomach.

'I really don't . . .' I started to say, but someone slid a metal tray on to the table with a dead frog on its back. Its skin was a bluish grey from being preserved in ice. It looked frozen.

'Concentrate, Lenah,' Ms Tate said. 'Your test begins now.' She turned away to deliver another frog to the table next to ours. I stared down at the tray. I wasn't expecting it to look like that – I wasn't expecting it at all. Its small belly was rounded and its legs spread wide.

Tony picked up a few pins and pierced the swollen frog's toes to a piece of blue fabric beneath its tiny body. Doing this exposed the belly so we could cut it open. I gasped and my body jerked in an odd kind of hiccup. *How odd*, I thought. This frog used to hop; it used to live. It had a life, yet here it was on the table. Dead and out of this world, yet somehow still in it.

I want to live, I thought. How many times had someone pleaded? How many times could I have let them go? My hands hung lamely by my sides. My pen fell out of my fingers, on to the table and rolled on to the floor.

'Lenah?' Tony asked.

I just stared at the frog's cloudy, unmoving eyes. For

this one inexplicable moment, I was this frog. I had been dead and lifeless for so long and here I was, enchanted and brought back to life.

'Did we not have moments of grace?' I whispered.

'What?' Tony asked.

I continued to stare at the frog's lifeless body. My heart beat and my eyes blinked. The frog moved out of focus and Tony's face came to the forefront of my mind. I could taste food dribbling down my throat, see Tony digging into scoops of his ice cream, an orange flower on Justin's tongue, the rain . . . the glorious rain.

'I want to live,' I said, refocusing on the frog.

I pulled out the pins, one by one, from the frog's tiny webbed feet. Then I pushed back in my chair and cradled its cold body in my left palm. I approached the windows that lined the side of the anatomy classroom. I unclasped them and pushed out. As though holding shards of glass, I held its limp body, close to me, keeping my arm near my ribs.

I leaned out of the window and reached down. Underneath a rose bush, a flower that symbolizes love, I lay the small frog on rose petals. I covered it with a few mounds of dirt, making sure its body was mixed with the earth and the rose petals. In Latin, I said, '*Ignosce mihi* . . . forgive me.'

I turned to face the class. Without a word, I gathered my books and bag and left.

Chapter 17

I sat on the Madame Curie statue's basin and looked out at Wickham campus but my eyes quickly lost focus. Even though I was staring at thousands of blades of grass, in my mind I saw the sculpted line of Vicken's biceps as he wielded his sword. I shook my head and looked back at the individual blades of grass fluttering in the wind. That soon lost my interest and another image from my past came to the forefront of my thoughts – Rhode's eyes. He blinked so that his long lashes barely grazed the top of his cheeks. The image burned me and I gasped for air. I sighed, shook my head and focused back on the campus. I could see the splits in the wood of the trees across the pathway. My breath felt heavy when I inhaled and then exhaled. Would I cry? I kept waiting for it to happen but it hadn't, not yet anyway.

I tried to concentrate on anything that would have been difficult to see with the human eye. If I was still seeing with my vampire sight, maybe I hadn't fully acclimatized? For the first time, I wished it was gone.

I continued to watch the wind rustle the leaves. Students walked by carrying books and backpacks. Teachers and groundskeepers passed me too. I watched them all – anything and anyone to distract myself from the event that had just happened in the anatomy classroom.

Then someone sat down on my right.

'You can rip a cat open with your bare hands but you couldn't cut the frog?' Justin asked gently.

'I couldn't cut the frog,' I admitted. I turned my head to look at him. I kept my hands clasped between my knees.

He took my hand into his and we sat in silence for a moment. Justin rubbed the top of my hand with his thumb. This sent a comfort through me. Justin had a way of making me feel as though everything, no matter what it was, would be all right. That anything could be fixed, even the ghosts of my past and all the ways I tried to escape my pain.

Justin, I could feel. I gripped tighter on to his hand – Justin I could feel with my whole body.

We sat like that for a few moments and soon everyone in our anatomy class filed past. Tony included. He stopped next to the basin.

'Len—' Tony started to say. His eyes darted to Justin's hand intertwined with mine. He looked forward, and embarrassment passed over his features. He glanced down at us again and then stalked away towards Hopper.

'I have to go in a minute,' I said with a sigh, and stood up. 'I have an appointment.'

'For what?'

'Family stuff,' I explained, kind of nudging my feet into the ground. I glanced back at Tony but he was almost halfway across the meadow.

'Listen. Two weeks from now is Halloween,' Justin said. 'It's a really big deal in my family because there's a football game at the local high school and my dad's the coach. I mean, he's a lawyer but he's a coach too. This game is a huge thing for him. Anyway,' he sighed. 'I'm going home for the game and I really want you to come.'

Parents. Justin's parents. In my mind was a gold earring in a palm – in the rain. I tried to shake the image out of my head.

'Your house?' I asked, and tucked a loose strand of hair behind my ear. 'For Halloween?'

'Yeah, the thirty-first. It's only an hour or so away.'

There was silence for a moment as Justin's words flowed through my mind.

Yeah, the thirty-first.

I placed my palm on my head and ran it over my hair. Heat suddenly swirled in my cheeks and I found it very hard to breathe smoothly.

'So do you?' Justin asked. 'Want to come?'

It's October . . . I thought.

My breath came through my nose in short wisps. My heart thumped so hard I felt it in my chest.

'Oh,' Justin grumbled, and then swallowed. 'You

don't have to come.' Justin must have been reacting to my silence. There was a fade in his eyes. He was still sitting on the basin even though I had stood up and slung my bag over my shoulder.

'No. I want to,' I said, though my voice was breathy. I started to back away from him down the path. 'Look, I have to go. I'll come by your room after my library shift,' I said. 'Around six?'

'Lenah, wait!'

I turned from him and ran up the path towards Main Street.

The truth was that I wasn't running away from Justin asking me to go to his parents' house. I was running from the date, the ticking clock in my head that I had let fall silent. Justin's invitation had set it back in motion because it was October and Nuit Rouge had begun.

I couldn't remember the last time I had been so distracted – Nuit Rouge had started and I hadn't even realized it! I walked slowly down Main Street, taking in the sites of the town I had now grown to love. I shoved my hands deep into my pockets as I passed by the marina and into the more residential part of Lovers Bay. It was surprisingly easy to let my guard down. Justin Enos, Tony and all that Wickham offered distracted my thoughts every moment of every day. I knew that as the days of Nuit Rouge passed I had to dive deeper into my human existence and leave the vampire world behind.

219

Just as Rhode had said – my life depended on it.

I stepped through the cast-iron archway of the Lovers Bay cemetery. As I followed the signs to the main office, I knew in my gut that I was doing the right thing. Once I stepped inside, I noticed it was very . . . white. Floral paintings on the wall gave the room a light pink glow. A woman stood up from behind an antique white desk. She was young, early thirties, with a facial expression that set her mouth pointed down.

'Can I help you?' she asked in a soothing tone.

'Yes, I would like to erect a tombstone,' I said. 'In memoriam,' I added, suddenly remembering Rhode's remains were hanging round my neck.

'Do you have a tombstone ready?'

'No,' I replied. 'Not exactly.'

The woman opened a brochure that she slid out from a stack on the right side of her desk.

'You can call this number here. They're local monument dealers. They can help you design a tombstone.'

I took out an envelope filled with hundred-dollar bills. As Rhode had said, I was to deal exclusively in cash. And let's face it, I had more than enough. The woman's eyes darted to the money and then to my face.

'How much is a plot generally?' I asked. The woman looked me up and down and then sighed.

'How old are you?' she asked, with a raised eyebrow.

'Sixteen,' I said.

'I really can't do this without a parent's consent,' she

said with an edge of power in her voice. I hated humans like this.

'This tombstone is for my parents. Both of whom are dead. So, if you want a couple thousand dollars for your cemetery, then you'll allow me to put it up. If not, I'll go somewhere else.'

'Oh,' was all she said, with a bow of her head so I couldn't see her embarrassed eyes. She pulled out a sheet of paper for the plot purchase. 'My mistake.'

She charged me $2,000 so Rhode's tombstone would rest under the branches of a sturdy oak tree. Even then, even while understanding the certainty of his death, I couldn't fathom that Rhode had ever been weak enough to die from the sun.

That next week, Justin and I walked towards the lacrosse field on a Friday afternoon.

'I'm glad you're coming home with me for Halloween,' he said, his hand wrapped in mine. Justin carried his lacrosse gear over his other shoulder. 'You haven't changed your mind in a week, right?'

'I'm excited to meet your family,' I said. Justin brought my hand up to his lips and kissed my knuckles.

Coming towards us across the meadow was Tracy and a group of commuter kids. Just as we passed her, one of them, a tall girl with black hair and dark-framed glasses, pretended to cough but said, 'Bitch,' under her breath. I ignored it. Tracy glanced back at us and she narrowed her eyes at me, tossing her hair over her shoulder.

The week after Justin had asked me to go home to meet his family, I wrote a paper for anatomy class. I had to write about the entire dissection process of the frog. Ms Tate said she understood what had happened in class (she would *never* understand, but I digress) and I was to write a paper instead. For a week straight, I only saw Tony during anatomy class. He wasn't home when I knocked for breakfast or lunch. His roommate always said he 'just wasn't home'. Tony didn't answer his phone either. How was it possible to avoid me so successfully? The art tower seemed a sacred place to Tony and I wasn't going to poke my nose around there when he was obviously avoiding me.

Another week passed and on that next Friday it was warmer than it had been. All I needed was a light sweater and jeans.

'My mom is cooking up this whole big meal in your honour,' Justin said.

We were back on the path and almost at the lacrosse field. It was about three in the afternoon.

'Your mother?' I gulped, feeling a stab of anxiety in my chest. I usually avoided the thought of my mother's eyes or how she'd smelt like wax candles and apples.

'Yeah, she keeps asking what you like to eat. And you eat a lot for someone so thin. So I told her to make my favourite. Pot roast.'

I wondered for a moment what Justin's mother would

look like. He kissed me on the cheek just as we got to the edge of the lacrosse field.

'We're gonna leave at, like, five thirty or so, does that sound OK?'

'Perfect,' I said, and sat down. Once I did, Claudia and Kate plopped down on either side of me. This wasn't a surprise – they had been doing that all week. That is, sitting down next to me when Justin was around and then virtually ignoring me when Tracy was with them. It must have been exhausting.

'Lenah! *Look* what we got,' Claudia said. Her eyes were wide with excitement. Around their necks were two tiny vials of pixie dust, the kind you can buy in a child's store.

'We tried to find some that looked like daggers, like yours. But we couldn't,' Kate added.

'Yeah, we thought we should try to coordinate,' Claudia said. 'Your style is definitely . . . unique.'

'Coordinate?' I asked, and rolled up my sleeves as the boys on the lacrosse team started to whizz up and down the field, passing the ball back and forth from each other's nets. I lifted my chin towards the sky. Claudia looked up at the sky too. She didn't know, but I was checking the time from the position of the sun.

'Enjoy it while it lasts,' Claudia said, stupidly assuming I was thinking about the weather. 'Wait until the team moves indoors for the winter.' I had on sunglasses as we lay in the field.

'It is so stinky in there,' Kate said. 'And, like, every girl comes to see the guys play. Losers.'

'Lenah! Look!' Justin said, drawing my attention to the field and pointing at Curtis's bright pink knee pads. I shared the laugh with him before the coach yelled for Justin to 'stop flirting with his girlfriend'.

'So, Lenah. You and Justin?' Claudia was leading. She smiled in a way that I realized she meant me to understand something that she was not saying aloud.

'What?' I asked, confused.

'You just came from Seeker. Together. Did you two . . .'

'Did we what?' I asked, lowering my chin to look at her over my lenses.

'Didn't he come from your dorm room?' Claudia asked.

I shook my head. 'He's never been in my room.'

'What?' Kate cried, sitting up. 'He's *never* been in your room?'

I shook my head again.

I watched the field. Justin ran towards the goal, cradling the ball in his net. When he got the goal in, Kate and Claudia sat up. We screamed in joy. We weren't losers. I was popular now. People watched me and Justin walk by wherever we went. But could I show him my room? The things in my life that made me . . . well, *me*?

Kate was right. Justin would start asking about the room eventually. Claudia leaned back on her hands to

224

enjoy the sun. She casually looked left in the direction of Hopper.

'Ew,' she said unexpectedly.

Kate and I both looked at her. She was peering up at the art tower.

'Stare much?' Claudia said. I twisted my body to look. I saw two almond eyes looking down at the lacrosse field from the art tower. Once I met Tony's gaze he turned into the darkness of the room behind him.

'He's been watching you all week. Assembly, class, now here,' Kate said.

'I didn't notice,' I said, and stood up. 'I'll be right back,' I said. I peeked at the lacrosse field again. Justin was about to run a play with the team.

'You shouldn't even bother, Lenah. It's leading him on,' Kate called after me, and pushed up the sleeves of the black sweater she was wearing.

'I'll be right back,' I said again, and peeked up at the art-tower window. It was now empty. I didn't know Tony had been watching me all week, though I wished I had known. Perhaps I could have told him that the Three Piece were spending time with me and not the other way round. It was Justin I cared about anyway, and I certainly wasn't a member of their group.

I walked across the meadow, into Hopper, and up the winding metal stairs of the art tower.

'Hello?' I called while climbing up. There was no response. 'Tony, I know you despise me now but you shouldn't stare and you shouldn't blow me off.' Still no response so I continued up the stairs. 'You can come to my room, you know—' I gasped when I stepped into the doorway.

Across the room, in the direct eyeline of the door, was the painting. I stopped where I was walking. I didn't know what to think or say. Tony had finally done it. My portrait. The perspective was from behind, from the middle of my back and up. My head was turned to the right, to show my profile, and I was laughing, open-mouthed and happy. The sky in the painting was blue and my tattoo was etched on my left shoulder. Not in a horrid way but in an artistic way. I knew the painting was taken from a photo; I had seen it in Justin's locker in Hopper just two storeys down from where I stood. It was from the day we bungee jumped. Unlike the photo, where I was wearing a T-shirt, in the painting, my back was naked, exposing my shoulders. I could see the deep curve of my spine and the smooth slopes of my shoulders. Tony hadn't just been practising his art, he had been studying my body – my soul.

'You like it?' Tony asked.

'It's beautiful,' I whispered. I couldn't take my eyes away from the painting. How on earth could anyone see me this way? As though I was someone to admire because of my happiness. 'That's not me. It can't be,' I said.

'That's how I see you.'

'Smiling? Happy?' I asked, turning my head to the right to Tony. He was standing next to me.

'You make me happy.'

I looked back at the painting, unable to look away from the radiance of my smiling profile.

'Lenah . . .'

Tony reached out and took hold of my right hand. His brown eyes looked into mine and his thin mouth was in a straight line, not smiling, not laughing, just being still. Usually his smile would lighten my mood; something funny was always bound to come out.

Tony's hands cupped my own and I saw that his fingers were not covered in paint. His baseball hat was backwards and his button-down shirt was spotless. He must have finished the painting days ago.

'I want to tell you before it's too late,' he said.

I looked at our hands, a sudden thought . . . realizing . . .

'Don't—' I tried to say.

'I—'

'Don't, Tony. Please.'

'I love you.' He said it quickly, like pulling a plaster off. He checked my gaze for approval. There was a silence that followed and I could tell from the way he looked at me that he wanted me to say something.

'Tony—' I started to say, but he jumped right in.

'I've loved you for, like, ever so there's no use in, like, convincing me it's not true. And I know that you think we're friends and we are, even though you've been hanging out with that idiot. But I want more. And I think I could have too. Maybe not right now but—'

'I'm going to meet Justin's parents. Tonight.'

Tony let go of my hands and backed away. He took his baseball hat off and ran a hand through his spiky black hair.

'Oh, that's cool. It's no big deal.'

'Tony, wait—' I reached my hands out.

He was almost at the stairs.

'Yeah. I gotta go.'

'Don't go. The painting. It's beautiful.'

He turned and walked down the stairs with a quick pace to his step that alerted me that I was in no way supposed to follow.

Chapter 18

Justin's family lived in . . . get this . . . *Rhode* Island. A small state between Massachusetts and Connecticut. I didn't know what to expect for the weekend so I brought way more clothes than I needed. When Justin pulled in front of Seeker, the sight of my suitcase was met with a brilliant smile.

'Do you really need all of this?' He opened the back hatch of the car. 'You OK?' he asked, noticing that I wasn't smiling as I normally did. He leaned forward and kissed my cheek.

'I had a fight with Tony.'

'About what? More portrait stuff? Is he ever going to finish it?'

'No idea,' I said. It wasn't my place to tell Justin Tony had finished his portrait.

'You'll talk after the weekend,' Justin said. 'He just needs to calm down.'

Curtis turned from the back seat. 'Hey, Lady.' That's what he'd been calling me lately.

Then a hand smaller and thinner than Justin's stuck up from the final seat row. He waved for an instant and

I realized Roy was lying down on his back. I got into the passenger seat and we were off.

I rolled down the window as Lovers Bay's Main Street became the entrance to Route 6, then Route 6 became the highway. We sped faster than any horse I'd ever owned and the trees seemed like a blur of evergreen. I put the window down completely and I let the pressure of the wind push my hand back. Justin looked over at me, smiled and squeezed my knee. I smiled back and lifted my chin to the dwindling sunlight.

Twilight lay over a long street flanked by oak trees with orange-tipped leaves. The houses had spacious lawns with pumpkins placed on white-painted verandas. Some were carved with jagged smiles, and candles lit the inside of their mouths.

'Guess Halloween isn't real popular in England, huh?' Curtis asked, pulling a light jacket over his T-shirt. We were headed up a sloped driveway towards a grey colonial mansion. 'You're looking at everything with your mouth open.'

Justin's house was three storeys with a light blue front door and pumpkins lining a stone pathway.

'We get tons of trick or treaters,' he said as he hauled both my suitcase and his bag up towards the front door. Justin opened it up, letting me inside first, followed by Curtis and Roy.

'Mom!' Justin yelled. The front foyer was huge, filled

with landscape paintings and mahogany furniture. Portraits and more paintings lined the walls. Justin's voice echoed up to the high ceilings and over the shiny wood floor.

'We're here!' Curtis yelled, and snuck past me. He headed to the right into a cushy living area. He plopped all of his bags on to the floor and clicked on the television. Roy dropped his bags too and found a spot at the other end of a long leather couch.

I, on the other hand, had never seen a modern house before. It was filled with electronics, some of which I had seen at Wickham, and plenty of modern artwork. The living room was just off the side of the main foyer. A grand staircase led up to the first-floor landing.

A woman in her mid to late fifties with fabulous blonde hair and laugh wrinkles came running down the staircase.

'Ah! You're here!' she said. Her sandals made a clacking on the wooden steps as she raced towards us.

'Hey, Mom,' Justin said, and placed his bag down by the front door. His mother, Mrs Enos, grabbed Justin into an embrace. Her hair fell about her face like feathers. She kissed his forehead and cheeks.

'I don't see you enough,' she said, squeezing his cheeks and kissing him again. Then she stepped back and looked at me.

'Wow,' she said, looking me up and down. 'You are one beautiful girl,' she said to me, and grabbed me into her arms. I hugged her in return and felt her palms press into my back. 'You weren't lying,' she said to Justin when she pulled away from me and walked into the living room.

Curtis and Roy got up from the couch and hugged their mother.

'Lenah, I want to hear everything, I mean *everything* about England. Tell me all about you,' she said when she turned from Curtis and Roy. 'Come watch me get the salad ready for dinner.'

Justin and I shared a glance and as I followed his mother into the kitchen I fielded the questions with grace and told her only as much as she needed to know.

After dinner, I came out of the bathroom freshly showered in jeans and a T-shirt. I held my bag of toiletries in my hand and was making my way down the darkened hall towards the guest bedroom. I took a step, then hesitated. There was a shuffling behind me but it stopped the same time I did. I spun round. Justin stood in the darkness.

Every human's skin is different. I know this from the thousands of times I'd sunk my teeth into someone's neck. Easy. Like a knife sliced through apple skin. But there in the dark Justin's skin glowed. He walked towards me very slowly. I watched the way the V-shape of his lower stomach muscles moved under his skin.

He had no shirt on and a pair of jeans hardly hung on to the sides of his hips. I looked up and instead stared at the sculpted definition of his arms.

He grabbed my hand and in an instant the door was closed and I was on my back on the bed. I was fully clothed but I wished I wasn't. Justin's hands were all over me. First they held my arms over my head so he could kiss my neck. Then he let me grasp him back and I held him close to me, wrapping my legs round his waist. He was groaning in my ear, almost a growl, as if he was going to devour me. I placed my lips right under his jawbone and licked him so I could taste the salt of his skin on my tongue. His palms ran up my thighs, his fingers fumbling to unbutton my jeans when –

'Justin!' his mother called from the base of the stairs.

'You have to walk around the neighbourhood,' Mrs Enos said to me as she took a sheet of cookies out of the oven. Justin and I shared a devious smile as we walked into the kitchen. I took a cookie that was offered to me and decided in that moment that chocolate-chip cookies had the most amazing smell ever. 'There are literally hundreds of kids in this neighbourhood and every house decorates for the holiday.'

'It's true,' Justin said. His cheeks were still red from our tryst in the guest bedroom.

Justin's mother ruffled his hair and stole a smile at me

233

as she walked out of the kitchen. The casual familiarity between them jolted a memory. The mornings in my father's house smelt like fresh tilled earth and summer grass. As I rested my head on my pillow dreaming away, my father would whisper, 'Lenah,' rousing me from sleep. We would walk through the orchards, discussing this and that, spending as much time together as we could before the day turned to work. Justin's mother – her one look said it all. I had forgotten what it meant to be a daughter. I had been queen for so long.

I could almost taste the apples in my father's orchard, feel the explosion of tart sweetness on my tongue when Justin's fingers gently grasped mine. The soft touch disrupted my thoughts and the images from my home blew away as all memories do, like smoke. We walked out of the house.

We strolled down the sloped driveway and then headed down the street. It was almost seven o'clock so children dressed in costume ran from house to house, up and down the long street.

'Do you ever dress up?' I asked him.

'I did when I was little,' he said.

'So why did you bring me here? To your family?' I asked, smiling at a little girl dressed as a witch. The street was about a half-mile long and brimming with children in costume. I looked at the many lights from front verandas and the children running from house to house.

'Because I think you're going to be part of my life for a long time,' Justin said. I wished we were back in the guest bedroom. We walked some more, hand in hand, munching on the cookies his mother had sent with us.

'I don't know much about your family,' Justin said. 'You never talk about them.'

A little boy with white fangs in his mouth ran by us towards a house nearby. I couldn't help but stare.

'They died. A long time ago.'

'But you said you had a brother. That day in the rain.'

'I did. But he also died,' I said, continuing to look forward. I could feel Justin's gaze on me. 'Anyone that I could call family has died in some form or another.'

Justin's cheeks reddened and his hands dropped from mine.

'Don't pity me,' I said quietly.

'I don't,' he said, showing me his palms in protest. He frowned and his eyes were hesitant to meet mine. 'I just think, I don't know. I don't know what I think. Everyone you love is dead. That must be lonely.'

'It is. But it's not something that defines me. I don't let it.' There was a pause. I listened to the children around us and the rustle of sweets in pillow sacks. 'I'm not lonely now,' I said, taking his hand back into mine.

Justin nodded, but it was an unsatisfied nod.

'Look,' I said. Now it was my turn to stop walking. 'This isn't something you can fix.'

'I want to.'

'I know. And if there was some way that it would be possible, I know you are the only person who could do it.'

Justin gripped my hand tightly.

We walked, and when we ran out of cookies we headed back. The night had ended in a calm silence. Justin's father came home and we said hello, then goodnight, because it was late and I wanted to lay my head down. Justin's shoulder would have been ideal but his family was always *around*.

After I'd trudged up the stairs, full of cookies and Halloween sweets, I closed the door to the guest bedroom and fell back on the bed. I thought about how I'd been accepted so easily into Justin's family. The memories of my own family were so faded and so difficult to access that they were just vague impressions now. Family wasn't something I'd had to create; I'd been admitted, warmly. As I took my clothes off, Justin's mouth and green eyes seeped in and out of my thoughts. When my head hit the pillow, I thought back on what he'd said in the street. That, if he could, he would fix my pain. No one could take back all of the horrendous things I had done. No one but me. But Justin Enos was a part of me now and that eased the grief still hiding in my heart. Somewhere, almost near sleep, I imagined Justin, in his room, on his back, thinking about me, hoping that I was up and awake, thinking of him too.

Chapter 19

That next morning, I could feel the chill in the air even in the bundles of blankets on the guest bed. I turned over on my stomach and lifted myself on to my knees. There was a small window behind the head of the bed and I lifted the curtains with the tips of my fingers. The sky was the colour of baby's breath so I knew it was too early for the Enos family to be up and debating breakfast. I decided to go for a walk in the neighbourhood alone. I pulled on my jeans, didn't bother to brush my hair and wore one of Justin's Wickham sweatshirts.

I walked down the driveway and stepped on to the street. The sky was now a blue grey and a thin mist hung over the trees. Justin's sweatshirt smelled like him. Sweet and woody, a comforting smell now.

I glanced back at Justin's house once I had walked a few feet down the street. I wasn't planning to go very far – just to explore the neighbourhood while his family was still sleeping.

My stomach did that lurching thing and I thought about eggs and coffee, something that I was sure Justin's mother would make. I smiled. Rhode Island. Of course

I had to be in *Rhode* Island. These days all I wanted was to stop thinking about Rhode and my vampire life. And I had in some respect. My ESP was gone, my vampire sight had started to wane and I wanted more than ever to move forward and be the human I was always meant to be and perhaps was finally becoming. Without my ESP, I was able to forget how separate I once was and participate in my life without knowing everyone's emotional intentions. Just when a glimmer of a smile spread across my face –

Something moved behind me.

There it was – the inherent feeling that I was being watched, no, let me make the distinction clear, the feeling that I was being followed. There is a sweeping realization when a vampire is present around another vampire. A hush of silence, like going deaf, and the sudden feeling of being covered in icicles. The hair on my arms rose and I found it difficult to swallow. I spun round.

There in the middle of suburbia, underneath a street lamp, stood Suleen.

I gasped. The air whooshed into my lungs, I held it and then there was silence. Suleen was so still, unmoving. He wore a white tunic, white trousers and gold leather sandals. A white turban covered his hair. He had a round face, and though his cheeks were full he did not nor could he ever look earthly. He almost seemed like a ghost in that morning light. He was so holy, so untouched by everyday worry, that he didn't have a wrinkle on his face. This is a man who had existed before Christ's birth.

How Suleen knew I was in Rhode Island I would never know, but there he stood. Instantly I felt safe, protected, as though a great white light circled us on that quiet street. Suleen is known in the vampire world for transcending evil, for living a life without the need to feed off humans. 'Only the weak,' Rhode had once told me of Suleen's life. 'He only drinks the blood of the reprehensible.' Suleen walked towards me, both of us silent, and he cupped my right cheek with his hand. He had no smell and his touch was perfectly lukewarm. His dark brown eyes gazed warmly into mine and he smiled.

'I am pleased with your transformation,' he said. His voice was slow, like molasses. From his pocket he pulled out a single sprig of thyme. Little purple flowers smaller than the tip of a finger attached to a long green stem. Thyme is used in rituals meant for the regeneration of the soul.

I gently took it with my thumb and index finger. 'To what on this good earth do I owe this honour?' I asked, stunned. Even in the highest days of my ranking as queen of a coven, Suleen had never visited me. He took a step back so there were a couple of feet between us.

'I come with a warning,' he said in his languid tone.

I slapped my hand over my mouth. My heart

pounded with such a force that Suleen looked at my chest because he could hear it.

'Nuit Rouge. My God. I completely forgot,' I said. 'Last night was the final night of Nuit Rouge. Today is November first. Nuit Rouge has ended,' I said, and looked to the ground, to the trees, to the sleeping houses that I wished I was in and then back at Suleen. 'Vicken has discovered I am not hibernating?' Suleen nodded once slowly in response.

I looked back towards Justin's parents' house in the distance. It was still dark.

'As a unit, your coven is unstoppable. Separated, as they are now, they will not succeed.' Suleen paused. 'The hunt for you has begun.'

It was back. My vampire extrasensory perception was overtaking my human consciousness. I assumed it was because of my close proximity to Suleen's power. An image, not from my own mind but from Suleen's, came to the forefront of my sight: Rhode's fireplace in my home in Hathersage.

'There is something else . . .' I whispered, looking at the fireplace in my mind. A waver in my tone gave away my fear. 'Something else you came to tell me.'

'They have found a clue in the embers. Rhode burned all his evidence of your transformation minus one. One word left on a charred and blackened piece of paper.'

'Wickham,' I said. I saw the image in my head. A

tiny jagged piece of paper from the school's brochure. The ESP connection with Suleen was extremely strong. I could feel Suleen's compassion, which surprised me, as I'd believed all these years that he cared nothing for trivial matters such as these. I felt my human and vampire connection to the event and somewhere through the images from Suleen I could almost feel Vicken's rage.

I had to catch my breath, but I couldn't. I bent over and placed my hands on my thighs. Suleen cocked his head to the side to watch me. My reaction must have been interesting.

'So –' I said between breaths. I stood back upright, holding a hand over my chest. 'They're coming for me.'

'They will come to reclaim their maker. They do not know you are human, Lenah.'

'That will be a surprise.'

Suleen's gentle eyes smiled, though his face remained stoical. His eyes travelled to the vial of dust on my neck. In a flicker of an instant, I thought I saw sadness in Suleen's face. He took a step forward and reached for the vial. He gently held the pendant in his hands.

'They have to figure out which Wickham and where, right?' I asked. Suleen let go of the vial and cupped his hand on my cheek again. He did not say anything in response. I knew as well as he did that it was only a matter of time before they found me. I was trying to rationalize.

'You were Rhode's brightest day,' he whispered. There was a stab in my chest when Suleen said Rhode's name aloud in the quiet street. 'Close your eyes,' he whispered next to my ear, and I did. After a moment he said, 'Go forth, Lenah, in darkness and in light.'

When I opened my eyes, the street was empty and Suleen was gone.

After a couple of days, the Halloween decorations came down and were replaced by the most ridiculous ornaments I had ever seen. Shops on Lovers Bay's Main Street were covered in turkeys. Pumpkins were still all the rage but there were also cardboard cut-outs of tall ships, strangely dressed people in high black boots and, top hats, and of course, more turkeys.

'Thanksgiving,' Justin explained. We were walking through campus on our way to the library to study for the maths SAT. Justin went into a long explanation of his family's Thanksgiving. I listened, though my mind was running in circles as it had been ever since Suleen disappeared on Justin's street.

Truth be told, I wanted to believe that Suleen was some kind of dream. That I had made it up. Despite Justin's attempt to study for the SAT, he couldn't distract me any more. All I could see and think about was Suleen's warning. I carried the thyme with me everywhere, always in my pocket.

'Look. The square root of eighty-one is nine, right?'

Justin asked. We were walking up towards the library to work in one of the private study rooms. Justin had begun enjoying those rooms because he could pull the blinds and kiss me for a half-hour instead of working on square roots.

'But I don't understand why we need to be able to answer these questions and then be tricked with other possible answers,' I replied.

'That's why these tests are evil. We have to take them . . .'

Justin could have been talking about anything and, as he kept speaking, I was back on his parents' street in Rhode Island. Suleen was cupping my face and I was imagining Vicken researching every possible explanation for Wickham that he could. I had let my new life distract me for too long. I was so foolish.

'You just concentrate on the problem and then look to the answers.' Justin was still explaining the best way to take the test as we walked up the pathway towards the library. I watched his mouth move, the way his hard, struc-tured jaw was oddly juxtaposed to his pouted mouth. His profile was relaxed and his hair had grown out a bit so the clean-cut sports boy was just a little bit messy.

It was time to tell him the truth.

'Let's go to my room,' I said, pushing the door to the library closed. Justin had one hand on the door handle to pull it open. 'To study,' I clarified.

Justin turned his head to look at me.

'Your room?' His eyes were a mix of shock and utter excitement.

'Not like that,' I said, and pulled him out of the doorway of the library so the students behind us could walk inside.

'I thought you didn't want anyone to see your room. Privacy or whatever you said.'

'Come on,' I replied, and led Justin back on the path towards Seeker. I wasn't exactly sure what to say or how I was going to say it, but it was time he knew what I had been hiding.

We climbed up the stairs towards my apartment.

'Hold on,' Justin said, and stopped in the middle of the stairwell. 'Is this why you haven't shown me your place?' He put out his hands as a gesture of disbelief. It was darker in the stairwell than it had been outside. The hotel-like lamps with their blue shades highlighted the stairs and his light green sweater with a golden glow. 'Because you live in Professor Bennett's old apartment? I knew that already.'

'It's scared everyone else,' I said, and continued up. The rosemary and lavender were still tacked to their usual spots. I could smell both of them as I unlocked the door and walked inside. Justin walked into the apartment behind me.

'This is amazing,' he said. 'You know, despite being a dead guy's place.'

I decided to give Justin time to take in the decorations of my small apartment, so I walked towards the balcony door. I pushed aside the curtain and looked outside. I watched the swaying trees with their falling leaves and some of the scattered and smashed pumpkins that were left over from Halloween celebrations.

'Whoa,' I heard, and assumed Justin had seen Rhode's sword. I turned and found that I was right. Justin stood a foot away from the distinguished metal. I walked back in and stood on his right side.

'Is that real?' Justin's voice was filled with awe and his eyes danced up and down the sword. Then he glanced at the iron wall sconces. They were made to look like roses and wire, bound together in a small circle.

'I need to talk to you,' I said, and took hold of Justin's warm fingers.

'I've never known a girl who was into weapons,' Justin said as he continued to look at the sword. He wasn't paying attention to me.

'OK,' I said. 'We need to talk.'

'Is this about Tony?' Justin said, and finally turned to me.

'Tony?'

'The fact that you guys aren't talking. I noticed. Everyone's noticed.'

'No,' I said, shaking my head. 'That's not what this is about.'

'Or why you haven't shown me your room before? I

didn't want to press it because it seemed so important to you to, like, keep it a secret.'

'Secret?' I asked.

'Yeah. Tracy kept saying how you're a millionaire or your family's royalty or something.'

I shook my head again and put my hands out so my palms faced Justin. 'I want you to look around this living room. I mean *really* look. And tell me what you see.'

'I did look. Kinda goth but that makes sense. You always wear black.' Justin smiled but the mischievous tone in his voice made me realize how little he actually understood about my true nature. 'Come on, are you royalty?' he asked, just confirming his ignorance.

'Please? *Really* look.'

Justin sighed and turned away from the sword. He spun slowly and looked at the adornments of the room. My bedroom was behind him and the door was wide open. A black quilt and simple wooden night table were in direct view. Then he turned towards the doorway and caught sight of the coffee table holding my sunglasses and car keys. He walked across the room and stopped at the bureau.

'You have a thing for old photography.' He bent over and picked up the photo of Rhode and me.

'Hey,' he said. 'I've seen that guy before.'

Silence.

'. . . What?' I whispered, not believing what I was hearing.

246

'A few days before school started. He was walking around campus. How do you know him? Old boy-friend?'

'No. Well, sort of,' I said, unable to hide my disappointment that Justin hadn't seen Rhode recently. Somehow, I still hadn't given up a sliver of hope.

'Sort of?'

'He's dead. 'Just keep looking, please,' I said.

He placed the photo down and started investigating the others. There were a couple of me alone, posing here and there around England. Then he picked up the one of the coven, the only one that existed. I wore a brilliant green gown (though the photo was black and white). Gavin and Heath stood on my right, Vicken and Song on my left. While Justin was examining the photo, I focused on Vicken's face. The strong cheekbones. His arm hung round my waist. It was just sunset, so the sky behind us was light grey and the castle decorated the back of the frame like a monster made of stone. I couldn't stop staring at Vicken's eyes, the eyes that had trusted me the night I'd taken him in Scotland. Now, in my absence, he was preparing to scour the earth to find me.

'How did you get this photo taken? It's not even a photo . . . it's weird.'

'It's called a daguerreotype. Earlier in history, pictures were made on glass plates. Around the turn of the last century.'

'They're all so real . . .'

I went for it. 'That's because they are.'

Justin turned to look at me. 'Where did you find someone to take them? You look like a superhuman or something. Is that your family?' Justin asked, pointing at the coven.

'Those men are the closest thing I have to family. That's my house in Hathersage.'

Justin examined the photo again.

'Why not just take the picture with a real camera?'

'They didn't exist back then.'

Justin's expression was incredulous.

'Exist?' he said. 'Photography was invented like a hundred years ago.'

This was going to be harder than I'd thought.

'Those photos *are* from a hundred years ago,' I said gravely.

'That's not possible,' Justin replied.

I stepped to the centre of the room, breathing in and out, as steadily as I could. I pointed. 'Look about you. Black curtains. Vintage decorations? Photos of me from a hundred years ago. Gothic art and portraits of me in my bedroom that are dated from the 1700s. Why aren't you asking me what I think is going through your mind?'

'What is there to ask? I don't know what's going on.' Justin was starting to panic. In the past I would have been enthralled to make him feel such fear. Now, I just

248

wanted to get to the point.

'Think. When we went snorkelling . . . why hadn't I ever seen the light reflect on the ocean?'

Justin swallowed so hard that I could see the muscles next to his ear clench. 'I don't know. You're sick? You have that weird disease where you can't go out in the sun?'

'Is it so easy to make excuses for me?' I asked.

'Jesus, Lenah. What are you saying?' Justin's naturally green eyes darkened.

'Those men,' I said, getting close to him, 'those men standing on either side of me and the man you saw before school started. Those men are vampires.'

Justin looked at the photos and then back at me. 'No . . .' he said. A general reaction, a common reaction. In fact, every human I'd ever told and then subsequently murdered had had the same exact reaction.

'Up until eight weeks ago I was a vampire. One of the oldest of my kind. Those men there are my coven.'

Justin placed a hand on top of the couch as though he needed it to support his weight.

'Do you think I'm a freak? That I would believe—' Justin started to say.

'This is the truth,' I said. 'You know me. You know I wouldn't lie.'

'I thought I did but I guess I don't know anything because right now I'm supposed to believe that you were a vampire. A blood-sucking, immortal vampire. That you killed people. Did you kill people?' His tone was sarcastic, even a little mean.

I swallowed. 'Thousands. I was the most powerful female of my kind. If you were to meet me as a vampire, I would not be myself as I am to you now. I would be ruthless. I would have used whatever tactics and means I had to hurt you. I was painfully sad about the life I'd lost. Rhode –' I gestured to the photo– 'believed that the closer a vampire felt to her life before she died, the more evil she would be as a vampire. And I was horrible. Those men in my coven were specifically chosen. Boys, just like you. I picked them for their strength, speed and ambition.'

'You found them? To, like, join you?' His sarcasm was painful.

'I wouldn't say *found*.'

'What would you say?'

'I *made* them . . . into vampires.'

'This is crazy!' Justin was yelling now. 'Why are you lying about this?'

I stalked over to the kitchen and took the tins out, opening the tops and showing him dried dandelion heads and the white petals of chamomile flowers sitting in the bottom of the tiny circular tins.

'How do you think I know so much about herbs? Or why I'm obsessed with medicinal healing. That I knew you could place that flower on your tongue and eat it.'

'I don't know,' Justin said, and took a step back.

250

'Or why I have a real sword on my wall.' I sighed and let my gaze fall from Justin's. He wanted to lace me into this perfect, innocent idea. Lenah, from England. Lenah, who couldn't drive. Lenah who was falling for a boy who took her to unusual places so she could feel alive. I stalked over to the bureau and took the urn. I opened it and a few pieces of glittering dust flew in the air.

'This is an urn filled with dust. The remains of a dead vampire. Why do I have this if I'm lying?'

'Why are you doing this?' Justin yelled.

'I'm trying to protect you!' I yelled back, throwing my arms out. The urn fell to the floor, hitting the ground with a thud, scattering Rhode's beautiful ashes in a pile on the floor. At the same time, my pinky finger hit the side of the sword. There was a searing zing. I screeched and fell to my knees. Pain, glorious, murderous, shocking pain. It was 592 years since I'd last felt mortal pain.

I turned my palm over. There was a hot pulsating feeling. I had sliced my fingertip. The cut was tiny but the blood oozed out. The flow was harmless yet there it was, the proof that I was human inside.

Justin stood across from me and came down to his knees. Together we knelt in Rhode's remains. I stared down at the tiny cut and did what I most desired – I brought my hand up to my lips, licked the blood and closed my eyes. Before it was the taste of satisfaction – one of the only flavours in my life. I leaned my head back and sighed, relishing the wonderful duality in the moment. I hated the rust, metallic flavour but I loved it that I remembered it so well.

I opened my eyes, sharing the silence with Justin. I looked at the blood, now just barely coming through and then up at Justin's gorgeous face.

'What is it?' he asked.

'It tastes different,' I whispered. The taste of the blood now, in this life, was just a momentary curiosity and a surge of familiarity. The relief dissipated into small waves of memories – barely making an impact on the person I was now. The vampire was gone; she had dissolved with the ritual.

'Different?' Justin asked.

'It tasted better before.'

Justin reached out for my hand and, as I snatched it away, my blood smeared on the inside of his wrist. Just a small rust-coloured line that ran from one end of the wrist to the other. Then in that moment, as my eyes lost their focus on Justin's skin, Rhode's voice echoed in my ears.

You cannot see what you have done!

Then Vicken came next.

Your features, Lassie, are not of these parts.

Then came my own impassioned voice that I recognized from the day out on the peaks.

God help me, Rhode, because if you don't I will walk out into sunlight until it scorches me to flames.

252

Then Justin, although he was sitting in front of me, spoke to me in my head.

Everyone you love is dead. That must be lonely.

How many memories can come through at once before they are just jumbled words and faces mixed together by years of pain?

The night I'd taken Vicken, I was transfixed by his happiness. Just as I was transfixed by Justin's happiness. I refocused on his wrist and my blood smeared across his skin. There, under the smear, was his vein, a bright blue vein.

'You would have been perfect,' I said. I ran my thumb over and across the blood. It was still sticky. 'I would have stalked you, watched you breathe with such specificity I could have timed the seconds between each inhalation. Even now, I do these things.'

I looked up into Justin's eyes. His gaze was fixed, his body unmoving. His large hands lay still in my grasp.

'Even now, I know you cross your ankles one over the other when you're relaxed. That it gives you a feeling of power. That the vein on the right side of your right wrist snakes out and then runs deep down your arm. It takes you two and a half seconds between each breath. Precisely. I know all of these things and thousands more. I would have killed you with pleasure. I would have killed you and then taken you with me.'

I looked to the floor but I knew that Justin had stood up. He said things like, 'Got to go, talk later,' and other assorted, useless comments. All I knew for sure was that the door slammed behind him.

Justin left sometime in the early afternoon but it was four thirty when I finally looked up from the floor. I rubbed at my lower back muscles, craned my neck and stretched my arms out. I pushed the curtain aside and walked out on to the balcony. The sky was starting to head towards sunset and I again thought of Suleen's warning.

The hunt for you has begun . . .

So I would face the coven and die alone. I was prepared for that. It was just a matter of when. I leaned against the ledge and watched so many of Wickham's students enjoying the afternoon. I hoped I would see Tony walk by and that I could call out to him but I knew that he would be avoiding my balcony. In fact, I only saw him in anatomy class. And then he only talked about the in-class experiments. Whenever I attempted to say anything different he would get up and go to the bathroom or make some snide comment about me being a lemming and the ringleader of the Three Piece. I shook my head and refocused on the trees. Either way, I missed him.

'You're leaving?' I said . . . only these words were a memory resurfacing in my mind. I wasn't actually speaking them out loud.

*

The Days of George II, 1740, Hathersage

'You are reckless,' Rhode hissed. He was walking away from the house and towards the endless sweeping hills.

It was when I'd lost interest in anything but the 'perfect' existence that I started to lose control of my mind. I became obsessed. I concentrated on the perfection when the pain became too much. It was the only way I could distract myself. What did perfect mean? Blood only of humans. No animals. Only strength.

'I know what I am doing,' I said, bringing my feet together and raising my chin up.

'Do you? Last night –' Rhode moved closer towards me so he was an inch away from my face. He whispered so his fangs bared at me – 'you murdered a child. A *child*, Lenah.'

'You always said that infant blood was the sweetest. Most pure.'

Rhode was horror-stricken. His jaw actually dropped. He backed away from me. 'I said it as fact, not as an invitation. You are not the same girl. You are not the girl in your father's vineyard wearing the white nightgown.'

'I saved that child from a life of sadness. She will never have to grow old. Miss her family. Her mother.'

'Saved her? In death? You murdered her after you let her play in this house!'

Rhode took a breath and from the way his eyes had a misty look I could tell he was formulating his thoughts. 'I told you to concentrate on me. That if you focus on the

255

love you feel for me, you can break free. But you can't do that – I see that now,' Rhode said. I tried to speak but he continued before I could do so. 'They say vampires after three hundred years or so begin to lose their minds. That most choose sunlight to bring them to their deaths rather than a slow insanity. The prospect of forever is too much. And for you – the life you lost has made you insane. Living on this earth for all of eternity has brought your mind to a place where I can no longer reach you.'

'I'm not insane, Rhode. I'm a vampire. You might try to act like it.'

'You make me regret what I did in that vineyard,' Rhode said, and turned from me, starting his long descent into the countryside.

'You regret me?' I called after him, looking at his retreating back.

'Find yourself, Lenah. When you do, I will return.'

If I could have cried, I would have. In that instant my tear ducts filled with a scorching pain, like acid rising and collecting in the eyes. I actually bent over from the shock of the agony when Rhode disappeared into the fields. I could have watched him leave. I could have followed his frame until he was out of my vampire sight but the pain was too much. Instead, I turned back to the house and walked into the darkened foyer. In the middle of the shadow on the tapestries and silver goblets, I resolved I would never be left alone again. That's when I decided to make the coven. So I went to London and found Gavin.

Chapter 20

Tap tap – tap. Three single taps on the door. I looked up from the ground. I had just finished sweeping Rhode's ashes back into the urn. How odd it was that all his wonderful life could be swept up in a matter of a few brush strokes. I walked to the bureau and set the photos so they stood upright.

Then whoever it was knocked again.

I wouldn't allow myself to think it was Justin. It wouldn't be. It would be someone looking for me, for homework, or for my library job. For one horrendous moment I thought it would be Vicken or a member of the coven. Despite the dwindling daylight I had no idea how strong any of them were any more. Perhaps all of them could be in the sun.

I placed the urn back on the bureau and opened the door. Justin stood in the doorway with one hand in his pocket and the other on the doorframe.

'How do I know you're not crazy?'

'You don't.'

Justin walked into the apartment directly over to the photos on the bureau. 'Explain to me why I've been walking around campus for the last three hours trying to talk myself out of believing you. Explain this to me. Why do I believe you?'

'I can't.'

'And those men are vampires too?' He pointed at the coven.

I nodded.

'You're not a vampire now?' He crossed his arms and leaned back on the bureau. His eyes were more relaxed. There was no furrowed brow or tense lips. Instead, his eyes looked into mine for answers.

'Definitely not,' I said as resolutely as possible.

'Let's say that I dare to believe you. That in some whacked-out universe this is true . . .' Justin took a breath. '*How* did this happen to you? Don't, um, vampires live . . . forever?' His words were clumsy; I could tell he was afraid of getting the information wrong.

'Generally,' I said with a hint of laughter. I felt the tension between us break apart and the air seemed to open up. A short wave of relief washed over my body and my shoulders relaxed. 'A very ancient ritual,' I said with a sigh.

'Ritual?'

'A sacrifice. A ritual older than Rhode and me combined,' I said, and sat down on the couch. I kept my hands near my knees but after a moment Justin was sitting down next to me.

'Rhode, the guy in that picture?' He nodded towards the bureau.

'He was my best friend,' I said, though my voice cracked. I cleared my throat. 'He died so I could be human again.'

'I don't understand,' Justin said.

We looked at each other a moment, the sheer uncertainty of what lay ahead of us resting in the air. 'Let's just take this one thing at a time.'

Justin nodded and he slipped his hand into mine.

'This is crazy,' he whispered. He ran his fingertips down my skin so goosebumps erupted on my arms.

'I know,' I replied, while relishing the glory of actually being able to *feel* my body. Was this joy or comfort? Maybe both. I smiled at our interlocking fingers. I didn't even ask if he was angry or wanted any more explanation from me. I was just glad he was there, and not leaving me alone to rationalize the shame and confusion of my former life.

'We could go out tonight,' Justin offered. 'Get our mind off this.'

'Yeah,' I said, perking up immediately. I sat up straight and smiled brightly.

'Come on, then. Let's go.'

'Where are we going?' I asked, standing up.

'My brothers are going to dinner. Then they're going out. I think we *need* to go out.'

I walked into my bedroom and strategically did not shut the door. I didn't get naked outright but I peeked out with just underwear on.

259

'Where do you usually go?' I asked.

'You'll see,' Justin said. His mouth dropped a bit at the sight of me and I tucked back behind the safety of the bedroom wall. 'Just make sure that if you decide to wear what you're wearing now, which I totally support by the way, that you wear comfortable shoes.'

To my surprise and delight we ended up in Boston. Once we got out of Justin's car, we walked as a large group up a long street flanked with grey stone build-ings. Claudia and Kate walked on either side of me. It was so odd how they had started to dress just like me. And it would be a lie if I said I wasn't somewhat flat-tered. That night I was wearing a short black dress with black heels. The girls, once they saw what I was wearing, ran back to their dorms to put on dresses.

Claudia linked her arm through mine. 'I hope the club's crowded tonight,' she said as we walked up the street. We approached a long line of people and stopped at the very end.

'What club?' I stepped away from the girls and asked Justin.

'We come here almost every Friday. We haven't lately but mainly we go to get out of Lovers Bay.' Justin mo-tioned to a building next to us.

'What kind of members do they have?'

Justin laughed and kissed my forehead.

'Not that kind of club,' he said. 'A dance club. I guess

in your time it would have been called a ball?'

'Oh,' I said, and it suddenly made sense. Justin put his arm around my waist and I cozied into his embrace. We were a unit, inseparable again, and he knew the truth. I was overjoyed, happy beyond measure, and I loved to dance, even back in the fifteenth century when I was human the first time.

We stood in line outside the club, called Lust, and awaited admittance. Around me women and men were dressed in tight clothes. Some of the girls had on short skirts and tank tops. It was the beginning of November and I knew they were shivering despite the unusually warm autumn.

This train of thought was going through my mind the moment I felt that tingling in the bottom of my stomach and the hush of silence. Yes, I was being watched. Considering Suleen's warning, this was not unexpected. I leaned on Justin's warm arm round my waist but my eyes surveyed the street. It seemed normal. Men and women walked from club to club, a street vendor sold hot dogs and pretzels. Cabs and cars drove up and down the street and the music from the many clubs filled the air with thumps and rhythms. Everything appeared normal.

Let's face it. Vampires, ones of Vicken's age, 200 or so, can see up to any horizon. I could have been leagues away from where he was standing. I turned to look down the street. Even though my vampire sight had waned, I calculated that I was able to see two miles into the distance. Five or six streets away couples walked together. It smelt like cigarettes, booze and hot dogs. I scanned the landscape, waiting for my eyes to fall on Vicken's, those brown eyes that mesmerized me and challenged my soul back in the 1800s. Perhaps it was Suleen keeping an eye out? That thought brought a momentary calm to my chest.

'Are you ever going to tell us what your tattoo means?' Claudia asked. I had taken off my coat, forgetting that on my left shoulder was the tattoo of my coven. 'My mom won't let me get one,' she added.

'Oh, um,' I began, but was saved from answering because we finally got to the door and Justin slipped something hard, like a credit card, into my hand.

'Just hand this over,' he whispered in my ear. 'You have to be twenty-one to get in here.'

Oh . . . the irony.

I looked down. My photograph was on a Massachusetts licence with a fake birthday so that it said I was twenty-one. 'Curtis made it,' Justin added, and I handed it to a burly bouncer. The bouncer was huge, like a body builder. Gavin, the last time I'd seen him, was bigger. I smiled in a genuine way and the bouncer waved me into Lust.

Once we walked into the club I could feel the bass of the music underneath my ribs. It pulsated inside me. Hundreds of people – no, it must have been closer to a thousand – crowded the club. Lust had two floors. The street level was actually the second floor of the club, though it had no dance floor and instead was a wrap-around balcony. Enormous paintings decorated the walls, all depicting couples in moments of passion. I gripped the bar of the second-floor railing. Justin stepped to my left.

'Your jaw's dropped again,' Justin said, and then he looked down. His skin highlighted green, gold, red and black from the interchanging lights on the ceiling.

'I've never seen anything like this before,' I said, and then I too looked below.

The people dancing looked as though they were all making love to one another. Bodies were pressed against one another so tight I couldn't tell whose belonged to whom. Hands interlocked, legs intertwined all in rhythm with the music blasting out of enormous speakers surrounding the club. People, in my time, never danced that way. Then the song changed. The rhythm was different to the one that had been playing before. The drums were so fast I knew they had to be a product of technology. Music made by machines?

Beat. Beat. Beat. The crowd started to jump. All of the bodies on the floor jumped up and down, up and down together. Then there was a mad dash to the dance floor.

Claudia, who I didn't realize was on my right, squealed with delight. 'Oh my Goooood!! I love this song!'

Immediately, she got on an escalator that was in the middle of the second-floor railing and rode it down to the bottom-level dance floor.

'Come on, Lenah!' Claudia called. She smiled at me and I felt a pull in my chest. She was so eager to share this with me but I had no idea how to move my body as the people did on the dance floor.

Curtis, Roy and Kate followed after Claudia. Actually a lot of the people on the second floor moved towards the escalators (there was one on either end of the balcony) and down to the dance floor.

Then Justin placed his hand into mine. 'Let's go.'

I pulled away from Justin. 'No way. I don't know how to dance like that.'

'No one here does,' he said, and pulled me on to the escalator. As we rode down, I tried to explain. 'The last ball I went to was before music could be played on a stereo. If you wanted to hear it, you had to go to a concert. Justin!'

Before I knew it we were in the middle of the dance floor. The rhythm of the song was fast then slow and then fast again. The moment we got to the dance floor it was slow again. Justin and I were surrounded by people, pressed together, everyone swaying, waiting for the moment when the song would pick up and really thud and beat everyone into a rhythm they could dance to. At that moment it was just a series of soft drumbeats.

'Just close your eyes,' he said. 'The song kinda slows down during this part and then really picks up. When it does, this place is gonna go nuts.'

I wrapped my arms tightly round Justin's back. I think I might have been bending my knees a bit, but compared to Justin I was basically standing still. He was amazing, pumping and thrusting his body to match the rhythm. The beat was rising, the pace of the drums was quickening and the bodies on the dance floor moved in sync.

A girl next to us kept her eyes closed while she danced and raised her arms in the air. As the rhythm picked up, so did her swaying and she moved so dramatically that her hips and arms knocked me out of Justin's grasp. So many people were coming on to the dance floor at that point, and the base was pumping so hard, I was pushed away from Justin before I even knew what was going on.

'Lenah!' he called, but I was stuck in between two couples pressed against each other. I stood on my tip-toes and I could see Curtis jumping up and down but not Justin. The music picked up so hard that it was thumping in my chest again.

I was squished in the middle of the dance floor, turning this way and that. People were dancing but I just stood. Then I heard someone whisper my name.

'Let go . . .' the voice said, though I wasn't entirely sure they were talking to me.

Maybe it was all in my head. I don't know. Maybe the whisper told me to calm down. But I took a deep breath. I smelt liquor, sweet perfumes, body odour. The last time I had been in a room crowded with people, I was setting them on a poor helpless woman. Someone to kill.

'Just let go.'

So I did. I was in the middle of the floor. I closed my eyes, let the rhythm of the song take me over and when the song really picked up and the entire dance floor was going nuts I was right there with them. My hands were raised above my head. I swayed. I jumped. I pressed my back against people I didn't know and felt them press back on me in return. Even though the song was pumping, my movements felt slow. I rubbed shoulders with strangers and someone even linked hands with me. The sweat dripped down my nose and back and I was lost in a sea of strangers. I didn't even know what I looked like any more. I didn't even care. No bungee jump. No solitary experience. Only something like this could make me realize it.

I was Lenah Beaudonte. No longer a vampire of the worst order. No more the leader of a coven of night wanderers.

I was set free.

Chapter 21

A Chinese vase shattered against a wall in a room cast in shadow. Vicken gathered his breath and collapsed into a lounge chair.

Through gritted teeth he snarled, 'Where is she?'

'Perhaps Rhode had trouble with the awakening,' Gavin attempted to rationalize.

'Nonsense,' Vicken spat. 'She was never here. Or, if she was, it was not for long.'

He got up and paced back and forth. They stood in the library. Every single book on the monstrous shelves was a book on the occult, a book on history, or a subject the coven felt was relevant to learn. I'd spent years perfecting it. A fire roared in the corner of the room. The coven sat in a semicircle though two chairs were empty: Vicken's and mine.

Vicken was pacing. His gait was smooth and he held his hands behind his back. He looked positively decadent in his designer clothes and modern haircut. In his hand was a charred piece of paper and on it, one word . . . Wickham. His hands were covered in dirt and some had collected under his fingernails. He had been digging in the soil with his bare hands.

'Perhaps she's dead,' Gavin said again.

'Fool. Don't you think we would feel it?' Vicken asked.

Heath nodded and Song grunted in agreement.

'Have we compiled the research?' Vicken asked. 'I want you to go through it again. I want to know every possible definition of whoever or whatever this Wickham is.'

'I think Rhode is dead. I feel that,' Gavin said.

It was Vicken's turn to nod.

'And no one has heard from or seen Suleen?' Vicken asked.

'He has ignored all of our attempts at communication. Do you think he would honestly show himself to us?' Heath asked. 'He does not meddle in these matters.'

'He is the only one who could answer my questions.'

'Not the only one,' Song said. 'There are others who could help.'

'I wouldn't call upon anyone else unless I had no other choice,' Vicken explained. 'Besides, Suleen is intimately connected. He *knows* Rhode.'

There was a collective silence.

'It's time,' Vicken said, and sat back in the chair. 'We're going to find her.'

I gasped and opened my eyes. The cold breeze from the window brushed my right cheek. I had leaned my head against the window and fallen asleep before the entrance to the highway. Then I felt a squeeze on my left knee. I looked at Justin and the images from my dream seemed to evaporate.

'You've been asleep for an hour,' he said. When I looked out of the windshield, I saw that we were back in Lovers Bay. We turned on to one of the driving paths through Wickham and Justin pulled his car into the spot in front of Seeker. He had dropped everyone off at their dorms and I had slept right through it. 'Did you dance at all?' he asked, and opened the SUV's sun roof. I looked up at the early autumn sky.

'That was one of the best times I've ever had,' I said, and leaned back into the seat. 'I wish Tony had been there,' I admitted, and brought my hand to my hair. I nervously attempted to make sense out of the straggly and sweaty parts stuck to my shoulders and forehead. I smiled after pulling my hair back. 'But thank you,' I said. 'Can we go again next week?'

Justin threw his head back and laughed out loud. He squeezed my shoulder with his right hand then we were quiet for a minute. I listened to the sounds of Wickham at night. Somewhere in the distance tiny waves rolled on to the Wickham shore.

'There's been something I've wanted to ask you for a while,' he said, and he moved his hand, which was still on my shoulder, and pressed on my back so I would lean forward a bit. 'What does your tattoo mean?' he asked.

The question was out of the blue, yes, but if I could

tell anyone it was Justin. I supposed he had never asked me before out of respect. Or maybe he didn't want to know the truth. I took a breath.

'Long ago, Rhode, the vampire you recognized in the photo, was a member of a brotherhood of knights. Sometime in the fourteenth century, men, healthy men, were dying. From the Black Plague. Huge pustules would cover the body. Children endured pain beyond belief. After seeing the devastation of the Black Death, Rhode decided to become a vampire. That complete story I do not know but when he returned he told his lord, King Edward the Third, what he had done. It is not easy to hide a vampire transformation.'

'Why?' Justin asked, his hand still on my back, only now his thumb was rubbing my skin.

'We look different in vampire form. Our features take on an ethereal quality. The amazing part of Rhode's tale is that King Edward accepted Rhode. Imagine discovering that your favourite knight, your number one, decided to join the ranks of the devil. When Rhode returned and told his lord what he had done, Rhode said, "Evil be he who thinketh evil," and thus the phrase was born. For Rhode, death was the ultimate . . .'

I stopped. My voice was breaking. I swallowed hard and my eyes burned. I blinked a few times and the burning went away. I looked up at Justin whose smile had faded, though his exhausted features calmly looked into mine.

'Death was not something he could face. So he protected himself from it,' I finished.

'He became a vampire so he would never die?'

I looked out of the window. The long winding path to the right of Seeker was dark and the trees swayed. Such peace lay outside the window.

'But he died for you,' Justin said.

'Yes, he did. Anyway, that phrase, "Evil be he who thinketh evil", became the calling card of the Order of the Garter, which still exists in England to this day. It also became the motto of my coven. Though I bastardized it to no end.'

I brought my legs up to my chest and rested my chin on my knees. I looked at the dashboard until all the small dials and lights were a blur.

'Rhode really believed that. To be evil you had to wield it. Mean it. From your soul.'

'Did you?' Justin asked.

'Yes.'

In my mind's eye I was looking at Rhode on the couch of my living room. His sunken cheeks and his strong masculine jaw were so bony, so breakable. And his eyes – the blue of his eyes had already burned its colour into my blood years before. But that night they had dimmed. I would still recognize that colour anywhere, in flowers, in the sky and in all the minutiae of the world. I tried to swallow but suddenly found that I couldn't. I had to get out – Justin's SUV was too small. I was too small. I was going to burst out of my skin.

'I should go,' I said, opening the door. I stepped into the Seeker parking lot.

Justin rolled down the window and called after me.

'Hey, Lenah! Wait.'

I heard the motor go silent, the driver's side door open and close, and the thud of Justin's shoes thump on the ground behind me. I turned to face him and clenched my fists. The lights from Seeker illuminated the benches and dorm entrance behind me.

I must have been a scary sight because Justin stopped two or three feet from me. My jaw was set in a hard clench, my eyes squinted down at the ground and I was breathing like a bull, through my nose.

'What is it?' he asked. 'What did I say?'

'You didn't say anything. It's me. I want to burst out of my skin. Take my mind and throw it into another body. I want to forget everything I've done up until three months ago.' I was saying all of this through clenched teeth. Spit came out of my mouth but I didn't care.

Justin's eyes reflected pure panic. His mouth dropped a bit and he scanned the ground and said, 'It's like bungee jumping.'

'. . . What?' This was perplexing to say the least.

'You're standin' there on a bridge and you know you're about to do something supremely stupid. But you do it anyway. You have to. To feel something. Because doing something that crazy is better than just standing around living life with all your mistakes and stupid responsibilities. You jump because you have to, because you have to feel that rush. You know you'll lose your mind if you don't.'

'You're saying that deciding to be human again after six hundred years as a ruthless vampire is like bungee jumping?'

We were silent for a moment.

'You don't see the connection?'

I couldn't help laughing. How did he do this? How could he make me see it this way? In the deepest moment of turmoil he made me realize that this life, the one I was in now, was full of laughter and happiness.

I threw my arms round Justin's neck and kissed him so deeply that when he moaned I could feel the vibration of the sound and it sent a chill through my body. I could feel it in my toes. I kissed the nape of his neck and the small space between his neck and shoulder. Then I pulled away so there was only an inch or two between us.

'Come upstairs with me,' I whispered before I even knew what I was really saying.

Justin's eyes widened. He smiled so his dimples were deeper than I'd ever seen them before.

'Are you sure?'

I nodded. I was sure.

After sneaking by the guard, Justin met me at the top of the stairs and I stood in front of the door. I slipped a finger into the bushel of rosemary at the door and took out a single leaf. I handed it to Justin.

'Press it. Keep it in your wallet. When you look at it – you'll remember tonight.'

Soon we were standing face to face in the middle of the living room. Around me were the talismans of my life. The sword, the photos, the vial of Rhode's dust round my neck.

'I'm glad you know the truth,' I whispered. 'You don't know. You can't know what tonight meant for me on that dance floor.'

Justin stepped forward and cupped his hand on my right cheek. Sheets of shivers rolled down my arms. Glorious touch. *Justin's* touch – one that I wasn't sure I could live without now.

'I love you, Lenah,' he said. I was shocked to see his eyes were watery.

'I've never said it to a human before,' I said, and looked down at the floor. I wouldn't dare look at the bureau where Rhode's eyes would meet mine. This was a different love, one that I could feel with my beating heart.

'It's OK. You don't have to say it,' Justin said, and leaned forward to kiss me again. I placed a hand on his chest to stop him and stepped back. I had to remove Rhode's remains from my neck. A respect thing. Maybe a vampire thing. I placed the necklace on the coffee table.

When Justin kissed me and then lifted me up so my legs wrapped around his waist, I knew he was headed towards my bedroom. Once we entered the room, Justin kicked back his leg and shut the door.

Chapter 22

'Lenah?' Justin whispered. He was stroking my hair with his hand. My head was on his chest and I listened to his heart beating, recuperating back to a normal speed. Outside, the sky was filled with stars.

'Yeah?' I replied. I was dozing, almost asleep under my warm and fluffy quilt.

'Will you go to winter prom with me?'

'Of course,' I whispered, sure I would fall asleep in moments. 'Justin?'

'Mm-hmm?' he said, moments from sleep himself.

'What's a prom?'

He laughed so hard that my cheek bounced up and down on his chest.

The late morning light shone through the bedroom window curtains. Something looked different. The things in my room seemed fuzzy – I rubbed at my eyes and slipped away from the bed as quietly as I could. Justin was still asleep, stomach down, so only his bottom half was covered by the quilt. I pulled a night-gown off a hanger from my closet. I slipped the black cotton dress over my head and rubbed my eyes until I approached the bay window in my bedroom. It was then that I noticed how different my world had become in one night.

Trees looked solid. I couldn't distinguish the fibres in the bark. Blades of grass moved in the wind by the thousands but their individual sways and vibrations were indistinguishable to my eyes now. I could see the beach in the distance but the details in the sand were muted and blurry. I could no longer see the chips in the paint of the chapel across campus. I rubbed my eyes again but the view remained the same. Rhode was right; I had lost my vampire sight and finally become the human he had dreamed that I would be.

I think hours passed as I sat on the window seat and looked out at the campus. At one point, I wrapped my shoulders in a blanket and just stared and stared. Then I heard the sheets rustle behind me.

'Lenah?' Justin asked, but he was sleepy.

I turned my body to see him in the bed. His hair was messy and his chest was bare. He held the sheets over his bottom half and joined me on the window seat. I turned back and kept staring out of the window. He looked out of the window and then at me.

'What is it?'

I turned my head to meet his eyes.

'It's gone,' I said, returning my gaze to the much different view out the window.

'What? What is?'

'My vampire sight.'

Justin sighed. 'Wow.' There was a moment of silence. 'Is it – um – my fault?'

I almost laughed aloud but I didn't. Instead I smiled and said, 'No.'

I refocused on the glittering ocean and the blurry rolls of the waves.

'Maybe this is why humans are so caught up in their own thoughts,' I said, still keeping my gaze forward. 'They can't see what the world is really like. If they could, they would look beyond their own dreams and preoccupations.'

I looked at Justin when he didn't say anything. His eyes, those wild green eyes that were always looking for the next daredevil trick, were still and calm.

'I love you, Lenah.'

I took a breath. It was my choice to love now. My choice to decide if I meant it or not. No curse binding me for all of eternity.

'I love you too.'

With that, Justin leaned forward and took the blanket from my body.

In the three weeks that passed after Halloween, autumn turned to winter very quickly. When everyone else went inside to get warm, so did Justin and I. We had become virtually inseparable. My thoughts of the coven were becoming more and more distant. Perhaps Suleen was wrong. Perhaps they had overlooked the ashes in the fireplace. Maybe Suleen was given the wrong information.

It's amazing what you can convince yourself of when you want to hide from the truth.

I was watching a lacrosse practice at the end of the season. It was only days before Thanksgiving break and soon practices would be moved inside. Music echoed from dorms. Students walked across the meadow and to and from the greenhouse. I no longer kept flowers in my pockets. The only trinket I kept was the vial of Rhode's remains round my neck. That day, I sat on the edge of the lacrosse field. I rested a notebook on my knees while finishing up a draft on an English paper. Justin ran up and down the length of the field, tossing the ball from the cradle of the net and back between other lacrosse players.

Claudia, who was walking back from the union holding a coffee for me and a tea for herself, sat down on my right.

'Tony Sasaki is leaning against Hopper. Like, staring over here.'

I took the coffee and turned to look.

A large oak tree stood tall next to the Hopper door. Except now, like the rest of the trees on the campus, it was starting to lose its leaves and only a few branches grasped on to drooping red and orange leaves. There was Tony with a black knit cap pulled over his hair. He met my eyes and motioned with a quick wave of his hand for me to come towards him.

I pushed up from the ground.

'I'll be back in a bit,' I said to Claudia, whose eyes said she knew that whatever Tony wanted to talk to me about it probably wasn't good. He had kept up his icy demeanour for weeks now.

'Hey,' I said, though I looked down at my coffee and then up at Tony's eyes.

'Can I talk to you about something?' he asked, but his mouth was set tight and he looked directly into my eyes.

'You haven't wanted to talk to me for about a month,' I said. A blast of icy wind whipped my hair around my mouth and cheeks. I gripped the coffee cup. 'Three weeks, actually.'

'Come inside,' Tony said, and turned to walk into Hopper. I glanced back at the field. Justin was turned towards me and in response I shrugged my shoulders. I followed Tony inside.

Tony's feet made his particular rhythm as he walked up the twisting stairs towards the art tower. I knew the heavy shuffle of his feet and the way that his boots sounded on the wood. I followed behind, my feet making considerably less noise even though I was wearing boots too.

When we walked into the art tower, Tony crossed the floor and turned left. The portrait was now framed and hanging on the wall. Tony stood to the right of an easel. Behind him were the large, open cubbies where students stored their pens and supplies. Tony's cubby was hidden behind the easel.

'So, what do you want to talk about?' I asked, still only a few steps into the room. I crossed my arms over my chest.

'I had to know. Doesn't make it right but I had to know. I mean, all this time, there was something different about you,' Tony said, as though he were rationalizing it to himself.

'What?'

'When you started spending all that time with the Three Piece and Justin. It wasn't you. At least, I didn't think you liked the kind of people that made fun of everyone else. Of me.'

'I got to know them, Tony. You hung out with them. They're not bad, especially Justin.'

'You made me hang out with them. I didn't want to.'

My cheeks got hot and I didn't want to look at Tony. His fingers, covered in their usual paint and charcoal, pushed the easel so the wooden legs made a scratching sound on the floor. Behind the easel, a red, velvet curtain covered Tony's cubby.

'What is this?' I asked.

Tony pulled the curtain to the right. Inside the cubby was a stack of eight or nine books. At the top was a thick hardcover book that looked very familiar. The metal cover, the gold leafing on the pages. It was the Order of the Garter book from the library and on top of it was the photo of Rhode and me.

'You tell me, Lenah. I know it's wrong. I know it is. And I'm not crazy or anything. But when I ran out that day, after I told you I loved you . . .' Tony said, taking the book and the photo from the cubby and putting them on an art desk. 'A couple of weeks ago, I was organizing my pictures, filing them away, whatever. In every single one, you're so pale. I mean, you're physically hiding from the sunlight. That was my first clue. So, I went to your room and I knocked on the door. But you hadn't locked it. So I turned the knob thinking maybe you didn't hear me. I went inside to wait for you. I sat on your couch and waited to apologize for just springing it on you when I told you . . .' He paused. 'When I told you I loved you. And that's . . . that's when I saw this.'

There was a red ribbon page marker in the book and when Tony opened it I felt my heart start to race in my chest. Tony used his index finger to open the book to the page with the engraving of Rhode. I gasped, a hiccupping gasp, the kind where you can't catch your breath fast enough because the shock is too great.

'This book was open on the table. I had seen it before but never made the connection. So I looked at the page you had left it open at. And then by sheer coincidence I looked up at your bureau. There was the same guy in a photo looking back at me.'

'You stole them from me? When?'

'Just a few days ago. I was desperate. I wanted to talk to you, be friends again, but once I saw this things just got out of control. I couldn't stop thinking about it.'

Tony pointed at the engraving.

'Explain this to me, Lenah. How could a guy who was alive in 1348 be the same guy in this photograph with you? And the sword on the wall. The vial of dust round your neck. You live in Professor Bennett's old apartment. You hate sunlight.'

'How could you?' I whispered. My ears were hot. My fingers shook. 'You won't even talk to me. *You* stopped being my friend.'

Tony fired off fact after fact . . . all of my secrets. Then he took off his cap and ran his hands through his hair. I was in the doorway. My breath was heaving, my eyes wide. I could feel the sweat gathering under my hat.

'Are you – Jesus . . .' He took a breath. 'Are you a vampire?'

I said nothing; we were locked in a stare. Outside somewhere students were blasting music and chattering with each other. I licked my lips. Everything felt dry.

'Come on, Lenah. You sat in the shade all fall; you still do. You know about bloodstreams, biology and dissecting cats.'

'Stop it.'

'You like knives. The first day I met you, you said you knew twenty-five languages. I heard you speak at least ten of them.'

'I said, stop it.'

'You are! Admit it!'

There was a rage in me that had been waiting so long to come out that when I raced across the room and slammed Tony into the wall of cubbies behind him I was sure he wasn't prepared for it. I pinned him by the throat with my forearm. He probably could have thrown me off but instead his brown eyes stared into mine and his mouth parted in shock.

'You want to know the truth? You want to know what I think? That you're a pathetic lovestruck boy who's jealous. You're already full of superstitions. This just feeds into it. You love me? You think you know me?'

I let him go and backed away, not moving my eyes from his. I snatched the photo off the table. Tony rubbed at his neck where I had pinned him to the wall.

'You were my friend,' I said. I let the stare linger between us and then I turned and ran from the art tower as fast as I could.

Chapter 23

Wickham beach was deserted but I sat on the stone wall anyway. The swells were small but they hit the beach in a comforting rhythm. There were white caps on the bay. I knew the reality of what had happened. If Tony had discovered my secret, it would only be a matter of time before everyone else would. I decided in the time it took to run from Hopper to the beach that I would go to a bank and store my vampire photos and treasures in a lock box. It was time to redecorate my apartment.

I unclasped the vial of Rhode's remains from round my neck and held them up to the sun. They glimmered and shone as brightly as they had on the day that he'd died. I toyed for a moment with the idea of putting the necklace in my pocket but I wasn't prepared to lose a piece of Rhode. Not yet. So I clasped it round my neck. Redecorating my apartment would have to be good enough for now.

Then someone sat down beside me.

I was completely distracted by my thoughts so I didn't realize that someone had been walking towards the beach wall. A few months before, I would have been able to sense it but everything had changed so much.

It was Tony.

'I . . . am a world-class a-hole,' he said.

I didn't say anything.

'A vampire?' Tony scoffed. 'What the hell was I thinking?'

'I don't know,' I said, though I couldn't help the burning shame that resided in my chest. I hated lying to him again and again.

'I got desperate, I guess. And you're right. I'm too superstitious.'

I nodded.

'But what about that guy in the photo? He looks just like the guy in that engraving.'

I felt the photo in my back pocket.

'It's a drawing, Tony. A coincidence, maybe.'

'Coincidence,' he said.

'Drop it, OK? I'm just an ordinary girl.'

Tony nodded.

'Buy you a coffee?' he offered.

'Yeah,' I said, and Tony stood up. He offered me his hand and he pulled me up from the cold stone wall.

I wanted to tell Tony, believe me. But with the warning from Suleen and the coven on my trail, I had to maintain silence. For myself.

Tony and I sat down at a table in the middle of the union.

'Did I mention I'm sorry?' he said, and placed his tray down across from me. On it was a steaming mound of turkey and gravy.

'About four hundred times.'

He took a heaping bite of his turkey so he looked like a little kid attempting to put too much in his mouth.

'I missed you,' he said after swallowing. His cheeks reddened as he said it.

I smiled and looked down at my plate. When I shifted my gaze, I caught a glimpse of Tony's boots under the table.

'Hey, I want to ask you something,' I said.

'What?' he said, and a piece of lettuce came out of his mouth and on to the plate.

'Are your boots new? How long have you had them? I've always kind of wanted a pair of combat boots.'

Tony swallowed. 'It's funny actually. I lost one boot last summer – *so* annoyed. But I got real lucky. I went back to the shoe store and they were selling the same boots for fifty per cent off. So I bought them again and put the other boot in my fish tank at home. Guppies loved it.'

Suddenly, Tony stiffened. He dropped his fork and stared behind me. I turned and followed Tony's eyes. Tracy walked by with a collection of girls from the senior class that usually gave me dirty looks because of my new association with Justin Enos.

'Tony?' I said.

He just kept staring. Then something happened I couldn't believe. Tracy turned her head and smiled at Tony. Not a big smile but a sly smile. One that said, *Well, come and get it.*

I leaned forward. 'Tony!' I whispered.

His eyes snapped down to his plate.

'Are you dating Tracy Sutton?'

'No,' he said with a mouth full of food.

'Liar!' I said with a smile, and started to dig into my own food. There was an air of mischief in Tony's eye and something felt right with the world.

'Well, she may have come and said hi to me the other day. And a couple days after that.'

'Do you actually trust her?'

'She's not so bad,' Tony said with a shrug, and took another bite of his food.

'You spend time with her? And have *actual* conversations?'

Tony kept looking at his plate.

'You're in love!' I said, and smiled.

Tony put down his fork. 'No way.'

I laughed and took a bite of my own food.

'Lenah, shut up. I am not.'

'Sure . . .' I said, laughing still.

There was a moment of silence then Tony said, 'I still have pics of her in her bikini.'

I almost spat out my food on my plate. Yes, something was finally right again in the world.

Chapter 24

A snowball came whizzing towards my face and smacked me square in the forehead. Claudia and Tracy fell back on to the mounds of snow that covered Wickham campus. They held their stomachs from laughing so hard. Tony was forming another snowball as I wiped my face with my warm mittens. It was 15 December and the night of the Wickham winter prom. In a couple of weeks it would be winter break and I was staying on campus for the holidays. It wasn't safe to stray too far from campus. Now that Nuit Rouge was over, and after that lovely dream on the way back from the club, I had to stay as close to Wickham as possible.

To my right, Justin lobbed a snowball at Tony then came closer to me. He whispered, 'But you haven't heard anything?'

I shook my head.

'That guy – Sul . . .?'

'Suleen,' I said.

'Yeah. He said they would come. Don't we have to sort of prepare?'

I scoffed and we both ducked from a whizzing snowball.

'How do you suppose we prepare to defend ourselves against four of the most gifted vampires in creation?'

Justin's expression fell. It wasn't like I couldn't relate. I would be utterly defenceless against them. There would be nothing I could do.

'If the coven comes, they'll be coming for me.'

'If they come for you, they might as well come for me. Will they try to kill you?'

'My gut instinct says no. They don't exactly know I'm human.'

I had explained the ritual in the best way I could days before. Though it wasn't something that Justin could easily wrap his head around.

'You said Rhode's ritual was a secret. Any ideas how he did it?'

'Some,' I said. 'First, you have to be five hundred years old and, second, you have to let the other vampire deplete your blood supply. The magic of the ritual lies within the vampire. It's the intent. If your intentions aren't pure, the ritual will fail and you both die.'

Justin's expression was hard to read.

'So what do we do?'

'Let's not try to think about it unless we have to,' I said. The truth was that if the coven came, and I was beginning to think they would not, it would be them and me. I would leave Justin behind if I had to – to protect him. And Tony.

A snowball slammed right into Justin's face, covering

his eyes and nose with sloppy slush.

'Yes! I am a snow god!' Tony yelled, and started running a lap in the Quartz meadow. He ran into Tracy and then tackled her to the ground.

'Tony!' Tracy squealed from the ground. Tony helped pick her up and then she kissed him on the cheek.

'Come on, Lenah!' Claudia called to me. 'We have to get our hair done.'

'Yeah, I'm all set with getting tackled for the rest of the afternoon,' Tracy added.

Once Tracy and Tony got together, things with the Three Piece and me kind of solidified. It wasn't like I was Tracy's closest girlfriend, but we were civil. I never quite decided if she was really interested in Tony or if she just missed the company of the group. I think she could tell how I felt because she was never mean to me again. Either way, if Tony was happy, I was happy. Tracy kissed Tony goodbye and Claudia, Kate, Tracy and I left the boys in front of Quartz dorm throwing snowballs at one another.

Claudia linked her arm through mine as we walked. 'Let me guess, Lenah,' she said. She smiled at me in a knowing way – her eyes fixed on me. 'Your dress is black, right?'

I gently pulled her closer to me as we walked up the path towards the dorms.

Once we reached Tracy's room, I got dressed. My dress was black and fell down to the tops of my feet.

Tony had helped me pick it out. I held a pair of dangling earrings to my face. In the reflection of the mirror, I looked at my hand holding the earrings to my cheek. My eyes lingered on Rhode's onyx ring.

'Those are perfect, Lenah,' Claudia said, distracting me from my thoughts. She looked like a movie star in her hot-pink gown.

When Claudia went over to help Kate and Tracy with their make-up, I had a minute alone. I looked in the full-length mirror on the back of Tracy's door. I was in my dress and wearing the highest black heels I had ever seen. I let my hair fall down past my shoulders, accentuating my long and lean body. The dress clung to my curves. I looked hard into my eyes. I reached behind my neck and unclasped the vial. I raised it into the air and focused on the tiny glints of gold within the ashes.

Anywhere you go, I will go . . . echoed in my head.

'I'm sorry,' I said to the ashes, and delicately placed the necklace in my bag. Then I looked back at my reflection. I touched the place on my chest where the necklace had lain for those many months. Like a faraway drum, I could feel my heartbeat under my fingertips.

A few minutes later I descended the stairs of the girl's dorm, and we waited in the foyer for the boys to arrive. Curtis and Roy, each in tuxes, turned the corner, holding boxes with a flower inside. Tony was next and when he saw Tracy he smiled, in the kind of wide-mouth Tony way that made a warm sensation pool in my chest. He looked at me even though he was hugging Tracy. The love Tony felt for me was evident in the expression on his face but it was the kind of love that would take us through the rest of our days. The kind of love shared between two best friends. Then Justin, in his tall languid way, stepped round the corner and into the foyer.

We walked slowly towards one another. He was dressed in his tux, his face somehow still bronzed. He smiled at me and I was filled with love, with admiration for his will for life, for the desire to love me and for showing me how to open up again.

'You are . . .' he said, just inches from me, 'so beautiful that I can't . . . I can't explain . . .'

I looked down. Justin held an orchid in a box that was attached to a wristband. All of the other girls had similar wristbands.

'It's a corsage,' Justin said as he opened the plastic lid. 'Um, you said . . .' He was nervous; it was so cute. He was looking this way and that. He was actually embarrassed. 'You said that flowers symbolize different things. So I picked orchid because it symbolizes—'

'Love,' I finished.

The winter prom was held in the Wickham banquet hall.

'You'd think they would shell out. Take us to a hotel or something,' Tony complained. We walked as a group up the snaking snow-covered path all the way to the hall. It was a modern building with panoramic windows that looked out at the ocean.

In front of the main entrance, delivery cars moved in and out of the campus. We opened the doors and walked down a long hallway. Music was already playing from a DJ booth in the room. When we walked in, I looked up. The room was filled with white shimmering snowflakes made out of all different types of material. Silver glitter and disco balls threw thousands of glints of light around the banquet hall. Lining the right side of the room was the run of windows and out of it I could see miles and miles of ocean. Well, I couldn't see miles of ocean any more but it was there and the moon was shining down on the icy water.

'You like it?' Justin asked, gripping my hand.

'It's perfect,' I said. Soon enough dinner was over and we were dancing so much that my legs hurt. We all danced together in a huge circle. We were impenetrable. Tony started kicking his legs out doing some ridiculous jig that made him look like he was having a fit. Around us were Ms Tate and our other teachers, including the insufferable Professor Lynn. They watched us from the perimeter of the room. Everyone looked so beautiful and the music kept almost everyone out of their seats.

It was late into the evening and I was sweating like mad. Some of my hair was coming out of its pins so I left the crazy dance circle to freshen up.

'I'm gonna go fix my hair!' I yelled to Justin with a

293

smile. Justin was glistening with sweat. He nodded and I turned to leave.

'No, wait, Lenah! No peeing or bathroom breaks. You haven't seen my best dance moves yet,' Tony said, pushing his butt out in front of Tracy. She wore a brilliant teal-blue gown. She slapped Tony's butt in time with the music and soon I was laughing hysterically.

I laughed so hard at Tony and Tracy that once I reached the banquet-hall doorway I had to stop a moment to catch my breath. I looked back into the ballroom and blew a kiss at Justin. He smiled and continued to dance with the group. He had to back up to give Tony more room.

I took one step into that hallway and the vampire soul within me reawakened. I hadn't felt it in so long, not since that cool October morning in Rhode Island when Suleen had come to me. Immediately, my hair felt electric. Even my eyesight felt sharper. Each breath I took felt hot.

There was a vampire in the building.

I stopped just outside the doorway. I stood in the corridor and slowly, very slowly, I looked to the right.

There, leaning against the wall at the end of the corridor, was Vicken. His hair was cropped short, like a modern-day young man – his white, pale face made my breath catch.

My whole body shook. The hot burning in my eyes that had tormented me for hundreds of years finally and inconsolably came up, and with a flourish spread over my cheeks. I brought my fingertips to my face,

294

disbelieving that this was finally my moment to cry. I brought my hand away from my face and looked at the tears; they glistened under the bright fluorescent lights. Tiny beautiful drops rolled down my fingers on to my palm. My hands shook, my eyes opened wide; I hadn't seen my own tears in six hundred years. Vicken walked towards me so slowly that my whole body was shaking by the time he reached me.

'So the rumours are true,' he said. I had almost forgotten the sound of his voice. His thick Scottish accent and grave tone used to ooze through me but now it chilled my soul. The rumours he meant were that I was human, and the tears had given me away.

He rested an elbow on the wall above me and leaned forward so his full lips and wide mouth nearly brushed my own.

'A high school? You make a fool of yourself, Highness,' he hissed.

'If you're here to kill me, then just do it,' I said through chattering teeth. My gaze didn't break from his black stare.

He bent next to my right ear and whispered, 'Twenty minutes, Lenah. Out front. Or the boy dies.'

I collapsed right there on to the floor. On my knees, I twisted to watch Vicken walk down the hallway and disappear out of the double doors without looking back. The music blasted from the ballroom. People were having an amazing time and I was crying with my back to the door. It was clear what I had done after Suleen's warning. I had recklessly put Justin, Tony – all of us – at risk. I should have told them all – protected them. Had I learned nothing? Would I always put myself first?

I took a few deep breaths. I had to get myself together. I only had twenty minutes. The prom music was so loud and I needed to think. Needed to make choices. The idea of Justin's death was the worst possible image I could conjure up. I had lost Rhode and now maybe Justin? I couldn't think of it.

I stood up and wiped my eyes. I would say my goodbyes and let fate have me. I had done so many incomprehensible things that it was time I paid for the bloodshed I'd caused. The loss was now mine.

I couldn't stop the tears now. It was too late. I held on to the ballroom doorway to support myself. The DJ played a slow song and, while Curtis and Roy paired up with Kate and Claudia, I looked at Tony and Tracy already wrapped around one another. Her nose was nuzzled into the nape of his neck. From the back I could see the way her long eyelashes pointed to the floor. Maybe I had been wrong about her – maybe what we all needed was for someone to care for us. Justin stood up from the chair at our table. When he caught my eye, his smile faded immediately. He jogged across the dance floor towards me.

'What's wrong?' he asked.

'Dance with me,' I said. I didn't want to make a scene and I knew I only had a few minutes left.

'OK . . .' he said, and we walked to the dance floor. Couples surrounded us and I was momentarily relieved to feel Justin's strong hands round my waist.

We started to dance and the tears started again.

'Listen to me. I have to tell you something very important,' I said. Every minute counted.

'Lenah, what's wrong?' He tried to wipe the tears away but they were pouring down now and I wouldn't have stopped those drops from falling for the world. 'The coven?' he whispered.

'You have to listen to me very carefully. OK?'

Justin nodded. 'If it's the coven—'

'Shh. I have to get this out,' I said. 'Everything that's happened. Meeting you. What you've done for me.'

Justin's face was a tragedy. He kept his mouth in a thin line. He had no idea why I was crying. I couldn't explain it. I wouldn't. I wouldn't set his anger and determination on a coven of vampires who would murder him in moments.

'You showed me how to live. Do you know what that means to a vampire? Do you?'

'I don't understand.'

'You brought me back to life.' I was sobbing now and I was almost out of time. I let go of his body and placed my hands on his cheeks. I looked into his eyes for a moment then kissed him so hard and deep I hoped it would give me the strength to walk away. 'I have to get some air. OK? I'll be right back. In a second.'

'Lenah—'

'Right back,' I barely choked.

I turned away and didn't look back. I couldn't. I walked out of the ballroom and into the long hallway. As I walked away, I lifted my head high, clenched my hands and pushed out into the freezing night. Directly in front of me on the pathway was my car, the blue luxury car that had been parked outside my dorm room for weeks. Vicken was driving *my* car.

The window came down and Vicken said, 'Get in.' The sound of that voice was ice cold.

I did as I was told and Vicken pulled away from the banquet hall, zipped through the campus as though he'd been there for years and pulled out of the school. I looked longingly out of the window at Seeker before we turned left and on to Main Street.

I refused to look at him. Instead, I placed a hand on the cold glass as I watched my favourite places zoom by. The sweet shop, the empty pavement where the farmers' market stood, the restaurants and dress shops.

'There is much to discuss,' he said.

'Where are you taking me?' I asked. My voice was a bit stronger. I wasn't going to let him see me cry again. Somehow, in that moment, I knew that Justin was outside the banquet hall calling my name.

'Why, darling. We're going home.'

In a matter of two hours we were on a private chartered plane and I was gone.

Part II

'My bounty is as boundless as the sea,
My love as deep. The more I give to thee,
The more I have, for both are infinite.'
— Juliet, *Romeo and Juliet*, Act II, Scene II

Chapter 25

Two days after my return to Hathersage, I leaned against a window frame and stared out at the fields through an upper-floor window. Snowflakes barely coated the top of the grass. Behind me, scarlet-coloured sheets and a matching quilt covered a claw-footed bed. A crystal decanter sat on a night table, though it was empty. I knew what it would contain soon enough.

It was a cloudy day but a dismal light strayed into the room. The blinds were modern, white, and I had pulled them all the way up. I had considered escaping through the window but as a vampire I had never installed a way to open or shut the house windows. They were bolted closed. The central air system kept the house at a cool temperature.

As I said, it was two days after the winter prom. While I looked out at the landscape, I thought of Tony dancing with Tracy and the looks on their faces under the glittering lights of the ballroom. I thought of our snow fight and the way coffee tasted as it trickled down my throat. I had been fed well for my first two days back in Hathersage but I was not allowed outside the mansion. I was given food ordered in from restaurants on the main strip downtown. I hadn't even known we had a main strip. I suppose that was something that was developed over the hundred years I was asleep. After we returned from the airport, Vicken walked me into the kitchen of the house and instructed that I call the school and tell them I would not return until the spring. It was only then that I would be able to collect my belongings. No one at Wickham seemed to mind when Vicken offered a hefty sum of money that the administration could not refuse. I wondered if word had spread. I wondered if Justin had knocked on my door, waiting, hoping that somehow I would answer.

I continued to look out of the window. The grass meadows still stretched as far as I could see. My precious fields had been spared modern-day development.

'Evil be he who thinketh evil,' Vicken said from the doorway behind me, though I did not turn round. 'Do you still believe that?' he asked. He sauntered into the room, wearing a T-shirt and jeans, though from the quality of the clothing I knew these were top of the line. Vicken never spared any expense on fashion.

I turned from the window and rested my back on the cold glass. It was hard to deny Vicken's power. He held his strength in his control – the slow movements, the calculated gaze. I had forgotten the sharp angle of his jaw and the strong point of his chin. I used to love to run my hand along his spine and ask him to name the constellations – just so I could forget myself awhile. No,

302

even then, standing in front of that window, I did not forget why I'd chosen Vicken.

'I told you, if you're going to kill me, then just do it,' I said.

I was surprised to see that the rest of the coven had taken up residence in the doorway. Gavin on the right, Heath on the left and Song in the hallway.

'Rhode always kept his papers here,' Vicken said. I stared them all down despite the fact that every molecule in my body pulsated with fear. 'Yet there was nothing. Nothing in this room, save the one scrap we found in the ashes of the fireplace,' Vicken continued. He fingered the quilt between his thumb and index finger. 'He really had no intention of returning.' The way Vicken said it, it was almost a question, though one I would never answer.

Vicken turned to the eyes of the coven.

'Leave us,' he said quietly. They followed his command and shut the door. He leaned on the opposite side of the window. 'He left no trace. No information about how to raise you from your hibernation. I should have known.' Vicken ran his hand through his hair. When I didn't respond or even move my gaze from his, he jumped at me, clutched the back of my head and kissed me. I thought I would lose my breath. His lips pressed mine apart. His tongue, cold and tasteless, wrapped against my own. I thought of Justin and I thought of the night after the club and the easy way he'd lifted me so my legs wrapped round his waist.

Vicken pushed me away from him so my back hit the frosty glass window.

'You dare think of that pathetic human?' he spat.

My heart beat in my chest as though to remind me just how much it wanted to be there. How badly it needed me to stay alive. I'd forgotten that Vicken's love for me was a curse – a link that would make him unable to kill me. He could make me a vampire easily and that would kill me, but he could not hurt me for his own gain. This was the magic and it had betrayed him.

'Oh . . .' He laughed, though it sounded more like a cackle. 'Pathetic human. My apologies.' He shot one more glance at me as he paced the room.

I sat down on the bed and looked at my feet. The heels of Vicken's shoes clicked on the wooden floor, then he was standing across from me.

'My God. Look at you. I'm at a loss what to do. The most powerful vampire in the world cannot even look her minions in the eye. Pathetic.'

I knew this tactic. Beat them down emotionally, then they'll fold. They'll want to be released from their pain. This was just phase one. But I didn't care. I was numb. Rhode hadn't meant to leave evidence. He had done so much to protect me. He'd even erased all the evidence of the ritual.

'Say something,' Vicken commanded, his voice rising.

'I have nothing to say,' I said, finally looking up.

'Why aren't you afraid? he yelled, so the chandelier

shook. 'Put up a fight!'

'Death is inevitable either way,' I said, though my voice betrayed my intentions. It wavered a little. Vicken walked slowly and sat down on the bed to my right. We held each other's gaze and the blackness behind Vicken's eyes reminded me that there was no soul inside the man in front of me. All I hoped was that the love Vicken felt for me was going to, even in some small way, make this less painful than it needed to be.

'You are not afraid to die?' he asked. I could see him looking at the base of my neck and then back up at my eyes.

I shook my head and a single tear escaped down my right cheek. Vicken watched it roll down to the base of my chin, hunger in his eyes. What all vampires wouldn't give for one tear to escape; what freedom to release the pain, even for one moment.

'Why not?' he asked.

I looked at Vicken. I mean *really* looked at him. Somewhere underneath the monster was the boy who loved maps and navigation. Who fought in a war and sang bar songs in a tavern.

'Because I finally lived.'

Vicken broke eye contact with me, leaned forward and pressed his lips against my neck. He started out kissing me, tiny pecks along the nape of my neck, then my throat until he was staring straight into my eyes. In a blink he ripped the nape of my neck, sucking my blood with such force that I couldn't breathe.

My heartbeat sounded in my ears. The rhythm – it was all I could hear until it began to wane. There was no pain, just hot, sticky breath around my neck where Vicken sucked the life blood out of me. Soon, I would be a vampire and I would only desire pain and hate. My fingers started to tingle and go numb and the muscles in my neck contracted in agony so sharp that I could barely keep my head up. Vicken held my head in the palms of his hands. Then the gurgling breaths started, the blood rose and seeped up through my lungs.

I concentrated on thoughts instead. That is, while I still had my mind. The mind was the last to go.

Justin's face at the winter prom. The sway of his hips in time with mine as we moved slowly on the dance floor. The constant smell of fresh grass on his skin and the pout of his lips. My eyesight failed next and the images I saw were only in my mind. I saw Vicken the night I took him in Scotland. I watched his father cup his cheek in his hand. I should have let him go to be with his family. Even though he was murdering me, I wished him peace and freedom. Last, my hearing went and the sucking sounds were silent. In the quiet, I saw Rhode. I wished, more than anything, that his soul, wherever it was, was protected. That he was free of worry and pain.

I hoped that all souls could go to heaven, even vampires who were victims of their own evil. Maybe one day I could go too. And in that moment of death I thought that maybe I would never be absolved of my atrocities, that maybe I would die and the transformation would go wrong. Hell wouldn't be so bad, would it? I'd made thousands live it. If I died, I wouldn't be able to hurt anyone else. I wouldn't murder or defile.

Then everything was black.

When I awoke, I blinked twice. Wherever I was, I was lying on my back. I would have thought I was in the bedroom with Vicken but above me was the sky. The sky was too blue, almost as though it was coloured in with a sea-blue paint – the colour of very deep ocean. There was no sun, though it was clearly day time. My hands lay at my sides. I looked down. Grass was all around me. But it was sharp and too green. I looked down at my legs. I was wearing the green dress, the evergreen one from the last Nuit Rouge.

I sat up quickly – my vampire sight was *back*. I was in the fields at my home in England but it was different. Dreamlike. I was at the bottom of the hill in Hathersage and ahead, a mile or so away, a familiar herd of deer ran through the open fields. If the deer were here, the green dress . . . could it be possible that . . .

My heart, in that moment, must have shattered. I spun round on the spot.

There at the top of the hill was Rhode. I smiled; all my teeth showed and the sides of my mouth hurt. Tears rushed to my eyes but, as expected, they did not fall.

There was no pain; maybe this was heaven.

There he stood. Rhode wore a long overcoat and his hair was short and spiky as it had been the last time I'd seen him at Wickham. He looked healthy and alive.

I held the sides of my dress and hurried up the hill. Although my Hathersage home should have been behind him there was just a meadow spread as far as the eye could see. It looked very much like the one in front of Quartz dorm.

I was mesmerized. I couldn't take my eyes off his. The joy coursing through me, the sheer amazement of seeing him in front of me, was a universe I couldn't understand. Was there a way for me to stay here forever? I would – I wouldn't question it.

'Having an adventure?' Rhode asked when we were face to face. Just inches from one another.

'Are you really here?' My voice was all breath.

He placed a warm hand on my right cheek. Suddenly, shame pooled in my chest.

'You must be so disappointed in me,' I said, not breaking eye contact.

'Disappointed?' Rhode clarified with a smile in his eyes. 'Just the opposite.'

'I failed you. Vicken remade me a vampire. I'm almost sure of it.'

'Our time is limited so I must be brief,' he responded.

Rhode started to walk and I kept pace with him along the edge of the hill where the fields and the Wickham-like meadow met.

'Tell me,' he said. 'What did you think of when Vicken was remaking you?'

'I don't know. I don't want to talk about that. You're here.' I held Rhode's hand as we walked. I never wanted to let go.

'You must, Lenah. Think.'

I closed my eyes and tried to remember my thoughts. Justin's face flashed in my mind, his smile at winter prom, Tony dancing and kicking his legs out. Then I thought of Vicken's family and his Scottish home and, of course, Rhode, in my mother and father's orchard. I hadn't thought of telling Rhode about Justin. It was odd to think I could tell Rhode about loving anyone besides him.

'I thought of you. That wherever you were – I wished you were safe.'

Rhode's eyes told me to continue.

'Then I thought of Vicken. That I wished I had left him that night. He should have lived his life.'

I stopped again. Rhode's slight smile said he already knew about Justin.

'Actually, I thought of Justin first. That I was sorry for the pain I was putting him through. And all my friends, for hurting them. Why are you asking me this?'

Rhode breathed a sigh of relief.

'Because you succeeded. And it has made all the difference in the world.'

'I don't understand,' I said. 'Where are we? Do all

vampires come here?'

'No. I sent for you. Though I knew the call would not be answered unless you were able to pass this test. And you did, even better than I thought possible,' he said, and then paused. He was staring at me with such intensity that it made all the world blurry. Nowhere else existed in that moment but the blue of Rhode's eyes. 'I come to you with a warning,' he said. 'The coming months are going to be filled with unbelievable challenges. You will be given certain –' he hesitated – 'gifts. Ones which will be powerful and dangerous. Do not be afraid of using them, whatever you do. They are going to save your life.'

'I'll be a vampire when I wake up from this. Evil again.' My breath caught in my throat. 'Will I kill those I love? Justin? Tony?' I gripped my chest at the thought.

'You must remember what I told you. No matter what – it is the intent that matters.'

'But I'll be evil. It won't matter.'

'I think you will find that is not possible this time.' Rhode ran a hand across my cheek, seemingly lost in a new thought. 'I missed you,' he whispered. He refocused on my eyes. Then he looked to the sky, seeing something that I could not. 'Why do you think I asked what you thought of during Vicken's ritual?' He was looking at me again.

I shook my head. Out of the corner of my eye I could see that the herd of deer was close, maybe only twenty feet away.

'Vicken was taking your life yet you thought of *his*

tragedy. You mourned for him. Then you thought of me, not to blame me, but in the hope that somehow I was at peace. And Justin, this boy? You wanted to save him from pain and grief. There was no thought of yourself.'

'I've done that enough.'

'It's the intent,' he said, leaning forward. 'Never forget that.' He kissed my forehead. When he did, I closed my eyes for a brief second. When I opened them, Rhode was backing away towards the Quartz meadow.

'Will I remain human?'

Rhode stopped.

'No, love. Even I cannot control a magic that ancient.' He pointed into the meadow. 'Look,' he said. 'Deer.' One of them was so close I could have patted the top of its head. When I looked back, Rhode was much further away, though I could still see his face.

'You're leaving?' My eyes went wide and I took a step forward.

'On the contrary, you are.'

He backed away some more. I ran towards him, but somehow he was so much further than I could reach, so I stopped after a few paces. 'There's so much I want to say. I miss you.'

Rhode smirked in response. He was almost out of my sight.

'Will I see you?' My voice cracked.

'Do not be surprised by your greatness, Lenah Beaudonte,' Rhode called. 'Be surprised that no one expected it.'

Chapter 26

One blink. Then another.

With my eyes closed, I ran my tongue over my teeth – they were smooth like ice. I opened my eyes. The ceiling tiles were a gleaming black. I turned my head to my right to see the night table. On it a crystal decanter was filled with deep red blood. I picked it up, ignoring the goblet next to it, and drank directly from the opening. I drank it fast. The blood was thick, thicker than tree sap, and full of iron. It smelt like rust and tasted like heaven and I let it fill me. But after two or three gulps, I found that I was full. Bursting actually, so that I couldn't take one more sip. Odd. Before, as a vampire, I would need cups and cups, at least a body's worth to feel this full, usually every few days. Now, all I needed were three gulps?

I placed the decanter back on the night table. I had my ESP back. It was quiet and I knew the coven was awaiting my awakening. I let my arms move slowly and I touched items delicately so as not to make a sound. A few moments alone were exactly what I needed to reacquaint myself with my surroundings.

What did Rhode mean by 'gifts'? As I let the questions about my brief encounter with Rhode swirl in my mind, I lowered myself back on to the bed so I wouldn't make the mattress squeak. I recognized my old armoire; I was sure Vicken had filled it with clothes for me. On the wall across from the bed was a flat-screen television and on the night table, a remote control. I could see the fibres in the floor as well as the microscopic air bubbles in the paint on the ceiling. There was a laptop, a desk made of the finest mahogany and the shine in the wooden floor almost burned my – oh . . . *my*. My appraisal of the room stopped immediately. I realized . . . I was *completing human thoughts*. I'd retained my soul. Ha! I giggled with my mouth open, then threw my hands over my mouth. I needed some more time alone to consider this. It was night, most likely 8 or 9 p.m. I could tell from the brightness of the stars outside. I sat up and pulled the curtains closed. I noticed that on the floor to the left of my bed was my prom clutch. I didn't even need to look. Inside was some money, the prom ticket, Rhode's vial and the dried thyme that Suleen had given me. I slipped it under my pillow. My legs were firm, my abs tight. I was rock hard and vampire-like. Yet my mind was a hundred per cent human.

I lay down on the bed and stretched my legs out. Nothing had a texture any more. No fabric could run along my arm and affect my nerves, sending chills. I was numb again but, from my memory, I knew this bed was soft. I waited and listened, but my heart was silent. I refocused on the ceiling tiles.

Do not be surprised by your greatness, Lenah Beaudonte. Be surprised that no one expected it.

What did this mean? I was a vampire who apparently needed only minimal blood to survive and I was able to keep my human thoughts. Were these my gifts? Seemed like an odd combination. I reached to turn on the lamp on the night table when a blast of light shone on the curtain pulled across the window. I sat up, my back rigid. I looked left at a dresser with a mirror on top of it and then looked right at the night table. The furniture was shrouded in darkness. There was only one lamp, the one next to me on the night table, and it was off. Where had that light come from?

I reached underneath the lampshade again to turn it on. My palm faced out towards the window and my fingers curled beneath the lamp shade. Another blast of light illuminated the curtain!

That's when I felt the heat emanating from my palms.

I sat on the edge of the bed and looked down at my hands. My vampire sight was back in full force and I could see all the tiny pores in my skin. Except, when I brought them close to my eyes, they were different. My pores were glittering. An odd shimmer, as though the pores were filled with . . . light.

I stood up, anxiety flowing through my skin. With the

blood giving me energy, I stared at my palms and threw my arms out as hard as I could. I stretched my fingers so my palms were tight. Light came through my hands and fingertips and out on to the wall and curtains. I did it again. Light as bright as the morning sun.

Then there was a knock on the door.

I spun round, shoving my hands under my arms.

'Lenah?' I heard Gavin's voice and the bedroom doorknob turned. He was always the softest of the four. I took a deep breath, reminding myself to hold up my guard. They couldn't know I had retained my soul. If they did, I would be killed instantly. That was part of the orchestration of the magic of the coven. If one of the coven retained even a semblance of their humanity, it meant they were weak. Weakness had to be killed and then replaced. I'd constructed the coven so that we would be powerful with *nothing* to hold us back. I had to be evil, like them. After all, they were expecting their queen.

'Come in,' I said, turning to face the door. My hair fell past my shoulders and I continued to hold my hands across my chest, my palms protected under my arms. Gavin was at least six foot with boyish features. I had made him a vampire in 1740 in England.

Gavin left the door open behind him. He bowed, just slightly, so I could see the top of his short brown hair.

'How do you feel?' he asked.

I walked towards him, not breaking eye contact. I

stopped and kissed his cheek.

'Perfect,' I said with a devious grin, and walked out of the door.

Keeping my mind focused, I walked down the hallway. I admit, while I'd been at Wickham, I'd forgotten about the glory of my mansion. It had four floors, each with a different theme. This floor was for my own personal use. I had some rooms decorated only with velvet, some in black onyx. I had a private bedroom, a study, a sitting room and a bathroom, though I never used it. My favourite room was the weapons room a few floors down.

As I walked, I could hear Gavin's footsteps behind me. At the bottom of a grand staircase, standing with his arms crossed over his chest, was Vicken and on either side of him, as though standing guard, were Heath and Song. I linked my hands behind Vicken's shoulders and pulled him towards me. We embraced while the others looked on. He pulled away from me just enough to look in my eyes. The love he felt for me surged through my arms and spread through my new body like a comforting heat. But I knew – on my side it was broken. When Rhode had made me human, the bond between us had broken apart. I hoped while locked in his gaze that he wouldn't be able to tell.

'Welcome back,' he said, stepping back and gripping my forearms. His touch was earnest and I could sense that indeed they were all happy. I embraced each vampire, making sure to look each in the eye to assure them that I was the evil vampire Lenah once again. I kept my head focused and my eyes still. As we walked into the living room, I stole one glance at the falling snow out of the window and felt a wrench in my heart. I could not allow this. The coven and I were linked again in magic and they might be able to sense what I was thinking.

Vicken tugged at my hand and held me back.

'Is it really you?' he asked as the others started a fire and organized our chairs in the living room. Vicken's glance was needy. He truly had transformed me back into a vampire for himself. Something I would have done.

'Fool,' I said, and took his hand and led him into the living room. He cackled and gripped my hand in return.

There was nothing. No burning in my cheeks. No desire for food. There was only a relentless desire to go back. If Rhode could wield the ritual, why couldn't I? I needed something to keep me occupied, to find a way to return home. To Wickham.

I spent my days researching Rhode's ritual. It helped time pass and it gave me an excuse to be alone. I made up all kinds of information to mislead the coven. I lied about how much I knew about the ritual. I claimed to have awakened at Wickham to find Rhode already gone – I said anything to throw them off. Vicken had a particular interest in the ritual and spent many days by my side while I worked in the library.

Days passed then weeks . . . snow fell and the coven threw parties in my honour. I did not venture out of the house. Truth be told, I'm not exactly sure I was allowed. The coven orchestrated my schedule. One day I would come downstairs to dead bodies strewn about the living room and the next I would find the coven reading, surrounded by books. Had I really been happy with this before?

Of course I could have overruled them at any time. I'd made them, I'd created the magic that bound them together, though I didn't test my boundaries – nor did they. If I had, my true nature would have been revealed and the hierarchy would have been broken. It was the rule. If a vampire in our coven retained their humanity, their capability to think rationally, they would have to be killed. It wouldn't have mattered if I were their queen or not. If I retained my humanity in any form, I weakened the link.

I wasn't sure exactly what had happened to me out on that field with Rhode.

At first, I drank one glass of blood every few days. I didn't ask the boys where they'd got it. I allowed them to provide it for me. Selfish, yes, but I knew what I needed and had no interest in killing anyone. Over time, the desire for blood waned. I only needed it once a week, then once a month. By the first of April, I had one glass of blood and found myself full. Just one glass for the *entire* month. The coven continued to bring me blood but I disposed of it in the sink.

Like I said, everything was heightened – my sight, my ability to comprehend thoughts – so reading was quick and easy. I was a super-vampire.

It was the end of April when I began to worry that Vicken suspected I was not myself. I was in the library, which was on the first floor of the mansion. I sat at a long table and a fire roared behind me. It would have been silent if not for the rain pelting the windows. Ancient candles in tall iron holders stretched up and down the table.

The book I was reading was written in Hebrew. I read it from right to left and followed the text:

. . . *The vampire can only break the bonds of the vampire existence in the five hundredth year* . . .

I already knew this. Rhode had discovered that a vampire had to be five hundred years old or else the ritual wouldn't work. I slammed the book closed. Dust from the ancient cover flew into the air, sending dust particles into the candle flames. In three months, I had acquired nothing I didn't already know.

'Reading again?'

I looked up. Vicken walked from the doorway down the length of the long table and sat down across from me.

'Had any luck?' he asked. He wore a crooked smile.

'If I said yes, that I uncovered that ritual, what would you do?'

Vicken folded his hands on the table and then leaned forward.

'I'd want to go wherever you are. Which is why I am here, in the library.'

'Well,' I said, looking back to the book in front of me, 'even if I found something, I couldn't wield it. The ritual calls for the vampire performing it to be five hundred years old.'

'You were very powerful – perhaps age isn't an issue for you.'

'What are you saying?'

'Don't you think it would work anyway?'

I leaned forward. 'Are you suggesting I attempt it despite the chance that I would die a painful death if it didn't work?'

Vicken said nothing. In some small way my response had overruled his position and he dared not challenge me.

I flipped the book open at a random page. I looked down at the ink but didn't focus on the words. 'I've found nothing,' I said.

'Perhaps you are not looking in the right places,' he said, gazing at the flames of the candles and then at me. 'You know, we installed lights when they discovered electricity.'

'And televisions and computers,' I said, leaning into

the chair back.

'Tell me what you've found. I know you've found something – you've been looking for months.' I kept my gaze fixed on Vicken. 'A hunch,' he confessed without me even asking. My position as his maker made it impossible for him to conceal this information from me. Something else came with that confession, an emotion I was not expecting to feel from him – longing.

'Why are you so interested? It would be ages before you could use the ritual.'

'What was your life like at Wickham?'

I admit I was shocked by the honesty of the question. My immediate reaction came in images: the green campus, Justin pushing through the water after he won the boat race and Tony's painting.

'Are you angry that I did not take you with me?' I asked.

His gaze was mesmerizing and I knew how Vicken felt immediately. His emotions came over me in waves. He wasn't angry; he was devastated that he hadn't been informed of the plan to make me human.

'Do you want to be human?' I asked. 'You've never expressed that before.'

'You were gone,' he said, leaning back in the chair. 'I hadn't thought about my humanity until I realized you wouldn't be here with me every day. Only then did I desire to go back.'

'We can't go back, Vicken. Even with the ritual. Not

really. Every age will always be a world in which we were never meant to participate.'

There was a silence between us. Though there was something in the air, it felt heavy; perhaps it was the many memories and intentions experienced within that library. Or perhaps it was all the invisible years that had passed between Vicken and I while at each other's side.

'You are not as you were before,' he said. 'You are different.'

I leaned forward again despite the anxiety creeping under my dead heart.

'I warned you that I had changed in my human existence. You fooled yourself into thinking I would be the same.'

'You do not feed or even desire to inflict pain. How are you able to deal with your thoughts?' Vicken asked.

I got up from the table and replaced the book. I gathered another couple in its place and set them down on the table while Vicken watched me.

'What I choose to do at my own pace, Vicken, is not your concern.'

Vicken sat back, his dark features focusing on the table.

'Of course,' he whispered, getting up. Before he reached the doorway he said, 'Tonight, a special treat for you, Lenah.'

I watched him leave and then opened another book.

At night I kept to myself. I ignored the knocks on my door or the calls of my name up the staircase. It was when the coven was occupied that I could think about Wickham campus. The trees. Justin's face. How my heart ached. How I wanted to punch through the windows and run out on to the fields until I couldn't run any more. I tried to dream of Rhode again but that visitation, or whatever it was, was a one-time thing. Precious, even. I knew now he would be gone forever.

When I was alone in my room, I practised. I stretched my fingers wide and light emanated out from me in a strong beam. I once accidentally clapped my hands together and the blast was so big I fell back on to the floor and cracked the vanity mirror. Luckily, the coven was not at home when that occurred.

That night, Vicken had promised me a 'special treat'. I watched the luxury car the coven drove snake out of the driveway. I took this as my opportunity to go and look in Rhode's room as I hadn't been able to up until this moment. It would have been a place where I couldn't keep my mind focused. Now, with the coven momentarily on an errand, I ascended the stairs to the topmost floor.

The room was the only one on the floor at the end of a long hallway. I walked, step by step, and finally stood in front of it. I pressed my hand on the door and it creaked open. His iron bed frame held only a stripped mattress.

The walls were bare and the only thing on the floor was an Oriental rug. I tiptoed in as though making a sound would disturb the peace in the barren bedroom.

I sat down on the mattress.

But there was nothing he'd left behind.

Could he have been so foolish not to consider the possibility? That perhaps Vicken would find me?

Across the room from the bed was a closet. Only hangers adorned the clothing rail. Hold on . . . yes, there was *something* in the closet on the wall. An engraving on the wood at the back of it. An engraving of a sun and moon. I got up and walked closer. I stepped into the open closet and stood inches away from the engraving. I knew the coven had seen these drawings. The images of Gavin and Heath running their hands along the walls came directly to my mind. I stayed and looked even though they would have already discovered if anything was special about the engraving. Perhaps Rhode's belief about intent was relevant here too. If their intent was to find the ritual and use it – they would never find it. More magic.

Instinctively, I raised my right hand, and knocked on the wall. First, the sun. It sounded solid. Just when my skin hit the wood, I realized that Vicken too had stood in this spot examining the engraving.

Stay . . . said a voice in my mind. A voice that sounded just like Rhode.

I knocked on the sun shape again. This time when

my knuckle tapped it, like a child's shape game the sun moved out of place in the wood. I used my fingertips to grip the circular shape and tried to wiggle it out of the wall. One wrong move and it could fall back into the wood or perhaps get stuck.

When I finally got my fingernails dug into the wooden shape, I slid it out. The small sun with its spiky perimeter lay in the palm of my hand. Behind it, in the blackness of the interior of the wall, was a piece of parchment, rolled with a red ribbon.

The creeping feeling of the coven's presence entered my mind. They were on their way back. I could see them in my head. I concentrated on the parchment. I unrolled it and found two pages. The first was a recipe.

Ingredients:
Amber resin
White candles
Blood from a vampire no younger than
    five hundred years . . .

I read the recipe. I would need assorted herbs, thyme and a silver knife to complete the ritual. At the bottom it said in bold handwriting, Rhode's handwriting, *INTENT*.

On the second page was a poem – no, at closer look, I realized it was a chant. The chant that Rhode must have said while completing the ritual.

329

I release you _____ (name of vampire)
(Vampire must now slice the wrist with a silver
blade.)
I release you _____.
I stand as your guardian. I cast away my being to
you.
(Vampire should allow other to take life blood.)
I cast away my life. Take on this blood.
Believe . . . and be free.

Beneath the chant, which was easy really, were special instructions about the candles and the herbs I needed to burn before the ritual. At the bottom of the page there was one more sentence and I knew Rhode hadn't failed me.

Lenah, be safe.

I didn't know if Rhode's words were meant for me to find or if they were just the thoughts he'd had in the moment and he wrote them down on the paper. I hoped he meant them for me.

'Lenah!'

It was Heath calling me from the first-floor landing. I stuffed Rhode's papers in the pockets of my trousers.

'Lenah!'

I called back and descended.

Chapter 27

'Come,' Heath instructed. Once I reached the first floor, we walked down a long hallway towards the ballroom. This was the same ballroom where I'd murdered the Dutch woman. The door was closed and the hallway had a grey aura. No lights were lit. Heath grasped the door handle, which was still shaped like a dagger pointed down to the floor. As the door opened, I saw the ballroom was dark, lit only by candles on the poles that supported the ceiling. Red candles, flickering against the shine of the parquet floor.

There, curled into a ball in the centre of the room, was a little girl, a child with hair the colour of sun-bleached beach grass. Standing in a semicircle, each smiling at me, was the coven. The little girl was curled in a foetal position on the floor. It took everything inside me not to rush to her and hold her against my chest.

Vicken, Gavin and Song stood in their crescent shape. I gulped when Heath shut the door behind me. I glanced at Vicken's dark eyes; he had done this on purpose. The vampire rage swelled inside of me. The burning irrational thoughts clouded my mind for one moment. So I walked, swaying my hips. I sauntered towards the girl. This pleased the coven. As I got closer to her, I saw that the girl was no more than five or six years old. I pointed to her.

'This is my welcoming gift?'

The coven, including Vicken, raised their heads in confidence.

'Four months late,' I spat.

This caused a shift. Song gulped. I made sure to keep my hands in my pockets.

'We were unsure, Lenah,' Song attempted to say. 'You have been so removed.'

'Leave us,' I commanded. The coven didn't move.

The little girl kept her hands covering her eyes.

'Leave us!' I yelled so that they had no choice but to obey. I was their maker, their queen. They turned obediently. Vicken was the last to leave. I spun round, my teeth gritted; I wished I could have spat fire at him.

'Mine,' I snarled, and bared my fangs. 'And do not let me hear you idling by the door,' I commanded.

I waited until I heard their footsteps and quiet grumblings. Only Gavin seemed to be pleased by my sudden anger. Once they were really gone to the third floor, I raced to her side.

'Look at me,' I whispered. The little girl was shaking uncontrollably. I held her close to me until it subsided.

'I want my mummy and daddy,' she cried into my chest. I could feel her tears soak through my T-shirt. I would have spilt rivers with her. I raised her face and when I watched her small blue eyes examine my face she broke into more tears.

'You look funny,' she cried. 'You look like them.'

'What's your name?' I asked.

'Jennie.'

'Well, Jennie. I'm going to take you home now.'

Her eyes lightened and she stopped crying for a moment, only to hiccup silently.

'What town do you live in?' I asked.

'Offerton.'

Great. Offerton was the name of a town near my home. The idiots didn't even go to another county.

The instant I took this child and sped off in the car it would be obvious what I had done. It would have shown with absolute certainty that I was no ordinary vampire. One act would reveal that I was no longer their queen and that I had retained my humanity. It would mean my instant death and it didn't matter. I had to do this. I stood up and Jennie followed, gathering her dress in her hands. Her patent leather shoes clicked on the floor.

'Jennie, you're going to have to help me. When I say so, you're going to have to scream at the top of your lungs. As loud as you can. Like you just fell at the playground. OK?' She nodded.

'I'm going to break the window and we're going to crawl out.'

She nodded again.

I picked up a metal chair from the side of the room. One of the many used during Nuit Rouge.

'Ready, Jennie? When I throw this through the window, you scream.'

My hope was that they would think I was torturing her, back in my 'old ways'. But I could only hope. I picked up the chair and threw it against the double-paned glass. Jennie screamed as loud as possible, and I could sense the coven's interest. They were on the move from the third floor back down to the ballroom. I brushed the glass out of the window by taking the curtain in my hand. She wrapped her legs round my waist and I climbed out. We ran, together, into the darkness of the night.

'Why did those men take me from Mummy and Daddy?'

We were in the woods, walking along the periphery of a main road. Jennie grasped my hand.

'Those men are dangerous and if you ever see them again you must run away.'

'What did they think you would do?' she asked.

I didn't answer.

Our steps brought us to the end of the main road. It had been four hours since I'd broken out of the mansion. When we turned with the road, we came upon a street with a dozen police cars in front of a small cottage. Two middle-aged people in evening dress paced in front of the house. The woman, with blonde hair like Jennie's, rocked back and forth on the ground, her knees to her chest, her high heels scattered by the front door.

'Jennie, listen to me. You go now. Will you promise me something?'

She nodded.

'Don't tell anyone about me, OK?'

'Where will you go?' she asked. 'Back to that house?'

'I don't think I'll ever go back there,' I said.

She hugged me, kissed me delicately on the cheek and ran down the long length of the street. Her dress bounced with her as she came closer to the house.

After a few moments, the woman on the lawn screamed.

'Jennie!'

The police swarmed around Jennie and her mother and I turned to face the woods. I walked into the thicket, into the brush and trees of the dark woods. The police would check the road and I had to get away from there. I walked even deeper into the woods. I didn't care; I would find my way out eventually. *Maybe I'll find Suleen*, I thought, when there was a rustle to my right, nearer, towards the road.

I turned. There, under the shadow of lush branches, stood Vicken. The woods shadowed his sharp jaw and the swollen curves of his mouth. His dark hair and long sideburns were black as tar. I could see his pain in the way he tightly clenched his jaw.

'What are you?' he snarled through gritted teeth.

'Changed.'

'What happened?'

'I retained my mind. My capacity for emotions and thought,' I said, finding no reason to lie. 'I feel no pain.'

'When?'

'When you remade me.'

'You forfeit your vampire life,' he said calmly, without emotion.

'I know the rules.'

He took a step closer to me so we were only a few feet apart beneath the canopy of the branches and the leaves.

'Lenah, my love for you prevents me from hurting you. But I cannot lie to them nor can I save you from what they will do. You know what will happen. They are bound to kill you.'

Flashes from Vicken's thoughts sifted in and out of my mind: the Scottish coast; the periwinkle gown I'd worn the night I'd made him; my profile, highlighted by the moon as we lay beneath the stars on thousands of different occasions.

Then my own thoughts came through: Justin's face smiling at me at prom. Another night, the night after the club and the way his arms looked as he lifted me up to take me into my bedroom. A new memory came next – a dangerous image, the parchment in my pocket came to my thoughts, the ritual scribbled in Rhode's languid handwriting.

I shook my head and refocused on Vicken's eyes.

'You,' Vicken said. His eyes held shock and his jaw suddenly set so firm. 'You have it,' he whispered. The dark branches canopied over us hid the beauty of the night sky but I could see the pain of betrayal in Vicken's eyes. His anguish was one that no human man could ever have the capacity to understand.

I tried to speak but I could not find the words to respond. I parted my lips but nothing would come out. Instead, Justin's face came back to my thoughts and I knew Vicken would see and feel what I was experiencing.

Red and blue flashes from the police cars lit up the side of Vicken's face. 'It doesn't matter if you have the ritual. I know where you will go,' he said.

'I would have gone no matter what,' I replied.

I could see in the brown of his eyes that Vicken was bound to the men back at my castle. A place to which I refused to ever return. I knew where I would go in that moment, where I probably would have gone anyway the moment I escaped from that mansion.

'Then I suggest you prepare yourself,' Vicken said. I was unsure if the next thoughts that came were

Vicken's or mine but Justin's broad chest and the way he glistened in the sunlight came to the forefront of my mind. Familiar words echoed in my head: *Twenty minutes . . . Or the boy dies.*

If Vicken was planning to kill Justin, there was no way I would put his life on the line. This was my fight, not Justin's.

'It is done,' Vicken said, echoing a phrase I had once wielded – the night I'd turned him into a vampire. What he meant was that it was the beginning of the end, the end of all the choices I had made that led me up to that moment in the woods. Letting go of a little girl I didn't have the evil to kill was just proof that whatever had happened to me during the second transformation was real and permanent. He walked away from me and was part of the darkness before I could respond.

Maybe it was always meant to be this way, I thought. *A fight to the death.*

I did not linger. I turned and raced into the darkness of the woods.

It was late afternoon in Lovers Bay, Massachusetts. It had been fourteen hours since I'd run into the woods away from Vicken. I followed the road and when I got to the airport I took an early morning flight and got back to Wickham by evening. Now that the coven knew I was alive, I had access to money again. I didn't care that they would be able to track the flight. They knew where I was going anyway.

I stood outside the gates of Wickham Boarding School. I could see the grounds, the meadows and the familiar red brick of the buildings. All of it was washed in a pink, spring sunset that lit the grass and everything within me aflame. Every blade of grass glinted yellow, then green. With a blow of the wind, a rippling gold. *If I were to ever get to heaven*, I thought, *it would look just like this.*

The time had come, so I walked through the Wickham archway. The metal facades and spiked points at the top of the gates reached towards the sky. I had to be calculated in my movements. Each Wickham tree was a friendly hiding spot. Vampires are naturally able to find places to blend into the landscape and Wickham campus had plenty of these to offer.

A couple of hours passed and stars started to twinkle in the blue grey sky. Students passed me but I never met their eyes. I was looking for Justin and Justin alone. By ten p.m. I started to worry. I knew that the coven would follow me. I couldn't hear their thoughts but I knew that Vicken had told them I had retained my human nature. This was a break in the coven's rules, the rules I had created. I was a vampire that could not be trusted, therefore I needed to die. I knew that Vicken was unable to kill me because of the love-bond between us but the other members of the coven could, and would, with ease.

I passed the student union. It was closed and dark. I stepped across the lit pathway and on to the meadow between Quartz and the union. A group of kids, seniors, scurried together in a tight group, trying to make their twelve o'clock curfew. I waited in the shadows next to the union.

I'm never going to find Justin like this, I thought.

I stepped across the meadow and was just a few feet away from the illuminated pathway in front of Quartz. I stopped in the meadow so my new appearance was still hidden in the darkness. Curtis Enos stepped out of the archway and lit a cigarette. He pulled out a cell phone and dialled. As he walked back in the direction of Seeker and the student parking lot, I trailed silently behind.

'Hey, man,' Curtis said to the person on the phone. 'You guys still at Lovers Bay Tav? You're gonna miss curfew again.'

He meant Lovers Bay Tavern, a bar at the far end of Main Street. I knew a lot of the upper classmen went there to drink if they had fake IDs. The smoke from the cigarette swirled up from Curtis's left hand. I never knew he smoked. I wondered when he had started.

'Is my idiot brother still there?' he asked the person on the phone. At the parking lot, Curtis turned right. A collection of students was coming out of their cars and walking towards the Seeker pathway. If I knew any of them, I didn't know how I would explain my new appearance. The last thing I heard Curtis say was, 'He's there almost every night now.' I walked back into the shadows of the trees.

Back in town, the late night was my friend. It made it easy to walk on the periphery. I stayed on the outskirts of the crowds, mostly sliding along against the stone wall. I tried not to seem conspicuous. To anyone who saw me, I would look more ethereal than anything else. I had white skin now, and blue eyes that looked like marbles. I walked past the simple shops that I loved: the dress shop, the sweet shop, the public library and finally, at the end of the street, I came upon the tavern. I checked the street, which, other than a few locals smoking cigarettes, was basically deserted. When they went back into the tavern, a rock song echoed out on to the silent street. Once the door closed, I moved from under the shadow of the trees and crossed the street.

I'd barely grasped the door handle when Justin exploded out on to the pavement. I backed away, ran across the street and watched him from the dark protection of the stone wall.

I stayed hidden underneath the trees. There was a street lamp to my right, far enough away for me to be in the darkness. I continued to watch. He was even bigger than the last time I'd see him. His chest was more defined but his face wasn't shaved and his hair wasn't short and trim. Long strands fell askew and the style

337

was kind of shaggy so it fell into his eyes. Nowhere was the collected, happy boy I'd left that winter. He held his hand over his stomach, bent over and threw up in a corner just shy of the doorway.

Justin sat down in front of the tavern with his legs stretched out in front of him. He spat once on the ground next to him and leaned his head back to rest on the brick wall of the building behind him. He closed his eyes. I stepped out of the shadow again and quickly crossed the street. He sniffed a bit so his sleek nose scrunched up.

I squatted down directly in front of him. Justin opened his eyes but the green pupils slid to the back of his head. He tried to lift his head and when he finally succeeded his eyes looked forward. He locked his gaze on me and narrowed his focus. His eyebrows furrowed. He jutted his chin out to really try and get a better look. His eyes went wide and then he started to laugh – hysterically.

'That's funny.' He pointed at me, laughed and pointed at me again.

We were inches apart; I could have licked his lips if I'd wanted to.

'What's funny?' I cocked my head to the right. The connection between us felt like a gold beam of light connecting us like a hot string.

'You're here. But I know you're not,' he giggled, and leaned his head back against the wall. He was laughing so hard his cheeks were bright red.

'All right. Come on,' I said, holding him from under his arms. In my vampire state, especially this state, I was considerably strong. Not superhuman, but strong. I got him up; he swayed but I helped hold his balance.

'Roy. Dude. Thanks, man.' Justin could hardly walk but I steadied him. 'Dude. I'm gonna puke again.'

He stumbled to the street and vomited. He leaned a hand on the car and when he was finished he lowered himself to the ground. I leaned on the bonnet and crossed my arms across my chest. It was late enough and I could care less now what anyone here thought of my new vampire appearance. Justin was here with me and that was all that mattered.

Justin looked up and squinted.

'Dude, Roy – I can't focus my eyes. But right now you look just like Lenah.'

I lifted him from the ground again and we trudged quite sloppily towards the Wickham campus.

Justin's single dorm room looked the same. Lacrosse sticks were strewn around the room, the nicest still tucked away protectively in the back of his closet. Dozens of trainers were scattered unmatched in front of the closet. Team uniforms and helmets were grass-stained and littered every available space. Somewhere on the first floor music played and echoed through an open window. I wondered where the dorm monitors were at this hour. I looked up: there was something new. Justin had stuck tiny glow-in-the-dark stars on to the ceiling. I looked down at the bed and watched him for a moment. He wasn't sleeping yet, but he was still. He brought his hand to his head and groaned. I lay down next to him softly, quiet so he wouldn't feel it. But he turned on his side and opened his eyes. I was shocked to see that they held tears. I knew he would be horrified for me to see him like this so I said nothing. He examined my face and the tears billowed over on to his cheeks.

'I know you're not here,' he said. 'But I miss you.'

I reached out to hold his cheeks in my hands but quickly brought them back to my sides.

'Lenah . . .' he croaked in a drunken whisper. And then in the next second he slept.

Chapter 20

The way the sun filtered through the blinds in Quartz was completely different to that in Seeker. Quartz was set back in a meadow and not blocked by any tall buildings, so the light was strong and bright. I sat on a bay window seat, my knees close to my chest. I leaned my head back as the light trickled into the room. It felt *good*. Like endless meadows filled with grass. Like summer days on an apple orchard. Like Rhode's voice in my ear. The light made me feel like I was home.

I kept watching the grounds but there was no sign of the coven. I only had one day to explain everything to Justin and keep him out of harm's way. There was no doubt in my mind that the coven was already in Lovers Bay. I just didn't know where. They too were guarded in their minds. Just when I thought I would have to wake Justin myself, he stirred.

'Ugh,' he moaned, and grabbed his head. He swung his legs sluggishly to the side of the bed and rested his elbows on his knees. He looked at the floor.

'How much did you drink last night?' I said, not moving my eyes from him.

'Jesus!' Justin jumped up and threw himself against the wall. A horrific realization passed over his face.

His mouth dropped, he laughed for a few seconds and then his face went completely blank. I hadn't noticed before but on the night table was a tiny vial filled with a clear liquid. He pulled out the stopper and sent the liquid flying at me so it splashed with force on to the floor. The vial cracked and glass exploded on the ground.

'*Are you mad?*' I asked, looking at the cracked glass and then up at Justin. He ripped a cross necklace from round his neck and held it out in front of him.

'Get back.'

'Have you lost your mind?'

It was like an onslaught of every vampire cliché. He leaned to his left and snapped the blind so the entire bedroom lit up and I was awash in sunlight. It felt like a warm bath after a cold morning. He threw a clove of garlic at me, which whizzed by and smashed on the opposite wall.

'Justin, stop!'

Justin was pressed against the wall, his palms spread and tight against the wood. He was panting. He fumbled with the night-table drawer and pulled out another vial of clear liquid. With a shaky hand he pulled the cork out of the top of the bottle with the cross chain dangling through his fingers. He tossed the contents of the bottle again so it splashed in my face. I wiped it slowly with the back of my hand. I stepped back.

Justin was balancing on the tips of his toes.

'Stay back,' he commanded.

'Was that holy water? None of that is going to work. Vampires are older than Christ.'

'You said if you were ever a vampire again you would be evil – reprehensible.'

Justin tiptoed sideways like a crab towards his bedroom door.

'It's true. I did say that. But I'm different.'

'What do you mean?'

'Something happened in the transformation. I retained my humanity, my soul.'

Justin stopped moving but kept his hands raised, a crucifix extended in his grip.

'How?'

'I have no idea.'

Justin's eyes narrowed and he examined my face.

'I swear,' I said. 'The only thing you can do is trust me.'

We were quiet. Voices of early risers echoed in the hall. Justin dropped his hands by his sides.

'You look different,' he muttered. His eyes darted from the floor to me and then back at the floor.

'The pores seal during the transformation. Tear ducts too. It gives us a glowing, waxy appearance.'

The way the light streamed into the room, a wash of morning shone over the wooden floor. All of Justin's

343

belongings felt suspended in time, frozen.

'We have limited time and I must tell you why I'm here,' I said, and gestured to the bed.

Justin, still with his back against the wall, scooted until he reached his bed again and sat down still with his back against the wall. I sat down a couple of feet away from him, almost at the end of the bed. I didn't speak just yet.

'I've thought about you coming back,' he said. 'Thought maybe I dreamed the whole thing. But other people remembered you and I knew all of Wickham hadn't lost their minds. But I thought maybe I'd lost my mind anyway.'

'You didn't.'

'I wish I had.'

That stung.

'That night at winter prom—' I started to say.

'I've just started to get my life back together,' Justin interrupted.

'I never meant to ruin your life,' I whispered.

'The absence of you ruined my life.' Hot shame oozed through my chest. 'Where did you go?' Justin asked.

'Back to England.'

There was a beat of silence but I continued.

'There is a reason I'm here. The fact that I retained my soul is a bit of a problem in the vampire world.'

I told Justin about Vicken, the coven, the whole lot. I told him of the young girl back in England and that once my true nature had been discovered by Vicken I'd left straight away.

'The bond between the coven magically binds Vicken to me. He cannot hurt me.'

'Because you loved one another a hundred years ago?'

'Yes.'

'But you can hurt him?'

I nodded. 'Once I was made human the bonds of love were broken. See,' I said, daring to rest my hand on the bed close to Justin's foot. Justin didn't jump away so I left it there and continued. 'Once a vampire falls in love, they are bound. For eternity.'

'Are you bound, to, um, humans?' Justin asked. The apples of his cheeks flushed red.

'No. Only vampires are cursed by that particular piece of magic.'

'So we're not bound.'

'Not in that way, no,' I explained.

Justin pressed his fingertips to his temples and rubbed them in small circles.

'What a day for a hangover,' he said, and got up from the bed. He looked out of the bay window at the sleepy campus.

'I'm here for your protection,' I explained.

'So they're coming? For me?' Justin asked. His tone was factual, not afraid, almost a little glib.

'No. They're coming for me.'

'I don't get it. Why come here?'

'The night of winter prom, I'm quite certain I saved your life. Vicken said that if I didn't go with him you would die. A few days ago, the night my true nature was uncovered, he saw into my thoughts. At least I think he did. The first place I thought to come was here. Vicken knows I would do anything to protect you. If I didn't come here, they'd come anyway just to check and kill you in the process. It's a catch twenty-two.'

A look of panic swept over Justin's face. He swallowed hard.

'OK,' he said, grabbing a lacrosse stick from the back of the closet as he paced. Unconsciously, he was cradling it like there was a ball in the net. 'So, we need a plan. How can we kill a vampire?' he said, looking more like the Justin I knew.

'You can kill a vampire by sunlight. The other classic ways are beheading or a stake through the heart.'

'I never understood that. The sunlight.'

'Vampires cannot be in sunlight because they are not whole. As I told you, our pores are sealed to protect the magic inside. When white light hits our skin, little fires ignite. The sunlight burns our sealed pores open, exposing the dark magic to the bright day, snuffing it out, as if it never existed. We are cold as ice, preserved in the darkness. Sunlight breaks these bonds down.'

'It sounds so clinical.'

'We are all born from the earth. It only makes sense

that something natural would kill vampires.'

'What about garlic cloves and sleeping in coffins?'

'Authors like to have fun with vampires,' I explained. 'Only the natural elements can kill us. And we can kill each other.'

We were quiet again.

'So this is you as a vampire?' Justin sat down on the bed next to me, the lacrosse stick still in his hand. 'Doesn't seem so bad.'

Justin's eyes did that twinkle that they did when he spoke softly. He reached his right hand out and placed it on my left knee. With his other hand he touched my cheek and turned my face towards him. We looked at one another and I could feel through ESP as well as my heart that he wanted to kiss me. He leaned forward and I did too. Just when his lips parted, I pulled back.

'We can't,' I said, looking at the floor.

'Because you're a vampire again?'

'That's the long and short of it,' I said, and stood up. I turned. 'There's something else.' I was facing him. 'Something else you need to know.'

I placed my palms together so the left side of my right hand was touching the right side of my left hand. If I had matched the life lines from the left to the right hand, they would have been perfectly connected. I tensed my palms so my fingers shook, like they were vibrating. Then, in a low hum, my pores opened and light came through. A white trickle of light then became a strong ray and shone up from my palms and on to the ceiling.

I watched goosebumps roll over Justin's arms. He stood up and squinted down at my open hands. Without looking away from the light shining out from my palms he said, 'Don't all vampires die in the sunlight?'

I placed my hands by my side, breaking the connection and throwing the room back into the light of the early morning.

'This is a particularly unique gift.'

Justin swallowed and said nothing.

'During the day you're safe,' I explained, trying to calm him down. 'Vicken is the only one strong enough to stand the sunlight. He wouldn't risk exposure in a place he doesn't know well. If for some reason we're separated, around five or six o'clock make sure you are indoors in a locked room.'

I watched goosebumps roll over Justin's arms again. His eyes darted to the window and the day breaking over the green trees that decorated his view.

'It's morning now,' he said. 'Everything's changed.'

And so it was.

Chapter 29

It took an hour to convince Justin that he needed to go about his day as though I wasn't there.

'I'll meet you at your lacrosse practice. In the woods that separate the field from the beach. Just come to the edge. I'll see you.'

When I finally left that morning, I tried to keep a low profile. I wore one of Justin's black baseball hats, jeans and a black T-shirt. Every few moments I touched the outside of my jeans, on my pocket, just to make sure that I still had the ritual tucked away safely. It was six in the morning so I knew as well as anyone that the campus was basically deserted.

Cherry blossoms dripped off the branches of the trees that lined the pathways. Daisies and tulips grew on every manicured lawn and the grass was greener than ever. I passed the crowded Wickham greenhouse; it was almost bursting with plants.

While Justin showered and got ready for his day, I had something I needed to see. The Hopper art tower. It wasn't that I hadn't thought of Tony while I was in Hathersage. Quite the contrary. If I'd thought of him, my focus would have come crashing down, revealing my true intentions to the coven. It was already a struggle not to think about Justin every time I blinked an eye.

I climbed the familiar art studio stairs, running my hand over the banister of the twisting and turning wooden staircase. I looked out of the small, square windows with a dull pain in my heart. I stepped quietly. I knew there was a banister beneath my hands but I could not feel the textured wood or the coolness of the air in the tower. Just that there was air in the stairwell and it entered in and out of my body.

Finally coming to the top of the stairs, I stepped into the art studio doorway. There, across the room, and in the same spot from that winter was my portrait. I walked towards it and stopped at the other side of the room. Unlike my sense of smell as a vampire before, which was limited to blood and flesh and occasionally herbs, this time, every smell was heightened. For instance, I could smell every single ingredient in the paints. I could tell just from taking a breath which colours were which. The pine green paint had more ammonia than the red. The brushes smelt clean, like soap. There were exactly 5,564 cracks in the wood of the wall behind the painting. These days the precision of my vision and the strength of my smell was too much to take. It was just another pain I had to endure.

I looked over the portrait. It was amazing how accurately Tony had depicted the muscles in my back and the exact curvature of my mouth. And the tattoo, as well. Tony had captured Rhode's handwriting. My eyelashes too, and the golden tint of my skin.

Thump thump, thump thump. Someone was coming up the stairs to the art tower. Because of a lumbering step, I knew that weight on the right side of the body was heavier than the left and remembered Tony's mismatched boots. He stepped into the doorway.

Tony gasped. I kept my back to him, though I turned my face so he could confirm for himself that it was me. I turned back to look at the portrait. He, on the other hand, was staring at the back of me. I could feel the intensity of his gaze. Although the normal human cannot see the vampire aura, they can feel it.

The air was still. The only sound was a rush of the breeze through the open windows. A whirr, then silence.

'Rhode Lewin,' I said.

Tony didn't move.

'He was a fourteenth-century vampire.' I stared at the features of my portrait. 'Original member of the Order of the Garter. A ring of knights under Edward the Third.'

Tony walked towards me. After a moment, he was standing beside me and we both stared at the portrait. Neither one of us looked at the other.

'Coined the phrase, "Evil be he who thinketh evil". He was the man in the engraving and in the photo.

He died in September.'

I looked to my right and met Tony's eyes. They widened as he searched my face. My vampire appearance must have frightened him – the sealed skin, and the radiating aura. Like a gleaming ghost. The blue of my eyes was like sea glass – hard and flat. Tony swallowed hard and kept his eyes on mine. In this state, in a dark room, my pupils were almost entirely closed, like a cat's in bright sunlight.

I examined Tony's face for the first time in four months, since I saw him slow dancing with Tracy at the winter prom. He looked the same except he had shorter hair and bigger gauges in his ear. It made his lobes seem even larger than the size of a quarter.

I looked back to the portrait, this time noticing the slope of my shoulder. Tony had depicted it exactly right. With the small dimple just at the joint of my shoulder. I could feel the energy coming off Tony, his heat, the sudden drops or changes in his body. I wasn't scaring him at all; he was anxious.

'Rhode once told me that when vampires first came into existence we really were just corpses filled with blood. Enchanted by whatever black magic curses us.' I paused and looked at Tony again. 'But we evolved, as all things do.' We shared a small, comforting smile. There was a beat of silence while I looked over the features of my former self. As I turned to leave, I added, 'Who are they to judge the damned?'

Once my back was to him he called, 'So that's it? You're just gonna leave?'

I turned back to Tony who remained in front of the portrait.

'I came to tell you the truth as I should have months ago.'

'Were you a vampire then?'

'No. Two nights after I left that night in December, I was remade.'

Tony swallowed. I walked to him but I could tell that once I was inches from him he was finally afraid. He took a step back but I placed both hands on his shoulders and looked directly at his face.

'Look at me,' I whispered, allowing my fangs to come down from my mouth. They weren't long; they were small but deadly.

Tony looked towards the floor.

'*Look* at me,' I repeated.

Tony's eyes darted from my boots, to the floor, up at my eyes for a fraction of a second and then back down at the floor.

'You deserved the truth. About me, about Rhode, all of it.'

Tony's eyes, the brown eyes that showed me kindness in moments when I really needed it, looked as though they would spill over with tears.

'You look so different,' was all he could say. He grimaced, probably to prevent himself from crying. He clenched his teeth and his nostrils flared.

'I know,' I sighed.

'Why didn't you tell me before?' Tony asked.

'I didn't know what would happen. You seemed so intent on finding out the truth. It seemed too dangerous.'

'Will you stay?'

'No – I must leave as soon as it's safe.'

'Where? I'll come visit.'

A dash of panic surged through me.

'No. No, Tony. I wish it could be. But you have to promise me you won't go looking for me. Your acquaintance with me will get you killed. I won't risk that.'

'I want to help you. I want to protect you,' he said, and a tear managed to escape down his cheek. I knew to expect this. I gripped on Tony's shoulders, not hard, just hard enough that he would stop trying to talk.

'Do you not understand? Can I not be more clear? I am here to protect Justin,' I said with urgency, 'and myself.'

'Why?'

'I belonged to a coven of vampires. They saw me with Justin at the winter prom. I have betrayed them and now they are on their way here to find me.'

'Here?' Tony's voice cracked. 'To Wickham?'

'Yes. Right now.'

Suddenly, the image of Tony sprawled on the floor, covered in bite marks, and drained of all his blood made my words disappear. I took a moment to formulate my words carefully.

'There is no protecting me against them, Tony. You will be killed and your death – God, I don't even want to think of it . . .'

My words seemed to stick in my mouth. The tears, the curse, all of it came up from the pit of my soul. Instead of tears, the fires of hell were coming up into my body. The relief from the tears would never pour down my face. I let go of Tony's shoulders and bent over. I held my stomach from the pain. That was the curse of the vampire. Punishment for wanting anything more than utter despair.

Once it passed, I stood back up. Tony wiped the tears from his cheeks with his fingertips. I felt a surge through me, to protect Tony. I loved so many things about him: that his fingers were always stained with paint or charcoal, his casual sense of humour and that he was loyal, to the end – even when I had lied so many times. He pursed his lips, highlighting his high and prominent cheekbones.

'This isn't some secret I'm trying to hide from you,' I said. 'This is a dangerous group of men who will be here by nightfall for one purpose. To murder me. I don't want you in the middle.'

'What are you going to do? How are you going to stop them?'

'I have a few tricks up my sleeve,' I said, and looked

up at the window when lines of light moved across the dark wooden floor. 'I must go,' I said.

'But it's early.' He looked to the window too.

'The instant the sun rises it also begins to set. The moment we are born we begin to die. All of life is a cycle, Tony. When you realize this, that vampires are outside the realm of natural life, you will understand. I'm sorry but I really must go.'

'I don't understand. Please stay . . .'

'I promise you, I will come to you, and tell you everything. My birth, my death and how I ever came to be at Wickham. As long as you promise not to meddle in whatever happens tonight.'

'When will you come back?'

'When you are just old enough to believe that perhaps this was all in your mind.'

'I'll never forget this,' he said. 'I'll never forget you.' I held Tony's gaze and just as I turned to leave he asked, 'Did it hurt? To be remade?'

'This hurts more.'

The corners of Tony's mouth turned down and tears ran down his face. I wanted to take his hand, run outside and suddenly be back in my life.

'You're still my best friend, Lenah. No matter what happens.'

'I am going to confess something to you,' I said. 'I don't think I've even said these words to myself. But I can tell you. Because you're you.' I smiled again, just for the quickest of moments. The silence gave me strength, propelling my words into the air. 'I wish I had never walked out to that orchard that night.' I took a deep breath just to give myself strength to say the words. 'I wish I had died in the fifteenth century as I was meant to. But instead I'm here, picking up the pieces.'

Although Tony would never understand what that meant, it didn't matter. It was irrelevant that he didn't know the story of my vampire making. Tony understood me and that's why I said it. I looked into Tony's eyes as long as I could before I would have to make small talk. I turned from him and walked down the winding wooden steps and back out into the world.

Chapter 30

'Rosemary,' I told the woman behind the herbs and flowers cart. I was on Main Street at about one in the afternoon.

After she bundled the rosemary into a tight bunch, she tied it together by a red ribbon. I took it and walked under the shaded branches. Humans strolled by me and no one knew, or at least didn't behave as though they recognized that I was different. I wore the baseball cap and kept my eyes to the ground.

Once I'd left the farmers' market, I checked the position of the sun again, making sure I had enough time before the coven emerged. I started on my way out of the commercial section of Main Street. I headed towards the Lovers Bay Cemetery and held the small bundle of rosemary in my left hand. I gripped it tighter, crossed the street and walked into the cemetery.

It was very quiet even though cars passed behind me on the street. Some headstones were ornately carved and weathered while others were sleek and modern. I manoeuvred through the grassy lanes. My thoughts rolled over Justin's face, Tony's promise and my hope that now, with the ritual in my pocket, I could go back. Maybe . . .

Even though I had the tombstone created before my hasty departure last winter, I hadn't seen Rhode's tombstone myself. *There*, I thought. I walked slowly down the end of the row. Facing me, in the direction of the sweeping grounds, was a horizontal, granite slab. It lay directly on the ground and did not stick up like the other headstones nearby. To the right of it was a dense wood filled with thin oak trees. Some of the branches jutted out so far that they dangled over the stone – as though they were protecting it from rain or perhaps direct sunlight.

RHODE LEWIN

DIED 1 SEPTEMBER 2010

EVIL BE HE WHO THINKETH EVIL

The birds chirped and the wind was light, throwing strands of my hair around my face. My eyes focused on Rhode's name. An ominous hush fell over my ears and I knew a vampire was close. That eerie silence. That inherent knowledge that something ancient and dead was nearby. My gaze slowly circled the cemetery. I made sure I kept my hands in my pockets for fear of my new 'power'. I scanned the perimeter of the woods again.

Through thick brush and a collection of dense green, Vicken emerged from the trees. Even though I had seen him in modern-day clothing in Hathersage, I was surprised by his contemporary appearance in Lovers Bay; he fitted in with his dark sunglasses and a long-sleeved shirt. No matter the circumstance, his strong shoulders and powerful build made him gorgeous. I looked back at the tombstone as though Vicken's presence made no difference to me. He approached me in silence and stood on my right. Together, for one moment, we looked down at Rhode's grave marker.

The only sounds were the birds chirping and the rustle of the leaves through the wind. Then he said, 'So. You've come to protect the boy.' I studied the etching on the tombstone, saying nothing. Vicken turned his head to look at me. 'That is monstrously stupid.'

Again, I said nothing.

'You know as well as I that despite my every intention, I cannot kill you. Though the coven has come to do just that.'

I turned to meet his gaze. 'Then you find yourself at quite an impasse,' I said coolly.

Vicken gritted his teeth.

'You ask me to betray my coven?' he said.

'My coven? *My* coven? No, you ingrate,' I yelled. 'It is *my* coven, born from the darkest of ideas. The lowest of beliefs. And fear.'

'They will murder you. Can you not see? Do you not see what you are doing to me? What you did to me just a few days ago with that child? Perhaps Rhode's voodoo set you free from our binding but not me!'

'I don't care.'

Now it was Vicken's turn to yell, 'They will kill you and I will be forced to watch!' Vicken's voice echoed into the silent, sunny cemetery. 'You are still evil, then, if you wish such torture on me.'

I said nothing. He was right – all of it.

'Once upon a time,' he continued, 'you told me you would be with me. Always, you said. How quickly you forgot when Rhode returned. I sat. I waited for you to awaken.'

I nodded but it was quick. I saw my own reflection in the silver of his sunglasses.

'Why are you here?' I asked. 'You're very brave to risk the sunlight.'

'I'm not afraid of that any more,' Vicken said.

'And the coven?'

'You know they cannot be in the sun.'

The momentary relief that spread throughout me was my realization that if Vicken was here, then he was not with Justin.

'If they will kill me,' I asked, 'why have you come?'

'You have two choices. You die by your own hand or they kill you,' Vicken said calmly.

I looked back at Rhode's tombstone, still keeping my new and powerful hands in my pockets. 'At least I have a choice,' I said, though every syllable was dripping in sarcasm.

Now Vicken turned his body towards me.

'I'm trying to make a deal with you, Lenah.'

'Vampires don't make deals,' I snapped.

'Use the ritual. Make me human and die at your own hand. Or the coven will kill you and the boy. Your death is inevitable. You cannot return to the vampire world.'

I could feel the warmth of the fire within me, the white of the light that now resided inside my soul and the love I had for Rhode, Justin and, some time ago, Vicken. I took a deep breath. I wouldn't let them hurt Justin. Vicken raised his sunglasses and I looked into his coppery eyes. The truth behind them was familiar to me and for one moment I understood Vicken completely. We could have been on the fields in Hathersage. I could have been Rhode.

'This humanity you desire cannot be wielded by me. Remember what I told you? The ritual calls for the vampire to be five hundred years old or more.'

'But you are powerful. Perhaps it will work.'

'I do not think so,' I answered.

'Do it anyway.'

'For someone who claims to love me you give my life up quite freely.'

'They will kill you anyway.'

'Rhode died for this!' I screamed. We were silent again. 'The ritual involves complete self-sacrifice,' I explained. 'Do you know what that means?'

'We were lovers once.' Vicken looked at me. Somewhere beneath the shade of darkness, my coven was preparing to fight me.

'Why do you want this?' I asked.

Vicken considered me for a moment.

'I became this monster *for you*. But you're gone. I am forced to love the ghost of you in either form.'

'So I die and you're free of me entirely?'

'I deserve it, Lenah. Don't I?'

'You do . . . but the ritual is clear. It's more than my age and blood. The person performing the ritual has to want to die. I cannot give that to you alone. My heart is broken in too many pieces.'

Vicken actually looked crestfallen. His dark eyes, the familiar look he gave me, the one that wanted me and hated me all at the same moment. He placed his sunglasses back on.

'Say your goodbyes, then,' he said, and turned on his heel. He disappeared into the trees.

I thought about calling out to him, calling into the branches and flowers that I knew smelt so good. If this were different, if this were how I wanted it, I would have sat with my friend and told Vicken how the earth in Lovers Bay rose to meet my feet in a way that nowhere else had. But I couldn't. Much to my surprise he called to me again. 'Go forth,' he said, from somewhere in the forest, 'in darkness and in light.'

*

The lacrosse field was washed in peach sunlight, a kind of late afternoon light that made the whole field glow. But I watched from the shadow of the trees. The leaves protected me and although I wasn't afraid of the sun I never risked standing in it directly. I looked at patches of the sky between the geometric angles of the leaves. I could tell from the sun's position that it was close to four in the afternoon. I leaned back against the bark of a large oak tree. After talking to Vicken it was clear the kind of battle this was going to be. Song would attempt to fight me physically, Gavin would try to spear me with a knife, Heath would use his words to distract me. But it was Vicken who would watch it – immobilized by the bond between us. The light was the answer – the only answer.

I turned my attention back to the field.

Justin sweated beneath his helmet and I could see tiny beads of perspiration resting on the top of his upper lip. He held his arms high in the air so his biceps flexed and pushed out from underneath the short sleeve of the lacrosse jersey. A line of girls, including the original Three Piece, sat on the benches to watch the practice. A burning tinge of jealousy shot through me but I shook my head quickly. That, more than anything else, was irrelevant now.

Beyond the field and across a pathway, I could see the greenhouse. I wondered if in some magical world I could walk in, hide and sleep amidst the nasturtiums and roses. Then Justin ran past my eyeline. He wasn't in his varsity uniform; he wore a jersey and shoulder pads. Justin cradled the ball, dodged through other players and finally shot it at the opposing goal. When he jumped up and down in victory, the coach blew a whistle indicating the end of practice.

Justin took off his helmet and when he did he looked to the trees. He ran off the field with his lacrosse equipment over his shoulder. He stood on the border of the trees that lined the perimeter of the field. To the right of me was more woods and, past that, the beach.

He stepped into the woods, and as the light from the sky shone on the ground I remembered the first time I ever saw him. The boat racing, the beach, the way he glistened. He was still glistening; I just wasn't a part of it any more. Once he'd stepped a few paces into the thick bush he saw me leaning against an oak tree.

'It's time,' I said.

'What's the plan?' he asked. 'What did you do all day?'

'Is your boat available? I want to go to the harbour near Wickham.'

'Why?'

'I'd like to keep watch on the campus. I think we can stay one step ahead that way. But I'll explain everything later. We have to go. This really is time sensitive.'

I took a few steps through the woods in the direction of the lacrosse field.

'I – um . . .' Justin stayed near the oak tree and readjusted the equipment on his back. His eyes were hesitant. 'I'm hungry,' he confessed.

'Oh, of course. I forgot—' I said, feeling very foolish.

'I'll be really quick,' he interrupted, and motioned his head to the right. I looked and he was motioning in the direction of the union. 'I'll grab a sandwich to go.'

'Sunset is at eight which means we must be on your boat by—'

'I know. I'll be quick, Lenah,' he said with a smile.

How could he possibly smile at me? I was a monster.

'Right,' I said, and stepped to the edge of the woods. 'Let's go.'

Chapter 31

'This way,' Justin directed.

I checked the position of the sun again; it was a deep orange and almost near the horizon, near six o'clock. The sun would set soon and I wanted to be well out on the harbour before the sun went down. Once the lights went out, the coven would be on the hunt. I got out of the car. Justin locked the door and placed his keys in his pockets. The gravel crunched under the firm soles of my boots. We walked in the direction of the docks.

'He wants to be human?' Justin asked, referring to Vicken.

'That's what most vampires want in the end,' I explained. 'To go back. To touch, smell – feel. Have rational thought. Most often too much time passes and everyone they love dies. The desire to become human again wanes. That's when the madness takes over.'

'What happens when a vampire loses their mind?'

'To explain who those vampires are would be very frightening for you. I'd rather we not talk about it.'

Justin asked nothing more. We hurried down the dock and on to Justin's boat where he packed some drinks for himself in a small cooler. As he turned the key and started up the engines, I climbed down into the comforting underbelly of the boat. We agreed that waiting in the harbour facing the school was the most efficient way for me to watch the school yet stay far enough away from the coven. They would never suspect the harbour. I was hoping I'd see them from afar and stay one step ahead.

I walked down the cabin hallway towards the bedroom at the back. I sat down on the edge of the bed. Everything was the same as the last time I'd seen it. The only thing that was different was my reflection in the mirror above a small basin. I could feel the rocking of the water under the boat and I looked down near my feet. A small stain had discoloured the blue carpet so it looked a deeper sapphire. It was the suntan-lotion stain. The oil had sullied the rich fibres of the carpet.

The motors slowed so the puttering and electric roars became just a purr.

'We're here,' Justin called. I heard him open the hatch and drop the anchor. I headed up to the deck.

With my vampire sight I could see the intricacies of Wickham beach, the tiny glints sparkling in the beige sand and the discarded soda bottles spilling over the rubbish bin next to the pathway. I scanned the campus.

I just kept waiting and waiting for the moment the coven would emerge from wherever they were hiding.

An hour or so passed and nothing. I knew Vicken was pacing. I knew he was waiting for the right moment when the coven would begin their hunt for Justin and me. If I closed my eyes and attempted to connect with Vicken the bond between us would allow me to see exactly where he was. Through the binding magic, he would be forced to show himself. But the connection could also be reversed, so I did not risk it.

Justin sat on the bow and I strained to search the campus as far as I could. I saw the empty entrance gates and security cars patrolling the campus. Most of the meadows and pathways were empty, though a few students walked here and there towards their dorms or the library. I decided to sit with Justin for a moment was OK, as long as I sat facing the campus. I sat down beside him. The water was still, barely moving the boat. I could smell the intricacies of Justin's flesh.

'So we're out here . . . ?' he said.

'It's nearly impossible for them to track us on the water,' I explained. 'We need to surprise them. They'll never expect us to come from the beach. Also, I need to prepare you for what must happen when we go to shore.'

Justin looked up. The moon cast wavering glows on the water. 'What are you gonna do?' he asked.

I hesitated, then spoke.

'We follow them and then lure them into an enclosed space. I was thinking the gymnasium. If we lead them on a chase, we're more likely to get them where we want them to go.'

'But, when we do that, what happens? To you?'

I looked down at the rolling water for a moment.

'I don't know what happens to me.'

I considered for a moment what this meant to Justin – I could feel his gaze on me.

'You know,' I said. 'I thought I would have a chance to come back here. But I see now that is not possible.'

'Come back? How?'

'The ritual,' I said. Justin's eyes widened for an instant as the memory of the ritual came back to him.

'Vicken knows you have it?'

I nodded. 'It doesn't matter. I have to kill all of them,' I said. 'Even Vicken.'

'But you said you were bound.'

'That binding has been broken on my side. Because Vicken is a vampire he is attached to that binding forever.'

'Lucky him,' Justin said. I smiled, just barely and it faded in the moments of silence that followed. 'So we'll fight all of them at the same time?' Justin asked.

'We?'

Justin faced me directly.

'Hell, yeah. You don't think I'm just gonna stand around while you fight off those psychos.'

I smiled. 'As you saw in your bedroom, I'm not exactly without a weapon.'

I ran my right index finger along the metal guardrail of the boat, sending a glow of light under my finger.

'The light?' Justin asked.

'One bright blast should do it.'

Justin reached towards me and I could feel his body temperature radiating on the right side of my body. His fingers shook and he hesitated for just a millisecond before he took my right hand from the bar and held it in his.

'Warm,' he whispered with a hint of surprise.

He brought my hands to his eyes and examined them. His gaze was easy and comforting. Then he did what I least expected him to do – he brought my middle and index fingers to his lips and kissed my fingertips.

Agony coursed through my body. My muscles tensed and my nerves contracted. Justin released me and held both of my cheeks in his hands. I closed my eyes. I could hardly bear him examining all of my vampire changes.

'You're still you,' he whispered, as though reading my thoughts. I finally opened my eyes and noticed that a line of tears poured from his eyes and on to his cheeks. Perhaps he wondered if tears would somehow make him less than a man but he was the best human man I had ever known. His bottom lip quivered and his nostrils flared a bit.

'I wanted you to come back,' he said, though his voice quivered. 'I needed it.'

Then his hands were running through my hair.

371

Even though I couldn't feel it, I was slipping back into the familiar touch that I loved so much. I did, even in this form, love Justin more than I could articulate. He gripped the back of my head and plunged his mouth on to mine. His tongue moved my lips open and we moved in perfect rhythm – that is until a man's scream echoed from the Wickham campus.

Once Justin was behind the wheel, we zipped towards Wickham beach.

Use your mind . . . my thoughts raced. *Where is the victim?* My own plan was working against me. I knew it was bait. They were luring me to the victim only so I would be next. Once the boat slid next to the dock, I slung one boot over the edge and started to run.

'Justin! You must stay with me! I can't lose sight of you!' I called.

'Lenah!'

There was no time to respond. The battle had begun. Justin slung one more rope over a cleat to secure the boat. I looked behind me and was comforted for the moment to see Justin trailing in my wake. He would catch up with me. As a vampire, I had no need to worry about my beating heart or catching my breath. But I was running fast up the path, past the science buildings, past the greenhouse, up the meadow. Justin ran beside me, pace for pace. I ran as fast as I could. Heavy footprints had trampled the grass. I threw my palm out, illuminating the grass. With my vampire sight I could see the shape of Song's footprint.

I ran towards Hopper. Because my gut told me to. When I reached the door, I tugged at it once and we stepped inside. We let it close behind us with a deadening thud.

The foyer was black. Dim light came from track lighting above us. Justin panted, trying to catch his breath.

'How –' he said between breaths – 'how do you know it happened here?'

'I just do,' I whispered curtly. I scanned the long hallway on Hopper's main floor. I knew with no doubt in my mind the coven was down that hallway. Then a feeling came creeping over me. Dread.

Oh no . . .

No. No. No. No. Not upstairs. But the coven allowed me to see. They allowed, perhaps insisted, that I know they'd murdered someone in the art tower. Someone I loved.

I looked up to the topmost landing. I knew I had to go up there because with every ache of my being I knew Tony was at the top of those stairs.

Twenty minutes . . . Or the boy dies.

Could I have been so stupid? Were they actually thinking of Tony? Not Justin?

Step by step we climbed. I reached back – Justin took my hand. Then the metallic smell came through, electrifying my vampire soul. My fangs started to come down. I shook my head to rid myself of the overpowering smell of fresh blood.

Oh, you stupid, stupid boy, I thought. *Please let it be someone else.*

'No!' I cried.

Tony stumbled across the room. He tripped over his own feet and slammed into the wall of cubbies. He was covered in blood. Head to toe. His blue shirt was a sticky red. It was unbuttoned, showing his torso. A torso that was covered in holes.

'Lenah!' he cried, his eyes widened in relief at the sight of me. He coughed blood and then collapsed on an easel, sending it to the floor. He fell to his knees.

I slid across the floor. Tony lay on his back like I had seen him do so many times while lying in the sun. Foolish boy held a crucifix in his hand. Why hadn't I thought to warn him of that?

I rounded on Justin and pointed.

'Stay back. Do not come into this room.'

'Lenah! Tony is my friend—'

'Modern criminology will implicate you if your fingerprints are found. Stay away.'

I looked down. Tony was barely breathing. His chest came up and then shuddered as he attempted to exhale. He was covered with bite marks. Everywhere. Down his ribs, his arms and his beautiful fingers. He choked so hard that more congealed blobs of blood came out of his mouth and clung to his neck and chest. They had not made him into a vampire. The thought momentarily entered my mind. But to be made a vampire means a transformation – rituals. They would have taken him with them.

It was clear this was simply a murder – in my honour. The coven had descended upon Tony and destroyed him. They'd only stopped because I was coming. I lifted him up and slipped my body underneath so his head rested in my lap.

'Len—'

'No.' I placed my fingers over his mouth.

'I –' some blood trickled from his neck and on to my jeans – 'I thought I could help you fight them but they found me first.'

'You were very brave,' I said.

I burrowed my hands under his back and lifted his dying body close to me. I heard sobbing from the doorway and I knew Justin was watching. Tony hiccupped and blood slid out of his mouth and down his chin. Trickles of red oozed from bite marks in his neck. This was it.

'I'm so cold, Lenah,' he whispered, and nuzzled his head closer to me. He was shaking badly now.

I placed my fingers over his eyes and the heat from within me projected outward and warmed his head. It was all I could do to comfort him in the last moments of his life. And then, in a last, shuddering breath, his eyes got large, wide; he looked up at me. He opened his mouth to say something and then . . . then he was gone.

I had spent so many months researching the ritual. To bring *myself* back. Really what I should have done was think of a way to protect those I loved when the coven, my coven, descended upon them. Why bother bringing myself back? Another selfish act. Another person I loved – dead.

I leaned over Tony and kissed his head.

'*Gratias tibi ago, amice*,' I said in Latin, and rubbed his forehead with my thumb. *Thank you, friend.*

I lay my head for one small moment on to Tony's chest. There would be no heartbeat – I knew that. Yet I rested my cheek against the fullness of muscles, which would soon harden, stiffen, and he wouldn't feel like Tony any more.

'Is he dead?' Justin whispered in shock. He stood in the doorway.

There, in the silence, in the draughty art tower, with the whirring of machines in the belly of the building, with the noises of Wickham and student life, a vampire named Vicken Clough laughed maniacally. It echoed up the hallway of Hopper and wound up the stairs so I could hear it loudly and most definitely clearly. Tony's death would be a ripple of relief in the agony of his pain.

The vampire inside me roared to life. I shot up, erect, my back tight. I laid Tony's body on the floor and my head snapped up. And when the rage within me poured out of me, my fangs came down so fast that Justin's eyes rounded and his hands pressed on to the wall.

'Let's go,' I said, my sight clearer than ever. I noticed the tiny flecks of chalk on the floor near the chalkboard. Stray hairs on the ground. Justin's pores and the shape of his skin across his bones. I was deadly.

'Lenah, we can't just leave him here.'

'We have to,' I replied. I was already out of the doorway and descending the winding staircase. I stepped off the stairs and started down the massive hallway away from the art tower. The coven was close; I could feel it.

'What's gonna happen? Lenah?' Justin asked.

I stopped walking in the middle of the stairs.

'Shhh,' I said to Justin gently, and then took a breath so I could project my voice. 'Killing a teenage boy,' I called into the darkness of the hallway. 'He was alone and unprepared. My, my, how we have lost our edge.' I taunted them on purpose. I could sense it, see their movements. They were on their way to me. I still couldn't accurately sense if they were in the building. The thoughts were abstract; I knew they wanted to find me, track me. And they would.

'Let's go,' I said to Justin, gripping his hand, needing his warmth more than ever before.

'But what about an enclosed space?' Justin asked, reminding me of my plan. But I didn't need reminding. The gymnasium was just at the end of the corridor – the perfect place. I looked back behind us down the long hallway. It was empty, but they were close, or I was close to them. I opened the gym doors, looked inside and pushed Justin in first.

'Go to the middle.' I pointed at the centre of the gymnasium floor. The gym was dark except for a dull glow from the line of track lighting along the top of the ceiling. The room was large and square with bleachers on opposite sides of a basketball court. A line of windows faced the Wickham beach. On the left and right side of the walls, behind the bleachers, were walls of mirrors. Whenever there wasn't a game, the dance team used the mirrors for their practices. It was exactly what I needed.

'Place your back against mine,' I commanded.

We stood back to back, my hands on his waist, his on mine. Our eyes searched, waiting for the chase to ensue.

'Promise me. No matter what I do – you'll listen to what I say,' I said, still scanning the gym.

'I promise,' Justin said, though I couldn't help but notice the quiver in his voice. 'Lenah,' he said, and we turned to face each other. 'I have to say this. I love you more than anything in this world. If I don't make it to-night. If one of us dies . . .'

Justin grabbed me into an embrace. Our mouths met and his lips pressed against mine. His tongue eased into my mouth and our kiss was rhythmic and perfect. It tasted like tears and sweat and blood and all of it was a momentary relief from the grief. I would see Tony's face for the rest of my days on earth. Yet in that moment, there was just Justin and me, and how he had saved me. How he had showed me how to live. Then there was a hushing sound, followed by silence and I knew . . .

'Justin?' I whispered. Our lips still grazed each other's.

'Yeah?' he answered, his eyes still closed. It was silent.

'They're here.'

Justin whipped round and we were back to back again.

Vicken, Gavin, Heath and Song stood in the shape of a crescent moon. They had come in from the windows. How or why, I would never know. They were dressed in black – some leather, some button-down shirts. Yet there they were, my mighty coven. Gavin, with his black hair and green eyes; Song, with his stout body and massive muscular build; Heath, blond and beautiful, stood with his arms crossed. He hissed something at me in Latin. Vicken stood all the way to the left, by the gym rafters.

'Fool,' Gavin said, and threw a knife past my head. The blade had just been sharpened and I watched its pointed end come flying past my eyes. It stuck in the door behind Justin and wobbled in the wood.

'You knew this would happen,' Vicken said, leaning a hand on the rafters. 'Bound to your fate, we had to

379

come for you. You knew this. The magic of this coven is sacred.'

Song took a step forward but this was it. The time had come. As I had taught them, they took very slow steps forward and soon, before we knew it, we would be backed into a corner. I needed the mirrors on the right and left side of the wall. I couldn't let them corner me. I needed to stay in the centre of the room.

'*Malus sit ille qui maligne putat,*' said Heath. What he said was the tattoo on my back.

Gavin cackled and Song crouched in a spider position. This was it, the moment before the attack. Justin was panicking; I felt his fear.

'Give it up, Highness,' Gavin whispered.

'Give up all this?' I said sarcastically, though I was stoical in my resolve. I had to concentrate, bring the power from within. Bring on the light.

We were surrounded and the moments were escaping.

'Hook your arm round my waist,' I whispered, though I knew the coven could hear every word.

'Oh, is she planning something?' Gavin teased.

'*Quid consilium capis, domina?*' Heath hissed.

Vicken took a step forward and I moved back with Justin behind me. I held my palms up in front of me, beaming sunlight out from every pore. The rays reflected on to the coven's faces, and each one retracted, shielding their eyes and holding their arms close to their bodies.

Vicken's eyes rounded. 'What dark magic is this?' he spat. He shook one of his hands, seemingly burnt.

'Sunlight,' I said. My eyes darted back and forth from Vicken to Gavin to Heath and Song and back again.

'How?' Vicken hissed.

Song propelled himself forward, jumping high into the air at Justin and me. His hands were like claws and his fangs were bared. I raised my hands again and pressed the light out. The beam was so strong that Song was thrown back against the line of windows. But, unexpectedly, the beam dulled.

Heath and Gavin took another step forward. I pressed the heat through my hands. The sun beamed from my hands once more, causing them to back up but, again, it waned, like the wick of a candle at its end – flickering then burning out.

'You can only keep that up so long, Lenah,' said Vicken.

Song cocked his head to the side. He was going to pounce again. Gavin reached his right hand ever so slightly into his pocket. A knife wouldn't kill me but his precision would murder Justin in an instant. I needed the sunlight to come in a blast. I closed my eyes and concentrated, just as I had done all those nights in Hathersage.

I took deep breaths, the white hot heat building inside me. Images came to my mind in a flurry: the first day at Wickham, the deer grazing out in the fields, Tony's smile when he scooped his ice cream. Then Vicken's words came to me and I felt the heat start to make my palms shake.

Use the ritual. Make me human. Then the images came back and my palms began to emit light. I could feel the burn on the sides of my thighs.

I looked into Vicken's eyes. The surprise and anger on his face was a mix of emotion I knew all too well.

I deserve it, Lenah. Don't I?

I closed my eyes to Vicken, concentrating on the moment, what I needed to do in order to gain the strength. Rhode's face illuminated the darkness in my mind.

Rhode on the hill in the dreamlike meadow, his top hat. His death.

I felt Justin's hands on my hips and my love for him surged through my body. I was almost there . . . the power vibrated through me.

'Lenah,' Justin said, warning me. The coven was so close. I opened my eyes, focusing on Gavin's hand.

He pulled back his hand, knife at the ready . . .

I looked up, locked my gaze with Vicken again and said, 'I suggest you duck.'

I raised my arms from my sides and brought them above my head with such a deafening clap that when my palms hit an explosive blast of white light reverberated throughout the room. Ripple effects caused the gym floor to crack in thousands of places, the windows shattered and a dust cloud mushroomed.

And then, for one moment, there was silence.

Chapter 32

'*Lenah?*' Justin's voice cracked.

'I'm here,' I said.

The room was filled with smoke. I was lying stomach down on the floor. When I raised my head, I could see that the smoke was actually dust. Thousands of particles of dust that filled the room so I could hardly see in front of me. The windows at the back of the room had been blown out and the dust was circling with the air rushing in.

A man in the corner groaned. I looked left.

I saw a pair of black boots, ankle, on top of ankle coming out from behind the bleachers. Vicken Clough had survived.

I waved a hand in front of my face, brushing dust particles away so I could see. An alarm started to echo and, once I'd cocked my head to the side to listen, I realized that it was coming from the art tower.

Then I noticed what was in the middle of the room.

'Get Vicken,' I said to Justin.

'Vicken? What?' I pointed. 'I thought you were going to kill—'

'Please, just do it,' I begged.

Justin ran to the bleachers.

The alarm blared on. Soon students would wake and the authorities would come. I took long strides to the middle of the room and looked down. There were three distinct piles of dust in the places where Heath, Gavin and Song had been standing. Except theirs wasn't glittering like Rhode's did. They were just dust, like fireplace ash. And then I heard a voice . . .

31 October 1899, Hathersage

'Lenah!' Song called to me from the front entrance. The sun had just tipped below the horizon. From the long hallway, I could see my coven congregating on the front step. Song was dressed all in black and Vicken looked dapper in his smart black trousers, heather-grey vest and black top hat. It was the fashion at the end of the nineteenth century. And we had the money to prove it.

A photographer stood in front of the open door. He readied a camera, which was shaped like a box on three long legs. The man with the camera waited for us to get into position for the photograph. He held the camera in the palm of both hands, and looked through a tube at the top, a view finder. I sauntered out of the front hallway into the doorway entrance. Next to me Song, Heath, Gavin and, of course, Vicken waited.

Vicken held a goblet. The red contents inside swished in the glass as he handed it to me. 'A fine English red,' he said with a smile.

My eyes darted to the cameraman. 'Ready now?' he asked me. 'While we still have the light?'

I raised my goblet in the air . . .

'Lenah!' Justin's voice broke through my memory and my eyes focused on the piles of dust. 'We have to go!'

I turned to see that Justin was holding Vicken up. The blast had knocked Vicken silly and his knees kept giving out. I had never seen this happen to a vampire before. The alarm shrieked on.

Somewhere nearby there were police sirens.

We started for the broken windows.

I took a swig from the goblet, swirling it in my mouth. Gavin, Heath, Vicken and Song stood in a circle round me.

'This photograph will commemorate our bond. It will represent all of the lonely-hearted, pathetic souls who will lie at our feet.' I moved so that I stood between Vicken and Song. Heath and Gavin took up position either side. We draped over one another like snakes in the heat dangling over branches.

I wrapped my arm round Song's back as the photographer readied the camera. I held the goblet in my left hand, lifted it into the air and then took one more sip before placing it down so I could pose for the picture. With a film of blood running down my front teeth, I repositioned myself between Vicken and Song.

'Evil be he who thinketh evil?' I said, lifting my chin to the air. 'Let them remember this.'

'Go! Go!' Justin called once we were out of the gym. I glanced one more time at the ashy piles of dust in the middle of the floor. The coven, my brothers, were gone. I held Vicken under his shoulder with Justin holding him up on the other side. We ran into the woods that separated the beach from the campus. Vicken tried to lift his feet but every time he took a step his legs would wobble. He kept looking at the ground as though he didn't have the strength to lift his head.

'Not the boat!' Justin said.

'Why not? We have to get out of here,' I said, while trying to hold Vicken up.

'No, we have to stay on campus. If we go on the boat, the cops will hear the motors. Just leave it. People park at the dock all the time.'

I could see the beach but Justin was right.

'Seeker,' I said, and we moved towards the pathway. Through the trees, back on campus, there were people swarming out of their dorms. I knew we would have to be careful.

'Lenah,' Vicken whispered. 'There's something wrong. My chest.'

'Stop,' I said to Justin.

'We can't. Look,' Justin said, and pointed. Police cars

screamed to a stop in front of the gymnasium. Lights flickered on in the nearby dorms, and campus security were already getting out of their cars. 'We have to get back to Seeker as fast as possible.'

I suddenly felt a tugging, something making my stomach feel as though it was turning in on itself, and I had to let go of Vicken. But we had to keep going and I knew what was wrong. I grabbed at my stomach for an instant.

It was the loss. The loss of the coven. The magic was breaking apart.

'You OK?' Justin asked as he held Vicken.

'Yes,' I said, retaking my position to carry half of Vicken's weight.

Then I looked far into the woods, down near where the chapel stood. Suleen stood in the darkness in his traditional Indian garb. He raised a palm to me and then brought it to his heart.

'Lenah, are you still here?' Vicken whispered.

I looked down at Vicken for just an instant. When I looked back to Suleen, he had gone. I didn't have time to wonder how and why he was there. I wanted to ask him so many questions but there was no sign of the vampire in white.

Justin started walking and we crossed over a pathway. We headed behind the science buildings back towards Seeker.

'Lenah?' Vicken said.

'Yes,' I said. 'I'm still here.'

*

Once we were far enough up the path, I looked back at Hopper. The rhythmic red and blue lights from ambulances and police cars filled the darkness.

Someone had to have found Tony by now. I wondered who would call his family.

My heart hurt.

After we broke into the delivery entrance of Seeker, I helped Justin carry Vicken up to my room. As we lifted him stair by stair, I knew why I had saved him. He was just like me. A victim, bound to love someone who was no longer available. He lived in an eternity of hell and I wasn't going to allow that to happen any more. Justin grabbed glances at me as he reached out for my left hand. He held it tight. We stood in front of my bedroom door.

'Tell me what you're thinking,' he whispered.

Vicken groaned. Both of our eyes darted to him. We could hear students running down the stairs below us, eager to find out what all the commotion was about.

'Lenah,' Justin said, and squeezed my hand to regain my attention. 'I have to know what you're thinking.'

I looked up at Justin's caring eyes and said, 'How would you feel if you'd just killed your family?'

We lay Vicken down on my bed.

'Lenah . . .' he called, but put his arm over his eyes. I closed the door behind me and Justin and I sat down on the couch. I put my head in my hands. Soon, Justin's strong palm was running up and down my back. I looked up at him and he smiled gently. I leaned over and rested my head on his chest. It was at least two or three in the morning.

As Justin sipped a glass of water, I stared at the curtain pulled over the sliding balcony door. With my head still against his shoulder, I thought of the morning that Rhode died and how the curtain had billowed in and out. That it had looked as though it was breathing.

'What should we do? About Vicken?' Justin asked.

I shook my head. 'I'm all he has. He wants the ritual so badly,' I said.

'But you already said you needed to be five hundred or older for it to work. And it killed Rhode.'

'It's really the intent of the ritual that is the most powerful aspect.'

'What do you mean? About the intent?'

'I mean,' I said, twisting the onyx ring on my ring finer. 'That I would want Vicken to live as a human. And I in turn would have to want to die.'

I looked down at the ring, realizing that I had forgotten I had worn it throughout this entire year. It had been my talisman, the one item, besides Rhode's ashes, that I took with me from place to place.

'Do you?' Justin asked. 'Do you want to die?'

'I want the cycle to end. And in some way it has,' I said.

In that moment, I knew what I had to do. Just as I'd known that night at winter prom when I'd left Justin in the ballroom. Even if I died, as Rhode said was a possibility, even if it didn't work, Vicken couldn't stay a vampire and neither could I. And maybe I'd known it all along and this was why I'd come back to Wickham and worked so long to find the ritual.

'I need you to do something for me,' I said, sitting up and looking at Justin. He was wartorn. His blond hair was slick with sweat and his face was smeared with dust, the dust of dead vampires.

'Sure,' he said, brushing my hair back with his palm.

'Will you go see if they have taken Tony's body? I can't do it but I need to know.'

'Sure,' he said, and kissed my forehead. 'I'll be back in a bit.'

Once he'd left and the door closed behind him, I opened the door to the balcony, allowing the air to scoot under the curtain and into the apartment. I went into the kitchen and stood in front of the black canisters that rested on the counter. Inside them were herbs and spices.

I unrolled the ritual parchment still hiding in my pocket. I picked out thyme, for regeneration of the soul. As I walked back towards the bedroom, I rose on to my tiptoes and took a white candle from the iron wall sconces.

I opened the door to my bedroom.

Vicken lay on the bed, his arm over his eyes. I shut the door behind me and pressed my back against the door.

After a moment he said, 'I feel as though I am split. In a thousand pieces. Drawn and quartered.'

'It will pass,' I said.

'Is that all I was to you?' He sat up slowly. His eyes were framed with black rings and his skin had whitened. He needed blood and he needed it soon. He leaned his back against the pillows. 'Just a victim? Of your dark age?'

I stepped next to the bed and placed the herbs and candle down on the night table. I tried to stay focused and refused to look at my bedroom, the shell of my life that I'd left behind in December.

'I do not think of you as a victim,' I said.

Vicken laughed but then swayed a little, drunk from thirst.

'Now what do we do?' he asked. 'Shall we return to Hathersage? Go back to our existence? I feel awful.'

I raised a hand and held my palm an inch or two above the wick of the white candle. Using the light from within me, I set the candle aflame. Vicken looked at the candle and then at me. I slid open the drawer in my night table and found my silver letter opener. Not a knife but it would have to do the trick.

'I release you, Vicken Clough.'

Vicken's eyes widened.

'No,' he said, sitting up, rigid. 'I was clouded. Insane. Lenah—'

391

I raised the blade in the air and slashed down on my wrist so hard that a gaping wound opened. The blood started to ooze, though, as expected, there was no pain. Vicken stared at my wrist and then licked his lips even though he shook his head. 'I don't want this.'

'I release you.'

'No . . .' he said, though I extended my wrist towards him.

This was what I wanted. To take back all of the hundreds of years of pain and suffering. To do something right for once. To set it right. So Vicken could live and Justin too. If Vicken stayed a vampire, I would spend eternity fighting him. He deserved more. He'd deserved it back in the nineteenth century when I'd promised him something I could never give.

Justin Enos was the reason I'd come to life. He'd given me that freedom. I'd danced with thousands of people, I'd made love and had friends. I'd been a full human and I had Justin and Tony to thank for it. And, if anything, I owed Vicken that same chance and I owed Justin the freedom to let me go.

'I stand as your guardian,' I said to Vicken.

I used the light from my right hand to ignite the herbs. Vicken took my wrist and placed it to his mouth.

'Believe . . . and be free.' The smoke swirled up from the herbs on the night table. I closed my eyes and did what I had to do. And in that moment, with Justin's face in my mind, I knew it was right.

Chapter 33

I stumbled out of my bedroom, closing the door behind me. I fell so my back rested on the wall. I tilted my head back, with my eyes closed. I was weakened beyond my wildest imaginations. Most of the blood was gone from my body. I was so exhausted that the room was off kilter and I couldn't focus.

To my right was the living room and beyond that the doorway to the balcony. Dawn had broken and the sunlight was peeking in from underneath the curtain. Vicken lay in the deepest sleep he would ever experience. When he awoke, he would be Vicken again. Not the soulless angry vampire that I'd created.

The front door opened.

Justin stepped into the dorm room. His beautiful pouted mouth pointed down; the energy in his eyes was extinguished. He didn't say anything at first. There was just the noise that silence makes that can never quite be explained.

'They took his body,' Justin said. 'The police.'

He finally looked up at me and his eyes rested on my right hand grasping my bleeding left wrist. He gasped and reached for me but I put up my left hand and he stopped.

'Tell me you didn't just do what I think you did. Tell me, Lenah, that you would have asked me first.'

'I can't.'

'Lenah . . .' Tears spilt out of Justin's gorgeous green eyes. His young face contorted with pain and the guilt surged through me. He would know heartache and grief and I was responsible for it.

He walked towards me but I kept my hand round my wrist, trying to keep the blood in. My body wasn't regenerating blood, it was escaping, and soon I would be empty entirely. Justin reached for me but I kept my hands close to my body. *Stay up*, I thought, and concentrated on maintaining consciousness.

He kissed me hard. I pulled away and, without a word, I slid off my onyx ring and placed it in Justin's palm. He looked down at it, thrown for a minute, and then back up at me.

'Don't you see?' I said, not removing my gaze from his. His green eyes were so watery with tears. 'I fell in love with you,' I continued. My knees buckled but Justin was there to catch me. He swallowed hard and another tear fell from his eyes. He wiped it away. I was seeing double. My time was running low.

'Lenah . . .' Justin was crying now.

I inched to the right, towards the balcony door.

'Don't do this,' he said, as if I could change it.

'In there.' I pointed at the bedroom door. While I was dying, the vampire within Vicken was evaporating and escaping his body. 'The intent was *you*. Your protection and freedom. That's all I want now – for you to be safe. You wake up tomorrow with no fear. It stops with me.'

Blood seeped through the grasp round my wrist.

'Please, go,' I whispered. 'You don't want to see this.'

'I'm not going anywhere,' Justin said through gritted teeth. 'I'm waiting here.'

If I could have cried, I would have. But there were no tears in me. I was nothing but a carcass. 'Just promise me you'll be here when he wakes up. It takes two days. Tell him my whole story. He'll know what to do.'

'I promise,' Justin said, just as the back of my heels hit the balcony doorframe.

I smiled; my hands were shaking.

'You brought me to life.'

Before he could respond, I turned to the door.

I thought I heard something as I stepped out into the dawn. I think it was Justin's knees hitting the ground. I pulled the curtain aside and a blast of morning light hit me square in the face. I raised my hands from my sides.

I would tell you that I felt fire, and hell and pain. It would be the only justifiable payback for the way I'd killed so ruthlessly throughout my life.

But I didn't.

All I felt were dazzling gold diamonds of light.

Acknowledgements

I'd like to thank the incomparable Michael Sugar. None of this would have happened without your belief in my work. Your generosity never ceases to amaze me.

I want to thank the fabulous Anna DeRoy who loved Lenah and her story from the start.

To the St. Martin's team, especially Jennifer Weis and Anne Bensson, for helping me fully realize this wonderful trilogy. Your dedication and hard work are one in a million.

A special thank you to Rebecca McNally at Macmillan Children's Books. Your editorial advice was extremely generous. You enabled me to write a better book.

Thank you, thank you, thank you to my unparalleled agent, Matt Hudson. You are patient, dedicated and brilliant. This book would not be what it is without you. (I'm probably calling you on the phone right now . . .)

To the CCWs: Mariellen Langworthy, Judith Gamble, Laura Backman, Rebecca DeMetrick, Macall Robertson and Maggie Hayes. Your feedback is invaluable.

I would like to extend a special thanks to the following people who have helped *Infinite Days* come to light: the talented Monika Bustamante, Amanda Leathers (the very first reader), Alex Dressler (Latin extraordinaire), Corrine Clapper, Amanda DiSanto, Tom Barclay, local history librarian at the Carnegie Library (the most generous librarian in Scotland), Joshua Corin, and Karen Boren, who taught me what it means to love fiction.

And last but not least:

For Henoch Maizel and Sylvia Raiken, who understood the beauty of words. I wish you could see this.